AN ENTICING INVITATION

She lowered her voice to a whisper. "Sometimes when I see ye smile, I think about kissin' ye. I wonder what your arms would feel like around me. How your breath would feel upon my cheek. What your lips would taste like."

In any other moment like this, he would have swept the woman off her feet, delved his hands into her hair, and ravished her mouth with passionate abandon. They would have ended up in an intimate embrace and a tryst between the linens.

But this wasn't any woman. This was Carenza. This was The One.

This work is a work of fiction. Names, places, characters and incidents are the product of the author's imagination or are used fictitiously. Any resemblance to actual events, locales or persons, living or dead, is coincidental.

LAIRD OF FLINT

Copyright © 2024 by Glynnis Campbell

All rights reserved. No part of this book may be reproduced in any form or by any electronic or mechanical means, including information storage and retrieval systems, without permission in writing from the author, except by a reviewer who may quote brief passages in a review.

Glynnis Campbell – Publisher
P.O. Box 341144
Arleta, California 91331
Contact: glynnis@glynnis.net

Cover design by Richard Campbell
Formatting by Author E.M.S.

ISBN-13: 978-1-63480-144-7

Published in the United States of America

Laird of Flint

The Warrior Lairds of Rivenloch, Book 2

DEDICATION

For anyone
who's ever felt like they
weren't enough...
you are enough.

OTHER BOOKS BY GLYNNIS CAMPBELL

THE WARRIOR MAIDS OF RIVENLOCH
The Shipwreck (novella)
A Yuletide Kiss (short story)
Lady Danger
Captive Heart
Knight's Prize

THE WARRIOR DAUGHTERS OF RIVENLOCH
The Storming (novella)
A Rivenloch Christmas (short story)
Bride of Fire
Bride of Ice
Bride of Mist

THE WARRIOR LAIRDS OF RIVENLOCH
Laird of Steel
Laird of Flint
Laird of Smoke

THE KNIGHTS OF DE WARE
The Handfasting (novella)
My Champion
My Warrior
My Hero

MEDIEVAL OUTLAWS
The Reiver (novella)
Danger's Kiss
Passion's Exile
Desire's Ransom

THE SCOTTISH LASSES
The Outcast (novella)
MacFarland's Lass
MacAdam's Lass
MacKenzie's Lass

THE CALIFORNIA LEGENDS
Native Gold
Native Wolf
Native Hawk

ACKNOWLEDGMENTS

A heartfelt thank you to

Amy Atwell, Kirby Anderson, and Jill Glass
for taking up the slack

The Jewels of Historical Romance
for being great listeners

Becca Syme
for keeping me out of burnout

My family
for giving great advice

Glynnis Campbell's Readers Clan
for their tireless cheerleading

CHAPTER 1

Rivenloch, Lowlands, Scotland
Autumn 1159

Hew's heart cracked.

He supposed he should have been used to the pain by now. He'd had his heart broken a hundred times.

But it always felt like fresh agony. Like a blacksmith had swung a sledgehammer into his breastbone. Shattered his ribs. Collapsed his lungs. Added another wound to his already scarred heart.

He let the scribbled missive fall from his fingers onto the rush-covered flagstones of the great hall. Anne's playful, flowery signature grinned up at him in mockery.

For a fortnight, he'd believed Anne was his ladylove. His life. His breath. His everything. She'd held his very soul in her hands.

Had none of it been true?

Had he only imagined she was as besotted with him as he was with her?

Bloody hell. Anger stung his eyes as he felt the familiar hollow ache begin in his chest.

At least the others had kissed him farewell. Or mumbled regrets. Or turned their tearful faces away as they explained their affection had faded.

Anne hadn't even had the courage to end their courtship face-to-face.

She'd sent a missive with a damned monk. A monk who'd been instructed not to wait for a reply.

Hew drew in a ragged breath and bent down to pick up the carelessly scrawled missive. Clenching his jaw, he crumpled it in his fist and tossed it onto the blazing fire. The page unfurled to give him one last taunting look at Anne's name before the flames licked at it, darkening and curling the parchment. Incinerating their love as if it had never been.

The page hadn't yet turned to ash when his younger brother Logan arrived with a pair of ales.

"I know that look," Logan said, handing him one of the cups. "Who is it this time? Gormal?"

"Gormal?" he growled. *"Gormal?"* Hew frowned as anger's sharp blade rushed in to try to protect his broken heart. "Gormal was three sennights ago."

Logan shrugged, unfazed by Hew's ire. "I can't keep up." Then he gulped down a large swallow of ale.

Hew supposed he shouldn't be vexed with Logan. Since summer, he'd enjoyed the company of a dozen different lasses. Indeed, if he hadn't given his heart so completely to each and every one, he wouldn't have been able to keep track of them either.

It was a truth known to all of Rivenloch that Hew du Lac had a serious weakness for women.

How could he not? They were so beautiful. Tender. Strong. Maternal. He loved their gentle touch. The sparkle of their laughter. The vulnerability of their tears. Their subtle curves. Their soft voices.

And he never met a woman he couldn't love. It didn't

matter if she was rich or poor. Young or old. Bonnie. Ugly. Widowed. Betrothed.

Indeed, it was lucky Hew was good with a weapon, for he'd gotten himself into more than one scrape, falling in love with another man's mistress.

"Anne. Right," Logan repeated, as if adding her to a mental list. "What happened? She didn't have a husband, did she?"

Hew pretended to bristle at the suggestion. "Nay."

"Come on," Logan chided. "'Tis me, your brother. Wouldn't be the first time."

Hew blew out a harsh sigh. "Nay, she wasn't married."

It had been three months since he'd unfortunately charmed the beautiful wife of Sithech the butcher. He was determined he wouldn't make that mistake again.

"That's good then, aye?" Logan said. "You won't have to kill anyone."

This time Hew didn't have to pretend offense. "I've never killed a man over a woman, and you know it," he grumbled. He *had* given Sithech the butcher a good clout in the nose. But that had been in self-defense.

Logan grinned at him over his cup. "I do know it. I'd just rather see you snarling than moping."

Hew narrowed his eyes meaningfully at his brother. "I *have* killed a man for testing my patience before."

Logan laughed. He wasn't afraid of his big brother, even though Hew took after their hotheaded mother Helena. Logan had inherited their father Colin's sense of humor, so he always knew how to incite—and quell—Hew's rage.

"Hey," Logan said, nudging him again with his elbow. He paused to finish off his ale, then wiped his mouth with the back of his arm. "Since you're not *otherwise occupied* with Anne," he said, raising his brows twice for effect, "why not come to the field and show me how to do that axe trick?"

"Maybe later."

While Hew appreciated his brother's efforts at cheering him up—Logan knew how much Hew loved demonstrating his axe skills—he wasn't in the mood.

This last heartbreak felt like the culmination of all that had come before. He'd been *so sure* about Anne. *So certain* this time he'd found The One, as his cousin Isabel liked to say. True, he'd said that at some point about most of the ladies he'd courted. But this time, he'd meant it. That Anne should so callously reject him for the feeblest of reasons—*I fear I grow weary of your company* the missive had said—felt like the final layer of the burial shroud wrapped around his love life.

"Forget her," Logan advised. "She wasn't good enough for you. You'll find another sweetheart soon enough. One more worthy."

Hew smirked at that. His brother almost always found a way to soothe his aching heart. But this time, Hew didn't think it was possible. He was weary of lust and loss.

"I'm going to take a vow of chastity," he decided, only half jesting.

"What?" Logan exploded. "Chastity? How can you say such a thing? You know you're my hero, right?" He shook his head. "Sard a bard, Hew, you're only one-and-twenty. Still in your prime."

Hew grunted. Today he felt like he was one-and-*forty*.

"On the other hand," Logan added with sly innuendo, "maybe with *you* off the market, *I'll* stand a chance."

"Who's off the market?" Their mother Helena strode into the room, clutching a rolled parchment in her hand.

"Hew," Logan told her. "He's taking a vow of chastity."

"Chastity?" Helena scoffed. "For how long? Two days? Three?"

"Maybe forever," Hew grumbled.

"What is it this time?" Helena asked.

"Another broken heart," Logan supplied.

"Ah. Done with Gormal?" she asked. "I had a feeling that wouldn't last."

Hew fumed in silence.

Logan rolled his eyes. "God's hooks, Ma. Gormal was three sennights ago. Keep up."

She scowled at Logan in disapproval. Then she arched a damning brow. "Out," she said in a voice that brooked no argument.

Logan trembled in mock fear. Then he called out "Farewell!" to Hew as he gave their mother a comically elaborate salute and made his exit.

When Logan had gone, Helena turned to Hew. Her face was grim. The sort of sober expression that told him she was about to make his day much worse.

"What is it?" he asked, eyeing the scroll she tapped against her thigh.

"News from Laird Deirdre."

"Ah. How fares my aunt?"

"Well enough, considering."

"Considering?"

"I'm sure you know about the king's...friendliness...with Henry."

Hew grunted. Scotland's King Malcolm had become far too genial of late with Scotland's foe, the English King Henry. Malcolm had taken Scottish soldiers to Toulouse, forcing them to fight alongside their sworn enemy, England, and against their old ally, France.

Most of the clans were deeply unhappy with the situation. It strained their loyalty and made them doubt the king's wisdom.

The Rivenloch clan had been fortunate. Since soldiers were always needed to defend the Scottish border, they hadn't been called upon to join the battle in Toulouse. Yet.

"Deirdre's not planning to send soldiers to France?" It would be a particular insult to clans like Rivenloch—clans that had held the border against the invading English for centuries—to be suddenly forced to join their ranks.

"On the contrary." She lowered her voice. "She's looking to protect the clan from Malcolm's...childish ideas."

Childish. That was accurate. The king was barely a man. He was two years younger than Hew. Malcolm had been but twelve years of age when he assumed the throne.

Hew shook his head. He'd heard the rumors about Malcolm's latest childishly romantic notion. "You mean the one where he wishes to be knighted by the English king."

"Vanity is a poor excuse for destroying an ancient alliance."

Hew agreed. "So if Laird Deirdre is not sending Rivenloch men to war..."

"She fears Malcolm may try to forge an alliance with the English another way."

"How?"

"Through marriage."

"The king might marry an Englishwoman?" The idea soured his stomach.

"Not the king. He's not quite *that* foolish. All his lairds would revolt."

Hew hoped so. Scotland had fought hard for its sovereignty. For Malcolm to reverse the gains of his forefathers was like a gauntlet blow to the face of Scotland.

"Who then?" he asked.

She didn't have to answer him. Her smoldering green eyes said everything.

"His most loyal vassals," he guessed. Then his already cracked heart plunged to the bottom of his belly. "Not me?"

"Not yet. But Rivenloch will doubtless be foremost in his sights. Deirdre is already planning to send your cousin away."

"Gellir?"

She nodded. "'Tis the curse of all his fame and fortune on the tournament circuit. Gellir's winning all his battles. Earning prizes. Gaining glory. He might as well carry a banner that says 'Most Eligible Knight.' If the king does indeed begin to marry off his vassals, Gellir will be the first one to catch his eye."

That was likely. Gellir was not only an illustrious tournament champion. He was the first son of one of the most powerful lairds in Scotland. And he was of marriageable age.

But Hew was the same age as Gellir. How long would it be before the king sought an English bride for *him?* He shuddered at the thought.

"Where will Gellir go?" he asked.

"To Darragh, I think. 'Tis remote enough that your cousin Feiyan can keep him out from under the king's nose."

"So what's this to do with me?"

"I think we'd be wise to follow Deirdre's counsel. Sooner rather than later."

"You think I should join him at Darragh."

Hew was fine with that. Now that he'd lost his ladylove, there was nothing to stay for anyway.

Besides, the west of Scotland was wild and beautiful. Darragh was an enchanting castle perched on a cliff overlooking the firth.

It would be refreshing to wake up to the sound of waves lapping on the shore and gulls screeing through the air. To breathe in the crisp scent of the sea. To see the sun set upon the gentle waves, gilding the crests with golden light. Or to watch from the parapet as a storm raged like a dark beast, lashing the rocks below with untamed force.

It would be good to see his cousins. He owed Feiyan a visit. And it would be fun to challenge Gellir the Tournament Champion to a skirmish or two.

Indeed, the more he thought about it, the more he looked forward to it.

Nothing was quite as invigorating as change. And after the heartache he'd endured in the last several months, Hew could use a change of scenery.

Perhaps he wouldn't have to consider chastity after all. Darragh would undoubtedly offer him a whole new array of eligible ladies. Ladies who wouldn't scoff at his sentimentality, laugh at his passion, or crush his heart.

Aye, Darragh could be the answer he sought.

"Nay, not Darragh," his mother said.

His enthusiasm sputtered out like a spent candle. He frowned. Not Darragh?

"Where then?" he asked.

"West of here. I've had a request for a warrior."

"Right." A good fight would keep his mind off of his broken heart.

"Someone very good with a weapon."

Good with a weapon. That was flattering. Especially in a clan full of warriors good with weapons. "Who will I be fighting for?"

"You're not going to like it," she warned, "though it may make your vow of chastity easier."

His frown returned. God's bones. Just how much worse could this day become? He sighed. "Where do you plan to send me, Mother?"

"To Kildunan."

"What's Kildunan?"

"A monastery."

He blinked.

A monastery.

A quiet, dull, boring place where he would be surrounded by quiet, dull, boring men who led quiet, dull, boring lives without so much as a glimpse of a woman?

No doubt his mother expected him to explode with

rage. *She* would have. Indeed, she'd already moved one hand to the hilt of her dagger, as if anticipating his resistance and planning to convince him at the point of a blade.

But Hew's spirit was too weary for resistance. Too broken for outbursts.

He'd jested with Logan about taking a vow of chastity. Now it was no jest.

"Perfect," he muttered, his voice dripping with sarcasm. "When do I leave?"

A fortnight later, on a cold and drizzly day, a quiet, dull, boring abbot with sparse white hair welcomed Hew to Kildunan monastery. Kildunan was exactly what Hew expected. Remote. Isolated. Lady-less.

At least he wasn't expected to actually take vows as a monk. He was only feigning an interest in the monastery with an eye toward higher ranks in the church.

The abbot had secretly requested a skilled warrior to deal with the thievery that had plagued the monastery for months. First, the silver cross upon the altar had gone missing. Then the gold chalice used for wine. A jeweled Bible had been taken from the nave, as well as several pieces of jewelry donated by wealthy nobles seeking to secure their place in heaven.

No one had been able to catch the elusive thieves. No one had even seen them. So the abbot had decided to use intimidation tactics. He figured a warrior from the Rivenloch clan would do nicely.

The abbot's eyes lit up when he saw Hew's mighty axe—sharp, gleaming, and deadly. And the generous donation of silver Hew brought from the Laird of Rivenloch only added to his enthusiasm.

The abbot knew if the thefts became common

knowledge, nobles would begin to distrust the monastery. And if that happened, donations like those from Rivenloch would dwindle. Despite taking a vow of poverty, the monks depended upon the generosity of patrons for their sustenance.

The abbot needed Hew to quietly apprehend the outlaws and, if possible, secure the return of the valuables. In exchange, he'd give Hew a private cell, two meals a day, and safe haven should the king's men come knocking.

His cell was a tiny, sparse enclosure with a straw pallet, a scratchy wool coverlet, a hook for clothing, and a single candle. Hew shivered as he dropped the satchel of his belongings onto the rush-covered clay floor. At least the room was dry. But with no hearth, it was as cold as a buttery.

Supper was barley pottage in a trencher and a cup of ale. He could have eaten twice as much, but the rations were scant. He made a mental note to snare a rabbit or two and see if there was a loch for fishing nearby to supplement the monks' stores.

After supper, he returned to his cell. There he huddled, fully dressed, under the thin coverlet. His feet hung off the end of the pallet. His teeth chattered. His bones ached from the cold.

What he really needed more than anything, he decided, was a woman to keep him warm.

CHAPTER 2

"Good morn, Hamish," Carenza softly cooed.

One big brown eye peered at her through the shaggy black strands of hair as Hamish plodded forward. His heavy hooves made dull thuds on the damp sod of the ferme.

"That's a good lad."

The other cattle, two dozen in all, followed behind Hamish, nodding their heads.

An outsider would have been horrified at the sight. The great dark beasts had horns almost as wide as Carenza was tall. The cattle descended upon her like a black cloud now, enclosing her with their enormous bodies.

Cainnech, her father's cooherd, would have scowled in disapproval. He constantly warned her away from the unpredictable animals.

She constantly ignored his advice.

But she currently limited her visits to Saturday morns, when Cainnech took a few hours off to meet his mistress in the village. Then Carenza could roam among the cattle in peace.

She also kept her visits from her father. If the Laird of Dunlop could see her now, he'd lock her in her chamber and throw away the key.

To him, coos were one of two things…

Dangerous beasts with foot-crushing hooves and belly-gouging horns.

Or supper.

But to Carenza, Hamish was an old friend. She'd raised him as a calf. Brushed him. Played with him. Taught him tricks. Comforted him when he'd had to be crogged and gelded. Told him stories she swore he understood.

Carenza wasn't afraid of Hamish.

She was afraid *for* him.

As far as her father knew, his daughter was simply fond of riding. On Saturday morns, she'd saddle her palfrey Leannan and gallop off across the Dunlop land. What he didn't know was that she always happened to ride to wherever the fold had gone to graze.

The grass was thin now. Snow dusted the tops of the mountains. Soon the cattle would be gathered to the stone-ringed close for the winter. And then...

Hamish nudged Carenza playfully with his nose, leaving a wet trail along her neck.

Carenza captured Hamish's great head between her hands and scratched behind his ears. As she gazed lovingly into the animal's enormous eyes, her own eyes welled with tears.

She would miss Hamish. But winter was coming. And sooner rather than later, she had to face the sickening truth.

Her father had explained it to her when she was a wee lass. He'd told her that the six-year-old cattle were always culled.

Never having heard the word, she'd secretly followed him out to the close to see what he meant. She saw a servant leading one of the coos to a stall away from the others. While Carenza watched through a gap in the fence, the man picked up a heavy mallet and swung it at the coo's head, knocking her to the ground.

Carenza screamed in terror.

She would have run to the animal's rescue. But her father prevented her.

Upset at her for following him, he scooped Carenza into his arms and strode away from the close. She kicked and pummeled him, begging him to save the coo. But his jaw was set. And when she peered over his shoulder in distress, she saw the servant cut the animal's throat.

Tears of shock and dismay sprang to her eyes. A wail of unimaginable woe escaped her. She collapsed against her father's chest, sobbing at first in horror, then with forlorn hopelessness.

He tried to soothe her. He tried to explain that it was the coo's time. That she'd lived a good, long life. That the clan would starve if they didn't have meat for the winter. He assured her that the servant had done his best to make the coo's death quick and painless. And that Carenza would have to learn about sacrifice and the cycle of life and death.

But the only powerful message she received from that day was that "cull" meant "kill."

Hamish snorted and nudged Carenza's shoulder, startling her from the horrific memory.

She smiled. "O' course I brought ye a treat."

She rummaged in the satchel she'd hung from Leannan's saddle, pulling out one of the shriveled apples she'd found among the fallen leaves in the orchard. She sliced the fruit into pieces with her dagger, distributing them to the coos, one by one.

The coos were exceptionally polite. They waited their turn, even when she had to return to the satchel for more apples.

Eventually the supply was exhausted. Most of the cattle, understanding she had no more, began to wander away.

Hamish remained. He liked Carenza's scratches and conversation as much as the treats she brought.

"I'm goin' to miss ye, lad," she said, letting her eyes brim over with tears as she brushed the hair back from Hamish's sweet face. "I'm goin' to miss your gentle eyes. And your curious nature. The way ye always trot up to keep me company and listen to my stories. How ye protect the new wee calves from the other coos."

She lingered a moment longer, resting her brow upon Hamish's brow, between his long horns, inhaling his peaty odor.

Then she sniffed back her sorrow and explained, "I have to go now. But I'll be back in a sennight." She added in sober tones, "Maybe sooner."

She rode away before Cainnech could return. Tomorrow was the Sabbath, his day off. That meant the cattle wouldn't be driven to the stone close for at least a few more days. Hamish was safe enough till then.

Meanwhile, she needed to pry from her father what day he planned to move them. And what day he planned to cull them. Nay, she corrected, to *kill* them.

It had been seven days since Hew had been in the company of a lass. Not since he'd *swived* one. Since he'd even *laid eyes* on one. In his entire life, he'd never experienced such famine.

But it was a challenge he felt compelled to undertake. After all, in the end, women had brought him only heartache. Suffering. Enslavement. Humiliation. He needed to forget about them for a while.

That might have been more bearable if the monks hadn't been such poor company. Though they weren't sworn to silence, they did revere quiet contemplation. Hew couldn't interest them in a game of draughts, a walk to the loch, or a hunt for coneys. Instead, they pored over religious tomes, prayed at all hours, and ate in silent reflection.

Chewing on a trencher of tough horsebread made of oats, rye, and peas, he regarded the somber faces around the table. The dull abbot. The stern prior. The boring monks.

He wished he'd been dropped into a convent rather than a monastery. Not that he would have tried to romance a nun. Even amorous Hew had his limits. Besides, he'd made that mistake once before. But after six days of staring at pasty-faced men, he would have been grateful for a glimpse of a rosy cheek, a pink mouth, a fluttering lash.

He swallowed, and the bread scraped down his throat, as if punishing him for his insufferable lust. He had to stop thinking about women. Stop dwelling on what he couldn't have.

Adding to his frustration was the fact he was half-starved. He'd always heard monks ate well. The monastery near Rivenloch was full of paunchy old men and soft-bellied youths. But these monks, raised on portions sized for a child, were gaunt and gangly.

To make matters worse, he hardly knew where to begin with his investigation. There wasn't much to go on. The monastery's treasures had vanished without a trace. The only way to discover the guilty party was to either catch them in the act or find one of the missing items. But that was as likely as locating a particular flea on an ox.

On the other hand, if he set out to scour the neighboring village for evidence, something might turn up.

And he might find some real food.

And he might get a glimpse of a feminine creature.

"Any progress, Sir Hew?" the abbot suddenly intoned, startling him.

Hew choked down the last rough morsel of bread. "Not so far. I'll venture to the village today to see what information I can acquire."

"The village?" the prior groused, gathering his bushy gray brows into a frown. "What do ye hope to find there?"

The vision of a table groaning with food and a lass feeding him grapes popped into Hew's head. He dismissed it at once.

"Clues," he replied.

"What sort o' clues?" the prior pressed.

The abbot placed a gentle silencing hand on the prying prior's sleeve. "I suspect a warrior o' Rivenloch knows what he's doin' and needs no help from us."

The chided prior's eyes frosted over briefly, but he said nothing, bowing his dutiful head.

"Still," the abbot said to Hew, "I hope ye'll be...discreet."

"Of course," Hew said. "Is there anything you need from the village?"

The prior frowned as if offended. "We have all we require."

The abbot smiled. "That won't be necessary."

Hew disagreed, and he suspected some of the monks did as well. They seemed like they could use a hearty roast. A barrel of strong beer. Perhaps a roll in the hay.

It was a four mile walk to the village. Hew frowned as he trod down the knobby road beneath the gray sky, his axe slung across his shoulders. His belly growled despite the horsebread. So he distracted himself by focusing on the crime he'd been hired to solve.

Three questions came to mind about the missing treasures.

First, who would have wanted to steal them?

They were obviously taken, not for their religious significance, but for their value. Anyone who needed or wanted wealth could have been responsible. Which left a lot of suspects.

And that led to his second question. What would the thief have done with them?

He might have sold them. The jewelry could be marketed to a merchant. But anyone could see the silver cross and gold chalice were religious items. So if they'd gone to a merchant, it would have to be a disreputable one.

He might have had them melted down. That would require a small crucible. Crucibles were used mostly by silversmiths and goldsmiths, who resided in the village.

He might have run away with them. But Hew didn't think so. The thief had returned again and again to the monastery. He likely lived nearby.

He might have hidden them to be sold later, when less suspicion would be roused. That would be the worst possibility. Hew couldn't very well ransack the whole village, searching for stolen goods.

The third question was how had the thief gained access to the monastery?

It was well known that nobles sent their valuables to monasteries for safekeeping since it was considered a mortal sin to rob a holy place. Most thieves would think twice before risking their soul by filching God's property.

The monks were up for worship all night and all day. Matins. Prime. Terce. Sext. None. Vespers. Compline. A thief would have to time his entry into the monastery to dodge the sessions of prayer.

A stranger wouldn't know the layout of the monastery. Where the treasures were kept. Who resided where. Which rooms were occupied at which hours.

Only someone familiar with the building could easily carry out such thefts. That meant the thief had to be someone who currently resided at the monastery, had lived there once, or visited regularly.

Hew would be sure to ask the prior who made deliveries of food and supplies. He'd learn which outsiders serviced the monastery in terms of cleaning or repairs or harvesting. And he'd ask the abbot whether any novices had recently changed their minds about entering the order.

Armed with those questions and his trusty axe, he figured he could get answers fairly quickly.

What he couldn't do so quickly was get past the appetizing array of lasses who populated the village streets.

He tried. He glowered as he walked along, training his eyes on the ground a few feet ahead of him.

Even then, his ear caught on snippets of conversation, feminine laughter, and a few speculative whispers as he passed.

He happened to brush a lady's skirts, and he lifted his gaze only momentarily to apologize. But the lass caught his eye and smiled. And of course, she was the most beautiful creature he'd ever seen. At least the most beautiful in a sennight.

Tightening his jaw, he murmured an apology and swiftly ducked into the first doorway he found for refuge. It was an alehouse. Perfect. He could use the distraction of a pint. And the local alehouse was the best place to collect gossip about a village's residents.

The place fell silent at the sight of his axe, as if they feared he was a Viking on the rampage. He supposed that was understandable. He was taller than most, with long straw-colored hair and pale gray eyes, and his sister said he was as broad as an ox. But he was Scottish, born and bred, not a rampaging Viking. It was his ancestors who had been the rampaging Vikings.

Hanging his plaid on a peg, he nodded a greeting to the attractive apple-cheeked alewife. She had a twinkle in her eye that told Hew she liked the cut of his trews. He tried not to think about it.

"An ale, I pray you," he said, averting his eyes. Then he reconsidered. "Got anything cooking on the fire?"

"Mutton pottage, m'laird," she said. "Warm. Tasty. And satisfyin'. Or so I'm told."

Hew couldn't mistake the innuendo in her voice. But he could ignore it. "A trencher of that as well then."

He chose a seat against the wall, propping his axe beside him, and nodded to the other inhabitants of the alehouse.

A velvet-clad nobleman scowled into his ale. A pair of laborers warmed their knees by the fire. Two dusky-skinned foreigners played at dice on a table. And three well-dressed commoners chatted animatedly in the corner.

Hew listened. The three were merchants, discussing the upcoming village fair. According to their discussion, they felt there were too many wool merchants being allowed in from other parts. Woolmakers Row, they said, was going to be crowded with competing vendors.

That wasn't useful to Hew. Wool merchants had no use for crucibles. Nor would they be likely to try to sell religious artifacts.

His trencher of pottage and ale arrived, and he dug in at once. He hadn't realized how hungry he was. But the simple peppery stew with its chunks of mutton, leeks, and kale tasted like food of the gods.

He suspected hunger had likewise clouded his judgment about the alewife's attractiveness. On second glance, she was at least a dozen years older than him and lacking two of her front teeth.

Finishing off the meal, Hew sipped at his ale and eyed the lone nobleman. He wore a jeweled ring and a silver medallion. His plaid was closed with a silver brooch, and a jewel adorned his velvet cap.

"Your pardon, sir," Hew said, "but may I inquire as to where you obtained your brooch? 'Tis a work of great craftsmanship."

The man gave him a cursory glance and decided Hew's

saffron leine and woolen trews were of fine enough quality to warrant further conversation. "'Twas made by a silversmith in the village by the name of Ingram."

"Fine work."

The man sniffed.

Hew nodded a good day, then retrieved his axe, donned his plaid, and headed into the gloomy morn to look for Ingram the silversmith.

He wasn't hard to find. But Hew discovered within moments that Ingram took great pride in his craft. He was horrified at the idea of melting down another silversmith's work for coin.

"Do you know of any in the village who might do such a thing?" Hew asked.

Ingram stroked his gray beard, possibly considering ruining a rival's reputation. But in the end, he was a man of solidarity. "No silversmith worth his craft would, m'laird, unless the owner wished the piece altered for his own purposes."

"I see."

"So if ye have silver ye're tryin' to profit off of," he said, arching a judgmental brow, "ye're better sellin' it to a Lombard or a chapman."

Hew had no wish to offend the man, so he nodded his thanks and continued on his way.

That left goldsmiths. He found only one. To his dismay, despite the sign indicating the shop was owned by William the Goldsmith, William had recently expired, and his widow had taken over his trade.

She was a sad and lovely lass with black hair and blue eyes. Of course. Any other day, he might have tried to coax a smile from her rosy mouth. But not today. Today he was on a mission.

"Tell me," he asked her, "did your husband ever melt down a gold piece?"

Laird of Flint

"Nay, not that I know of," she said, confiding, "But I'd be willin' to do it, if ye have coin."

By her tone, she was hungry for work. Perhaps her husband's patrons didn't trust her skills. In Hew's experience, a member of the guild was a member of the guild. It didn't matter whether a goldsmith was young, old, male, or female.

"How much is that?" he asked, nodding to a tiny gold ring decorated with intertwined vines.

"Twenty shillin's."

Twenty shillings was enough to buy two coos. But the woman's sad blue eyes were troubling him. So he dug the shillings out of his coin purse and saw her face light up with hope as she wrapped the ring in a linen scrap and pressed it into his palm.

What he was going to do with it, he didn't know. It was too small for his fingers. And since he'd sworn off women for the moment, he wasn't going to gift it to his next sweetheart. He tucked it into his satchel. Perhaps he'd give it to his little sister, Nichola.

Over the next few hours, he visited the handful of shops where used goods were sold. Though all of them featured jewelry—it was a common item to sell for those needing quick coin—the pieces didn't match the abbot's descriptions.

No one had a silver cross or a gold chalice, though one unsavory shopkeeper boasted a splinter of the true cross. A splinter that had probably come from the ruins of a henhouse.

By the end of the day, discouraged by his fruitless search, Hew headed to another alehouse to feed his belly and gather more information. This time he chose a dingy, cheap place where serfs and laborers might gather and more could be had than just ale. It seemed like the kind of spot where nefarious thieves who would steal from a monastery might gather to brag about their spoils.

As he expected, within the alehouse were several unsavory characters. This time when he appeared with his axe, he saw several men clap hands on the hilts of their own weapons, as if they expected a fight. He ordered an ale and a trencher and sat in a corner to observe them.

As the heavily-wrinkled, gruff-voiced alewife brought him his supper, she told him she had a pair of daughters if he had another kind of hunger, giving him a broad wink in case he didn't catch her meaning.

Hew seldom turned down female attention. But he never paid for it. Not only did it trouble his romantic nature. Seeking companionship in a place like this was risking the pox. Besides, he was on a strict no-female regimen. So he muttered in the negative and turned his attention to his supper.

The pottage tasted like it might have been made with mouse meat. But it was cheap, and he was hungry enough to choke it down.

Two rough-looking men in mud- and blood-stained leines whispered over their ales. He could only hear fragments of what they said. But it seemed to do with pigs and how busy they'd been lately with the autumn butchering.

At another table, a nervous young man with an older brother had taken the alewife up on her offer of more than supper. They were waiting for their turn with the daughters. Hew was tempted to warn them away. But the older brother was intent on ushering his sibling through this rite of passage, so there wasn't much Hew could do.

A shamefully drunk merchant lolled in one corner, and his apprentice kept stealing coins from his purse. It was wrong, of course, but most merchants didn't compensate their apprentices fairly. The lad might filch a penny from his master once in a while. But Hew doubted the lad made a habit of thieving churches.

Hew took a final swig of ale. He was getting nowhere. Then a new man entered the alehouse and hung his plaid on the wall. He had a broad back and shaggy brown hair. The pig butchers waved him over.

"Cainnech!"

Cainnech nodded and joined them. "How's pigs?"

The men groaned in mutual exhaustion.

The alewife set an ale down in front of the newcomer. "Still comin' to town for Mary, are ye?"

"Every Saturday," Cainnech replied.

"Pah!" she groused. "Ye let me know when ye get an itch for one o' my daughters."

All three growled and waved her off.

"How are the coos?" one of the pig men asked Cainnech.

"Haven't driven them to the close yet."

"Better watch for caterans," one of the pig butchers warned. "I heard Boyle's lads have been reivin' this year."

Caterans. Hew doubted there was any connection between stolen cattle and stolen church treasures. Caterans were usually just troublesome lads who routinely crossed over clan borders to take their neighbor's animals. Still, he'd keep listening.

"Och aye, the Boyles," the other pig man concurred. "That clan's had a grudge against Dunlop for years."

Cainnech disagreed. "Not anymore. Boyle's made peace with Dunlop. He's got two sons o' marryin' age now, and they've set their eyes on Dunlop's daughter."

"Carenza," one of the pig men said on a sigh.

"Everyone's set their eyes on Carenza," the other replied.

"A real beauty, that lass," the first said.

Cainnech scoffed. "But her da's ne'er goin' to wed her to a Boyle. He's got his sights set higher."

They all drank to that.

Then Cainnech volunteered, "Truth to tell, I'd just as

soon sell the cattle before Martinmas than deal with butcherin' 'em."

"Wouldn't we all?" the pig butchers agreed, raising their cups in a second toast.

The mention of selling cattle made Hew remember he meant to procure food for the monastery. A coo on the hoof would make a wise purchase, providing milk, butter, and fresh cheese every day. He almost regretted spending so much coin on the gold ring.

The hour was growing late. The alewife led the two brothers to a back room. The merchant had dozed off. His apprentice was gulping down the second trencher of pottage he'd bought with the coin he'd pilfered. The pig and coo men were now discussing the weather. Hew didn't think he'd get any more useful information today.

He had to find the village butcher shop before it closed. He'd made up his mind. He'd purchase a slab of ham with the coin he had left.

CHAPTER 3

Carenza peered into the square of polished steel that served as a mirror. She was dressed now from her bath, which she'd scented with lavender to disguise the smell of cattle. She combed each strand of dark hair into a tidy braid that hung to her waist. Pinched her cheeks. And practiced the wide-eyed gentle smile that pleased her father.

It was her duty, after all, to keep him happy.

Ten years ago, she had been devastated by the loss of her mother.

But her father had been utterly ruined. The death of his wife had left him deeply melancholy. Dangerously depressed. Inconsolable.

Carenza learned as a young lass she had to tread carefully around him. God forbid she should complain. Or weep. Or counter his commands.

She feared if she made him unhappy, he might leave her as well. And then she would be all alone in the world.

But as long as she kept him happy...

It wasn't too difficult.

She only had to be the perfect daughter.

She smoothed her brows and checked her teeth. She adjusted the pearl pendant around her throat. Then she tugged her leine into place on her shoulders, adjusting the soft arisaid of muted gray tartan that brought out the smokiness in her eyes.

Out of the corner of her eye, she caught the reflection of a wee beast behind her. A brown rat. Standing on its hind legs in the middle of her chamber floor. Sniffing at the air.

She lowered the mirror and turned to face the animal.

"Ye're early, Twinkle," she told him. "I haven't a crumb yet."

The rat settled back down onto all fours.

"Come back in an hour," she said. "I'll be back from supper and bring ye a nice treat."

Twinkle's whiskers twitched. Then, as if he understood, he turned round and returned to the shadows of the garderobe.

That was another thing she had to hide from her father. He knew she had a fondness for animals. But he didn't realize how all-encompassing her affections were. In the last ten years, under her father's nose, she'd kept a menagerie of pets. At any given time, her chamber might be crawling with pups, kittens, ducklings, doves, coneys, mice, rats, toads, or lizards.

She'd gone through so many shrieking lady's maids that she finally told her father she'd rather tend to herself.

In spring, she visited the lambs and kids, piglets and calves, stots and colts. She fed the birds in the forest and had a crow that liked to bring her treasures in return—bits of pottery and ribbon and coins. She studied the bees in their hives. Butterflies hatching from their chrysalises. Chicks emerging from their eggs. And tadpoles turning into frogs.

Because she couldn't bear the thought of disappointing her father with her strange interests, she was careful not to let him see too much.

She also worked exceptionally hard in the hours she wasn't tending to her fauna to ensure she was as well-educated as her noble peers. As well-mannered as her father expected. Skilled with a needle. Accomplished at the lute. Softspoken. Kindhearted. Everything one could wish for in a lady and a daughter.

Perfect.

She glanced in the mirror again and brushed a stray eyelash from her cheek. Then she set the steel square down on the table beside her ivory comb. Holding her head high and smoothing the wrinkles from her pale yellow skirts, she pasted on a brilliant smile and left her chamber to greet her father for supper.

The clan's chatter lowered to murmurs as Carenza entered the great hall. Her father turned to her, and approval shone in his eyes. Breathing a sigh of relief, she smiled and sat beside him.

"Ye look lovely, as always," her father murmured.

"Och, Da," she teased, "ye're still blind as a bat."

He laughed.

She liked making him laugh. Laughter kept his grief at bay.

The new kitchen lad approached with oatcakes and ruayn cheese, setting them down before her with shaking hands.

"Thank ye, John," she said.

He seemed surprised she knew him. But he'd soon realize she knew all the servants by name. After all, being considerate was the hallmark of a proper lady, and there was nothing more considerate than remembering a person's name.

She spread cheese on an oatcake and took a tiny bite.

"How fares the midwife?" her father asked.

"The midwife?" She took a moment to swallow. And think.

"Aye. Ye said ye rode out to visit her this morn?"

"Och aye." She'd told him that when he'd asked where

she was riding. It had been the first thing she'd thought of. But she hated lying. It was unladylike. And there was always a risk of getting caught. "I must have missed her. Maybe she was deliverin' a bairn somewhere. Or sleepin'." Then, to throw him off her scent, she asked, "How was your day?" She took another bite of oatcake.

"Good," he said proudly. "We got the last o' the cider into barrels today. We'll be smokin' eels o'er the next few days. Then 'twill be near time for the cullin'."

The oatcake abruptly congealed in her throat. She couldn't seem to swallow it or reply. She could only nod.

"Not a moment too soon," he added, shaking his head. "The Boyle lads are up to their usual antics, reivin' cattle."

Her heart caught. What if the Boyle brothers stole Hamish? "Do ye think they'll come after ours?"

"Not if what I heard from their da is true."

"What did ye hear?"

"He said the lads are lookin' to catch your gaze, Lady Carenza," he confided.

"Mine?"

Her eyes widened. The Boyle brothers? Gilbert and Herbert Boyle were a pair of dimwitted bullies who had terrorized her since she was a wee lass. Throwing chestnuts at her. Pulling her braids. Chasing away the birds she tried to tame.

"Don't fret," he assured her. "Neither o' them are fit to kiss the ground ye tread on. But as long as their da thinks they have a chance, they'll leave our cattle alone."

She forced a conspiratorial grin to her face. Her father was clever. Too clever. She took a measured sip of ale.

"So ye'll bring the fold to the close soon?" she asked with casual indifference.

"Aye, in a sennight or so, when the grass is gone."

She nodded and managed to squeak out, "And the cullin'?"

"Sometime betwixt Samhain and Martinmas."

She gulped. Young John brought the next course, barley pottage in a rye trencher. But she'd suddenly lost her appetite. She ended up sneaking bites to her favorite hound, Troye, under the table.

There was no time to waste. She couldn't wait until Cainnech drove the cattle to the close. It was too risky. She had to do her work before they were rounded up.

As Hew expected, his gift of ham for the monastery instantly endeared him to the monks. The next day, as the cook sliced it up for their Sabbath supper, only the prior frowned in disapproval at such excess. The abbot, however, allowed it. He was wise enough to realize Hew's strategy. After all, a man who filled a monk's belly might gain his confidence.

Indeed, after supper, Hew engaged several of the monks who were clearing tables in the refectory in what appeared to be casual conversation.

From one, he learned that the silver cross had disappeared sometime in the middle of the night, between vespers and compline.

Another told him the gold chalice had gone missing once before from the sacristy, but had been found in the library and returned. The following week, it was gone, this time for good.

A third volunteered his theory that the chalice was in truth the Holy Grail and that a Templar had come secretly to claim it.

The prior, a particularly ascetic fellow, believed the thefts were a sign from God. A lesson to them all to reject the earthly trappings of wealth. He didn't offer any ideas, however, about who he thought had done God's work.

More than one said they'd seen the abbot's key to the

coffer of jewels left in the lock, though none of the jewels had gone missing at those times. The key had been immediately returned to the abbot, who hadn't realized he'd accidentally left it in the coffer lock.

Most knew nothing about the thefts. But after a succulent supper, thanks to Hew, they were willing to offer what help they could.

At Hew's request, the prior made a detailed list of all deliveries made to the monastery, along with the names of those who delivered them. Hew meant to question each one.

But the more he heard, the more he was convinced the thief was someone close to the monastery. Someone who had both knowledge and access. Perhaps one of the novices who hadn't yet embraced the Commandment about stealing.

Despite a full day and a full belly, when Hew settled onto his pallet, he couldn't sleep. After an hour of shivering in the cold, tossing, turning, and staring at the plaster ceiling, he decided to do some investigating around the monastery.

Armed with his axe, he circled the inside of the perimeter wall. There didn't seem to be any gaps in the stone. Or loose panels of stained glass in the windows of the church. Or gates in disrepair. No secret passageways were in evidence.

He walked through the moonlit cloister with its central well. The square yard was bordered on the west by the monks' cells and on the east by the prior's and abbot's quarters. To the north was the church. To the south was the refectory.

It was possible that a catapult fired from outside the monastery might launch a thief into the midst of the cloister. Otherwise, it was inaccessible to anyone not living within the walls.

He searched the library, where the missing gold chalice had once been seen. But, located in the heart of the monastery, it was the most secure chamber. And none of its small treasury of books, chained to the walls for safekeeping, had been taken.

The only other building was the infirmary, which was at some distance from the other structures, adjoined by its own tiny chapel and kitchen. Mainly for monks who fell ill, it was also open to a few devout outsiders who were at death's door. But most hadn't the strength to walk. Much less steal anything.

Hew's exploration reinforced his view. The thefts had been accomplished, not by a stranger, but by someone with easy access to the monastery.

Stealing back to his cell across the grass of the cloister, he heard a scuffle along the wall. In one smooth motion, he shrugged the axe off his shoulder and gripped it in both hands before him.

It was probably just a monk on his way to matins. But Hew was not a man who liked to be caught unawares.

Narrowing his eyes in the faint moonlight, he saw a low shadow hobbling awkwardly beside the stone wall. Not a monk. An animal.

He lowered his axe and smiled in self-mockery.

A waddling hedgepig snuffled through the leaves.

"You're not the thief, are you?" he whispered. The wind rose, making him shiver. "Let me know if you find a warm place to bed down. I may join you."

The hedgepig never obliged him. So Hew endured another chill and restless night. Nonetheless, he set out for the village early the next morn. Armed with his axe and the list the prior had given him, he trudged down the frosty road.

More than sleep, he could use a decent fire to warm his bones. And the apple-cheeked alewife's establishment had a cheery enough hearth. For a few pennies, he could break his fast.

By a stroke of luck, when he peered above the doorway of the alehouse, he saw the sign matched a name on his list. The Bell. This was the alewife who supplied the monastery. According to the prior's list, her son Peter visited twice a week to deliver the ale.

He didn't have to request an interview with Peter. As soon as he walked in with his axe across his shoulder, the lad, perhaps twelve years old and as apple-cheeked as his mother, rushed up in wide-eyed wonder.

"Can I look at that, sir?" he asked. "Your axe?"

"Peter," his mother chided, "leave the patrons alone."

"Is this your lad?" Hew asked.

She nodded.

"I'm happy to show him my axe." He whispered to Peter, "Let's sit by the fire where the light is better."

"I've just made oatcakes," the alewife offered.

"I'll take a pair then," he said.

She brought him the oatcakes and an ale while he showed his axe to Peter.

"I like the designs," Peter said, tracing the carvings along the handle with a finger.

"They're Viking runes."

Peter's eyes widened. "Are ye a Vikin'?"

"My ancestors were," he said. "What about you? Do you have warrior kin?"

"Nay," he said. "My da died when I was three."

"I'm sorry to hear that."

Peter shrugged. "I don't remember him. But we do just fine, my ma and me."

"You help her with the alehouse?"

He straightened with pride. "I do the deliveries."

"Deliveries," Hew said, pretending to be surprised. "Where do you deliver?"

Laird of Flint

"All over. To the hermit at village end. To the monastery. Even," he confided in a dreamy whisper, "to Lady Carenza herself."

There was that name again. Carenza.

"Sometimes she gives me a penny," Peter told him. Then he leaned closer to murmur, "Sometimes she kisses my brow."

"Peter," his keen-eared mother scolded. "I'm sure she kisses all the wee lads' brows. She's the laird's daughter. 'Tis her duty."

For an instant, Hew wished the dutiful Lady Carenza would kiss *his* brow. Then, deciding that would be a mistake, he cleared his throat.

"You deliver to the monastery, you said?" he said. "That's where I'm staying."

"Ye are? Aye. I go every Monday and Thursday."

"You go into the monastery proper?"

"Nay, the cellarer meets me at the gate after midday Mass."

The alewife called out to him. "Ale's ready for Dunlop, Peter."

"I have to go," Peter said, scrambling up from the table. "Don't like to keep Lady Carenza waiting. Maybe I'll see ye at the monastery?"

Hew nodded. But he'd already ruled out Peter as a suspect. The lad was enterprising, but he didn't seem like the sort to steal from a monastery.

He'd only polished off one of the warm, chewy oatcakes when patrons began wandering in. The Bell was surprisingly popular for this early in the day. But considering the quality ale and decent fare, it was probably a good way to prepare for a long, hard day of work.

He checked the prior's list. When the alewife refilled his cup, he asked her about the man who visited the monastery once each season to deliver spices. "Do you

39

know where I could find Absalom the spice merchant?"

"Absalom? When he's in town, he comes most every day. He should be along any time."

No sooner did she say the words than a dusky-skinned, black-haired man came through the door in a cloak thickly embroidered at the edges with bright thread.

"That's him," she murmured.

Absalom seemed rather richly dressed. Was that thanks to his talent as a spice merchant? Or his dexterity as a thief of religious artifacts? Hew wasn't sure.

He stood and greeted the man. "Absalom?" he asked.

"Aye."

"I'm told you deliver spices to the monastery not far from here?"

"That's right. Kildunan. Four times a year." He paused to call out to the alewife. "Ale and an oatcake."

"On its way," she called back.

"Can you tell me," Hew asked, "who takes the order?"

"The kitchener comes to the gate." Then he frowned, eyeing Hew's axe. "Why? Is there a problem?"

"Nay. 'Tis only..." He drew closer, confiding, "I'm staying there, and the food..." He wrinkled his nose.

Absalom nodded. "All the spices in the world won't help a bad cook."

"I was afraid of that," Hew said, saluting him with an oatcake.

Absalom gave him a nod of farewell, then called out to a man at another table before joining him. "Bernard."

Bernard. Hew glanced at his list. There was a Bernard who sold parchment to the monastery. Could it be the same man?

He didn't dare confront Bernard while he was sitting with Absalom. That would be too suspicious. No doubt the alewife was already wondering why this stranger with an axe was asking so many questions.

Laird of Flint

As he leaned back against the alehouse wall, he closed his eyes briefly, waiting for Bernard to leave. By the time he started awake, the man was gone.

"Did ye have a nice wee nap?" the alewife teased.

Shite. How had he drifted off? And how long had he been asleep?

"Can ye tell me where the parchment shop is?" he asked.

"At the far end o' the village," she said, adding pointedly, "downwind."

He thanked her, snatched his plaid, and hurried out the door.

He understood what she meant when he reached the end of the lane and entered Bernard's shop. The air was heavy with the stench of greasy sheepskin.

The proprietor furrowed his bushy brown brows at him. "Aren't ye the fellow who was snorin' at The Bell?"

Snoring? Hew didn't snore. At least he didn't *think* he snored. It was hard to know, since he was asleep.

"I was at The Bell, aye."

"Huh." He waved his arm at the goods stacked on shelves. "Ye need parchment?"

"Nay."

Bernard licked his lips and eyed his axe. "Then what are ye here for?"

"A few questions."

Bernard's gaze flitted nervously to the door. "Is this about the laird's daughter?" he blurted. "I only sold her parchment. I swear. If anyone said 'twas anythin' else..."

Hew lifted his brows. Was everyone entangled with Lady Carenza? "Nay."

"Oh." Bernard's shoulders dropped in relief. "What is it then?"

"The local prior told me you provide parchment to the monastery."

"Aye."

"You take it there yourself?"

"I do the delivery, aye."

"Directly to the prior?"

He shrugged. "Sometimes the prior. Sometimes a monk."

"You go to the scriptorium?"

He shook his head. "They meet me at the gate. But why do ye want to know all this?"

"I'm staying at the monastery, trying to make myself useful," he invented. "If I can save you the trouble of carting your wares to the monastery..."

"'Tis no trouble," Bernard assured him, adding quietly in confidence, "and just so ye know, the cost is the same, whether I deliver it or not. I'm already givin' the abbot a good price." He glanced at Hew's weapon again. "Ask anyone."

"Of course." Hew nodded. "Thank you for your time."

Bernard seemed like an untrustworthy sort. But it was probably true he'd given the abbot a good price. A man as paranoid as Bernard would likely try to buy his way into heaven.

So far, Hew was not convinced any of the vendors were guilty of the thefts. None of them were in the habit of entering the monastery. But interviewing everyone on the prior's list was the only way to eliminate suspects.

Mabel the cloth merchant only delivered goods to the monastery twice a year. She was a pious woman who walked with a crutch and considered the trip a pilgrimage of sorts. Hew mentally eliminated her.

The next two frequent visitors to the monastery were Brother Cathal, who collected the alms from Kildunan to distribute to the poor, and Father James, who oversaw the monastery with a monthly inspection. They would naturally be given free access to the monastery. Their presence in the most private chambers would never arouse suspicion. Indeed, Hew was rather surprised the prior had put them on the list at all.

Still, logistically, they were likely suspects. And Hew wanted no loose threads. Not only did they have access. They might have worked as a team, which would have made the thefts easier. And the fact that they both traveled widely, collecting alms and making inspections at various monasteries, meant they could hide their plunder almost anywhere.

They weren't in the village at present. A servant at the church said they had gone together to see the construction of the new monastery at Kilwinning.

That aroused Hew's suspicions even more. He began to wonder if Kildunan wasn't the only monastery to have treasures go missing. If all the monks were as secretive about the loss of valuables as the abbot of Kildunan was, there might well be serial robberies taking place.

As he left the church, Hew spotted the butcher shop where he'd purchased the ham. The village butcher was the last entry on his list.

When he swung open the door of the shop, the butcher waved his bloody hand in greeting.

"Ye again," he said with a wink. "Did ye finish off the ham already?"

Hew laughed. "Not quite. I've come to ask you a few questions."

"Questions?"

"About your deliveries to the monastery."

"Ah, ye mean Alan's deliveries to the monastery."

"Alan?"

He beamed. "My son. Ten years old, and he can already wield a butcher knife as fast as Sir Gellir o' Rivenloch can wield a sword."

Hew smirked. He wasn't going to tell the man that Sir

Gellir of Rivenloch was his cousin. His mother was right. Gellir was known everywhere. "Is your son here?"

"In the back." He turned and yelled, "Alan!"

The stout lad looked like a smaller version of his father as he came out in a butcher's blood-smeared apron. "Aye, Da?"

"This fellow wants to speak with ye."

"Me?" he squeaked.

"You take meat to the monastery every fortnight, aye?" Hew asked.

"That's right." He spotted Hew's axe. "I didn't miss a delivery, did I?"

"Nay, nay. I'm just wondering, when you deliver that meat, do you take it into the kitchens?"

"Och nay," he said, very gravely. "I'm not allowed inside. I give it to the monk."

"What monk?"

He furrowed his brows in deep thought. "The one in the...brown robe?"

"I see." Hew's lips twitched as he repressed a smile. Any lad who took his trade so seriously was an unlikely suspect. "Well, Alan, apprentice butcher, what would you recommend I purchase for..." He peered into his purse. "Two pence?"

Alan screwed up his face, considering. "A brace o' coneys?"

His father said, "We sold the last to Lady Carenza, remember?"

"Och aye," Alan gushed, turning bright scarlet. "I for-, forgot."

Hew frowned. Had the lady kissed him on the brow as well? Evidently she had the power to reduce wee lads to stammering fools.

"Go on, son," the butcher nudged.

Recovering from his fluster, Alan suggested, "How about a leg o' mutton?" He glanced over his shoulder to check that with his father, who nodded his approval.

"Good," Hew said.

Carrying the wrapped meat over one shoulder and his axe over the other, Hew yawned as he strode back up the street. He figured he'd arrive at the monastery after midday Mass and before the first meal of the day. So he'd have to decide whether he wanted to eat or sleep. At the moment, despite his earlier nap, sleep was winning.

He wasn't sure the prior would approve of the sudden increase of meat in the monks' diet. But a "rampaging Viking" like Hew had to eat well. Especially if he was required to travel from monastery to monastery to continue his investigation. Besides, he doubted the monks would complain.

CHAPTER 4

Carenza was simultaneously pleased and ashamed that the ragpicker in the village believed her story. It was an outright lie, after all. Carenza had no intention of making clothing for the poor with the scraps of wool and linen she'd purchased from him.

She meant to make a disguise for herself. Something dark. Warm. Bulky. Something that would render her unrecognizable.

She quickly found what she needed. The shopkeeper tied it into a parcel. When she exited the shop, Symon was across the lane, chatting with a friend. Her father had insisted she bring the servant along for safety.

The street was busy now. Everyone knew the laird's daughter, of course, and they all paid their respects. Vendors bobbed their heads as they carried parcels here and there. Young lads gaped as they scurried past, making deliveries and fetching coffyns for their masters' dinner. Women paused to smile and nod at her as they shopped, counting out coins for autumn apples and hard cheese and fresh fish. Carts rolled past, brimming with hay or stacked with barrels, and their drivers tipped their caps to her. She beamed at all of them.

Then she stepped into the road. All at once, a man

rushed by her so closely and in such haste, she felt the breeze of his passing.

With a tiny squeak, she recoiled.

"Sorry," he muttered, continuing on.

She frowned. The rude oaf didn't even bother to turn around to make sure she was unharmed. He just kept taking gigantic strides down the middle of the road, as if he owned it.

Who was he anyway? She knew everyone in the village, and she didn't recognize his tree-like height, his ox-wide back, or his tawny gold hair.

And that axe. Who carried a fierce battleaxe over his shoulder like that? He looked like a marauding Norseman.

He had something else over his other shoulder. Something round, wrapped in waxed cloth.

She smirked. Maybe it was a head. Aye, that was it. The marauding Norseman had cut off someone's head and was carrying it back to his longboat.

Then, shaking off her silly wandering thoughts, she continued carefully across the road. There was much to do and no time to waste. She couldn't afford to be distracted by marauding Norsemen.

"I'm ready to return now," she told Symon. She'd already purchased a brace of coneys, a dozen beeswax candles, lavender bath oil, and a pair of hair ribbons, mostly for cover.

He tied her last parcel onto his horse and helped her onto Leannan.

Unfortunately, as they rode out of the village and onto the main road, she discovered they were traveling along the same route as the Viking.

When she drew up within sight of the striding giant, she was tempted to seek revenge, to terrorize him by spurring her horse and grazing past him at a gallop. But she resisted the urge.

He looked quite formidable, even from the back. The cloth of his leine strained around his bulky arms, outlining each impressive muscle. The hand gripping the parcel on his shoulder looked massive. His hair gleamed like gold over broad shoulders that funneled down to narrow hips. A leather belt hung low across his buttocks, and it shifted with each long and confident stride.

She told herself he probably had the face of a monster. Scarred from battle. Fierce with berserker rage. Bloody from the beheading he'd just done.

But she'd never know. After all, it was unladylike to gawk at strange men.

So she rode past in silence, fixing her eyes on the road before her and focusing her mind on the daunting challenge ahead.

When Hew returned to the refectory with the leg of mutton, he expected a glare of disapproval from the prior. But the prior was engaged elsewhere. The abbot had the meat whisked away to the kitchens for later use.

The meal was silent as usual. But that was fine with Hew. He'd rather not discuss the fine points of his investigation with the abbot, since his two most likely suspects so far were members of the church.

Perhaps he would mention his suspicions to the prior. After all, the prior was the one who had put their names on the list in the first place.

"Where is the prior?" he murmured to the monk beside him after they'd finished eating.

"In the infirmary."

"Is he ill?"

"Nay. He's lookin' after a layman."

"A layman?"

The monk nodded and leaned closer to whisper, "A local

merchant. The physician's been summoned. But they're fairly certain he'll need last rites soon."

Hew nodded. That was one of the advantages of making generous donations to a monastery. When a wealthy man was about to die, he could call in favors from the church and live out his days in relative comfort. The infirmary had a dozen soft beds. A warm hearth. Better food than the monks got. Servants to see to a dying man's every need. And holy men to look after the deceased's soul.

It was a good arrangement.

"Oh," Hew suddenly remembered, "do you happen to know what day the almoner turns over donations to Brother Cathal?"

"Thursdays."

"And when does Father James visit?"

"He ne'er announces his arrival. Just shows up."

That made sense. Hew's mother never announced inspections of the armory either. It kept men honest.

Hew drank the last of his ale. Then he stifled a yawn. The lack of sleep last night and a hearty extra meal today had caught up with him. Since Brother Cathal wouldn't come by for another few days, there was not much else he could do. He might as well take a long, leisurely nap.

In his cell, he'd just settled his head into the recess he'd punched into the pallet when his eyes flew open.

The physician.

The prior hadn't put the physician on the list.

It was probably just an oversight, not an omission. After all, a physician would only be needed when someone was seriously ill. He would visit the infirmary, which adjoined the monastery.

The monk had told him the prior had *summoned* the physician. So where had he come from? And could he have something to do with the missing valuables?

Hew sat up. He wasn't going to be able to sleep now.

Not with that new possibility nagging at his brain.

Emerging from his cell into the cloister, he cast his gaze in the direction of the infirmary. It was tempting to simply charge into the building and start questioning the physician.

But a man was dying there. And the infirmary was isolated for a reason. Peace and quiet.

To be fair, the whole monastery seemed peaceful and quiet to Hew. Especially compared to the lively atmosphere at Rivenloch. But he supposed interrogating a man in the infirmary would be frowned upon.

When Hew saw several of the more seasoned monks begin to file past, heading toward the infirmary, he figured the dying man's time was nigh.

Would they send the physician home soon? And where was home?

He cornered one of the younger monks in the library. "The physician in the infirmary. Do you know who he is?"

"The physician? Peris."

"Where does he come from, do you know?"

"I don't. He only comes when someone's about to..." The monk gulped, as if saying the words aloud might make it so.

"Who *would* know?"

"The abbot?"

Hew was fairly certain the abbot was seeing to the dying man as well, since all of the senior monks seemed to be gathering at the infirmary.

He supposed he'd just have to wait until the man expired.

Hours passed. He was served a silent dinner of thin mutton pottage. The sun sank in a gloomy sky. The cloud-ringed moon emerged. Still no one returned.

He retired to his cell and stared at the plaster ceiling, dimly illuminated by the filtered moonlight.

He was glad he was a warrior. Warriors didn't suffer through lingering death watches or questionable cures. They went out in a blaze of glory.

If Hew had his way, he would never have need of a physician.

Maybe to mend his wounded heart, he corrected. That was something that wouldn't heal on its own.

He drifted off, dreaming of all the women he'd loved and lost.

Carenza rubbed her aching eyes and scooted her stool closer to the hearth. It was difficult to stitch late at night by firelight. But she didn't have a choice. She couldn't exactly piece together a disguise by daylight in front of witnesses.

Fortunately, no one would be inspecting her handiwork. It was truly rushed and haphazard. Her stitches were crooked and uneven, and she didn't bother to finish any of the seams.

But it only had to last one night. Afterwards, she'd rip it apart into unrecognizable rags.

Besides, its rustic quality made it a better disguise. No one would suspect the stout beggar hobbling along the hill in tatters was in truth the laird's daughter.

She tied one final knot in the garment and snipped the thread with scissors. Then she shook out the cloth and stood to hold it up to her waist.

A few nights hence, she'd be in a hurry to dress. She needed to try everything on before then.

She'd never worn men's trews before. They were surprisingly comfortable. The waist was a bit baggy. So she dug through her chest to find a leather belt to hold them up.

Over her leine, she slipped the voluminous patchwork shirt she'd sewn. The garment, padded in the shoulders and at the front to add bulk, fell to her knees.

She pulled up the thick woolen socks she'd borrowed from her father's winter chest.

Then she let out a jagged breath. If her da could see her now, he would lock her in her room and throw away the key.

She'd procured a pair of sturdy boots from the stable lad. She'd told him she meant to have them repaired and cleaned for him. Which she would. After she used them to tramp through the muddy hills.

But when she picked up the left boot, it was occupied.

"Oh!" she cried. "Blancmange, what are ye doin' in there?"

She gently dumped the wee hedgepig out of the boot onto the floor.

"Ye can't make a nest in that."

Undaunted, Blancmange waddled toward the second boot.

"Nor there either," she said, picking it up out of the way.

As she watched the hedgepig continue on toward her discarded slipper, she felt a tingling at the back of her neck.

They weren't alone. She was being watched.

Sliding her gaze warily to the left, she glimpsed a second spiny beast huddled on her bed, regarding her with beady eyes.

"Pokerounce," she scolded in a whisper, "ye're not allowed on the bed, and ye know it."

She picked up the wriggling hedgepig and placed her on the floor next to her sister.

"Ye two are naughty wee lasses tonight."

Then she smirked. They weren't the only ones.

She clucked her tongue at the adorable pair of hedgepigs. She'd rescued them last spring when their mother had been killed by a hound.

Lately they'd had a strong nesting instinct that had led them to snuggle in her skirts, hide in the peat pile on the hearth, and burrow into her pallet. She supposed she'd have to do something about that soon.

Meanwhile, she plucked out the vials of bath oils from her willow basket and propped the basket upside down in the corner for them. They immediately toddled over and made themselves at home within the makeshift nest.

The boots proved roomy but serviceable. She snatched up the hood she'd fashioned out of brown scraps and pulled it over her head. It was perfect. Deep enough to both warm her ears and keep her face hidden under the cold, bright moon.

When she held her mirror out at arm's length, a wave of shame washed over her again. She looked nothing like the daughter her father was so proud of.

The woman in the reflection was someone even Carenza hardly recognized. A wayward, willful, disobedient scruff of a lass who was about to embark on a mission that was disgraceful. Dishonorable. Deceitful. And dangerous.

When Hew awoke the next morn, it was over.

The man had died in the middle of the night. The abbot had delivered last rites. The monks had prepared the body. And the physician had gone home.

At the midday meal, Hew was finally able to ask the bleary-eyed abbot where the physician came from.

"Peris? Dunlop Castle," the abbot replied. "He's the laird's own physician."

Dunlop again.

"Why do ye ask?" the prior said.

"The physician wasn't on your list," Hew pointed out.

The prior gave him a humorless smile. "I didn't feel it necessary to include him. He's here only on occasion."

"Of course. Still, we must leave no stone unturned in the pursuit of justice."

"O' course."

"I'll need to make a visit to Dunlop," Hew decided, "to speak with him."

"He's likely exhausted," the prior argued. "He was up all night, carin' for a dyin' man."

"He's right," the abbot agreed, which pleased the prior, until he added, "But 'tis a few hours walk, and ye could go later today."

"I'll go with him," the prior volunteered. "I can make introductions."

The abbot's brow creased. "I may need ye here. We still have the burial to complete."

"The burial will be on the morrow, aye?" the prior reminded him.

"Och. Aye." The abbot rubbed at his sleepy eyes. "I've lost track o' the days."

"Besides," the prior said, "I can take Dunlop a jar o' the honey he likes so well."

The abbot waved his approval.

Hew was not happy with that decision. He'd hoped to make the journey alone.

As expected, the dour prior proved poor company. The instant they passed through the gate, 'twas as if the prior was no longer bound by the silence of the monastery. He began to chatter incessantly, preparing Hew to meet the physician as if he were going to meet the Pope.

He warned Hew that Peris was a nervous man who didn't like to be questioned about his methods. He said that a death was always traumatic for a physician, so he should not be judged by his fragility today. He stressed that the monastery appreciated the physician's services and wanted to keep them.

To make matters worse, the prior's sandal-shod shuffle lengthened the journey. What Hew could have covered in an hour of long strides took twice as long at the prior's slow pace.

But as long as the prior had insisted on accompanying him, Hew supposed he should make good use of the time.

"Tell me what you know about Brother Cathal."

"Brother Cathal? He collects the alms once a week, on Thursday, and distributes them to the poor."

"Where does he go to collect them?"

"The chapter house."

"So he goes within the monastery walls?"

"Aye, but..." The prior halted on the road and drew his brows together. "Ye don't think Brother Cathal is the thief?"

"He has access."

The prior looked troubled. He stroked his chin thoughtfully and resumed walking. "Brother Cathal." He shook his head. "'Tis possible, but..."

"Did any of the thefts occur on Thursdays?"

"They *may* have. 'Tis hard to say. Sometimes the objects aren't missed for days." The prior mulled over the idea for a moment. Then he said, "Ye don't suppose he's been stealin' the alms as well?"

Hew shrugged.

"Sweet Mary," the prior said, "if he's been stealin' alms all this time..." He let out a pained sigh. "Brother Cathal's been collectin' from Kildunan for two years."

Hew thought the prior was getting ahead of things. Brother Cathal's guilt hadn't been established. Access didn't prove the crime.

"What about Father James?" Hew asked.

"Father James?"

"He was on your list as well."

The prior straightened indignantly. "Father James is beyond reproach. I only put him on the list because he makes regular visits to the monastery."

"Random visits, not regular visits."

"Well, aye. But he comes every month."

"And what is his access?"

"He has access to all o' Kildunan," the prior scoffed. "As he should. After all, he's in charge o' the monastery."

"Have any of the valuables gone missing after his inspections?"

The prior gasped at the suggestion. "Are ye insinuatin'—"

"I mean no offense. But you can't flush out quarry without beating about the bushes."

The prior huffed at that. Then he said in hushed tones, "Ye mustn't let Father James know ye're 'beatin' about the bushes.' The abbot has made it clear. The father is not to be alerted to the thefts. Not yet." He added sharply, "Especially since ye're accusin' him o' bein' the thief."

"I'm not accusing him. I'm only crossing the names off *your* list," Hew pointed out.

The prior muttered something under his breath.

"Tell me this," Hew said. "Are there times when Father James and Brother Cathal come to Kildunan together?"

"Aye. Sometimes. Wait. Ye don't think..."

Hew filled in the possibility. "They could be working together."

He expected an outburst of disbelief from the prior. But there was none. To Hew's surprise, the prior's voice was distraught as he murmured, "As much as I don't want to believe it, ye may be right. No one else has the access they do. No one would question their goin' into the church. Or the library. Or the cloister."

Hew suddenly felt sorry for the prior. The possibility that Father James, a man revered by the monks, might be a common thief was obviously upsetting to a man who lived and breathed his faith.

He was about to offer a morsel of compassion when the prior pointed and announced, "Ah. There 'tis."

Through the thinning trees, Hew glimpsed a castle strategically perched atop a hill. It was of modest size, compared to Rivenloch. But its sandstone walls gleamed golden. Proud banners topped each corner of the keep, snapping crisply in the breeze. And dozens of figures dotted the hillside, as busy as ants. The castle was small, but it seemed efficient and well-maintained. Dunlop likely owned much of the land surrounding it as well.

At the barbican, the guard waved the prior through the gate, though he gave Hew and his axe a dubious scowl. Indeed, once they were in the courtyard, several clanfolk gave Hew a dubious scowl. Women with children also gave him a wide berth.

The prior plunged ahead to address a pair of men-at-arms standing beside the keep. "Do ye know where Dunlop is?"

"Inside," one of them said, nodding toward the great hall.

"Come," the prior said to Hew. "I'll introduce ye. While ye're makin' the laird's acquaintance, I'll find out where Peris has gone."

The great hall was packed with people. Maidservants wielded besoms, polished tables, and carried trays of oatcakes. Lads placed candles in sconces, wrangled loose hound pups, and poked at the coals on the hearth. Wee children played with wooden dolls. Noblewomen giggled over them. Warriors drank ale by the fire.

"There he is," the prior said, nodding toward the far stairs.

Hew followed his gaze. A middle-aged nobleman towered several inches above the rest of his clanfolk. He was pleasant-looking, with a neatly trimmed black beard and fine clothing, as crisp and well-maintained as his castle. Though he wasn't built like a warrior, he looked confident and calm. It was clear he was the leader of this clan.

Then Hew's eyes fell to the young maid on his arm.

Suddenly he couldn't move. Couldn't think. Couldn't breathe.

She was The Most Beautiful Woman He Had Ever Seen in His Entire Life.

CHAPTER 5

The lass was so breathtaking, so knee-weakening, so heart-melting, Hew actually let the axe slide off his shoulder. It almost hit the man standing beside him.

"Hey, mind your blade," the man growled.

"Sorry," Hew mumbled, fixated on the impossibly lovely woman.

Then the man saw where he was looking. "Och. Lady Carenza. She's a head-turner, for certain."

Carenza.

In the village, her name had been on everyone's lips. The alewife's lad's. The parchment-maker's. The butcher's son's. In The Bell, the cooherd had been talking about her.

What had he said? That the Boyle lads wanted to court her, but her father had his sights set much higher.

No doubt. An angel that magnificent deserved nothing short of a king. Maybe a saint.

Traffic moved around him as he stood in stunned admiration.

Her father had her in a close grip. Hew couldn't blame him. If he owned such a treasure, he'd hold onto her tightly too.

She looked as pale and delicate as an apple blossom. Her forest green gown clung to her gentle curves. She walked with such grace, she seemed to glide through the hall. Her dark waist-length braid was draped coyly over one shoulder.

But what caught at his heart and stopped his breath was her brilliant smile. Welcoming, warm, and full of delight, it made everyone around her smile in return. Like a candle moving through the shadows, she lit up everything she touched.

Hew could feel his heart stirring, waking, coming to life. A rush of emotion surged through his veins, warming his blood. The familiar gush of pleasure filled his body, melting his bones. His eyes softened as he gazed at her with the sudden certainty that he was sincerely, deeply, helplessly in love.

Again.

This time, however, she was The One. He was sure of it.

She continued on while he stood there, dumbfounded. Perhaps it was best that her father steered her up the stairs, for if Hew had crossed paths with her at that moment, he might have done something foolish. Like fallen to his knees and begged for her hand on the spot.

He gave his head a sobering shake.

What the hell was wrong with him? Had he no bloody self-control?

He'd vowed he was not going to fall in love. Not again. And he meant it. He had no intention of subjecting his heart to damage again just because he'd seen a lass with a bonnie face.

He took a deep breath. Gathered his wits.

When the laird emerged from the stairwell again, he was alone. Thank God.

But before they could engage him, a pair of merchants called Dunlop aside.

As they drew near, the laird's eyes widened at the

sight of Hew's axe. Hew lowered his weapon, planting it harmlessly between his feet. The laird resumed his conversation with the merchants, finally dismissing them to greet the prior.

"Prior," the laird said, "I hear ye had a rough night at Kildunan."

"Aye, we lost another man o' faith," the prior said, making the sign of the Cross, "God rest his soul."

The laird glanced at Hew. "And who is this?"

"M'laird," the prior intoned with a bow, "may I present Sir Hew o' Rivenloch. He's stayin' at the—"

"Rivenloch," the laird interrupted. "Ye're a Rivenloch warrior?"

"Aye, m'laird," Hew replied.

The laird reached out to clasp Hew's hand in both of his. "'Tis an honor, sir." Hew couldn't help but remember those hands had just touched the sleeve of that beautiful angel. "Your reputation precedes ye."

Hew belatedly realized that the prior probably shouldn't have revealed his clan name. His presence at the monastery was supposed to be a secret.

Nonetheless, he gave the laird a polite nod. "The honor is mine, my laird."

"Your pardon, m'laird," the prior interjected, "can ye tell me where I might find the physician?"

"Peris? Ye'll likely find him near the kitchens, tendin' to John's burns." He shook his head. "I suppose all kitchen lads get a baptism o' fire, aye?" He gave the prior a wink.

The prior didn't see the humor. "Ah." He held up the jar of honey he'd brought and said, "Shall I leave this with the cook then?"

"Is that Kildunan's famous honey?" the laird said. "Pray do so."

Then the prior turned to Hew. "I'll fetch the physician for ye."

"Ye need the physician?" the laird asked when the prior had gone.

"I just have a few questions."

"About last night?"

Hew gave him the easy answer. "Aye." Then he changed the subject. "'Tis a fine castle ye have, m'laird."

"Not nearly as fine as Rivenloch, I'm certain," the laird argued. "Is it true the armory is the size of a tournament field?"

Hew chuckled at that. "Not quite, though 'tis nearly as big as your great hall."

The laird whistled in amazement. "How are ye kin to the laird?"

"Laird Deirdre? She's my..." He faltered as, out of the corner of his eye, he spotted the vision in green emerging again from the stairwell. But he dared not let his gaze drift to her. "My aunt."

"So your mother is..."

Hew couldn't think. Not while the green blur behind the laird was smiling and carrying on with the maidservants. "My mother is..." he repeated. Fierce? Hot-tempered? Deadly with a sword? What did the laird want to know? Ah, her name. "Helena."

"So your father is...Colin?"

"Mmm."

It took all Hew's willpower to keep his gaze trained on the laird when he heard a trickle of gentle laughter that had to belong to the delicate lass. Laughter like a bubbling burn. The soft sprinkle of spring rain. The melodious plucking of a harp.

"...are ye not? the laird said.

Hew flushed. He hadn't heard a word. And the swelling in his trews was proving a powerful distraction. "I'm sorry. What was that?"

Laird of Flint

The laird grinned. "I think we need a larger hall. The Dunlops are a noisy bunch. I said, then ye're cousin to the great tournament champion, Gellir, are ye not?"

"Aye." Hew stiffened. He hoped the laird wouldn't ask him where Gellir was. He'd already said too much.

"He's got quite the reputation with a sword." The laird pointedly lowered his gaze. "Though ye seem impressively endowed yourself."

Hew's eyes widened with horror. Was his arousal so obvious? Then he realized the laird was looking at the axe he'd planted betwixt his feet.

Expelling a relieved breath, Hew hefted the axe up, holding it so the laird could inspect the handle. "She's served me well in battle."

The laird ran his fingers over the carvings. "Vikin' runes, aye? What does it say?"

"'Tis the Rivenloch motto. Love conquers all." Hew furrowed his brows. At the moment, he didn't exactly believe that.

"Curious inscription for a weapon o' war."

It wasn't the first time someone had told Hew that. Nor the first time he'd quipped in reply, "No one forgets the kiss of my axe."

"No doubt," the laird agreed, eyeing the sharpened deadly blade.

A few yards away, the lass giggled again. Hew clenched his jaw as he focused on the laird, trying not to look at her. But in his peripheral vision, he saw the green gown weave in and out and finally disappear into the crowd. Now perhaps he could think.

"Supper?" the laird suggested.

Hew silently cursed. His eyes might have been trained on the laird, but his mind had wandered again. What had he missed? "Supper?"

"Aye." The laird drew close to confide, "I hear they don't feed a man enough to fill a flea at Kildunan. My cook can make ye a proper meal."

"'Tis a tempting offer," Hew said. "But the prior needs to return for the burial on the morrow."

"Send him back to Kildunan. Ye can stay for supper and return on the morrow if ye like. 'Tisn't every day we get a renowned warrior at Dunlop. Ye could regale the clan with tales o' Rivenloch."

The last thing Hew needed was to be the center of attention. No one was supposed to know he was here.

"I'm grateful for the offer. But I promised the abbot I'd return this eve."

"Perhaps another time then?"

"Perhaps."

"Well, ye should at least meet my daughter, Carenza." He began to scour the hall. "Where's she gone?"

Hew was saved from that unthinkable ordeal when the prior returned with the physician.

As the prior had warned, Peris was as skittish as a dove loosed among hawks. He licked his lips. Darted his shifty eyes. Clasped and unclasped his hands before him.

"Peris," the prior said, "this is Sir Hew. He wishes to ask ye a few questions."

"Peris," Hew said by way of greeting.

The physician's eyes flitted to Hew's weapon. He visibly gulped. Hew wondered, if the man was so bothered by the sight of an axe, how he managed to do surgery.

"Sir Hew wants to ask ye about your visits to Kildunan," the prior said.

The laird was still casting about for his daughter. "I'll leave ye to your questions then. I've got to find out where Carenza's gone." With that, he left.

"'Tis loud in here," Hew told the physician. "Is there someplace we can be alone? Perhaps the wall walk?"

LAIRD OF FLINT

Peris gave the prior a panicked glance, as if he thought Hew intended to push him from the battlements.

The prior assured him, "I'll come with ye."

They climbed the steps to the top level of the keep, where a single guard patrolled the wall. There, the only sounds were the rippling of the banners and the distant chatter of the bustling courtyard below.

"I did all I could, sir," Peris volunteered out of nowhere. "I swear. It must have been God's will."

"O' course ye did," the prior said. "No one is blamin' ye for his death."

"Right," Hew agreed. "I want to ask you about the others."

"The others? What others?"

The prior placed a calming hand on the man's shoulder. "Like I said, he wants to know about your visits to the monastery, that's all."

"I'm not blaming you for any deaths," Hew clarified.

The physician rubbed his chin. "All right. What do ye want to know?"

"How often do you come to Kildunan?"

"Not often. Just every time there's a..." He paused to glance at the prior.

The prior finished for him. "Every time there's a serious illness."

"Right."

"Do you come alone?" Hew asked.

"Aye."

"And where do you go?"

"Where do I go?" Peris said. "To...to the infirmary, o' course."

"O' course," the prior echoed.

"And do you go anywhere else?" Hew asked.

"Think hard," the prior suggested.

While the physician was thinking, a furtive movement

65

from the courtyard below caught Hew's eye. It was her. The angel. The vision. Carenza.

She had slipped behind the wall of the stable and was hunkered down in the shadows beside a small animal. He couldn't make out what it was. A kitten? A pup?

"The refectory," Peris said, "if I'm there for more than half a day."

"To take your meals," the prior explained.

"Aye, and the garderobe," he said, "in case I...ye know."

What *was* that creature? It was very small but quick and reddish in color. She seemed to be feeding it.

"The library."

That caught Hew's ear. "The library?"

The prior explained. "The monastery has a few medical texts."

"That's right," Peris said.

"Where else?" Hew said.

"The cloister."

"The cloister. Why?"

"To fetch water from the well."

Hew nodded. "Go on."

Peris continued trying to recall all the places he'd gone.

Meanwhile, the creature Carenza was feeding scampered onto her lap. He could see now it was a squirrel. How she'd convinced the wild thing to let her feed it by hand he couldn't fathom. But she was playing a dangerous game. If it bit her...

"I think that's all," Peris concluded.

Hew hadn't really been listening. But it was clear Peris basically had access to the entire monastery. After all, a monk could fall ill in any quarter of Kildunan.

"Do you know on which days you've come to the monastery?" Hew asked.

"The days?" Peris chewed at his lip.

"'Tis all right if ye don't remember exactly," the prior

said. "Ye've been comin' to the monastery for a long while now."

"Aye," Peris said. "Nigh a year."

Hew frowned. A year wasn't that long. And the thefts had taken place within the last year. "What days do you remember?"

"I remember the first time was a few days after Candlemas. I was there just before Beltane and sometime in midsummer…"

The prior finished, "The last time ye came was on Michaelmas. I remember that."

"Aye, for Sir Patric," Peris recalled. "That was a big one."

The prior gave him a sharp look. "His…size…is no doubt what led to his demise."

"Och." The physician nodded. "Aye."

Hew would have to compare the dates of the physician's visits with the dates of the objects' disappearances.

He glanced down toward the stable. The lady was gone now. He saw the trailing hem of her gown disappear between two holly bushes. The squirrel, its belly full, was skittering across the stable roof, probably on its way back to the forest.

He furrowed his brows. The lass shouldn't have fed the creature. Now it would return, expecting more. And one of these days, if she didn't have a morsel to give it, it would likely take a bite out of her hand.

"Is that all?" Peris asked.

He looked over at the physician, who was sweating as if he thought Hew might grab his axe and behead him at any moment.

"For now." He didn't have anything else to ask the physician. Not yet.

He might return if the dates seemed to coincide. But he felt like Brother Cathal or Father James were more likely suspects. Their visits were scheduled. They had plenty of time to plan a robbery. They didn't have to rely on someone falling ill.

"Carenza! There ye are."

Carenza nearly jumped out of her skin. She hastily nudged the squirrel away from her. It skittered under the holly bush. Then she rose to greet her father, dusting the dirt from her skirts.

"We should have plenty o' holly boughs for Yuletide," she proclaimed, as if she'd been inspecting the holly and not feeding a wee wild beast a few oatcake crumbs out of the palm of her hand.

"Ah. Good." Then he sighed. It was a sigh of mild disappointment. "I wish I'd found ye earlier."

She hated disappointing him. "Why? What's happened?"

"Ye missed our guest."

"Guest? What guest?" She'd been too busy feeding her squirrels to notice anyone's arrival.

He gave her a smug grin. "None other than a warrior o' Rivenloch."

Rivenloch. She thought she knew the name. But not as well as her father apparently did. She pretended to be impressed. "Rivenloch? Really? Here?"

"I know," her father said, his eyes gleaming. "And he's stayin' at the monastery."

"Ah." Why a warrior would be staying at a monastery, she couldn't guess.

"But ye'll be glad to know I've invited him to supper."

"Tonight?" She was absolutely not glad to know that. First, his timing was awful. She had to finalize her plans tonight. And second, why was it men always expected a woman could whip up a special supper for guests with a snap of her fingers?

Laird of Flint

"Nay, not tonight," he said. "Sadly, he had to return to the monastery."

Sadly for her father. Carenza was relieved. "Another time then."

"As soon as possible."

Carenza smiled, but she was doing calculations in her head. She needed to be sure nothing conflicted with her scheme. And a supper guest sounded like a conflict.

"He's cousin to Sir Gellir, the tournament champion," he told her.

"Ah." That name sounded familiar. Her father may have mentioned it before. But he followed tournament contestants. She did not.

"And a nephew o' the laird."

Her smile grew brittle. Why was he going on and on about this Rivenloch man? A man who was the cousin of a champion and the nephew of a laird, yet somehow resided at a monastery?

"I think ye'd be quite impressed," he said with a knowing lift of his brow.

Then she understood. He wanted her to meet him because he thought the man might make a suitable suitor.

Part of her wanted to scream. She had far too much on her mind to feign fascination with a possible future husband.

But part of her felt a tender admiration for her father. It must be difficult for him to consider marrying her off. In vulnerable moments, he'd often said she was all he had. The idea of giving her up to another man couldn't be easy.

"Ye know," he continued, "the Rivenlochs are one o' the oldest border clans in service o' the king. The oldest and the richest. Plenty o' land. A formidable keep. And the warriors...well, if ye'd seen this one..." He shook his head in wonder.

A border warrior sounded like the sort of man Carenza despised. Violent. Overbearing. Heartless. That kind of man certainly would have no patience for a maid who rescued spiders and fed squirrels and saved coos.

Her father continued. "Ye could see the Norse in his blood. Tall he was. Golden-haired. And broad o' shoulder. With a great battle axe that had runes carved into—"

"An axe?" she choked out.

It couldn't be. Could it? Was this Rivenloch warrior the man she'd seen on the road?

"Aye, just like a Vikin'."

"What was he doin' here?"

"He and the prior had some questions for the physician."

"What kind o' questions?" She wondered if he'd asked Peris how best to preserve the head he was carrying about in a sack.

He shrugged. "Somethin' about the death at the monastery last night. But that's not important. What's important is he's stayin' nearby for a while."

Carenza could see she wasn't going to weasel out of hosting the man for supper. It seemed she'd find out what he looked like after all. But there was one way she could both please her father and put her own heart to rest. She could manage the timing.

"I know, Da," she said, her eyes sparkling with feigned enthusiasm. "Do ye think he'd like to celebrate Samhain with us?"

"Brilliant, lass!" he exclaimed, lighting up. "I daresay Samhain at Dunlop Castle will be a bit more...festive...than All Saints Day at the monastery."

"Wonderful," she said, clasping her hands together under her chin. "I look forward to meetin' him then."

Her father kissed her brow in farewell.

Good. For a few days at least—until Samhain—she

could put her mind at ease. She could banish all thoughts of warriors and marriage and focus on what was truly important.

By nightfall, she had her plans well in hand. She managed to drift off to slumber and dreamed of happier times when Hamish was a wee calf.

Unfortunately, her dreams curdled into nightmares. She woke in the dark, gasping from a horrifying vision of a Viking with an axe chasing after her beloved coo.

She couldn't get back to sleep after that. So she wrapped her arisaid about her and opened the shutters to stare up into the cold heavens, where stars winked through the threadbare clouds.

She'd make her move tomorrow night when the moon was full.

Once it was dark, she had to escape unnoticed from the castle. Locate the fold of cattle. Lead Hamish to his new home beyond the hills. And return without getting caught.

She sighed. The task seemed impossible.

But she had no choice. She wasn't going to let her father kill Hamish.

The wind rose, stirring strands of her loose hair. The cold air made her eyes water. The stars, once steadfast, now blurred and shimmered, untethered and unstable, as if to show her her fate was likewise uncertain.

CHAPTER 6

As a youth, Hew always relished the glorious rites held at Rivenloch whenever a noble warrior perished in battle. Because the clan was comprised of Viking invaders, Norman knights, Scottish warriors, and one intrepid assassin from the Orient, he was never certain whether the deceased was headed to heaven, hell, or Valhalla. Any ceremony on Rivenloch land was bound to be a melding of Viking tradition, pagan superstition, and Christian doctrine. But the event was invariably celebrated with fire and feasting, singing and storytelling.

So it was a disappointment to learn that burying the deceased layman at Kildunan involved none of these. Indeed, the ceremony stipulated even more decorum and prayer, less food and drink.

The dead man had no living kin. Still, the monks gave him a lengthy and somber service in the church. The man had apparently donated enough wealth to earn him a grave within the monastery walls.

Halfway through a day of burning candles and monotonous chants, Hew had had enough. His belly was growling. And the litany of prayers made him wonder if the monks intended to recite the entire Bible.

But then the elusive Father James made a surprise appearance.

At his arrival, the abbot fawned over the elderly priest. He welcomed him into the church and remarked on what a blessing it was to the deceased to have him present.

Hew studied the man. White-haired and wizened, there was a spark of intelligence in his snapping eyes. Withered he might be, but he missed nothing. His gaze immediately settled on Hew, and Hew could almost hear his thought... *What is* he *doing here?*

Just as quickly, the priest turned his attention back to the matter at hand. He blessed the body and began intoning words of prayer as monks wafted incense over the shroud.

Hew used the opportunity to sink back into the shadows and observe.

Could Father James be the thief?

Was he devout or devious?

Did his holy vestments hide a black heart?

Was his practiced genuflection an indication of his light-fingered habits?

Suspicion must have shown in Hew's furrowed brow, for beyond Father James, the prior glared pointedly back at him, wordlessly reminding him not to let on that anything was amiss.

He supposed that was wise. A watched outlaw was always careful. Hew needed the thief to think he was safe. Overconfident robbers made mistakes.

The priest didn't stay long, and it seemed neither the time nor place to inquire about his visits to Kildunan. But Father James did speak at length to the abbot and the prior. And once or twice he glanced in Hew's direction. Clearly, he wished to know who the stranger at the monastery was. Hew wondered what they were telling him.

According to the prior, when a monk died at Kildunan, he was buried in an unmarked grave in the orchard. But there was a special graveyard behind the orchard for notable guests. Two rows of small gravestones were embedded into the sod there like crooked teeth. At one end was a new hole gouged into the earth where the latest body would be buried.

By late afternoon, the rites were over. The monks dispersed from the grave until only the prior and he remained.

"Well?" the prior asked with a smirk, raising one judgmental brow.

Hew frowned. "What?"

"Ye can't possibly think Father James is..." He glanced cautiously about the orchard for stragglers. "Ye know."

"The thief?"

The prior winced. He obviously didn't want to speak the words aloud. "Aye."

Hew wasn't ready to say. "I'm not certain yet."

The prior thinned his lips in disapproval.

Hew had a question of his own. "What did you tell him about me?"

"Just that ye were visitin' the monastery."

"You didn't tell him I was from Rivenloch?"

"I did not."

"Good."

"The abbot, however, might have mentioned it."

Hew growled.

Bloody hell. Loose-lipped monks would be the death of him. Soon all of Scotland would know a warrior of Rivenloch was hiding at Kildunan. And when the king found out, he'd no doubt come running with a betrothal. A betrothal between Hew and some milksop daughter of an English lord.

Hew wanted to punch something. But he'd resist the

urge. He didn't want to alarm the prior. He needed the man's trust and cooperation. The sooner he could get it, the sooner he could solve the crime. The sooner he could solve the crime, the sooner he could leave this purgatory and find a safer place to hide. Hopefully with his cousin Gellir at Darragh.

So he reduced his temper to a low simmer. "Brother Cathal comes on the morrow, aye?"

"Aye."

"I'll want to question him."

"O' course."

As he left to find something to eat, he called back over his shoulder, "And henceforth, I wish to be introduced simply as Hew."

Since he'd had little to eat all day, Hew treated himself to double portions of supper, ignoring the scowls of scorn from the prior. Afterwards, he borrowed the monastery's rarely used wooden tub, filling it from the well. Then he coaxed the cook to heat a cauldron of cinnamon-infused water for him to add to the tub. An hour later, he sank into his first decent bath in a fortnight and scrubbed off the cloying scent of incense and the lingering stench of death.

The steaming, fragrant water lulled him to drowsiness. He bathed, dried off, and cracked open the shutters to let in the fresh evening air. Then he fell into bed, asleep almost before his head hit the pallet.

Sometime in the middle of the night, through the gap in the shutters, a shadow falling across the full moon abruptly awakened him.

His eyes flew open. But he lay motionless, listening.

Were those footfalls?

He wrapped his fingers around his axe on the floor beside him and rose without a sound.

Peering between the shutters, he spied a dark figure stealing across the cloister.

Then he mouthed a silent curse. When he'd gone to bed, he'd assumed he was done investigating for the night. It appeared he'd assumed wrong. He needed to find out who the mysterious figure was and what he was up to. But first he had to get dressed. Quickly.

He wrenched his leine over his head and pulled up his trews, cursing as he struggled to tie the points. He shoved his feet into his boots. Finally, whirling his plaid over his shoulders, he crept out of his cell. Thankfully, the moon was bright enough to follow the path of bent grass where the man had trod. It led straight to the monastery gate.

Hew gripped his axe tighter as he cautiously nudged open the unlocked gate. Who else but an outlaw would steal out of a monastery in the middle of the night?

He spotted the figure far in the distance on the westward road. The man had wasted no time fleeing Kildunan. And he was making haste now. Hew's delay meant the outlaw was not much more than a faraway speck.

But that was good. It was best that Hew keep his distance and make sure the man didn't know he was being followed.

An hour later, he was still headed west. In the direction of Dunlop Castle. And Hew began to have doubts about the man and his motives.

What if the figure was not a thief, but the physician returning to Dunlop?

What if he'd only arrived in the middle of the night because someone in the monastery had taken ill?

What if his visit hadn't been for a robbery, but a mission of mercy?

The man crested the grassy hill before the castle. Hew continued his pursuit, staying close to the trees. When he ran out of trees at the clearing, he stopped to watch.

The barbican gates of Dunlop would open for either the physician or a man of God. As Hew expected, the man swiftly disappeared within the castle walls.

Axe-wielding Hew, however, was not likely to be welcomed by the guard.

Sooner or later, if he'd come from monastery, the mysterious visitor would need to return. Likely before dawn.

Hew settled down onto the hard ground to wait.

For Carenza, the full moon and the cloudless sky were both a blessing and a curse. The light would help her find her way across the courtyard, out of the castle, and over the hills. It would also leave her visible—and vulnerable—to anyone else who happened to venture forth on the clear, crisp night.

But too much misgiving spawned cowardice. And Carenza was not a coward. Besides, she'd gone too far to turn back now.

Still, before she committed to the challenging journey, she had to finish one less complicated task.

Entering the shadowy garden, she crouched between the apple trees, juggling the pair of squirming hedgepigs in her hands.

"Winter's comin'," she explained in a whisper, "and I can't hide ye in my chamber anymore. Ye've got to go on now and make your own cozy nests."

She set Blancmange and Pokerounce down in the soft mulch, just a few feet away from the garden wall, where she'd left a jumbled stash of willow twigs. To her simultaneous dismay and relief, they toddled off without a backward glance, eager to investigate.

Letting her animal wards go was always bittersweet. But Carenza was under no illusions. They were not hers to own. None of them were.

As she watched them waddle away, she felt a twinge of envy. They were on their own now. Free.

The only way Carenza could be free to roam where she willed was if she did it behind her father's back. Which was why she'd been reduced to sneaking out like this in the middle of the night.

She understood his protectiveness. He didn't want to lose her. He needed her to be his adoring daughter. To bring him light and laughter when the world grew too dark. To be the dutiful lass who fulfilled all his hopes and expectations. The compliant young lady he would one day surrender to another man. A man to whom she'd become an adoring wife.

She would always be some man's pet, she supposed. Such was the fate of a laird's daughter.

Still, she longed for more.

And she couldn't help but feel spoiled and selfish for wanting that.

After all, she lived in luxury. She was well-fed. Well-dressed. Bedecked with jewels. Blessed with good health. Spoiled by servants and tutors. Provided with entertainments. Given all she desired.

Perhaps being a man's pet wasn't so bad. A pet was beloved. Well cared for. Treasured. As long as Carenza stayed obediently on her leash and didn't bite, she would always be protected and cherished.

Why then did the prospect of being kept in luxurious captivity depress her so?

She sighed heavily, making a soft mist in the chill air.

She gazed up toward her father's window. She certainly wasn't staying on her leash tonight. Fortunately, the laird was asleep. His window was shuttered. If all went well, he'd never learn about her midnight adventure.

As she eased open the garden gate, she saw movement beyond it. She froze. Someone was striding across the courtyard.

She narrowed her eyes. It was a monk. What was he doing here?

She watched as he headed toward the keep and was let inside. Perhaps someone in the clan was ill and had summoned him—for prayers, a blessing, or to administer last rites. She was just grateful she'd lingered in the garden. The last person she needed to encounter on her sinful enterprise was a man of the cloth.

She shivered.

Not from the chill in the air. She was well protected from the cold. Her bulky garments made a thick if unwieldy barrier against the weather. She'd thrown an old plaid over her shoulder. If anyone spotted her at a distance, they'd assume she was a short, stout, crusty old fellow.

Nay, she shivered because, of all the clandestine excursions she'd made under the laird's nose, this was the most daring. The most perilous. And the most illicit.

Lifting her eyes to the barbican, she saw the guard slumped against the wall. She wasn't proud of the fact she'd fortified his beer with aqua vitae at supper. But the strong drink assured he'd sleep for the rest of the night. Plenty of time for her to slip in and out of the castle unnoticed.

Still, her heart pounded with trepidation and excitement as she passed through the barbican gate and hiked down the slope. She wondered if this was how the hedgepigs felt, released into the wild.

It was a long trudge over several hills to where the coos slumbered for the night. But Carenza wasn't afraid. She knew about the wild animals that roamed the countryside in the dark at this time of the year.

The only danger she might face was a pack of wolves. And they would generally rather pick on small, timid prey.

Not full-grown coos with sharp horns. And not someone who looked like a substantial, barrel-shaped crofter, tramping boldly over the hillocks.

She took large, confident strides across the grazed slopes. Despite the warmth of her makeshift garb, it was heavy, and her labored breath made frosty curls in the air.

Finally she spotted the cluster of dark forms beneath the pines. Hamish and the rest of the fold, drowsing in the grass.

She approached with stealth then. She didn't want to startle the beasts.

Hamish was the first to rouse. He tossed his shaggy head, as if shaking off the cobwebs of sleep, which woke the others. But since the cattle were accustomed to her presence, once they caught her scent, they settled back into slumber.

Only Hamish stayed awake, waiting for her to come and give him a scratch.

She meant to be strong. But her eyes filled with tears as she rubbed the furry spot behind his crogged ear. She remembered what a brave wee calf he'd been when he had to be marked and gelded. How he'd rested his head in her lap afterwards. How he'd let her sing him to sleep.

She remembered how she'd occasionally sneak a turnip from the kitchens to take to him. How his eyes rolled with excitement as he crunched the special treat.

She remembered how he always lowed for her that first day after winter when the fold was driven to the ferme to graze. And how eagerly each fall he trotted back to the stone close, knowing Carenza would visit him every day.

A sob escaped her as she brushed the hair out of his handsome face. If all went as planned, Hamish would come back to the close no longer.

She needed him to stay safe. To move on to greener

pastures. To leave Dunlop and civilization. To find a wild herd and never return again.

Sniffling and wiping a tear from her cheek with her palm, she murmured, "Are ye ready, lad? Are ye ready to go with me on an adventure?"

She looped the rope she'd brought around his head, dodging his horns and cinching it around his neck. She planned to lead him northeast to the mountains beyond Dunlop. She knew of a secret spot where herds of wild coos sometimes passed. A lovely glen hidden between two high peaks. A glen where a steer could feed to his heart's delight. Where he could live out his days in peace. Where nobody would find him. Least of all, her father, who meant to cut his life short.

The ground was hard. The air was cold. But Hew didn't mind. The blood of Vikings flowed in his veins. Besides, it was no less comfortable than his cell at the monastery.

He stretched out his legs, crossing his boots, and draped his plaid over them for warmth. Then he set his axe on his lap, folded his arms over his chest, and leaned back against the trunk of the pine to wait.

He'd barely settled in when the barbican gate swung open again.

He sat forward, unfolding his arms and seizing his axe.

It wasn't the man he'd followed. This figure was smaller and stouter and walked with a shorter stride.

Hew frowned. Was Dunlop a gathering place for mysterious nighttime travelers?

This stocky fellow wasn't even using the road. He clambered down the slope and began hiking off across the hill.

Where was he going?

Hew came to his feet.

The figure strode surely through the wet grass, as if he knew exactly where he was headed.

Hew hesitated.

He didn't want to leave his post. The man he'd followed could emerge at any time.

On the other hand, perhaps *this* man was the thief. Perhaps he was on his way to a robbery right now.

The man from the monastery had only just arrived. If he was the physician, he'd remain within. If he was a man of the cloth, he'd surely spend at least an hour inside.

Meanwhile, Hew would follow this new stranger and see what mischief he was up to.

After a long trek over fell and dale, it seemed the man at last found what he sought. A fold of cattle sleeping beneath the trees. They stirred when the man approached, then settled back down to doze.

"Sard me," Hew muttered in self-disgust.

The man was obviously just a cooherd come to watch over the laird's cattle. Hew had wasted time, following the fellow.

Still, it was curious that he'd come in the middle of the night. And his behavior toward the coos was odd. He was standing far too close to one of them, scratching its head between two horns that could have easily tossed the man heels over head clear across the glen.

Perhaps the cooherd was soft in the head.

He sighed. It wasn't Hew's affair. He had a thief to catch.

But then, just before he turned to go, he saw the cooherd lead the familiar beast away from the others while the rest of the fold slumbered on.

Where was he taking it?

His interest piqued again, Hew crept down the hill after the cooherd. And the farther he got away from the rest of the fold, the surer Hew was that this was not a cooherd after all, but a cateran, a cattle reiver.

LAIRD OF FLINT

He'd never seen one work alone before. As a lad, he and his cousins had occasionally thieved cattle from the neighboring clans for sport. They were chided by their parents and always returned the coos. Just as often, the neighboring clans stole Rivenloch coos. In the Lowlands, reiving cattle was considered harmless fun.

But there was a bit of danger in it. Not only from the coos. Sometimes drunk or angry clansmen took the thefts too seriously and came after young caterans with their fists or swords. That was why they always went reiving in groups.

Reiving alone was risky.

Another curious thing was that the cateran had come out of Dunlop, but he was leading the coo *away* from the castle.

Before he could wonder further about that, he spotted something the cateran hadn't seen yet. Two figures had emerged from the woods and were scrambling down the hill after him. They were probably the cooherds who watched over the fold.

Hew grimaced. There were two of them and one reiver. They were twice his size. Young and brawny. When they caught him, they would likely pummel the poor fellow to within an inch of his life.

Hew couldn't stand by and watch that happen.

As the pair closed in on the unwary cateran, Hew sidled down the hill to intercept them.

Hamish snorted and lifted his wary head.

Carenza froze, alert.

"What is it?" she whispered, praying it wasn't a pack of wolves.

Hamish chuffed out a foggy breath on the chill air. But he wasn't afraid. Hamish was vexed.

She scanned the hillside, looking for the source of his ire.

Then she heard scuffling behind her. She turned to see two men clambering down the slope, headed straight for her.

She nearly leaped out of her disguise. Her worst fears were confirmed. She'd been seen. Not by the monk. Not by a guard. But by two men who must have been waiting near the coos.

Neither of them were Cainnech, the cooherd. When the weather turned this cold, Cainnech left the cattle on their own until it was time to bring them to the close.

Who were they then?

"Stop, thief!" one of them commanded.

"Hold it right there!" the other said.

Hamish startled at the sudden noise. If she hadn't had an arm around his muzzle, he might have bolted and run off.

But the other cattle were not so restrained. If the pair of barking fools charging down the hill weren't careful, they'd panic the beasts and wreak havoc.

One of them sneered, "That's Dunlop's coo."

She recognized the voice. It was a Boyle. Gilbert or Herbert. She couldn't tell which. She didn't dare lift her head to look.

What were they doing here, in the middle of the night, on Dunlop land?

The second brother shrugged a rope off his shoulder and chimed in, "And we're goin' to take the beast—and ye—straight to the laird."

She gulped. Not her father. That was her worst nightmare.

"But first," he added, punching a fist into his palm, "we're goin' to show ye what we do to filthy caterans."

Carenza gasped.

Sweet Mary! Did they intend to beat her?

Fear drained the blood from her face. She couldn't breathe. Couldn't move.

For one horrible instant, she wondered if she would die on this hill. If all her father would find of her when he went out riding the next morn would be her bloody and battered corpse.

Then, as the bullying brothers grew near, she glimpsed their bloodthirsty sneers and their vicious eyes. She suddenly saw them for what they were. Spineless, entitled cowards who preyed on the weak.

Slowly, her fear curdled into rage. How dared these dunderheads trespass on her father's land? How dared they threaten her with violence? Who did they think they were?

She wasn't going to let them ruin her best-laid plans.

She couldn't fight them on her own, of course. She had neither the muscle nor the mass to do battle against this ox-sized pair of brutes. But she had friends who did.

Still calming Hamish, she began waving her free arm about wildly. Then she took a deep breath and let out a loud, long, wolf-like howl.

As she expected, the sound pushed the rest of the cattle to the edge of panic. Lowing in alarm, they rocked up onto their hooves. They danced in confused agitation, kicking up moss and gravel as they bolted in all directions.

The Boyles, intimidated by the deadly thunder of hooves rumbling on the sod, yelped and separated, fleeing for their lives.

Carenza wasn't afraid. She knew these beasts. They might charge about wildly for a while, shaking off the dregs of fright. But they'd never hurt her. Carenza was practically part of their clan.

And while the brothers were looking after their own safety, dodging the rush of cattle, she could steal away into the night as planned. Unrecognized. Uncaptured. Unbeaten.

Allowing herself a small smile of triumph, she gave Hamish a soothing scratch behind the ear and tugged him forward. "Come on, Hamish. 'Tis all right now."

"Stay where you are, lad!" a new voice called out to her. "I'll come to you!"

Carenza's smile instantly drooped into a frown. Now what?

She wasn't about to stay where she was. She'd already outsmarted the Boyle brothers. She wasn't going to let anything else stand in her way.

But before she defied his command, she *would* steal a sidelong peek at the new arrival.

Her breath caught.

He was big. Bold. Brawny. His hair shone like wheat in the moonlight as he strode across the sod between the great black charging beasts. He had the face, not of a berserker as she'd expected, but of a god.

For a brief yet impressionable sliver of time, she stood stunned. Breathless. Enthralled. Overwhelmed by the magnificent cut of his jaw. The furrowed determination in his brow. The dark promise in his eyes. Then, in the next instant, her gaze fell to the axe clenched in his fist, and fear struck her heart.

This must be the Viking warrior. Sir Hew of Rivenloch. The prospective bridegroom she was supposed to invite to Samhain three nights hence.

Thank God they'd never actually met. If a Rivenloch warrior discovered the daughter of Dunlop reiving cattle, her reputation—and that of her father and her clan—would be ruined.

Ballocks. This was a disaster.

CHAPTER 7

hew tightened his grip on the axe.
There was a benefit to being hotheaded. Passion made one fearless.

It was passion that had made him boldly follow the monk to Dunlop.

Passion that had pushed him to brazenly track the cateran across Dunlop land.

Passion that had urged him to brashly insert himself between two brutes and their victim.

Now, suddenly, one glimpse of a familiar delicate moonlit cheek, the sweet curve of a jaw, the flutter of an eyelash, the open gasp of a soft mouth, drained that passion. For one awful moment, his hotheaded fearlessness wavered. He was stunned by sheer terror for the cateran.

He told himself it didn't matter that the thief wasn't a lad, but a lass.

It made no difference that the lass was not just any lass, but Lady Carenza.

He told himself these things. But his heart still pounded with icy fear for her. His breath still froze in his chest as more of the raging black beasts swirled around her.

Thank God, he was a trained warrior. His heart might be tender, but fierce blood pumped through it. He would protect her. And he would die before he'd reveal her secret.

"Stay there," he repeated.

To his shock, she ignored his command.

Not only did she ignore it. She did the exact opposite of what he instructed. She turned her back on him and resumed leading her captive coo away.

The foolish lass seemed not to notice she was surrounded by stamping, snorting beasts that were twice her size. Beasts that could crush her in an instant.

He dared not cry out to her again. That would only further agitate the cattle.

There was only one thing to do. Dropping his axe, Hew let passion convince him to charge into the maelstrom of wild cattle.

No sooner did he enter the fray than his shin was struck by a stray hoof. The tip of a coo's horn grazed his shoulder as it passed. And he was nearly crushed between two beasts determined to collide.

Dodging the lunging, darting cattle, he picked out the fastest, the one that looked like the leader. He shadowed the animal, running alongside until he could catch the base of its long horn in his bent arm. Then he dug in his heels and pulled back with all his might, slowing the coo and steering it aside.

It slipped and skidded on the sod, and its eyes still rolled in panic. But it finally stopped running.

"Easy," he commanded breathlessly, slowing it to a saner pace. "Easy now."

Once the first coo calmed, the others began to settle. Eventually he was able to circle the animal back in the direction of the woods. The rest of the fold gradually followed.

Still, by the time he swung around to seek out Lady Carenza, she'd gained a hundred yards. She was blithely continuing on her way with her spoils in tow, which both relieved and infuriated him.

Taking bold strides across the field toward her, he scooped up his axe and tossed it over his shoulder without missing a step.

"Wait!" he called out.

Her shoulders jerked in surprise, which gave him some satisfaction. She probably assumed the cattle had trampled him to death.

But when she wheeled around to confront him, he glimpsed a fearful plea in her eyes. A plea that caught at his heart. Dissipated his anger. And dissolved his conceit.

"Let me take the beast back, lass," he murmured. "I won't reveal your secret."

She flinched once, hearing him call her lass. Then she tightened her grip on the rope around the animal's neck.

"This one's mine," she whispered. "Ye can't have him."

It was as if her soft voice wrapped around the shell of his ear and breathed an enchantment into his soul. He lowered his axe, resting the blade on the ground. Suddenly he wanted nothing more than to grant her wish.

Of course, reason dictated otherwise. It was possible the lady was fleeing an unhappy home. It was possible she was giving her father's coo away to a crofter in need. But if both the lady and the coo went missing on the same night, it wouldn't take a scholar to figure out the connection. And Hew had no intention of subjecting the beautiful lass to a cateran's punishment.

But before he could discuss options, the lady's eyes abruptly widened at something behind him, and she pulled her head back into the shadows of her hood.

Hew heard the cooherds approaching from behind.

"Who the hell are *ye?*" one of them demanded.

With a grim frown, Hew turned.

If there was one thing Hew hated, it was a bully. Now he confronted two of them. Worse, they appeared to be the sort of brutes whose bodies were too big for their brains.

The dunces were standing but a dozen yards from the lady, in full moonlight, yet they were too thickheaded to notice that she *was* a lady.

He supposed that was a blessing in this instance. She obviously didn't wish to be recognized.

He didn't bother answering their question. Instead he warned them, "You should walk away."

The one with the beard puffed up his chest. "And ye should stay out o' this."

Hew ignored the threat. "You don't want me to even the odds."

"What's that mean, even the odds?" the beardless one said, leering in challenge.

In answer, Hew casually swung his axe up where they could see it, resting the blade on his shoulder.

The lad's leer drooped. His companion let out a low whistle.

The once leering lad whined, "We're not even armed."

"This?" Hew said with a shrug. "I don't need this." He swung it around with a showy flourish and hurled it into the ground in their midst with a resounding thud. "But I won't stand by while two swaggering brutes threaten a wee lad half their size."

"That 'wee lad' is a God-cursed cateran," the bearded one argued.

Hew smirked. "So neither of *you* have ever reived a coo?"

They scowled, but couldn't deny it. Every lad in Scotland had reived a coo. It was practically a rite of passage.

"Let's settle this here and now," he told them. "No fists. No bloodshed. Take the beast. Return it to the fold. I'll take the naughty lad to Dunlop." Of course, he had no intention of turning the lass in for the crime of reiving cattle. But they didn't know that.

Laird of Flint

"We're the ones who caught the thief," the bearded one said. *"We'll* take him to Dunlop."

Hew crossed his arms. So they wanted credit for the capture? "Give me your names. I'll tell the laird 'twas you who caught the cateran. But I'm not going to turn him over to you so you can bloody your knuckles on his face." Then he had a second thought. "Besides, don't you have cooherding to do?"

The beardless lad took offense at that. "Cooherdin'? We're not cooherds."

Hew blinked. They weren't? "Then what are you doing out here?"

The bearded one straightened. "Watchin' for outlaws like him." He nodded his head toward the cateran.

Hew narrowed his eyes. "How do I know you're not outlaws yourself?" he wondered aloud. "Maybe you were planning to reive the coos when this one came along and beat you to the fold."

"We're not outlaws," the bearded one sputtered.

"Maybe you are. Maybe you aren't," Hew said. "Are you even in the Dunlop clan?"

The other one lifted his beardless chin. "We're the Boyles. Their neighbors."

Boyle. He recognized that name. Weren't those the brothers who thought they were worthy of the affections of the beautiful Lady Carenza? The idea was laughable.

But suddenly he realized why they were watching over the Dunlop coos. They hoped to do just this—catch a cateran and be rewarded by the laird of Dunlop, perhaps with a betrothal to his daughter. Indeed, they should be grateful Hew had saved them the humiliation of having bloodied their fists on the lass they intended to court.

"Wait," the bearded one said, furrowing his brows in concentration. "How do we know *ye're* not a cateran? We've ne'er seen ye before."

"Aye, that's right," the second chimed in. "How do we know *ye're* not after the coos?"

"Maybe ye're this one's accomplice," the first Boyle deduced, jerking a thumb toward the cateran.

"Me? I offered you the coo," Hew pointed out.

"We *are* goin' to take the coo," the bearded Boyle said.

"Not now you're not," Hew informed him.

"What?" he barked.

"Don't be tellin' *us* what to do," the beardless Boyle said. "Our da is a laird." He made a move toward the coo.

Hew blocked the way.

"How dare ye!" the other bellowed, his beard trembling with rage. "When our da finds out about this..." He made a lunge toward the animal.

Hew blocked him as well.

Their frustration erupted in a spate of cursing and spitting and jostling that made Hew feel like he was trying to contain a pair of wildcats chasing after a mouse.

Carenza had heard enough.

She didn't intend to turn Hamish over to anyone. Nor would she be dragged back home to face the laird. Not even by the handsome axe-wielder who had somehow made his way unscathed through a rioting mass of cattle in a misguided attempt to rescue her.

He couldn't protect her for long anyway. Any moment, one of the Boyles would recognize her and run tattling to her father.

Desperate times called for desperate measures.

While the three fools were scuffling and swearing like suitors fighting over the same maid, she made a bold move.

Surging forward, she took hold of the axe handle in both hands and wrenched it out of the ground. Then she swung the heavy weapon in a wide arc toward the knot of brawling men.

They split apart at once, leaping back with yelps of surprise.

She stepped forward and swung again.

The Boyles squealed. Herbert staggered backwards. Gilbert fell on his arse.

"Hold on," the Rivenloch warrior said, lifting one palm to her.

It was a brazen gesture. She could have lopped off his hand with her next swing. Not that she would have. Carenza wouldn't harm a flea. But he didn't know that.

"You don't want blood on your hands," he told her.

She wasn't afraid of the Boyles. They were cowards. Already they were scrambling away, slipping on the wet grass in their panic.

This man, however, seemed undaunted by the fact he was unarmed while she possessed a weapon that could split him in half.

He took one cautious step forward, and she shook the sharp blade before her in warning.

"Don't be foolish," he growled. "You don't want to hurt anyone. Hand it o'er."

Another time, she might have succumbed to the lethal power of his voice. He was right. She didn't want to hurt anyone. She wouldn't even kill a spider.

But Hamish's life was at stake.

She shook her head, refusing him.

"I won't turn you in," he promised.

She didn't believe him. She jabbed the axe forward again.

He took a judicious step back.

"Why do you want the coo?" he demanded.

She clamped her lips shut. She didn't have to tell him. He wouldn't understand anyway.

Then he gave her a quizzical look and asked, "Do you know these lads?"

She paused, then gave him a subtle nod.

Then he raised his voice so the Boyles could hear. "These two," he asked, "do they belong here?"

Carenza hesitated. She had a choice.

She could admit that the Boyles were indeed welcome on her father's land. Though they'd always been a source of annoyance to Carenza, especially lately, they were amicable enough neighbors.

But they were up to some sort of mischief. Skulking around in the dark. Messing about with her father's cattle. Bullying people half their size.

If they'd known who she was, they would have been mortified. But they didn't. So she could command their fate as she willed.

She shook her head. Nay, they didn't belong here.

The Boyles sent up a loud protest.

"Are ye goin' to believe a cateran?" the beardless one complained.

His brother added, "When our da hears what ye've done—"

Hew silenced them with an upraised hand and spoke to her.

"I'll make you a trade," he offered, stepping forward.

She shoved the axe quickly toward him again, forcing him back.

He bit out a frustrated curse. Then he nodded toward Hamish. "Take the coo. Just give me that rope from around his neck. And leave me my axe. I'll tie these two up. The laird can find them on the morrow."

"What?" Herbert squeaked.

"Nay!" Gilbert bellowed. "We'll freeze to death."

"You can cuddle with the cattle," the warrior called back over his shoulder. "They'll keep you warm enough."

Laird of Flint

The Boyles weren't going to linger long enough to be tied up. They beat a hasty retreat, heading back toward the woods.

He turned to Carenza. "Are we agreed?"

His offer was tempting. He had an honest face. A noble bearing. Earnest eyes that seemed to pierce her soul.

She blinked. She shouldn't trust him. Why would he simply let her go?

He nodded as if reading her mind. "I know you don't trust me, lass," he murmured. "But I'm a knight of Rivenloch, and I swear on my honor I will keep my word."

She considered his oath. She believed the illustrious Rivenloch tournament champion, Sir Gellir, was probably a man of honor. But she knew nothing about the rest of the clan. They could be a pack of wild savages for all she knew.

Still, the passionate sincerity in his gaze...

"Pray make haste," he urged. "They're getting away."

She decided she'd trust him enough to give him the rope. But not the axe.

She nodded. Then she made a slow retreat, brandishing the weapon before her, until she could reach Hamish's head.

The man stayed obediently rooted to the spot while she ducked under Hamish's horns and loosened the rope around his neck. But she kept her eye on him.

Once the rope was off, the man's impatience showed. He waved his fingers toward her.

"Hurry, lass," he said. "They're halfway up the hill."

But she had one more precaution to take. Something to ensure her safety.

She slipped the rope off Hamish's horns with her left hand. But before she tossed the coil to the warrior, she reared back her right arm and, with all her might, hurled the axe as far as she could across the field.

It arced impressively through the sky, catching the

moonlight on its sharp blade as it tumbled end over end before clattering onto the ground.

Ten yards away.

She sighed in exasperation.

He was too polite to comment, but she detected a gleam of amusement in his narrowed eyes.

After that, she may have thrown the rope at him with more force than was necessary.

His reflexes were good enough to keep it from smacking him in the chest. After he caught it, he hurried off after his quarry.

This was her chance to escape.

All things considered, the odds were still in her favor.

No one knew who she was.

She had the coo.

And tying up the Boyle brothers would keep the Viking occupied long enough for her to flee with Hamish.

It was tempting to retrieve his axe and keep it for herself. But she was a woman of her word. Besides, he was a Rivenloch warrior. While he might eventually lose interest in tracking a common cateran, he'd likely follow her to the ends of the earth to get his precious weapon back.

Nay, she'd proceed as planned. Just her and Hamish and the journey ahead.

Without the rope, she had to coil her fist in the thick hair of Hamish's neck to guide him. It wasn't ideal. The rope would have given her greater control. But she knew he would stay close. He would sense the slightest shift in her bearing and follow her without question.

With a whispered prayer for safe travels, she guided him onto the path through the mountains.

Centuries ago, a crack in the rock had widened into a deep ravine running alongside the narrow trail that traversed the stony slope. As the path progressed, the steep shards of slick, moss-covered walls grew taller on one side and deeper on the other. Anything dropped into the chasm was gone forever. Anything and anyone.

Stray lambs sometimes slipped into the ravine. Now and then, an unwary traveler stumbled and fell to his death. Children were warned away from the path. Still, every few years, some drunken lad lost his life trying to negotiate the path blindfolded on a dare from his fellows.

But tonight, the ravine's treacherous nature made the route the perfect choice. No one with an ounce of sense—no one but intrepid Carenza—would attempt to take a great beast like Hamish through the perilous passage. And more importantly, no one would ever try to bring him back.

Containing the Boyles took longer than Hew anticipated. There was no loyalty lost between the brothers. One was perfectly willing to flee while his sibling was captured and tied to a tree.

Eventually, Hew chased and tackled the second brother and managed to secure them both. Then, annoyed by the bearded one's incessant caterwauling about freezing to death, he tore off a piece of the lad's leine and stuffed it into his mouth.

But now, the lady and her coo were long gone.

Still, he wouldn't give up. The Boyles might not have recognized who she was, or even that she was a lass. But he knew. Which meant someone else would eventually find out. If news spread that the daughter of Dunlop was reiving her father's cattle, it would bring shame upon her and her whole clan.

On the other hand, he'd promised he wouldn't turn her in.

There was only one thing to do.

He blew out a determined breath, loping toward the spot she'd disappeared, pausing only to retrieve his axe.

There was a primitive footpath nestled against the mountain which led away from the field. That was where she'd been headed. It must be where she'd gone.

She couldn't travel very quickly with a coo. There was a good chance he could catch her before she got too deep into the mountains.

Increasing his pace, he moved swiftly from the wide moonlit grassland to the narrow shadowed path. The trail sloped abruptly upward. But as he climbed, the mountain on his right rose even more steeply.

The moon, hidden now behind the mountain's peak, provided no light. Only starlight illuminated the path, which constricted more with each step.

On his right loomed a sheer face of rock, carpeted with moss and fern.

To his left plunged a crevasse as black as peat. How deep it was, he couldn't tell.

But the narrower the trail became, the higher it rose and the darker it got, the more he worried about Lady Carenza.

Had she really come this way with the great beast?

Did she realize how dangerous this path was?

As if to prove his point, his heel slipped on rubble, scraping perilously close to the edge of the abyss. A taunting trickle of pebbles dribbled down the side, fading far below.

"Shite," he muttered in disgust.

Was this how his life would end? Would the fierce Sir Hew du Lac fall to his death, not in battle, but on a mountain pass, chasing after a lass with a coo?

He managed to regain his footing and braced himself against the wall.

Then his heart wrenched as a horrible thought knifed through his soul.

What if the lady hadn't made it this far?

What if she'd already met with an unspeakable accident?

What if the beast had misstepped as he had?

What if it had tumbled headlong into the crevasse, dragging its mistress down to her death?

The bitter taste of terror filled his mouth. It was too awful to contemplate.

Instead, he shook off the fear and donned the scowl he wore into battle.

By God, he was Sir Hew du Lac. A Rivenloch warrior. Fear only fed his resolve.

Steeling his nerves, he blew out a determined breath, pushed away from the wall, and swung his axe up over his shoulder.

Unfortunately, the weapon never made it to his shoulder.

Instead, the blade caught on something—a root or a rock—beside him. The halted momentum made him stagger and lose his footing. He fell to one knee. As he tried to lever up with the other leg, the earth gave way beneath his boot, launching a hailstorm of rocks into the crevasse.

He slammed his left hand forward, grasping for purchase. But his palm scraped across the ground as his weight began to pull him over the crumbling edge.

Grimacing, he scrabbled at the slick growth for a handhold and found none.

His last prayer as the earth opened its dark maw to devour him was that the lady had not met a similar fate.

CHAPTER 8

Carenza heard the rockslide behind her. She gasped and froze.

Something or someone was on the path. Or *had* been on the path. That much rock sliding down the hill could mean they'd fallen into the ravine.

But who or what was it? A wolf? A lost lamb? That meddlesome knight of Rivenloch?

She immediately regretted calling him that. After all, he'd protected her from a beating at the Boyles' hands. He'd kept her secret, not once revealing to them that she was a lass. And he'd sworn on his knighthood he wouldn't turn her in to the laird.

Still, it would be terribly convenient for her if he... disappeared. She entertained the idea for the space of a heartbeat.

But despite her desperation—desperation that had driven her to nefarious behavior like sneaking out at midnight and thieving cattle—at heart she was still Lady Carenza. Her father's pride and joy. Her clan's inspiring figurehead. The laird's daughter, who brought love, light, and kindness to everyone she met.

She didn't have a ruthless bone in her body. And she had no appetite for violence, whether it was against coos, spiders, or even rampaging Vikings.

Laird of Flint

She sighed in surrender. If she didn't turn back, she'd never forgive herself.

Silently cursing her soft heart, she found a wide part of the trail where she could turn Hamish around. Slowly and carefully, assuring his hooves found solid ground, she began leading him back down the mountain.

As she descended, she began to hope the Rivenloch warrior hadn't fallen into the chasm, despite the inconvenience of his presence. She couldn't say why exactly. After all, she didn't even know the man.

But there was something she'd glimpsed in his eyes that told her there was more to him than just his Viking's body and a warrior's lust for battle. Something honest. Something direct. Something pure, intense, and worth investigating.

No one had ever looked at her like that before. Men either leered at her in open admiration or shyly shunned her gaze. But the warrior had regarded her with respect, with honor, with...

"Argh..."

Carenza hurried in the dark toward the sound of gasps and groans. It was indeed the Viking. And her eyes widened when she saw his predicament.

"Och!" she cried.

He hadn't fallen into the ravine. Not yet. But he was hanging by one arm, gripping his axe, which was caught on the narrow lip of a boulder. Every muscle strained as he fought to keep from twisting and dislodging the blade.

She crept cautiously forward, kneeling beside him.

Once, long ago, she'd saved a lamb from falling into a well. She'd managed to grab one of its forelegs and hauled it up over the stone wall.

"Here," she said, extending her arm. "Take my hand."

He shook his head. "I'll only...pull you down...with me."

He was probably right. The warrior was no lamb. He was as big as an ox.

An ox!

"Hamish," she decided. "Hamish can pull ye up."

"The coo?"

"Aye."

"Do you have...a rope?" he gasped.

She grimaced. He'd used her rope to tie up the Boyles.

"Hold on," she said, wondering if he could. He'd already held on a long while.

She shrugged out of her plaid. Then she began tearing off the rags of her disguise, knotting them together.

His axe blade made a forbidding scrape as it slipped, grinding against the boulder.

He held his breath. His arm shuddered.

Her heart pounded as she tied the rags with frantic fingers.

"Almost," she breathed, securing her plaid to the last rag.

Shivering in her thin leine, she rose on trembling legs to loop the tied rags around Hamish's neck. She ducked under his head to secure the line. Then she fed out the makeshift rope and dropped it gingerly over the edge toward him.

The fingers of his free left hand could barely reach the cloth of her plaid.

She clucked to Hamish to summon him closer.

The axe made a sinister shriek as it twisted again on the rock.

Hamish stepped forward.

The plaid lowered toward the warrior another few inches.

Then, with a loud crack, the edge of the boulder chipped off, and the axe fell away.

At the last instant, the warrior seized the plaid in his left fist.

Laird of Flint

She gasped as the rag rope suddenly went taut. But Hamish, the loyal beast, stood steady, as if rescuing warriors from certain death was something he did every day.

Coaxed a few more paces forward along the path, Hamish hauled the Viking up out of danger. The man was able to crawl onto his hands and knees to catch his breath.

It was then Carenza noticed he'd never let go of his axe. She supposed it was a warrior's instinct to die with his weapon in his hand. But now she wondered if she should be worried.

It was then she also realized, in her zeal to make the rag rope, she was now half-naked, clad only in her trews and thin leine.

He seemed to realize that at the same time.

But his concern was not for her modesty. "You must be freezing."

He quickly untied the plaid from the rest of the rags and gently wrapped it around her shoulders.

Then he looked into her eyes with that penetrating gaze again. The one that seemed to read her thoughts and divine her emotions.

"I owe you my life," he breathed.

She blushed. Not from his statement, which was true. But from the passion with which he'd uttered the words, as if his next words might be "so now I'm your slave forever."

She gulped.

But then she remembered her mission. Saving Hamish.

Averting her eyes, she murmured, "If that's true, then let me go."

Hew's first thought was, *Never.*

He didn't say that, of course. He didn't want to frighten the woman.

But deep in his soul, he knew he could never let her go. She felt like his destiny.

He tried to blame that strong belief on gratitude. Surely, he was only shaken by his close brush with death and grateful to the lady for saving his life.

But that wasn't true. His warrior maid cousin had saved his life once. He didn't feel that way about *her*.

Nay, this woman felt like his fate. His heartmate. The One.

Somehow she was different from all the others.

Yet even as he had that thought, a dark voice inside him sneered a reminder... *Isn't that what you always say? Isn't that how you got your heart broken the last time? Didn't you swear off women?*

Besides, that wasn't what Lady Carenza meant by "let me go." What she meant was she never wanted to see him again. She wanted him to give her the coo, go away, and forget any of this had happened.

He sighed. "I can't do that."

Her chin trembled, and it was hard to tell whether she was on the verge of tears or holding back rage. He wondered if she was tempted to push him back into the crevasse.

"'Tisn't safe for you," he explained. "The Boyles may not have recognized you, my lady. But I do."

She inhaled sharply. "How..."

"I saw you when I visited Dunlop yesterday. I believe you were feeding a squirrel."

She looked momentarily discomfited. "I see." Then she furrowed her brows. "So ye naturally intend to return the coo to my da." She added bitterly, "For what reward? My hand in marriage?"

He frowned. She'd pricked his temper now. What kind of a conniving oaf did she think he was?

"I'm not a Boyle," he grumbled. "I'd never stoop to such tactics."

"Then what is it ye're after?"

"After?" he scoffed. "Naught. Bloody hell, I'm only trying to help you."

"Ye think turnin' me in to my father as a cateran will help me?"

"I'm not turning you in," he fired back. "I'm turning myself in."

"What?"

"I'm turning myself in as the cateran. 'Tis the only way. 'Twould only bring shame to your clan for the laird's daughter to be exposed as a thief," he explained. "The Boyles may be dunderheads, but they're not cattle reivers, so 'tisn't right *they* should take the blame. Still, they know my face now. They'll surely tell your father I'm the one who stole his coo and tied them up. 'Tis far better if I return the coo myself and confess to the laird before they have the chance to accuse me."

For a moment, she only stared at him in amazement.

Then she said, "Ye would do that? Ye would take the blame for my thievin'?"

Her surprise irritated him. Had he not just said so? What else would she expect him to do? Did she not know about chivalry? About honor? What kind of a villain would not protect a lady? But he replied simply, "Of course."

"But ye'll bring shame upon your clan."

He shrugged. "'Twouldn't be the first time." His impulsive actions were always getting him into awkward scrapes. "They're used to it by now."

Her gaze softened. She lowered her shoulders. And when her lips opened with a grateful sigh, it took all his willpower not to pull the awestruck woman into his arms and capture her mouth with his own.

"That's so very honorable of ye," she gushed, "offerin' to sacrifice yourself for my sake."

He dismissed her praise with a grunt. "I wouldn't be much of a knight if I had no honor."

"And I'm grateful for the gesture. Truly I am. But..."

"Aye?"

"I won't return my coo."

And just like that, her enchantment over him shattered into a thousand pieces.

"What?"

"I won't give him back."

Ire began to bubble under the surface of his stolid demeanor. What was it about this coo? Was it some sort of magical beast? He'd gone out of his way to come to the lady's rescue. And now he was offering to bend over backwards for her to keep her out of trouble. To think she was refusing his help...

He clamped his teeth together hard enough to crack walnuts. It would do no good to lose his temper with the lass. He had to try to use reason.

But before he could explain to her that she couldn't keep the coo, that stealing was wrong, she blurted out, "I can't return him. I don't expect ye to understand why. Nobody does."

Her words—so raw, so hurt, so vulnerable—shot him straight through the heart, wounding him to the core. His ire dissolved like iron in a crucible.

If there was one thing Hew prided himself on, it was understanding women.

He knew they sometimes felt small and powerless. Insignificant and unheard. As if their thoughts and hopes and dreams didn't matter.

But they did matter. They mattered to him.

"I want to understand," he told her.

"Ye don't mean that."

Laird of Flint

"I do."

She blinked in surprise, then lowered her gaze. "Ye'll only think me foolish."

"Tell me." He clasped her arm. "I pray you."

Carenza never let men touch her unbidden. She was skilled at diplomatically ducking away from their attempts. She could peel their fingers off of her person, smiling all the while. Make them feel as if they'd earned her affections even while she sidled out of their reach.

But the Viking's massive hand wrapped around her arm didn't feel like a dalliance or an intrusion. It felt curiously like a comfort.

Through his touch, she could feel the warmth of his blood. The strength of his muscles. The sincerity of his words.

She had no desire to wrest free of him.

Indeed, she *wanted* to tell him her reasons for keeping Hamish, even though she knew he wouldn't understand.

She gazed at the ground and murmured, "My da means to kill him."

His thumb rubbed along her arm as he considered his response. "He *is*...a coo."

She sighed. She knew that.

"And he's, what, five, six years old?"

"Six."

"And your clan," he ventured, "they have roast for supper, aye?"

She nodded, and her eyes began to fill with tears. She knew he wouldn't understand. She hardly understood herself.

"And you?" he asked softly. "You eat roast for supper?"

"Aye," she confessed, sniffling as she spoke her hypocrisy aloud. "But 'tisn't Hamish. 'Tisn't the coo I raised from a calf...who lays his head upon my lap...and lets me sing him to sleep. 'Tisn't the beast who comes trottin' across the field to me when I call. Who lets me scratch him behind the ears...and helps me watch o'er the new bairns."

"He does all that?"

She nodded.

"Ah, my lady," he said, giving her arm a reassuring squeeze. "But I do understand. You have a gentle nature and a kind heart. 'Tis a commendable thing in a person."

The compassion in his voice was unexpected and moving. Still, she sensed there was a "but" coming. And she refused to be swayed by his sweet words, no matter how comforting or reasonable they seemed.

"But what do you think will—"

Before he could come up with some perfectly convincing counter argument, she seized the front of his plaid in her desperate fists and blurted out, "Ye have to let him go. Hamish saved your life. Ye owe him his."

Her gesture startled him. His eyes widened as he stared back into hers. Then his gaze drifted toward her lips.

For an instant, she wondered if he meant to kiss her.

Even worse, she wasn't sure she wouldn't have welcomed it.

Hew knew, if he stood there another moment, he'd toss all his honorable intentions into the abyss, gather the wet-eyed woman in his arms, and kiss away each and every tear. In this intimate situation, even the beast roaring in his braies didn't believe him capable of restraint.

But he dared not let that beast have its way. Instead, he had to follow his heart.

Unfortunately, his heart was foolish and weak-willed.

And that was how the next unwise words spilled from his careless lips.

"Fine," he croaked out. "I'll do it. I'll save your coo."

She let out a soft, grateful cry. The sheer joy that shone in her face was worth the offer he'd made. At least in the moment. Later he'd have time to regret his promise. But for now, the way she unfurled and pressed her hands against his chest, the way her mouth fell open in wonder, the way her liquid eyes poured into his with thanks and adoration, she made him feel like her hero.

In the next moment, of course, she grew aware of their improper proximity. She was a titled lady, after all. Her father might guard her with an iron glare. But even without his supervision, she would naturally follow society's rules.

Except, apparently, when it came to coos.

She took a judicious step backward and lowered her gaze. "My thanks, sir."

He managed a sickly smile and let out a long breath.

God's bones. What had he done? This was just the sort of reckless behavior that always got him into trouble.

What was he going to do now?

He had no intention of doing what she wanted most—walking away and letting her continue on her perilous journey alone through the mountains.

And he certainly couldn't go with her. It was bad enough to confess to reiving cattle. He couldn't afford to be accused of abducting a noblewoman as well. Not again.

"You need to return to Dunlop," he told her. "It grows late. Your father will miss you."

"But Hamish..."

"I'll take him."

"Ye don't know the path or where I was goin'. Ye don't know Hamish. And he doesn't know ye. What if ye fall again?"

He grimaced and rubbed the back of his neck. She wasn't going to like his answer. Hell, *he* didn't like his answer. But it was the only way.

"You—I'm taking back to Dunlop. The coo—I'm taking to the monastery."

"What? Nay."

"I'll keep him safe," he vowed, wondering how on earth he was going to do that.

"Ye'll sell him," she accused.

"Nay, I won't. I promise."

"Or ye'll slaughter and eat him."

"I told you, I'll protect him."

"Ye swear?"

"On my honor."

"But for how long?"

He didn't know how to answer that. "It grows late. Let's chat on the way," he said, nodding down the trail.

"He'll need food," she said, coiling her hand in the coo's fur to guide him along the path while Hew followed. "The grass at the monastery is nigh gone. So ye'll have to purchase hay."

Hew frowned. Purchase hay? Already this was sounding like far more responsibility than he'd anticipated. Not to mention that what went in came out. The abbot certainly wouldn't put up with a cloister covered in coo shairn.

"I'll send ye coin for the hay, o' course," she assured him. "I can't imagine ye brought much if ye're staying at the monastery."

He grunted.

"Why *are* ye staying at a monastery?" she asked.

He wasn't at liberty to say. He'd promised to keep the monastery thefts secret. Instead he told her the first thing that popped into his head. "I'm thinking of...of taking my vows."

She coughed. Or choked. Or laughed. He wasn't sure which.

After a long and uncomfortable silence, she finally replied, "Ye should probably tell my father about your vows then. He's invited ye for Samhain supper, and I fear he has hopes ye will offer to court me."

Hew suddenly regretted his pathetic lie. On the other hand, he supposed the lie would help him keep his vow of chastity. Besides, it was too late to repair the damage.

They traveled in silence after that, focusing on the dimly lit path.

By the time they descended and emerged upon the field again, the Boyle brothers could be seen snoring away on the hillside, surrounded by the cattle.

By the time they reached the woods at the entrance of Dunlop, Hew figured the visitor had already departed and returned to the monastery.

He nodded toward the castle, whispering, "How will you get back in?"

"I can steal past the guard."

"He must not be a very good guard."

"I may have spilled aqua vitae into his beer earlier," she confessed.

He raised a brow. The lass's lovely and innocent face clearly concealed a devious mind.

But she instantly turned back into a supplicant angel with guileless eyes, beseeching him, "Pray take good care o' Hamish."

He could no more refuse her than he could turn down a challenge to battle. "I will."

She gave the beast a final squeeze of farewell. Then she glanced at Hew. He wondered if she meant to give him a hug goodbye as well.

But she only nodded. "On the morrow, I'll send someone to the monastery with coin for his hay."

Then she whirled away.

"Come along then, Hamish," Hew said, threading his fingers through the coo's shaggy hair to guide him down the road.

Each step away from Dunlop was fraught with more misgiving.

As with most of his plans made in the heat of passion, Hew hadn't thought anything through. He'd only wanted to return the smile to the lass's face.

Now he was saddled with a huge hulking coo stolen from the local laird. A useless animal he could neither sell nor butcher. A male beast he couldn't even claim he'd purchased for milk and cheese. Going to a monastery that had no ferme or cattle of its own.

What would he tell the abbot?

Where would he say he got the creature?

Where would he pasture it?

And where would it sleep?

He shivered. As cold as it was, it was tempting to let Hamish curl up with him in his cell.

And not for the first time, he wished he'd taken the *coo* to Dunlop and brought the *lady* with him.

CHAPTER 9

It was still dark when Hew roused to the sound of the normally silent monks gathering to pray at matins. Tonight, however, their soft footfalls were accompanied by a low rumble of murmurs which slowly grew into a rolling thunder of exclamations.

With a sigh, he sat up, scrubbing at his gritty, sleep-deprived eyes. He wrapped the coverlet around himself and prepared to face the mob. He'd hoped to catch a few more hours of sleep before this confrontation. But it was apparently not meant to be. The abbot would want to know immediately why on earth there was a coo in the cloister.

It was tempting to claim it must be a miracle. Clearly, God had seen how the monks suffered from a lack of meat and had gifted them with provender on the hoof.

But he'd promised Lady Carenza he'd keep Hamish safe.

So he had to come up with a different story.

Hew hated lying. It was dishonorable. Cowardly. Sinful. And it felt like a lie told in a monastery was more damning than one told on less holy ground.

But when a man was faced with the prospect of twisting the truth in order to salvage the reputation of a lady as lovely as Carenza, the price of his soul seemed fair.

The instant Hew emerged from his cell, the abbot demanded, "Do ye know aught about this beast?"

He pointed to what admittedly resembled a hulking horned demon guarding the church well. To his credit, Hamish sat in quiet compliance, looking as tame as a lady's palfrey.

The other monks waited to hear Hew's answer, probably glad to be distracted from their usual boring prayers.

But Hew decided the less said, the better. "I do, but..." He glanced meaningfully around at all the other witnesses.

The abbot received his unspoken message and waved the others off. "To matins."

The prior looked particularly displeased at being excluded from the conversation, but he obediently herded the others along.

When they were gone, the abbot asked, "So what's this about?"

"'Tis part of my investigation into the thefts."

His brows shot up. "A coo?"

"Aye."

"How? Do ye think a coo stole the treasures?"

"I can't explain yet," he said grimly. "But I assure you in time 'twill become clear."

"A coo."

"Aye," Hew replied with even more conviction.

The abbot gave his white-tonsured head a dubious shake, but mumbled, "I suppose ye know what ye're doin'."

Just then a sharp and piercing wail came from across the yard.

The abbot frowned in concern.

But warrior Hew's instincts kicked in first. He bolted forward, leading the way toward the sound, wishing he'd brought his axe.

As it turned out, there was no need for a weapon. One of

Laird of Flint

the young novices had simply tripped over his robes in the dark passage. He'd fallen and broken his arm.

It was severe enough that the prior decided the lad would need the services of the physician from Dunlop.

Carenza woke with a silent scream stuck in her throat. Her heart pounded like a fuller's mill. She'd had the chilling nightmare again, the one where the Viking of Rivenloch was chasing after Hamish with his great axe. Only this time, since she'd met the warrior face-to-face and hefted his formidable weapon herself, the details were far more vivid.

"'Tis only a dream," she rasped out, repeating it thrice to convince herself.

She rattled her head, still clouded with cobwebs. She felt as if she'd lain awake all night. But she could see light through the shutters. She had to rise at her usual time if she didn't wish to arouse suspicion.

Her eyes burned, her muscles ached, and her head throbbed. Still, her father would expect her to break her fast with the clan. And Troye the hound would expect his usual scraps. So she staggered out of bed and splashed water on her face, shivering as the icy drops shocked her awake.

She chose her rose-colored surcoat. The one her da liked so well. The one that would best disguise her sleepless pallor. Then she quickly braided her hair into two plaits, fastening them with the new ribbon she'd bought in the village.

She pinched her cheeks to give them some color and dabbed a generous amount of rosewater onto her skin to hide any lingering scent of cattle.

Her main task today was to act oblivious. To be her own cheery self. To behave as if nothing unusual had happened.

And to be completely dumbfounded and appalled when it was discovered that a cateran had stolen one of her father's coos.

Emerging from her chamber and down into the great hall, however, she realized it was later than she thought. The castle folk were already finishing up their ale and oatcakes and leaving to do their chores.

Meanwhile, the Boyle brothers had been discovered and freed from their bonds. They stood in the midst of the hall. Red-faced with indignant fury, they gesticulated wildly, explaining to her glowering father what had happened.

Her first instinct was to hide, to retreat up the stairs and tuck back under her coverlet until they were gone.

Then she reminded herself they had no idea she was the cateran. In their minds, the laird's daughter had likely spent a peaceful night slumbering in furs and dreaming of faeries.

So she glided forward with her usual serene smile and placed a hand upon her father's sleeve.

"What's happened, Da?"

"Naught to worry ye," he said, patting her hand.

But Gilbert Boyle was eager to impress her. "Caterans stole a Dunlop coo, m'lady."

"Sweet Mary!" Carenza exclaimed, pressing a hand to her bosom.

Herbert chimed in, "Lucky we were watchin' o'er the fold, or it might have been more."

"Ye were watching o'er the fold?" she asked.

"Aye," Gilbert said, puffing out his chest to explain, "'Tis the neighborly thing to do."

"We would have caught the filthy dastards too," Herbert boasted. "But they outnumbered us."

Carenza's brows shot up.

"Aye," Gilbert agreed. "And they had an arsenal o' weapons."

"Faith!" Carenza bit her twitching lip. "How...how many were there?"

"Dozens," Gilbert said.

"At least," said Herbert.

"And they took just one coo?" she asked with ingenuous wonder.

Her father cleared his throat. It was clear he didn't believe the magnitude of their story. But he was a good diplomat who wouldn't expose the Boyles' penchant for exaggeration. Instead, he gave them a look of concern. "I'm just grateful they didn't use their arsenal o' weapons on the two o' ye."

Herbert gave Carenza a sidelong glance. "They did tie us up, though, and left us for dead."

"How dreadful." Carenza clucked her tongue in sympathy.

"But ne'er fear, my lady," Gilbert announced. "We'll find them. We'll track the brazen scoundrels to the ends o' the earth."

"Anythin' for the Dunlop clan," Herbert added.

Her father nodded. "Your dedication is appreciated."

Carenza, however, didn't like the sound of that. She didn't want the Boyles poking around, looking for Hamish.

She clasped her hands under her chin and furrowed her brows in feigned worry. "I pray ye don't endanger yourselves. Better the loss o' one coo than two of our dear neighbors."

The Boyle brothers beamed at that. But she feared it would only renew their determination to get to the bottom of the cattle theft.

Eventually they left, mollified by her father's praise and Carenza's attention.

When they'd gone, the laird murmured to her, "Do ye think they hired someone to do it—steal the coo and tie them up?"

"Why would they..." Then she realized what he was thinking. "Ah. So they could get the coo back and save the day."

"Seems likely. Men will go to great lengths to impress a lady." He gave her a wink.

She grinned. A man would certainly have to go to great lengths to impress her. After all, she'd been raised by a man who was clever. Kind. Honorable. Patient. It would take a special person indeed to be the sort of man her father was.

Unbidden, the image of the Rivenloch warrior's face crowded into her thoughts. Was he that sort of person? He had definitely been clever, outwitting the Boyles. He'd also been kind, agreeing to take care of Hamish. There was no question he was honorable, the way he'd offered to take the blame for her crime.

But patient?

That he was not. She'd seen the spark of anger flash in his eyes, like a knife striking flint. Felt it rippling off of him like waves of heat off a fire. With that kind of rage boiling inside him, he seemed ill-suited to be a man of the cloth. She wondered how long he'd last at the monastery before his temper betrayed him.

"Heavens! That's thrice in a fortnight," her da said, shaking his head. "What is it this time?"

She hadn't been listening. What was he talking about?

Then she realized he was addressing Peris the physician.

"One o' the novices fell and cracked his arm," Peris said.

The laird frowned. "Perhaps the monastery should get its own physician, save ye the trouble o' makin' the trek."

"Och, 'tis no trouble," Peris hastened to say. "I'll be back in a wink."

"Ye're goin' to Kildunan?" Carenza asked.

"Aye."

Laird of Flint

"I need to send somethin' with ye."

"Oh?" her da asked. "What are ye sendin' to the monastery?"

She was sending the coin for Hamish's hay. But thinking quickly, she told him instead, "Ye wished to invite the Rivenloch knight to Samhain supper, aye?"

"Och, aye. Good plan. Peris can take the invitation."

Returning to her chamber, she scribbled out a hasty missive. Her father would have found her sloppy hand atrocious, considering the small fortune he'd spent on her education. It said simply, *Rivenloch – Purchase hay. Come to Samhain supper. Lady Carenza.*

She squinted at the words. Would he think he was to bring hay for supper?

No matter. There wasn't time to rewrite the note. Besides, the warrior would assume someone else had penned the missive for her. Her ability to read and write was a rare talent in a woman.

She tucked the note into a purse with the silver she'd promised him and gave it to the physician to deliver.

Aside from struggling to stay awake, the rest of Carenza's day was fairly ordinary.

She stitched a row of daisies along the hem of a coif. Took Troye the hound out for a game of fetch the stick. Played chess with her father. Left crumbs for her usual menagerie of pets. Sent lads out to gather wood for the Samhain bonfire. And recited the tale of Beira, the goddess of winter, to a group of wee children.

By supper, she began to flag. She fought to keep her eyes open, fearful she might fall face first into her pottage.

But when Cainnech the cooherd approached the laird after supper, she grew instantly alert.

"'Tis my fault," he said to the laird. "I should have been watchin' o'er the fold."

"Nay." Her father put a hand on Cainnech's shoulder.

"'Twas a scheme by the Boyles. I'm sure of it. They'll miraculously 'recover' the coo in a day or two and expect to be rewarded for their efforts."

Carenza gulped. She'd forgotten. If Hamish never returned, poor Cainnech would hold himself accountable.

"But ye won't do that, will ye, m'laird?" Cainnech asked, glancing pointedly at Carenza. "Ye won't reward them?"

"Hardly," the laird said, arching his brow at her.

"Good."

Inside, Carenza bristled at the idea of the two men discussing her as a reward. But she dared not betray her affront. She gave her father an indulgent smile instead.

Then, hiding a yawn behind her hand, she wondered how soon she could steal off to bed without arousing suspicion.

The door of the great hall suddenly opened, letting in a breath of fog along with the physician, returned from the monastery.

He looked concerned as he rushed forward through the throng.

"M'laird, I fear I have unwelcome news."

"The lad's arm," her father said on a sigh. "Was it beyond repair then?"

"Nay, 'tis splinted."

Carenza guessed, "Rivenloch refused the invitation?"

It wouldn't surprise her. She'd told him her father's intentions. He certainly wouldn't want to waste the laird's time wooing her if he meant to take holy vows.

"Nay. He said he'd come."

Her father frowned at her. "Now why would ye think he'd refuse? He's a healthy man in need of a wife. And ye're the loveliest eligible lass in the Highlands."

"Och, Da," she chided, squeezing his arm with affection.

"'Tis somethin' I saw at the monastery," the physician said.

"What is it?" the laird asked.

"They've got a coo in the cloister, one that wasn't there before, and I'd swear its ear was notched with the Dunlop mark."

Carenza couldn't breathe. Her smile congealed on her face.

"Is that so?" her father said in surprise, chuckling. "So I'm to believe the caterans are an army o' monks?"

"M'laird?" the physician said, blinking in confusion.

"Ne'er mind, Peris. Perhaps I'll pay a visit to the monastery myself in the morn," he decided, "save the Boyle lads the trouble o' retrievin' the beast."

"I'll come as well," Carenza blurted out. Why she said that, she didn't know. It wasn't as if she could stop the ugly confrontation sure to occur. It just didn't seem fair to leave the Rivenloch man without an ally.

"Is that to your likin', Laird Hamish?"

Hew scratched the beast behind its ear as it chomped down a breakfast of fresh hay. It was a pleasant enough animal, despite its intimidating girth.

Lady Carenza had sent coin along to keep the coo fed. So while the physician tended to the novice's broken arm, Hew picked up a cartload of hay from the village.

By the time he returned, Brother Cathal had arrived as scheduled to collect the alms.

Hew questioned the brother with careful diplomacy, commending him on his charitable profession and feigning an interest in how the funds were equitably distributed.

Brother Cathal, however, was reluctant to share details. Unwilling to make conversation, he wouldn't even meet Hew's gaze. He was a man of few words and little time. Driven to do his work and move along, he picked up the donation from the chapter house, slung the satchel over his shoulder, and made his way briskly across the cloister. He flinched in surprise just once when he saw Hamish grazing beside the well, then continued on his brusque way out of the monastery.

Hew wasn't sure whether the man's manner was efficient or suspicious.

Brother Cathal had unlimited access to the monastery. The monks let him come and go as he pleased. He could have easily stuffed something extra into his satchel on any of his visits.

But he didn't seem conniving enough to pull off such a theft. He wasn't exactly feeble-minded. But there was something different about him. An odd sort of self-absorption and disconnection from the world around him. He seemed intensely focused on one thing, the task at hand. And anything that distracted him from that task—like a coo in the cloister or a layman asking too many questions—rattled him.

If Brother Cathal *was* involved in the thefts, it could only be as an unwitting accomplice. An accomplice to someone aware he had access to the monastery's wealth. Someone who could be directing him to bring them certain items.

Could it be Father James?

It wasn't out of the question. But anyone on the outside might be capable of manipulating Brother Cathal.

Hamish lowed suddenly, and Hew jumped, startled by the loud sound. A moment later, the bell at the gates of the monastery rang out, indicating a visitor.

A pair of monks bustled to open the gates.

Hew gave Hamish one last pat and then retreated to his cell. Unless it was a sickly patron, the visitor probably wouldn't be let in. But one day, he feared, it would be the king's men coming with an English bride for him.

So it surprised Hew moments later to hear the sounds of raised voices coming from the cloister. Seizing his axe, he peered out through the crack of his cell door.

Shite.

On one side of Hamish stood the Laird of Dunlop. On the other appeared to be the Dunlop cooherd. The cooherd was inspecting the animal's ear notch.

The Boyle brothers paced nearby, bellowing and pointing accusatory fingers at the abbot and the prior, who paled in shock.

Monks milled about in distress and confusion.

And in their midst, like a delicate flower blossom dropped onto a field of thistles, stood Lady Carenza, looking distraught. Out of place. Achingly beautiful.

Though she uttered not a word, he could see the silent misery in her face. Her eyes filled with tears, but she bravely held them back. And she had a white-knuckled grip on the stones of the well.

Hew couldn't let her languish. He had to come to her rescue.

Without a second thought, he flung open the door and stormed out.

The monks gasped and scattered.

He felt an instant of remorse. After all, monks weren't used to seeing a warrior crossing the cloister with an axe. Not since his forefathers had raided monasteries centuries ago. But when he beheld the gratitude in Carenza's face, he knew he'd done the right thing.

The Boyles behaved like a pair of untrained hunting hounds, uncertain whether Hew was a fox for them to chase or a wolf they should fear, and looking to each other for support. They ultimately decided to stand their ground.

"That's him. That's the cateran," the bearded one declared. Then he glanced at Carenza. "The *main* cateran. There were dozens."

"Dozens," the beardless one confirmed. "Aye, but I recognize this one's axe."

"Now hold on," the laird said, stopping them. "So ye're sayin' this man and dozens of his fellows reived my coo last night, and he brought the beast here?"

"Aye," the Boyles replied together.

The laird shook his head. "Lads, I think ye want to be careful who ye're accusin' of—"

"They're right," Hew intervened before the laird could reveal his name. He lowered his axe, planting it between his feet.

"What?" The laird's jaw dropped open.

The Boyles looked astonished as well.

The abbot was mortified. "Explain yourself, sir."

Silently praying for mercy for telling yet another half-truth, Hew said, "'Tis fairly simple. Last night, I was unable to sleep. While ranging afield, I happened upon three caterans fighting over a coo."

"What?" the bearded Boyle exclaimed.

"We told ye last night we weren't caterans," said the beardless one.

His brother gave him a hard elbow in the ribs, realizing he'd said too much.

Hew continued. "I seized the beast, and they scattered, so I ne'er got a good look at their faces." He glanced at the Boyles, who were wisely silent. "Then, not knowing who the animal belonged to, I brought it to the monastery until the matter could be sorted out."

The laird nodded, satisfied. Then he turned to the Boyles. "Ye see? A perfectly reasonable explanation."

Hew noticed Dunlop asked no further questions of the Boyles. He was a wise laird indeed, not wishing to stir up trouble with neighboring clans.

As for the Boyles, they didn't dare reveal any more of the story and seemed happy to let it lie. Indeed, they decided to leave straightaway for home.

As the laird bid them farewell, Hew let his glance fall on the woman for whom he'd just borne false witness.

He expected her to be relieved. Awestruck. Grateful.

She was none of these. Instead, she looked more miserable than before.

He frowned. Then he realized, of course...

He hadn't solved her problem.

He'd only solved *his*.

The laird of Dunlop would take Hamish home now. He'd slaughter the beast along with the rest of the six-years, as planned.

In her eyes, all of it—her efforts, their plan, his rescue—had been for naught.

"Ye can take the hay for your cattle, m'laird," the abbot offered. "We won't have any use for it."

Hew kept hearing the lady's words in the back of his mind. *Hamish saved your life. Ye owe him his.*

It was that haunting refrain and the hopeless look in Carenza's eyes that made him act impulsively yet again.

"How much for the beast?" he blurted out.

"What do ye mean?" the laird asked.

"How much would you take for it?"

The laird blinked. "Ye wish to purchase it."

"Aye."

The tightfisted prior scoffed. He had an opinion on that. "We can't keep a coo."

The abbot lay a hand on the prior's forearm, probably envisioning months' worth of roasts in his future. "If Sir Hew wishes to purchase the animal, who are we to argue with his generosity?"

"How much, my laird?" Hew repeated.

The laird gave him a figure, far less than the beast was worth, perhaps thinking to endear himself to the powerful Rivenloch clan.

"Here is double that," Hew said, handing over his purse to the laird.

"Double?" the laird exclaimed. "Ye're certain ye want to do that?"

"Aye."

One glimpse of Carenza's relieved smile made it all worthwhile.

It was hours later—watching Hamish in the midst of a diminishing pile of hay and increasing piles of coo shairn—that he realized he was now the proud owner of a beast about which he knew almost nothing.

CHAPTER 10

It had taken all Carenza's willpower not to rush up to Hamish this morn and rest her cheek against his shaggy head. She hadn't realized how much she would miss him. But she was grateful he was at least safe. And alive.

She still couldn't believe how the Rivenloch warrior had explained his way out of an impossible situation. He'd not only emerged the hero of the story, but he'd silenced the smug Boyles as well. He definitely had a gift for deception.

Of course, if he wished to join the monastic order, he'd have to curb his deceitful ways.

She took another bite of salmon and leeks. It was her favorite meal, and there was always an abundance of salmon in the nearby river. Why the clan couldn't do without roasts made of her four-legged friends when fish was freely available, she didn't understand.

Her father suddenly narrowed critical eyes at her. He used the corner of his table linen to wipe a spot of sauce from her chin.

"Can't have ye dribblin' like a bairn at supper on the morrow, aye?" he chided. "Not with a warrior o' Rivenloch at the table."

She managed to give him a gracious smile, despite his lighthearted ribbing. He smiled back, unaware of how his penchant for perfectionism affected her.

It didn't matter anyway. The Rivenloch warrior didn't intend to court her. She could spill frumenty down her leine, dip her braids in her pottage, and lick her fingers, and, as a monk, he'd be obliged to overlook her sins.

"'Twas generous o' the man to buy our coo," her father said.

"Aye."

"Though if he'd waited, I might have given it to him as a dowry," he added.

"Da!" she scolded.

He chuckled.

She shook her head. "I'm afraid ye're in for a disappointment. He's not interested in me."

Her father laughed so hard at that, he choked on a leek and had to take a sip of ale. "Och, darlin', the day a man isn't interested in ye will be the day the sun rises in the west."

She sighed. Her father truly did believe she was flawless. "He plans to take his vows, Da. That's why he's at the monastery."

Her father narrowed thoughtful eyes at her. "We'll see."

His confidence gave her pause, because the laird was usually right, at least when it came to human nature. He always knew which way the royal winds blew. He could sense when clan conflict was brewing. He could tell when a man was lying to him.

Indeed, his only blind spot was where Carenza was concerned. He never suspected his sweet, obedient daughter was in truth a perverse and headstrong wench who'd resort to reiving cattle to save her beloved pets. It would break his heart to know who she really was.

But what if he was right?

What if the Rivenloch warrior did take an interest in her?

The idea gave her a strange feeling.

Laird of Flint

She'd always known she'd marry someone of her father's choosing. It was naive to think otherwise. After all, she was the daughter of a laird.

But somehow she'd imagined her husband would be a stable, quiet, boring man. A man who would satisfy her father's requirements for protecting her. A man who would keep her well supplied with servants, gowns, trinkets, and bairns. A man who would busy himself with manly pursuits—hunting, hawking, sparring, riding, fishing—and leave her to her own pastimes.

The idea of being wed to a man like the Rivenloch warrior made her breath quicken and her heart pound. He seemed dangerous. Unpredictable. Far too exciting. Too interested in her affairs. Too willing to insert himself into her life. Faith, she would have no life of her own, anchored to such a man.

Still, she would never have to doubt his loyalty or his dedication to her. He'd already proved he was a man of his word.

And to wake up to him each morn?

She blushed the color of her salmon as she recalled his handsome face.

She hadn't seen his features well on the night they met, just an impression of a chiseled jaw, deep-set eyes, and long blond hair.

But this morn at the monastery, she'd beheld the stern furrow between his brows. The grim set of his mouth. The flinty gray of his eyes, sparking with fire as he charged across the cloister, axe in hand.

He had been magnificent, like a fearless Viking come to conquer.

Then, after the conflict was over—after his jaw relaxed and his lips softened—he'd turned to her, and the tender affection in his misty eyes had left her breathless.

What would it be like to be wed to such a man?

What would it be like to *bed* such a man?

"...don't ye think, Carenza?" her father said.

Startled, she dropped her knife onto the table. "I'm sorry. What?"

"I said, don't ye think 'twas generous o' Sir Hew to keep the monastery in beef this year?"

"What?" Her head was still spinning. "Beef?"

"'Tis about time someone fattened up those monks."

Her heart plunged. She felt sick. Was that true? Had the warrior changed his mind? Had he broken his oath to her? Did he mean to butcher Hamish to feed the monastery? Or was that only an assumption on her father's part?

She managed to give him a feeble smile in return.

Then she looked down at her supper. The normally tempting fare now turned her stomach. She wiped her mouth and asked to be excused.

"Do ye feel well?" her father asked. "Ye look a bit pale."

"I'm fine," she lied. "But I'd like to retire early this eve. There's much to do for Samhain supper on the morrow."

"O' course."

Surreptitiously tearing off a small crumb of her trencher, she left the table.

She managed to make it to her chamber without losing her supper. But she still felt sick inside.

When she opened the door, Twinkle was waiting for his crumb. She gave him a fond greeting, but as she fed the sweet little rat his morsel of bread, her eyes filled with tears. Tears of pain and despair, anger and frustration.

She'd been a fool.

Of *course* he meant to butcher Hamish. It was probably how he was paying for his stay at Kildunan.

To imagine a fierce warrior like Hew of Rivenloch would care a whit about her beloved coo was ridiculous. Men like him slew other men without a second thought. How much less could he care for a coo?

Laird of Flint

Twinkle finished his meal, then washed his face and scampered off to his home in the crack of the wall.

Carenza palmed away her tears. Then she began to pace, winding one braid around her finger.

She couldn't allow Hamish to be slaughtered.

What could she do?

It was too late for another midnight raid to rescue the animal. She couldn't fortify the guard's ale again. Her costume was in tatters. Besides, the monastery would be locked up tight.

As she undressed and climbed into bed, she vowed she would muster her courage on the morrow. She'd stand up to the Rivenloch warrior. She'd remind him of his promise in no uncertain terms. And refresh his memory about his debt to Hamish.

She'd have to confront him when he first arrived. Alone. Where her father couldn't see the venomous fire in his gentle daughter's eyes. Or hear the sharp edge in her sweet voice.

At least it wasn't raining, Hew thought as he traveled along the rutted road to Dunlop the next morn. He'd bathed at dawn and dressed in the finest clothing he'd brought—a fresh white leine with dark gray trews and a gray and black plaid over it all.

It was appropriate attire, he thought, for a Samhain supper.

It was not so suitable for leading a shaggy coo down the road.

But he didn't intend to let Lady Carenza fret another day over her animal. He knew she likely suffered every moment she was away from him.

"I suppose I look like a simpleton, eh, Hamish, dressed in my best to deliver a coo?"

Hamish had no reply.

"Well, it might surprise you to know, it wouldn't be the first time I made a fool of myself for love."

That stopped him abruptly in his tracks.

Love?

What the devil was he saying?

This wasn't love. He'd sworn off love.

Hamish mooed, then plodded forward again, pulling him along.

"Oh aye, I know your mistress is a beauty. She's also kind. Gentle. Sweet. Bright. Sensitive. Generous. The kind of woman any man would be proud to have by his side. But I don't need to tell you that, do I, Hamish?"

He gave the beast a fond pat.

"Nay, 'tis only that I'm through with women. Oh, they seem innocent enough, luring a man in with their honeyed words and their soft bodies. But they ultimately only break a man's heart."

Hamish seemed disinterested.

Hew murmured, "I told your mistress I mean to take my vows at the monastery. 'Tisn't true. But I do mean to keep my vow of chastity."

He shuddered. When he said it aloud like that, it sounded so stark. So severe. So final.

Carenza had nearly paced a rut in the wall walk, watching for the warrior's arrival.

Her father was in the northern field, supervising the lads stacking wood for the great bonfires to be lit tonight. Cainnech was driving the cattle down from the hill into the close. Servants crisscrossed the courtyard, carrying baskets of barley, cabbages, leeks, and neeps, offerings that would be left at the castle doorways to appease the spirits.

The scents of roasting boar, baking oatcakes, stewing apples, and brewing ale wafted through the keep. Tonight the tables would creak under the weight of the year's final harvest. On the morrow, the culling of the cattle would begin.

Carenza didn't want to think about it. She narrowed her eyes at the spot where the road emerged from the woods. Was that movement? A figure approaching?

She straightened.

Then her heart plunged to the bottom of her stomach.

Hamish.

The warrior had brought Hamish *here.*

There was only one reason to bring an animal to a Samhain celebration.

Her father was wrong. The man didn't mean to kill Hamish to feed the monastery.

He meant to offer him as a Samhain sacrifice.

Horror filled her veins.

She began shaking.

Gathering her skirts, she flew down the steps. She dodged through the milling clan folk in the courtyard and burst out through the gates.

She had to stop the warrior. She had to force him to keep his promise. She had to convince him to turn around and return Hamish to Kildunan. No matter what it took. Shame. Guilt. Begging. Insults. Threats.

And she had to do it before her father caught sight of him.

For one lovely, lingering moment as he approached Dunlop, Hew imagined the beautiful enchantress in blue was rushing toward him out of eagerness. She'd seen him bringing Hamish, and gratitude had overwhelmed her.

His heart leaped. His breath caught. A familiar, warm tingling started in his belly. The sensation of being loved.

In that moment, he forgot about all his past broken hearts. His swearing off women. His vow of chastity.

He smiled.

Carenza's skirts rippled behind her like the caparison of a galloping warhorse. Her breast heaved as she narrowed the distance between them. Breathless from exertion, she had the pink-flushed cheeks and open mouth of a lass freshly swived.

In that lovely, lingering moment, he believed she was going to leap into his arms. Declare her undying love for him. Gratefully cover his face with kisses.

Then the moment vanished.

Instead, she skidded to a stop before him.

Her smooth brow was crossed with lines of worry. Her mouth was tense. Her wide eyes reflected an emotion he couldn't discern. Dread? Confusion? Disappointment?

But all she could gasp out was, "Don't do this. I beg ye. For the love o' God, go away. Go back to Kildunan, and don't come back."

He blinked. The warmth that had been tingling inside him congealed into a cold, hard lump. Like his ballocks when he dove into the icy loch.

Before he could respond, she continued in a hiss. "Have ye no honor, ye bloody traitor? Did your word mean naught? Is this how the craven knights o' Rivenloch keep their vows?"

Now she'd pricked his temper. There was no need to call his good name into question. "Now wait a—"

"To think I came back for ye, ye churl, that I let Hamish save your worthless life." She shook her head, adding in a murmur, "I should have let ye fall."

That felt like a punch in the gut.

Suddenly, from across the field, the laird of Dunlop sang out, "Welcome, Sir Hew!"

Hew dragged his gaze to the laird and managed to give him a weak wave in return.

"Shite," Carenza muttered under her breath.

Hew's brows popped up. He assumed the delicate flower was incapable of cursing.

"What's this?" the laird asked as he loped up, nodding at the coo. "A sacrifice for Samhain?"

Hew froze. A sacrifice? Of course. Why else would a guest bring an animal to a harvest celebration? No wonder Carenza had been reduced to nasty expletives and trying to shoo him away.

"Oh. Nay. Nay." He glanced at Carenza, who waited for his explanation with her lip caught under her teeth. "'Tis...a gift."

"A gift?" the laird echoed.

"Aye." Hew licked his lips, preparing to make up yet another sketchy story for which he'd owe penance. "'Tis a Rivenloch tradition. At Samhain, a visiting guest is expected to bring the gift of a single coo to the lady of the household," he explained, adding quickly, "a coo that must be kept and ne'er slaughtered—to appease the gods and bring good luck in the coming year."

Carenza was staring at him as if he'd grown an extra head. She clearly didn't believe him.

But her father did. And that was all that mattered.

"Is that so?" the laird remarked.

"Aye."

"How interestin'."

"Aye, 'tis been so for as long as I can remember." He wondered how hard his clan would laugh when he told them about this ancient Rivenloch tradition.

"Well then, it appears this is a lucky coo indeed," the laird said, grinning at Carenza, "and we are equally lucky to be blessed by your presence today, Sir Hew. Aren't we, Carenza?"

Carenza hardly knew what to say. How her father could believe such a blatant fable she didn't know. But he'd swallowed the warrior's lie as readily as a puffin gulping down herring.

As for Sir Hew, his talent for prevarication was remarkable and more than a little unsettling. He would have to spend years in confession if he had any hope of becoming a man of the cloth.

More than anything, however, she was grateful to him for saving her beloved Hamish. He had kept his word, after all. And now that the matter was settled, she could smooth her ruffled feathers and be the polite hostess her father wished her to be.

"We are blessed and *honored* to have ye with us, Sir Hew," she said, placing a humble hand on her bosom. "And I cannot thank ye enough for the gift. I will treasure it forever."

Her father nodded in approval.

But the Rivenloch knave winked at her.

Her cheeks grew hot. She averted her eyes, training them on the road ahead, hoping her father wouldn't notice how flushed she'd become.

He didn't notice. Instead, he initiated a boring subject. "So, Sir Hew, tell us about the Lowlands. Are ye constantly battlin' with the English?"

Sir Hew replied, but Carenza wasn't much interested in the conversation, so she was left to her thoughts.

The warrior really was devilishly daring. It was one thing to sneak around in the middle of the night in a disguise, reiving coos. It was quite another to tell an outrageous, barefaced falsehood to a laird. And he'd done it without even blinking.

But it wasn't only his boldness that left her blushing. It was also the glimmer of mischief in his eyes when he winked at her. His sly, one-sided, conspiratorial smile. The breathy growl of his voice. The way his freshly washed tawny hair curled around his ears. How his leine cleaved to every impressive muscle. Even the spicy scent of cinnamon that lingered on his skin.

It truly was a shame the man didn't mean to wed.

Not for her sake, of course. He was far too wild and impetuous for her.

But another lass would certainly appreciate his boldness. His unpredictability. His intensity.

And what woman wouldn't be thrilled by his warrior's body? His wide shoulders. His massive hands. His chiseled jaw. His lush mane. His smoky eyes. His broad back and the way it narrowed down to his firm and muscled...

"Carenza?" her father said.

She started. "Aye?"

"I said, tell Sir Hew about your education."

"Education?" Shite. All she could think about were the warrior's taut buttocks. "What would ye like to know, Sir Hew?"

But her father couldn't wait. "She can read and write," he boasted, "and she knows her numbers. No one will pull the wool o'er Carenza's eyes when it comes to matters o' the household."

Carenza had to bite her tongue. Her father was being painfully transparent, extolling her virtues to the man he hoped to snag as a bridegroom for his daughter.

"'Tis commendable," Hew said. "What's your favorite subject?"

She blinked. No one had ever asked her that. Most men were intimidated by her knowledge. Especially warriors, who rarely wasted time on books and study.

She opened her mouth to speak, then closed it again. She longed to tell him all about her interest in the natural world. How she studied butterflies and frogs and sparrows. How sometimes, when everyone thought she was stitching embroidery, she was actually working on her own bestiary. But that kind of conversation would trouble her father.

So she said, "I'm fond o' readin', I suppose."

"Me too," he replied, to her surprise.

"A warrior who reads," her father marveled.

"Most o' the Rivenloch clan reads," Hew told him. "'Tis useful for negotiations along the border."

Carenza couldn't help herself. She had to know. "The lasses as well?"

"Aye. Some of our lasses grow up to be lairds."

Her father frowned. "Sir Hew's own aunt is the laird o' Rivenloch."

She could tell by her father's tone that she should have known that. But her studies were learning letters and numbers. Not memorizing who was laird of every clan in Scotland.

Thankfully, Sir Hew saved her from the embarrassment of silence by filling in his family history.

"The Rivenloch clan is ancient, born of two cultures that gave equal power to men and women," he explained. "It began with the marriage of a Viking warrior and a Pictish princess."

"Och aye," her father said. "Many Vikin's took Picts as wives when they invaded."

"In this instance, 'twas a rare love match," Hew said. "The Viking was shipwrecked and heartsick, and the Pictish princess was exiled and alone. She took him captive for barter, but as fate would have it, they fell in love. Thus was born the Rivenloch motto."

Her father replied, *"Amor vincit omnia."*

Love conquers all, she silently translated.

"Aye," Hew said. "It remains to this day, and our tradition of equal power has remained as well."

"Interestin'," her father said, which was always what he said when he wasn't sure he approved.

Carenza was too astonished to comment.

Equal power. How freeing would that be? If she had equal power, she'd keep pets openly in her chamber. And decree that beef was off the menu. And formally announce that she intended to choose her own husband when she was ready.

"And what do you think of that, my lady?" Sir Hew asked.

She knew better than to voice her actual thoughts in front of her father.

"Interestin'," she said, giving him a noncommittal smile.

Then he gave her another knowing wink, and she glanced away before her blush could betray her.

Meanwhile, her thoughts churned like a raging river.

Equal power. The idea was intoxicating. If she married into the Rivenloch clan, would she be endowed with such power? Would she be free to make her own decisions?

Sir Hew had made it clear. He was destined for the church. But could he have an unmarried kinsman? One who was more ordinary, even-tempered, and predictable than the axe-wielding warrior monk? Perhaps a brother? Or even better, a twin who shared Sir Hew's good looks, captivating gaze, muscular body, broad shoulders, powerful hands, firm buttocks...

She must find out.

If there was another eligible Rivenloch bachelor, she could direct her father toward him. If they suited and eventually married...

She might be able to follow her dreams.

Keep a menagerie of animals.

Finish her bestiary.

Steer her own fate.

CHAPTER 11

The Laird of Dunlop believed Hew was a well-connected noble in need of a wife.

Lady Carenza believed he was a man about to devote himself to the church.

Keeping the threads of those two narratives separate required the skills of a master weaver. But Hew was accustomed to doing that. He'd had to appease cuckolded husbands and contrite mistresses enough times that he knew how to keep them from becoming an inextricable knot.

What was challenging was keeping his heart out of things.

This evening he could feel it thrumming every time he glanced down at the lovely lady supping beside him. Every time he glimpsed the delicate curve of her wrist. Heard the breathy murmur of her words. Inhaled the floral scent of her hair.

These things were impossible to ignore. And he didn't necessarily want to ignore them. After all, if the circumstances were different, he would leap at the chance to court the laird's daughter. And he couldn't rule out the appealing possibility that the king would approve such a match in the future. Keeping in Dunlop's good graces was essential.

Laird of Flint

But Hew had already declared to the lass that he was monastery-bound. What kind of scoundrel would she think he was if he made improper advances?

He was accustomed to women familiar with the reputation of the warriors of Rivenloch. Who trusted in their honor. Their loyalty. Their decency. Who took them at their word and believed what they said, simply by virtue of their clan name.

But Carenza questioned his chivalry at every turn.

For the first time in his life, he had to prove his worth to a woman, not by his reputation, but by his deeds. Beginning with being true to what he'd told her. He had to act as if he intended to become a monk. At least until he solved the monastery's thefts. After that, he could conceivably and reasonably change his mind about the church.

Only then would he be free to pursue Lady Carenza with all his heart. And he was almost certain she would return that love in full measure. After that, all he'd need to do was get his aunt, Laird Deirdre, to secure the king's permission for him to wed the Laird of Dunlop's daughter. Then the two of them would live blissfully ever after.

The thought made him smile as he cut another bite from the slice of roast in his trencher.

"Ye like the boar, aye?" the laird guessed, nudging him with a companionable elbow.

"Aye," he agreed, shoving the succulent morsel into his mouth. Then, reconsidering, he stopped mid-bite and inclined toward Carenza, muttering, "'Tisn't one of your friends, is it?"

She smiled and shook her head.

That sweet expression instantly convinced him of two things. One, that he'd gladly give up meat and dine on peat roasts and smoked plaster if it would make her happy.

And two, that the beast rousing in his braies was more starved than his belly.

"Sir Hew," the laird said, "Pray tell us about the great battle at Darragh."

The battle at Darragh. Hew knew that would bore Carenza. But it would appease the laird. And it would distract the rutting beast of lust.

He began with a humble, "I was but a youth at the time, so the battle was waged mostly by others of my clan."

Carenza knew the subject of warfare thrilled her father. But aside from sword-wielding Rivenloch women, she didn't find the discussion of battle tactics particularly engaging. Still, she listened intently for mentions of Hew's other kin, in the event there was a man suitable for marriage.

Unfortunately, she'd already had to dismiss his cousin Gellir, the tournament champion. When it came to animals, she assumed he would stab first and ask questions later.

Gellir's younger brother Brand sounded like a shadow of Gellir, so she was forced to reject him as well.

Another cousin, Adam, was apparently a master of disguise who'd once feigned to be a royal escort. He sounded even more dangerous than a man who'd lie about cattle reiving while standing next to a priest. So she crossed him off the list.

As Hew continued describing the warfare at Darragh, he mentioned his cousin Ian. At first, Ian sounded like a possible match. He was bright, quiet, serious, and inventive. But it turned out he was only fifteen years of age and just as much an agent of destruction as his warrior cousins. It had been his idea to fabricate and launch the mysterious and horrific flaming phoenixes that had finished the battle.

"Such a marvelous tale," her father exclaimed.

"Marvelous," Carenza echoed, glad it was over. "What about your other kin? Brothers? Cousins?" She licked a drop of honey from the corner of her lip.

When she glanced up at him, his gaze was fixed on her mouth. His eyes were smoky. His jaw was tense. His nostrils flickered.

There was no mistaking his thoughts.

He wanted her.

Nay, he hungered for her.

Her breath caught audibly.

In the next instant, he blinked. And the fire went out.

"Kin?" he croaked. "Aye."

She lowered her gaze. Still, the heat of his regard lingered. The rest of his words went into her ear and vanished in the misty maelstrom of her brain. At the end of a long list of recited names, she said simply, "I see."

Her father added, "'Tis a bit overwhelmin', is it not, Carenza?" To Hew he explained, "Carenza has neither brother nor sister."

"That may explain her good nature," Hew said. "No battle was more fierce than those the Rivenlochs siblings waged against each other."

"That may be true. Carenza only caused trouble a handful o' times."

She squirmed. She hated it when her father talked about her as if she wasn't present.

Hew turned to her. "Only a handful. Is that true?"

She sensed his amusement. After all, he'd seen her at her worst. Disobeying her father. Skulking about in the middle of the night in crofter's rags. Reiving cattle. Cursing.

"Once when she was very young," her father said with a chiding cluck of his tongue, "she 'borrowed' the jars o' tempera from a visitin' artist."

Carenza paled. He hadn't told that tale in years. Apparently, her father still believed she'd eventually returned the jars to the artist. She hadn't. Instead, she'd offered the man a very expensive brooch in exchange and kept the tempera. She still used it to illustrate her bestiary.

"Ah," Hew said, saving her again from humiliation by changing the subject, "a budding artist. Do you like painting?"

She loved painting. But she wasn't going to say so in front of her father. As far as he knew, she owned no artist's tools.

"I do stitchery," she said.

"She does beautiful work," the laird said. "See the sleeves o' my leine?"

Hew dutifully examined the ivy border she'd stitched along the wrist edges of the linen. But she was sure he wasn't impressed. She might wield a needle against linen and silk with some skill. But his mother wielded a sword against enemy flesh.

So she was surprised when he said, "This is quite clever."

And annoyed when her father chimed in, "I'm sure she could do somethin' similar for *ye.*"

"Oh, I couldn't ask—"

"Nonsense. 'Twould be my...*our* honor. Would it not, Carenza?"

"I'd be delighted," she lied with a delighted smile.

It seemed like an utter waste of time. After all, he'd soon be trading in his fine linen leine for a scratchy wool cassock. But she had to remain gracious.

"What figures would ye like?" she inquired. "Flowers? Axes?" Her lips twitched. "Coos?"

His eyes twinkled in return. "Perhaps flames."

"Flames?"

"Aye. My brother Logan is e'er teasing me about my hot temper."

"Logan?" Her ears perked up. Had he mentioned his

brother before? Was he of marrying age? "Tell me about him."

"We're as different as night and day. I always had our mother's quick temper. He got our father's sense of humor. But we've managed to make it work, like *they* do."

Her father leaned forward. "Ye have a hot temper? I've yet to see it."

"Now that I'm no longer a child, I find 'tis less of a temper, more of an intolerance for injustice."

"Ah," her father said, lowering his voice to confide, "injustices like seeing the Boyle brothers get away with lyin' about the cattle theft."

Carenza drew in a quick breath. So her father knew they'd lied. She supposed it shouldn't have surprised her. When it came to outsiders, her father was quite perceptive.

Hew nodded.

Her father wiped his mouth and left his linen on the table. "Now that I'm no longer a young man, I find the road to justice is sometimes windin' and very long."

Hew smiled and raised his cup in agreement.

"Speakin' o' no longer bein' a young man…" Carenza tucked her own linen under her trencher. "I fear the wee lads are gettin' restless to light the bonfire."

An hour later she and her father led the Dunlop clanfolk, bundled in thick woolen plaids against the chill wind, as they climbed up the frosty hillock to the blazing bonfire. Their offerings of crops and slaughtered fowl were carefully placed on the fire to appease the spirits and guarantee a good harvest in the following year. Tongues of flame licked the black sky, keeping evil souls at bay and reminding winter that the light of spring and new life would return.

At the spring celebration of Beltane the wee lads would be allowed to run and frolic around the fire. But Samhain was a somber time, and with the wall between this world and the next so narrow, most were afraid to incur the wrath of departed spirits. So there was little chatter. Instead, the air was filled with the crackle, roar, and snap of the fire consuming everything thrown into its greedy maw.

As the heat scorched Carenza's face, the bright flames drew her gaze upward. She saw what appeared to be the dark souls of the dead circling above the bonfire.

"Look!" a young lad cried out. "There they are!"

"Hush!" an old woman hissed. "Don't look at them or ye'll follow after!"

Soon the clanfolk began murmuring quiet blessings, while the wee children shivered in fear, shielding their eyes and whispering.

"As the wheel turns..."

"The veil thins..."

"Spirits o' those departed..."

"Keep us safe from..."

"Take these gifts..."

"Till the light returns..."

"Protect us from those who would..."

"Evil spirits."

"The souls o' the dead."

But Carenza knew what they were.

They were her treasured secret. Her favorite part of Samhain.

And for some curious reason, she felt compelled to share that secret with Hew. She clasped him by the forearm and nodded toward the top of the fire.

He followed her gaze in silence and then narrowed his eyes as he saw the dark forms.

She grinned. "Bats."

He furrowed his brows.

"The firelight draws insects," she explained in a whisper. "And the bats feast on them."

"I won't tell," he promised. "Though how can you be certain they aren't the evil souls of dead bats?"

That made her laugh, which immediately earned her a scowl from her father, standing near the bonfire.

Ashamed, she sobered at once.

Carenza only half-believed the story of Samhain. But for her father, of all the rites celebrated at Dunlop, this was the most significant. A time when the veil between the worlds was nearly transparent. A time for somber reflection. For regret and remembrance. For mourning and forgiveness. The time when he felt closest to Carenza's departed mother.

Clasping her hands and lowering her head, she ignored the bats and peered guiltily into the flames, which danced manically now, as if to leap free of the confines of the bonfire.

Nothing was going to bring her mother back. Why did her father foolishly insist on tormenting himself with renewed grief and false hope?

Still, it had been rude of her to find levity in a moment when he was suffering in despair.

Burdened by remorse, she murmured to Hew, "I must see to my father."

She left Hew's side and came up behind the laird. She slipped his hand into hers and gave it a squeeze.

He closed his eyes. By the orange light of the roaring bonfire, she saw a tear seep out, rolling down his cheek and into his beard.

They stood there in silence a long while as the wild wind urged the fire higher.

Eventually, he sniffed back his anguish and gave her hand a pat.

"So what do ye think o' this knight o' Rivenloch?" he murmured.

She spoke cautiously. "He's...a good man."

"I think your mother would have liked him."

She tensed, but managed to reply, "My mother would have said no one was as good as my father."

He smiled, but was not deterred. "Ye could do worse. Rivenloch is one o' the oldest and most respected clans in Scotland. Sir Hew is wealthy and powerful. Strong o' body and clever o' mind. Marryin' him, ye would want for naught."

"I told ye before, Da, he's bound for the church."

"'Twasn't brotherly reverence I saw in his eyes when he looked at ye at supper tonight."

"Da!"

"And 'tisn't virtuous piety I see in yours when ye look at him."

She gasped, glancing about to see if anyone else had heard his frank words. Then she spoke between clenched teeth. "Be cautious, Father, lest ye draw the evil spirits near tonight."

He leaned toward her and whispered, "Those are bats."

She sighed. Of *course* he realized they were bats. He might believe he could commune with his dead wife on Samhain. But he was as driven by truth as she was.

"Anyway," she said, "I'm sure the monastery is keeping him busy with..." What *did* monks do all day? "Prayin' and chantin' and...and takin' vows o' silence."

He made no comment on her obvious contradiction. "Ye won't discourage him, though, will ye?"

"From the church?" she asked, intentionally misunderstanding him. "O' course not." She crossed herself for good measure.

"From pursuin' ye."

"Ye've seen me, Da." She fluttered her lashes. "I've been nothing but gracious and welcomin'."

That he couldn't argue with. Mostly because he hadn't seen her threatening to let the man fall into a crevasse to his death.

He tried once more to convince her. "He really would make a good match, Carenza. And ye know how I am about these things."

He might be intuitive about others. But about her? He was as blind as the bats circling over the bonfire. She no more belonged with a wild and reckless warrior than a kitten belonged with a hound.

"He suits ye," he continued. "I sense deep honor in him. Integrity. A love o' justice. A good mind. And a good heart. He would make a fine husband. A fine father. The son your mother and I ne'er—"

His litany of praises was cut off abruptly when "the son he'd ne'er had" bowled violently into him, sending the laird tumbling away from the fire to sprawl in an undignified tangle of plaids and arisaids and clanfolk.

CHAPTER 12

Hew's heart beat like the wings of a trapped falcon. Faster and harder than it ever had for Gormal, Anne, or any of his past lovers. It slammed painfully against his ribs as he turned to Carenza with purpose in his furrowed brows.

There was no time for tact.

He lunged toward her. Seized her about the waist. Heaved her up over one shoulder. And packed her off like his Viking forefathers packing off the spoils of war.

At a safe distance from the bonfire, he lowered her gently but swiftly to the damp sod.

She gazed up at him in startled shock, unaware of the peril.

But Hew had spotted it at once. Whipped up by the wind, the flames of the bonfire had leaped onto Carenza's gown. They'd begun to greedily consume her leine and lap at the edges of her arisaid.

He started beating at the fiery fabric with his bare hands. Trying to extinguish the destructive flames. Scarcely noticing the heat.

From afar, the laird—seeing only a warrior attacking his daughter—cried out, "What the devil? Unhand her, sirrah!"

But those closer to Hew slowly realized what had happened. Gasps of concern rose around him.

Finally Carenza sat up, shrieking when she saw she was ablaze. She thrashed. Kicked. Tried to squirm away. Which would only make it worse.

"Nay!" he roared.

He forced her down with one hand and held her there. With his other sleeve, he fought to smother the fire.

Finally, after what seemed an eternity, the flames made one last sparking gasp of surrender and smoldered out.

With an exhausted sigh, he released her and rocked back on his heels.

She rose to her elbows, staring at him in wonder.

His heart still pounded. Panic continued to race through his veins. His body shuddered with residual fear.

Behind him, her father sobbed, "Carenza! Dear God, what hap—"

He cut himself off with a gasp when he saw the ragged edges of her leine, curled and blackened by fire, and the wisp of smoke rising from her scorched arisaid.

"I'm all right, Da. Just a bit singed." Her grateful gaze settled on Hew. "Ye saved my..." Then she lowered her eyes. They widened in horror.

Hew followed her gaze. Below his shoulders, the sleeves of his leine were burned away. The flesh of his exposed arms, from shoulder to wrist, was bright red. The palm of his right hand was blistered.

"Ye're hurt!" she said.

He didn't want her to fret. "It looks worse than 'tis." It wasn't a lie. Not really. He could see there was damage. But at the moment, there such an intense current of residual terror flooding his body, he could feel no pain.

The laird crouched beside him with a worried frown. Then he turned and bellowed out over his shoulder, "Peris!"

Was the laird calling his physician on Hew's behalf? Or for his own injuries? After all, Hew had walloped Dunlop with all the force of a battering ram in his effort to snatch Carenza from the blaze.

"Here," the laird said when the physician arrived. "He's been badly burned. Take him to my chamber."

Hew scowled. Surely he wasn't badly burned. Just a bit seared. He needed no special treatment. He was a battle-seasoned knight. The warriors of Rivenloch shrugged off injuries like a duck shedding water.

"That won't be necessary, my laird," he muttered.

The laird ignored him, adding, "Quickly, Peris."

Carenza sat up and pressed a hand to her breast. "I pray ye do as he says," she begged him. Her lips trembled. Her pale brow was etched with care. Her wide eyes were wet and full of fear.

Her urgent entreaty softened his frown. Melted his pride. How could he argue with an angel?

He gave her a reluctant nod.

And now that the excitement was over, now that the fire was out and Carenza was safe, Hew's pulse could calm at last.

Carenza's brow creased again as she perused his injuries. "They must be terribly painful."

"I've had worse," he said, giving her a wink.

This time it *was* a lie. Now that the danger was past and the tension flushed from his muscles, the pain seeped into his blood like swift poison.

He was accompanied to the castle by the three of them—the physician, the laird, and Lady Carenza.

By the time they reached the keep, Hew's arms felt as if they were engulfed in liquid flame.

By the time they entered the laird's chamber, he had to clench his jaw against the pain.

And by the time he sank down onto the laird's pallet, sweat began to pop from his brow, chilling his fevered skin and making him shiver uncontrollably.

The physician performed with clean, quick efficiency. His manner was completely at odds with the nervousness he'd displayed when Hew had first questioned him. He opened his leather satchel, pulling forth vials with calm, collected expertise.

"I'll need a bucket o' cool water," he said to the laird. "Butter. Honey. And a cup o' wine."

"Ye can have the bottle o' Bordeaux on the table," the laird said. He turned to Carenza before he left the chamber. "Stay with him?"

"O' course." Carenza drew near, wringing her hands. "How can I help, Peris?"

He handed her a wee vial. "Pour out a cup o' the wine. Then add three drops o' this. No more. No less."

While she fetched the wine, the physician carefully removed the remains of Hew's leine.

"'Tisn't too severe," he proclaimed as he studied Hew's damaged flesh. "The worst is your hand. Your arms should heal within a day or two. But ye won't be able to wield an axe for a while."

When Carenza returned with the wine, the sight of his injuries must have shocked her. She fumbled the cup in her hands and nearly dropped it.

"Does it look that bad?" Hew rasped out.

"Nay," she rushed to say, turning as red as his arms. After that, she wouldn't meet his gaze, though her eyes flitted frequently to his bare chest.

"Have him drink it down quick," Peris said.

Hew hated the way he was shivering. Doubly hated that he wasn't able to even hold his own cup.

But the compassion in her eyes, the light breeze of her sweet breath upon his face, and the touch of her delicate fingers on his chin as she tipped the cup up for him almost extinguished the fiery pain searing his arms.

The wine did the rest.

Whatever was in the vial, it worked quickly. Once he laid back on the pallet, his shudders subsided. The burning in his arms lessened. And lethargy drained the strength from him.

When Carenza drew near to mop his brow with a cool rag, he looked up at her with glazed eyes and smiled.

She was a mess. She was still clad in the blackened shreds of her leine and the scorched arisaid she'd adjusted for modesty. Strings of her dark hair, strewn with dead grass, had escaped her braid and now hung like a frayed mantle over her shoulders. Her hands were filthy. Her pendant was askew. Ash smudged her perfect nose and painted her rosy cheek.

But his last thought as he drifted off to a land of oblivious euphoria was that he had never seen a more beautiful woman.

Samhain had been cut short after Carenza's accident. But before the clanfolk retired, they took the time to snatch branches from the bonfire to light their own hearths for good luck. The sacrifices from the harvest had worked to appease the dark spirits. No evil entity had dared to venture past the bright fire of the living to do harm. Unless you counted the wicked flames that had licked at Carenza's gown.

Now, with Hew sleeping soundly, Peris and her father chatted quietly by the fire.

"O' course he'll stay at Dunlop to mend," her father announced.

Carenza was afraid of that.

She could feel things happening in her heart that did not bode well for the future. Things like the way it had softened, knowing Hew had sacrificed his own safety to keep her from harm. Things like how it pounded when she beheld his bare chest, bold and magnificent. Things like the way it ached when she thought of the kind warrior wasting away in a monastery instead of taking a wife.

She sighed. She needed to listen to the voice of destiny. Hew's fate was spoken for. By a higher power than she possessed.

It was hard to remember with temptation so close at hand.

"But he'll miss All Saints Day," she argued, "and All Souls Day."

"'Tis best not to move him in his condition," her father said. "Besides, the physician is already here."

"But they have an infirmary with beds at Kildunan," she told him. "Ye can have your bedchamber back."

She knew she was grasping at straws. Her father was perfectly content to sleep on the rushes in the great hall with his clanfolk.

"Don't worry about me," he said.

"He's goin' to need watchin' o'er, day and night," the physician warned. He held up the vial. "He'll need drops o' this every few hours."

"Right," Carenza agreed. "At Kildunan, they have dozens o' monks who are up all night, prayin'. Surely they can—"

"I insist," her father insisted. "'Tis the least we can do for the man who saved your life." To the physician, he said, "Ye'll o'ersee his care. And if ye're called away, Lady Carenza can look after him." He uttered the words with far more enthusiasm than Carenza deemed appropriate.

She clenched her teeth even as she curved her lips into a pleasant smile, as if that weren't the worst idea in the world.

It was obvious what fueled his satisfaction. The laird schemed to make a match between her and her Samhain hero. A feat that would be so much easier with the prospective bridegroom sleeping in the laird's chamber for several days. And Carenza serving as his nursemaid.

"'Tis settled then," the laird decided.

She wished she could say the same thing about her heart.

An hour later, after she'd dressed for bed and given Twinkle a last treat for the night, a maidservant scratched at her door. As fate would have it—or perhaps as her father had arranged—a messenger from the monastery had come to Dunlop to summon the physician. A wealthy patron had arrived at Kildunan's infirmary. He'd fallen from his mount in a hunting accident, and it was feared he might die.

Wrapping her arisaid around her, Carenza went to her father's chamber, where Peris gave her hasty instructions for Hew's care. He was to be given a cup of wine with three drops of the tincture—no more, no less—at each canonical hour. The dressing for his hand—a poultice of butter and honey—should be changed daily. And he should be watched for fever and signs of infection.

A pallet was brought in for her, though she could hardly sleep. Not with the magnificent warrior of Rivenloch slumbering so near. She crept close and gazed down at him.

He truly was a stunning figure of a man. Even in repose, there was a fierceness in his face that probably made his enemies quake. He had a few light scars—one on his brow, one high on his cheek, one along his jaw—where a blade had kissed his flesh. But they only added character.

His pulse throbbed in his throat. His ribs rose with each slow breath. As her gaze traced the smoothly sculpted muscle of his chest, she felt heat rise in her face.

This was not good.

Catching her lip under her teeth, she stealthily pulled up the coverlet to cover him. She told herself it was because he might be chilled. But she knew the truth. She found Hew attractive. Alluring. Irresistible. And she knew the fewer temptations she had to face, the better.

Perhaps she should invent a new history for him. One that would portray him as a repugnant villain instead of an irresistible hero.

Hew of Rivenloch probably ate kittens for breakfast, she decided. He wrestled with wolves to prepare for battle, killing them with his bare hands. And he drank the blood of his enemies.

After all, he and his clan had come from Viking parentage. They were probably berserkers who raped and pillaged their way through the countryside. Burning down churches. Sacking castles. Destroying villages. Stepping on spiders.

It was only right to despise the vicious son of Vikings, who wreaked havoc wherever he roamed. Any civil person would hate the hound-beating, horse-whipping, lamb-slaying savage who never traveled without his killing axe. It was natural to loath the deceitful and duplicitous monk who had invaded her home and deluded her father.

Then she made the mistake of glancing down at his face.

Lord, he was handsome. As handsome as the Devil.

A subtle furrow creased his brow. His eyes fluttered beneath his lids. A quick intake of breath parted his lips. He was stirring in his sleep.

And now she'd given herself a fright, endowing him with the traits of a wild Northman.

How long was it until matins? How long before she should give him another cup of wine? Should she rouse him when the time came? Or would he wake up, screaming in pain?

She gulped.

The physician had laced his wine with opium. What if he was not himself when he awoke? What if he *was* the berserker she imagined? What if he thought she meant to harm him? What if he tried to harm her?

Should she give him four drops? Five? More?

In the next moment, his brow eased. His breath calmed. His eyes went still.

She exhaled in relief. Then she realized she'd let her imagination get the best of her. Sir Hew was not a villain. He was an ordinary man. He'd shown her nothing but courtesy. Decency. Generosity.

With a self-mocking sigh, she gazed down at his peaceful face, framed by a shining golden mane.

His hair looked soft. She liked the way it curled around his ears and caressed his neck. She wondered, while he was safely asleep, if she might...

With a tentative hand, she reached out and lifted one lock from his throat. She rubbed it gently between her fingers. It *was* soft. Velvety. Silky. Like the fur of a kitten. Or the down of a duck. Or—

Before she could finish the thought, her wrist was seized in his iron grip.

She squeaked in surprise and then dragged in a loud gasp. But she couldn't wrench free.

His eyes were half open. His brows collided. He opened his mouth to speak.

"Drink," he croaked.

Then, his strength spent, he released her. His arm dropped back down to the bed.

"Och. Aye."

The distant bells for matins rang out then.

"'Tis time for more wine anyway," she told him.

She poured the Bordeaux and stirred in exactly three drops from the vial. Then she sat beside him on the bed to help him drink it down. As she lifted his head, she noted again the soft texture of his hair, at odds with the hardened muscle of his body.

But she wouldn't think about that. Especially since he would shortly have it tonsured. Nor would she think about the way his mouth opened eagerly to receive the drink.

The way his brow creased in concentration. And the way his lids lifted drowsily, revealing smoky, glittering eyes that pierced her very soul.

He finished off the wine. By the time she returned the bottle of Bordeaux to the table and added more peat to the fire, he was snoring beneath the thick fog of slumber.

It was a soothing sound. When at last she climbed between the linens of her own pallet, the rough, measured music of his breath lulled her to a dreamless sleep.

Hew awoke in the dark to the soft sawing sighs of a woman. He smiled. One of his favorite joys was rousing after a tryst to the peaceful sounds of his satisfied lover. He was too drowsy at the moment to recall who the lovely lady was or what they'd done. But he'd doubtless made her happy.

It was only when he rolled onto his side, brushing his arm against the linens, that pain brought him fully alert. He grimaced as his hand throbbed and memory came flooding back.

He'd been burned. The Samhain bonfire had ignited Carenza's leine, and he'd extinguished the flames with his arms.

The recollection magnified the sting of his flesh. Heat emanated from his arms. His blistered palm pulsed like boiling lead with every beat of his heart.

He clamped his teeth against the pain as he recalled more.

He'd been brought to the laird's chamber. The physician had given him wine. He'd drifted off shortly after that.

So who was in the room with him now?

The fire had gone out. It was too dark to see.

It must be either the laird or the physician.

He edged carefully onto his back again and closed his eyes, listening and willing the pain to subside.

That was definitely a woman's breathing. He'd heard it

enough times to know. He strained his ears, trying to detect more.

In the distance, muted bells rang, waking the breather.

"Prime," she announced to no one.

He recognized her voice at once. Lady Carenza. But he wondered why the lass would care about monks' hours. Unless she needed to pray several times a night to atone for stealing her father's coo.

Not wishing to startle her, he feigned sleep as she scrambled out of the pallet and crossed the chamber.

He heard her poking at the hearth. The shadows on his closed eyes lifted as fresh firelight illuminated the room.

She poured something and approached him.

"Sir," she whispered faintly.

Sir? Was she calling him *sir?* Surely they were on less formal terms. After all, she'd apparently spent the night in this chamber with him.

He ignored her.

"M'laird."

M'laird was worse. They were practically accomplices in crime.

He didn't move a muscle.

She softly cleared her throat. Twice.

He continued breathing evenly. Which was no easy task when she reached out and pressed a finger to his brow. Even more difficult when she tapped it twice.

She withdrew her finger and finally mumbled, "Hew. Hew. Wake up."

Ah, there it was. The arousing allure of a woman murmuring his name. He pretended to stir and let his eyes flutter open.

His mind's eye hadn't done her justice. She was still disheveled and sooty, with red-rimmed eyes and tangled tresses. But the concern in her face and the kindness in her gaze made her as lovely as an angel.

"Drink this," she said. "Peris said 'twill help with the pain."

What helped with the pain was her heavenly presence. With her beside him, he almost forgot he felt like he was burning in Hell.

"Thank you," he said, reaching for the cup before he remembered his injured hand.

"I'll hold it."

He took a sip. It tasted nasty. "'Tis bitter."

"'Tis the opium. But it seems to work, aye?"

He nodded and forced it down.

She took the finished cup to the basin to rinse it.

"You stayed with me," he called out to her. "Why?"

"'Twas the least I could do, considerin' ye saved my life."

He settled back onto the bed. "Well, you saved mine, so I suppose we're even."

"Nay. Ye saved Hamish's life as well."

"Right. But let's not keep flirting with death just to even the score."

"Agreed."

To Hew, it seemed rather reckless for the laird to leave him alone with his daughter. But then maybe she'd told him Hew was bound for the church and therefore unassailable.

"Where is Peris?" he asked.

"He was called away to Kildunan."

"Again? What was it this time?"

"Somethin' about a wealthy patron and a huntin' accident."

That seemed curious. Rivenloch was a warrior clan, and they didn't keep their physician as busy as did Kildunan. "Does the monastery infirmary usually have so many visitors?"

"I'm not sure."

"But Peris is the one they call when someone arrives?"

She nodded.

"And how often does he visit Kildunan?"

"At least once a fortnight. Someone contracts a fever or twists an ankle or eats bad meat." She narrowed her eyes. "But why so many questions about Peris? Has he done somethin' wrong?"

"Nay. I just..." Hew could already feel the effects of the wine. It was loosening his tongue and wrecking his judgment. Perhaps it would be best to steer her aside before he revealed too much. "If I'm to stay at the monastery, I'd like to be of help. It seems like Kildunan could benefit from having their own physician."

"Not *you?*" she asked, incredulous.

The idea of him as a physician made Hew chuckle. "Nay. I'm a warrior. I do all my bloodletting with an axe."

She arched a brow and murmured, "Ye won't be doing any bloodlettin' at all if ye join the order."

He sighed. For one morose opium-addled moment, he regretted his decision to quit his warrior ways to become a monk. Then he remembered that wasn't true. It was just a story he'd made up.

"I hope ye're not thinkin' o' stealin' Dunlop's physician," she said. "We need him here."

The wine was washing away his pain. Now he was feeling quite good. Giddy even. If he wasn't careful, he might blurt out something inappropriate. Something dangerous.

"I don't need Peris. Not with a beautiful angel like you by my side."

Like that.

CHAPTER 13

Carenza had been called "beautiful" hundreds of times.

Sometimes the word was used as a sort of currency by suitors and flatterers who wanted something for their efforts.

Sometimes it was spoken on a sigh, an involuntary reaction to the particular arrangement of features with which she'd been blessed.

"Beautiful" had become a description with little meaning for her, like the repetitive warble of a sparrow that knew no other tune.

But she was well aware that—wrecked by fire, smelling of smoke, with her hair hopelessly snarled and her face smeared with ash—she was as far from beautiful as a boar was from a butterfly.

But he saw past all that. Hew peered into her soul and called her "beautiful."

It took her breath away. On Hew's lips, it became a new word. Sweet. Pure. Honest. Imbued with deeper meaning.

Normally, she responded to praise with a humble dip of her head, a smile of gratitude, and words to the effect of "How kind o' ye to say so."

But hearing Sir Hew offer the compliment with such gushing sincerity, she was left speechless.

It was just as well. He wouldn't have heard her reply anyway. Thanks to the strong wine, he'd already sunk into the murky depths of ease where he was free of pain. Free of care. Free of having to answer for speech that was completely contrary to the virtuous intentions he claimed.

For Carenza, however, his words echoed in her head, tormenting her.

It could be, she reasoned, that his brain had simply been muddled by opium. That he was confused. That he'd temporarily forgotten about his monkish aspirations.

He might have imagined Carenza was someone else. A past acquaintance. Or perhaps a real angel.

But she couldn't shake the feeling that what he'd said in that moment had come from the heart. And it made something inside her quiver with delight.

What would it be like, being the "beautiful angel by his side" *forever?*

To be wed to a true hero who had snatched her from the jaws of death?

To be wife to a champion who would protect and defend her with his life?

To wake up to his sweet words of praise every morn?

To tuck her head into the warm and welcoming crook of his massive shoulder each night?

They could forge a beautiful future together. A future of which even her father would approve. One that had started with the bridegroom rescuing the bride, just like in the stories of old.

They could have a perfect life. A life full of bairns to raise. Precious pets for her. Grand tournaments for him. Salmon for supper every night.

Perhaps her father was right. Perhaps Sir Hew could— and *should*—be dissuaded from his holy pursuits.

She climbed back into bed with a smile. She could

dissuade him. If anyone knew how to use charm, it was Carenza. She'd been taught to be a perfect daughter. A perfect lady. A perfect hostess.

How much harder was it to be a perfect prospective bride?

She was too excited to sleep.

If Hew had called her a beautiful angel when she was a charred mess, what would he say when she was freshly bathed and dressed in her finest clothing?

Ordinarily, she wouldn't wrest a servant from their bed. Especially not after the late night revels of Samhain. But these were special circumstances.

So, using the excuse of it being the Sabbath and All Saints Day, she coaxed a servant to heat water for her bath, which she would take in the solar. Then, stealing past her snoring father, who had commandeered her bedchamber in her absence, she dug through her chest to find her favorite gown. It was of silk imported from Lucca, but the best thing about it was its color. It was a rare shade of vivid blue, almost as violet as a thistle. And her father told her it matched her eyes perfectly.

By the time the lavender-scented bath was ready, the servants were up and about. A maidservant helped her bathe and scrubbed the ash from her hair. Then she fashioned it into a flattering style that swept her waist, with loops of tiny braids and white ribbons as decoration.

She finished dressing just before the bells of prime. With a smile that for once wasn't forced, she left the solar and glided along the passage toward her father's chamber.

She was astonished to find the door ajar.

Who had entered the chamber?

Peering through the crack of the door, she saw Peris, hovering at Hew's bedside. Hew was still asleep. The physician was putting drops of opium into a cup of wine for him. She didn't want Peris to think she'd abandoned

Hew. But she didn't want to disturb his critical measurements. So she hesitated.

He slipped in one drop. Two. Three. Four. Five. Six. Seven. Eight.

Her jaw dropped. She accidentally leaned against the door, pushing it open.

Startled, Peris quickly righted the vial of opium tincture and swirled the cup of wine as if nothing was wrong. But he reddened and scowled.

"There ye are," he said, refusing to meet her eyes. "I didn't know if ye were comin' back."

"O' course."

She didn't want to alarm him. Maybe he'd miscounted or drifted off while putting in the opium drops. Maybe it had been an honest mistake. She didn't want to embarrass the physician. But she had to make sure Hew didn't drink the deadly wine. And for that, she had to put Peris at ease.

"Was the man in the infirmary hurt badly?"

He stoppered the vial and replied snappishly, "He fell from a gallopin' horse, so aye." Then he put the empty Bordeaux bottle on the table. "He'll likely die on the morrow or the next day."

She lifted her brows. "But ye're a skilled physician. How can ye be so sure?"

"I always do the best I can," he grumbled. "But 'tis God's will who lives and who dies."

"O' course."

She wondered if he thought it was God's will to put extra opium into Hew's wine.

"Ye must be tired," she said. "Ye can't have had much sleep." She stepped forward and reached for the cup. "I can take o'er if you like. Ye can rest."

The bells of prime rang out then. Peris, startled, snatched back the cup before she could wrap her hand around it.

Hew began to rouse. Peris shot a sharp glance at him.

"Och, ye're awake," he said in a rush. "Time for your wine."

Carenza had no intention of letting him poison Hew, even if she had to take drastic measures. Acting on instinct, she stepped forward as if to help.

"Would ye like me to—"

Then she pretended to trip over her skirts. She gasped and knocked the cup aside with the back of her hand.

The clay shattered on the floor, splattering wine everywhere. Including in a dark red splotch on the front of her favorite blue-violet gown.

"Lucifer's ballocks!" Peris cursed as drops of dark wine rolled down his beard and onto his leine.

"Och nay," she lamented, looking down at her gown. Her despair was only half feigned. That stain would never come out of the Lucca silk.

Awakened by the crash, Hew lifted his head and narrowed groggy eyes at her. "What happened?"

"Just a wee spill," she said.

He closed his eyes and sank back onto the pallet.

Peris was shaking, whether with rage or fear, she wasn't sure.

"Don't fret, Peris," she said sweetly. "I'll clean this up and mix another cup for Sir Hew. Ye go on and find your pallet. After all ye've been through, ye deserve a rest."

He couldn't argue with her. Instead he used a linen to dry his beard and groused, "'Tis only that there's always so much to do. The hours. The responsibility. The travel. The sickness. The death."

"Ye know, Sir Hew was remarkin' that Kildunan might be better off hirin' their own physician."

"Nay!" Peris erupted, then thought better of his outburst. "Nay. I can manage. 'Tis an act o' service and a labor o' love."

"One for which God will surely reward ye," she cooed.

"Reward?" he scoffed, then added in a mutter, "Och aye, I'm certain of it."

Carenza quickly ushered him out of the chamber. "Will ye send someone up with a bottle o' wine and a cup?"

He grunted in reply.

After the door closed, Hew opened his eyes. "Peris seems...ill-at-ease."

"Ye were awake?"

"Enough to hear the edge in his voice."

"'Tis likely exhaustion. He was in the infirmary again all night."

"The hunting accident?"

"Aye. Peris fears the man will die."

"That's two in a sennight."

"Aye." She started picking up the shards of the cup. "By the way, we're even now."

"Even?"

"I saved your life again."

"You did?"

"Aye." She placed the broken pieces on the table. "When I came in, Peris was addin' a deadly amount of opium to your wine."

"What?" Hew glowered in outrage. "Did he mean to poison me?"

"I'm not sure. It may have been an accident. But I couldn't let ye drink it."

"Did you knock the cup out of his hand?"

"I did."

His mouth curved slowly up into a heart-melting, delicious, conspiratorial smile. And she found there was something liberating about not having to keep up appearances for Sir Hew. Something thrilling about sharing her mischief with him. So she couldn't help but grin back.

LAIRD OF FLINT

Lady Carenza's charming innocence was going to get her into trouble. The lovely lass had no idea how her smile lit up a room, plucked heartstrings, and made a man grow hard with longing.

Hew felt that way now.

Sometime last night, she'd bathed and dressed. Aside from the garish wine stain marring her skirts, she looked flawless. The color of her gown matched the jewels of her eyes. Every strand of hair framed her face perfectly. Every inch of her skin was radiant. She smelled like a field of summer flowers.

He longed to court her with pretty phrases and gentle caresses. To whisper praise into her ear and slip the silky strands of her hair between his fingers. To sweep her into his arms—his burns be damned—and cradle her winsome body against his chest.

But his careless vow of chastity kept him in a prison of his own making. He would have to avert his eyes and temper his desires.

"How are ye feelin'?" she asked. "Any better?"

He nodded. His arms still stung. His hand burned. But the pain seemed negligible when compared to the throbbing in his braies.

"I need to change your poultice," she said.

He nodded. That was what he needed. Pain to distract him from lust.

Her fingers were surprisingly gentle as she unwrapped the linen bandage. She winced more than he did when exposing the greasy, blistered palm of his hand. But it appeared to be no worse than before.

"Perhaps 'twill hurt less if ye do this yourself," she said, offering him a clean rag to wipe away the old balm. "Take care not to burst the blisters."

After he was done, she dabbed a honey-butter mixture over his clean skin with a feather-light touch. Then she tenderly swaddled his hand in fresh linen.

Someone came to the door to deliver a bottle of wine. He watched as Carenza poured out a cup and carefully added three drops of the tincture.

Then he frowned.

What if Peris's measurements hadn't been an error? What if he meant to do Hew harm? Hew had made the man nervous with the questions about his monastery visits. At the time, he'd assumed it was because the physician was unused to being interrogated by a warrior. But perhaps it was something more.

"Do you think Peris is hiding something?"

"Hidin' somethin'?" she said, swirling the cup of wine. "Hidin' what?"

He shook his head. "He's been acting uneasy ever since I questioned him that first day."

She considered this for a moment and then asked, "Why *did* ye question him?"

He couldn't tell her the truth. At least not all of it. "I...wanted to know what he does at the monastery. How often he goes. What kind of access he has."

"Why?"

"Why?" he echoed.

He couldn't divulge details about his investigation. So he had to invent something. Fast. Not an easy feat when one was indulging in regular doses of opium wine.

"Because if Kildunan wishes to hire their own physician, they'll need to know such things."

"Perhaps Peris is afraid ye mean to replace him."

"Perhaps. But is that cause to poison me?"

"I do think it may have been an accident."

He sighed. He wasn't so sure. "I don't trust him."

She popped the stopper back into the bottle of wine and

turned away to set it on the table. "Is that why ye were skulkin' about the hills o' Dunlop in the middle o' the night?"

That he didn't expect.

And he didn't have an answer for her.

So he did what any clever adversary would do.

He created a distraction.

"Ahh!" he cried out suddenly, doubling up with a grimace of pain. He lifted his injured hand and gasped as if someone had just lopped it off.

It worked. With a look of horror, Carenza rushed toward him with the cup of wine.

"Here," she said. "Drink this. Ye should feel better soon."

He drank it down all at once while she paced, fretfully wringing her hands, distressed by his distress.

But the silence he'd purchased with his suffering couldn't last forever.

Eventually the opium began to work. Soon he couldn't recall why he was so concerned. In fact, he felt very calm. Pleasant. Delighted.

"Is the pain gone now?" she asked.

He smiled. Her voice sounded like bells.

"Aye."

"'Tis my fault," she said. "I should have given ye the wine sooner."

"Nay, y're not t' blame." The relief in her face made him happy, so he added, "Y're…perfec'."

She blushed at that. But he could tell the compliment pleased her. And suddenly he wanted to please her more.

"Y'r gown matches y'r eyes. Did y' know that?" He could tell his words weren't as smooth and polished as usual. But he wasn't sure it mattered.

"So I've been told."

"And y'r hair," he murmured, gesturing with his uninjured hand. "How'd y' get it in such wee braids…an' coils…an' loops?"

"'Tis my maid's handiwork."

"Ah." He took a deep breath. "I like the way y' smell. Like...roses?"

Her eyes twinkled. "Lavender from my bath."

He nodded. "Y'r eyes look like stars." Then he hesitated. "Did I already mention y'r eyes?"

"Ye did. But now I have a question o' my own." As it turned out, the wily lass hadn't been distracted at all. "Why *were* ye skulkin' about Dunlop that night?"

"I wasn't skulking." It came out like the voice of a petulant child.

"What were ye doin'?"

"I was... I was..." He scowled, trying to remember. What *had* he been doing? Oh aye, he'd been following someone from the monastery. But he wasn't supposed to tell her that, was he?

Why? Why wasn't he supposed to tell her?

He let out a long sigh. It seemed pointless to keep secrets from Carenza. After all, they already shared secrets. They were already accomplices in crime, weren't they?

"I'll tell y'," he decided. "But y' mustn't tell anyone. C'n I trust y'?"

"Aye."

"D' y' swear it on y'r honor as a knight? Y' won't tell a soul?"

"I'm not a knight."

He rattled his head. "Argh." Of course she wasn't. "D' y' swear on y'r honor as a lady?"

"Aye."

Checking the corners of the chamber just to be sure there were no witnesses lurking about, he beckoned her near.

She came close, and for a moment he was distracted by the sublime perfume of her skin.

Then he whispered, "At the request o' the abbot o' Kildunan, I'm investigatin' a series o' thefts from the monastery."

Up until now, Carenza had mostly been amusing herself with Hew's intoxication. The opium wine had worked quickly to ease his pain. But it had also made him a bit daft. He was indulging in wild conspiracies. Garbling his words. Spewing awkward compliments.

This, however, was intriguing. Furthermore, it sounded true. It made little sense for an esteemed warrior of Rivenloch to be sent to a sleepy monastery just to sample the life of a monk.

"What kind o' thefts?" she asked.

"Big ones. Mon'st'ry treasure. A silv'r cross. A gold chal'ce. A jewel'd Bible."

Then she straightened, realizing what he was saying. "Ye think someone from Dunlop took them?"

"Nay," he said. Then he screwed up his forehead. "At leas' I don't think so."

"Then why were ye here in the middle o' the night?"

He yawned. The opium was making him drowsy. "I w's followin' someone."

"Who?"

"I'm not sure. He left the mon'st'ry, so I followed him."

"Ye thought it might be the thief?"

"Mm-hm."

"And he came to Dunlop?"

He nodded. "But turned out 'twas a monk."

"A monk? What was he doing, comin' to Dunlop in the middle o' the night?"

"That's wh't I wanted to know. Which 's why I was followin' him."

"And?"

"When I saw 'twas a monk," he mumbled, letting his eyes drift closed, "I figured someone needed...last rites or somethin'."

That couldn't be. No one had died at Dunlop in months.

"What happened then?" she asked.

His words were slurring badly now. "Y' came out o' the keep then. Took off 'cross the hills. So I thought..."

She could guess. "Ye thought the scruffy beggar was a more likely suspect."

He nodded, sinking deeper into the pallet as his breathing slowed.

She watched him as he slipped away to the land of dreams, considering everything he had told her. Then an awful thought occurred to her.

"Ye don't *still* suspect I'm the thief, do ye?"

But he was already asleep.

CHAPTER 14

Normally, All Saints Day meant that Carenza would spend several hours in the chapel, praying. Her father thought they should set a good example for the rest of the clan. Most of her devotions went to Gertrude, Cuthbert, and Modestos, the Saints who loved and protected animals.

But she was admittedly relieved when, shortly after dawn, the physician was called back to Kildunan and she had to take over Hew's care again. It meant she'd have an excuse to avoid kneeling in the chapel all day. It also meant she could learn more about this secret mission of Hew's.

As she strode along the corridor to where Hew was sleeping, she promised God she'd pray extra hard for the Saints on the next Sabbath.

The bells of terce tolled in the distance. She quietly entered the chamber, bearing a linen cloth stuffed with oatcakes.

Hew was still dozing.

His bare arms, atop the coverlet, looked less red now. Perhaps they were healing.

Below the coverlet, his chest rose and fell. His breath cut through the silence like a carpenter sawing through wood.

A smile tugged at her lips. She wondered if he always

snored like that or if it was only the medicine making him sleep so deeply.

She almost hated to wake him. But it was time for another portion of wine. He should eat something as well. And most important, Carenza needed to find out if she was a suspect in the Kildunan crime.

She placed the bundle of oatcakes on the table. Crossing to the hearth, she stirred the embers to life and placed several more chunks of peat on top.

By the time the fire was blazing cheerily along, Hew had roused.

"Good morn," she said as she mixed his opium-laced wine.

He grunted.

She could see he was in a foul mood. It would be best to placate him first before diving into the deep waters of interrogation.

"Your arms look better already." They looked magnificent, if she were being honest, though she wasn't going to say that. "But ye need to break your fast. Ye haven't eaten enough to keep a flea alive." She loosened the knot on the bundle of oatcakes.

He winced. "I need—"

"I know. Ye need your medicine. But 'tis best taken on a full belly." She offered him an oatcake.

"Nay," he said, turning his head away. "First I need—"

"Come, be a good lad," she said, waving the oatcake in front of his face like a taunt. "I promise I'll give ye the wine as soon as ye—"

"Nay." He pushed the oatcake aside and threw back the coverlet.

"What are ye doin'?"

He sat up on the edge of the bed and arched a brow at her. "I need to piss."

Mortified, she bit her lip, lowered her head, and took a meek step backwards.

When she stole a glance at him, he was shaking his head in amusement as he rose to visit the garderobe.

Meanwhile, she threw open the shutters to let in the morning light, then spread honey-butter on an oatcake for herself.

She was mid-bite when he emerged again with a frown.

"You," he proclaimed, "are a wicked thief."

She half-choked on the oatcake. Snapping up the cup of wine, she took several gulps to wash down the crumbs.

So Hew *did* suspect her.

And he wasn't mincing words.

He'd come straight out with a bold accusation.

Then he shook his head and clucked his tongue. "Pilfering my healing balm to sweeten your oatcakes." He picked up the bowl of the honey-butter concoction. "Well, I won't turn you in," he said with a wink, "as long as you share."

Somehow she regained her composure. Somehow her heartbeat resumed its normal pace. She even managed to imbue her gaze with a twinkle of amusement she didn't feel.

Then she rasped out, "O' course."

He sat on the edge of the pallet and watched her spoon honey-butter onto an oatcake for him. Ordinarily, it was a task she did with ease. Today, however, she was as nervous as a kitchen lad on his first day.

Now she understood why Peris had been so anxious. It was unnerving to be suspected of a crime one hadn't committed. Especially by a fierce warrior with a passion for justice and a menacing axe.

She offered him the oatcake.

"Are you all right?" he asked.

Was her worry so obvious? "Aye," she lied. "But ye... How are ye feelin'?"

"My arms are better. But my head..." He grimaced.

"Ye're probably cravin' the opium," she said, reaching for his cup.

When she peered down at the contents, she realized with horror she'd drunk three-quarters of it.

"Och." It was all she could say, lowering the cup.

When he saw it was mostly gone, he glowered at her with feigned outrage. "Are you stealing my medicine as well?"

Her heart dropped. She was too panicked to even pretend to find humor in his words.

She'd never taken opium before. What would it do to her?

Would she lose her good judgment?

Her carefully constructed control over her emotions?

Would she embarrass her father?

Shame her clan?

Her worry must have show in her face, for Hew's manner changed at once.

"Oh, sweetheart, what's wrong?" His voice was tender. Earnest. Full of concern.

He should not have called her 'sweetheart,' of course. It was far too familiar a term. But the endearment touched her heart and brought tears to her eyes.

"I've ne'er taken..."

"Opium?"

She nodded.

"To be honest, neither have I...until now."

"What if I make a fool o' myself?"

"Did *I* make a fool of myself?" he asked.

She shook her head. He hadn't. Not exactly. He *had*, however, grown rather loose-lipped. For him, it was of little consequence. He didn't have the responsibilities or expectations that she had.

"I won't let you do anything foolish. I promise," he assured her. He took the cup from her and set it back on the table. "Do you trust me?"

LAIRD OF FLINT

That was a hard question. She'd known him such a short time. And he'd proved himself a capable liar. But he was aspiring to the church. Her heart and her instincts told her he was worthy of her trust.

"Aye."

"Then you'll stay here with me, and I'll look after you."

"Ye'd do that?"

"Of course," he scoffed.

"But how will ye stay awake?"

"I can do without the medicine."

"But your hand..."

He shrugged. "I've been hurt worse in battle."

"Ye have?" She couldn't imagine. She'd seen a few men who'd been hurt worse. They'd died shortly afterwards.

"Aye." Then a glimmer of mischief entered his gaze. "I'd show you the scar. But 'tis in a spot not meant for innocent eyes."

Her face grew instantly hot, and she looked shyly away. But she couldn't help wondering exactly where he'd been wounded and if he was still whole.

"Eat another oatcake," he suggested. "It might dilute the effects of the opium."

That was a good idea. She would eat another oatcake. Then she would lie down on her pallet. With any luck, she would drift immediately off to sleep.

Under no circumstances would she do what Hew had. Blurt out her secrets. Confess her sins. Share her dreams. Or bare her heart.

Not today, but soon, Hew was going to break his vow of chastity.

He could feel it.

His head throbbed. His hand burned. His forearms sizzled with pain. But the desire flowing through him overpowered all earthly discomforts, like a soothing balm for his heart.

Many made the mistake of thinking Hew was a cuckolding rake, trysting with women for the sport and thrill of it.

But it was never so. Never had he lain with a woman he didn't love, heart and soul.

Trysting was but the culmination of the fierce and powerful love that came before. A union born of passion and devotion. A heavenly merging of bodies that echoed the merging of spirits. It simply happened more swiftly for Hew than for others.

Even now, his affection for Carenza was growing rapidly out of his control. Every glance, every smile, every touch she bestowed upon him took root in his heart, spreading through his veins like an intoxicating elixir.

How then could he resist her?

And if she felt the same way about him...

He sighed. He'd be lucky to last another sennight.

Carenza swallowed down the last of her oatcake and met his gaze. Realizing he'd been staring at her, he averted his eyes, but not before the image of her licking a drop of honey from her finger was imprinted on his brain.

"I think I should lie down," she decided.

Hew thought so as well. In this bed. Next to him. Naked.

"That's probably best," was what he said.

She tucked herself modestly into her own pallet and pulled the coverlet up to her chin.

Without warning, intense pain pressed down on him like an ocean wave breaking over his head. Pain far worse and demanding than the discomfort of his burns.

It wasn't from his accident.

It was from the medicine.

He would somehow have to endure the throbbing, because he planned to take no more.

He had no desire to become like a few men he'd known—men who had never found relief from their pain except in greater and greater measures of the poisonous flower. Better he should endure the anguish of his injuries than inflict new wounds where there were none before.

Besides, it was a sacrifice he'd gladly make. There was nothing more rewarding than serving as a guardian angel, watching over the one he loved.

Even as he had that thought, he silently cursed his eager heart. Already he was calling her "the one he loved" when she'd given him no assurance of her affection. None whatsoever. Only gratitude for what he'd done in saving her and her coo.

Her coo.

Thinking about the great beast touched off a memory.

In the wee hours of the morn, when he'd been in the throes of opium, they'd spoken about the night he'd first seen Carenza at Dunlop.

But what had they chatted about? He strained to recall.

Oh aye, she'd asked him why he'd been lurking about the castle.

He'd told her he was following someone from the monastery.

He exhaled on a groan. God's eyes. Why had he told her that?

Naturally, the curious lass had immediately wished to know why that should interest Hew.

He'd had no choice but to confide in her.

Nay, that wasn't true. The opium had made it feel like the right thing to do. As if confiding in the lady would be wise and sensible.

Holy hell. Just how much had he shared with her?

Enough, he decided.

Enough to know that in doing so, he'd flagrantly broken his word to the abbot.

Enough to put his investigative process at risk.

Enough to endanger his discovery if Carenza couldn't be trusted with his secret.

The lass asked too many questions. And she no doubt had many more.

This entire scheme of hiding Hew from the king by stashing him in a monastery and putting him to work hunting down a thief had been ridiculous.

First of all, keeping a secret in the Dunlop clan was impossible. Already, half the Highlands knew Sir Hew of Rivenloch was staying at Kildunan. And now Carenza was privy to his highly confidential mission.

Would she keep that confidence? Or compromise his efforts?

How long would it be before Father James began to suspect the odd guest at Kildunan was up to more than taking his ease at the monastery? How long before news of Hew's whereabouts reached the king's ears?

He sighed. His head had begun to throb again.

Despite the pain, he resolved that he was done with opium wine. It made him far too vulnerable.

"Sir Hew?" Carenza called softly.

"Aye?"

"I'm beginnin' to feel...strange."

"Are you?"

"Aye. Like I'm floatin' on a cloud."

"Where else would an angel dwell?"

"Awww." She sounded pleased.

That pleased him. But flirting with her was a mistake, considering how easily aroused he was.

"Ye, sir, have a smooth tongue," she said.

All the better to lick your delicious skin.

That was what he thought. But Carenza was an innocent. Not some randy wench to be wooed with nasty innuendos. So what he said was, "You inspire me, my lady."

She giggled. It was an adorable sound. The opium must be relaxing her.

"I feel so...so happy."

He couldn't help but smile at that. "What makes you happy?"

"My animals," she said on a sigh. "My animals make me happy."

Animals, as in more than just Hamish? How many did she have?

Before he could ask her, she began listing them, poking up a finger for each one. "I have Hamish the coo. But ye already know him. I feed a squirrel named Scarlet who comes to the courtyard. I've just set Pokerounce and Blancmange free to sleep for the winter. They're hedgepigs. I give table scraps to Troye, my favorite hound. In the courtyard, there's a crow who likes to bring me gifts. And a friendly fox comes round now and then if I've got a bit o' meat." She paused to emit a luxurious yawn. Then she stopped counting and continued in a drowsy voice. "O' course, I'm fond o' the new wee lambs...an' piglets...an' calves. I haven't named them all. I used t' have a spider called Tidy who kep' my window free o' bugs. An' Twinkle the rat comes to m' chamber ev'ry night for a wee bite."

He raised a brow. "You have a rat in your chamber?"

"Mm-hmm." Then she gasped and lifted her head to look at him with wide eyes. "Och! Don't tell my Da. He'll be so upset."

Hew thought the laird would be far more upset over his daughter reiving cattle than feeding rats. But he didn't tell her that.

"I won't breathe a word."

"Y're a good man." Her eyes turned all soft and dreamy. "I'm so glad y're here."

"I'm glad I'm here too."

Mostly because someone had to keep her from leaving the room in her condition.

The opium had definitely taken control of her. Opening her mind. Softening her heart. Relaxing her tongue.

"Y're very handsome," she said.

His lips twitched with amusement. "Thank you."

"An' strong."

He nodded, not knowing how to respond.

"Good-hearted. An' generous. An' full o' honor."

"You're too kind."

"Bold an' brave." She pondered hard. "An' handsome. Did I say handsome?"

"I believe you did."

"*Very* handsome." She caught her lip under her teeth. "I like your hair. An' your eyes. An' the way ye smile." Then she waved him forward with a flutter of her fingers. "Come 'ere. I have somethin' to tell ye."

He couldn't refuse. He came up beside her pallet and hunkered down beside her.

Her eyelids dipped and opened again slowly. "Come closer," she murmured.

He drew as near as he could. Near enough to see the languid glaze in her amethyst eyes. Near enough to smell the sweet lavender on her skin. "What is it?"

She lowered her voice to a whisper. "Sometimes when I see ye smile, I think about kissin' ye."

He gulped.

"I wonder what y'r arms would feel like aroun' me," she confessed. "How y'r breath would feel upon my cheek. What y'r lips would taste like."

Hew could only gape at her in slack-jawed silence.

In any other moment like this, he would have swept the woman off her feet, delved his hands into her hair, and ravished her mouth with passionate abandon. They would have ended up in an intimate embrace and inevitably in a tryst between the linens.

But this wasn't any woman. This was Carenza. This was The One. And she wasn't in her right mind.

She lifted a finger and placed it on his mouth. "Do y' think about it too?"

He didn't trust himself to speak. So he nodded.

She traced his lips with her finger, lingering on them with a limpid gaze. Then she whispered, "Do y' think about other things?"

His throat closed. The raging beast below his waist was thinking of them. In fact, it was demanding them.

She withdrew her finger and gave him a sultry smile. "Y're goin' to make a terrible monk."

She wasn't wrong. But for now he had to behave like one.

Making light of her comment, he replied, "And you, my lady, are going to make a terrible cateran."

"Me, a cateran." She flashed him a gleeful grin. A grin that ultimately melted into a yawn. Then a crease settled between her brows. "Y' don't think *I'm* the monastery thief, do y'?"

So she *did* remember their conversation from the wee hours.

He was about to reassure her that nay, he didn't think she was the thief. Who could ever believe Carenza was a common outlaw?

On the other hand, she'd stolen her father's coo, let the Boyle brothers take the blame, and deceived the abbot. She wasn't exactly without sin.

Could she have stolen the church treasures?

There was only one way to find out. Ask her directly.

"*Are* you the monastery thief?" he asked.

"Nay," she replied.

She closed her eyes. He figured that was the end of it.

Then she opened them again and said, "But I'm goin' t' help y' find him."

Hew frowned. "I don't think that's a good idea."

"Why?"

"'Tis too dangerous."

"No more dang'rous than reivin' coos."

She had a point. But the last thing he needed was a lass getting in the way of his investigation, especially when it involved powerful members of the church. And if Carenza was anything like the last three women he'd courted, she'd be unable to resist sharing her clandestine mission with her maid.

Soon the whole clan would know what they were up to.

The abbot would find out Hew had been indiscreet.

And the gossip would reach the king's ear.

Nay, it would be best if she forgot everything she'd heard about the monastery thief.

"I work better alone," he told her.

"No one w'rks better 'lone." As she grew sleepy, her voice trailed off.

But what she'd said was true. And it made him think.

"Wait. What did you say?"

She smiled. "About kissin' y'?"

He couldn't help but smile back. But this was important. "You said no one works better alone."

"Did I? Mmm."

He began to think aloud.

"Working with a partner does make things easier. Whether 'tis fighting in a clan battle or digging a cart out of the mud."

"Or stealin'."

"Right. It makes sense that the thief has an accomplice. Someone to cover for the theft or provide a distraction."

"One t' steal it an' one t' hide it."

He froze. Of course. There were *two* thieves.

He'd been searching for a person who had both access to the innermost chambers of the monastery and the freedom to come and go as he pleased in order to stash the treasure at a remote location.

But if there were two thieves, only one would need to have access to the treasure. He might be any monk within the walls. The second thief would simply receive the stolen goods from the first and transport it elsewhere. That person could be any vendor or visitor who came to the gates of Kildunan.

His mission had just gotten a lot more complicated. But for the first time, he believed he was on the right path.

"My brilliant lady," he declared, "I think you may be right."

But his new partner in the investigation was already asleep.

CHAPTER 15

All the day and half the night were gone when Carenza awoke. She'd never slept so long. She'd missed supper. Skipped feeding her animals. Neglected to tell her father goodnight.

As far as she could tell, the opium had had no other lasting effect. But it had certainly made her feel strange. Deliciously relaxed and deliriously happy. As if she hadn't a care in the world. As if she were perfect just the way she was.

And Hew… Her heart softened. The loyal warrior had stayed with her. Watched over her.

Like her noble champion. Her perfect hero. Making sure she didn't make a fool of…

Then she remembered.

A silent scream slowly built inside her throat as the words she'd blurted out in her opium-induced state crashed down on her with vivid clarity.

She *had* made a fool of herself. In front of Hew.

She'd utterly lost control. She'd dished out ridiculous flattery. Uttered unmentionable things to him. Revealed her heart's secret longings. Let ribald remarks glide across her tongue. Lord, she'd behaved like a doxy.

She'd never be able to look him in the eye again. Not after that. What kind of wanton must he think her?

She pushed up off the pallet and stared into the darkness. She could hear his rough breathing from the bed.

Dawn was several hours away yet. But she didn't want to be here when he woke.

She quietly left the chamber and made her way down the stairs.

She was hungry. There would be bread and cheese in the pantry.

Dozing clan folk nested in the rushes on the floor of the great hall. She picked her way through them by the dim light of the banked fire. Then she climbed down the steps in the corner of the hall to the lower level, darker and chillier than the floor above. A narrow passageway cut into the stone opened onto four storage rooms.

One was the buttery where casks of ale, bottles of wine, perry, cider, and mead were kept.

The second held tallow and beeswax candles, bottles of scented oils, and spices—pepper, saffron, ginger, cinnamon, clove, cubeb, nutmeg.

The third contained her mother's things. Things her father couldn't bear to part with. He'd locked the room long ago and probably never revisited it. Carenza imagined it was full of rotted leines and moth-eaten arisaids.

She entered the fourth room, the pantry. On the shelves were a few day-old loaves of bread, several crocks of butter, and dozens of blocks of cheeses in neat rows. In one corner hung several hams.

She helped herself to a large chunk of bread, using her eating dagger to slather it with butter.

While she was choosing which cheese she wanted, she heard voices. The furious whispering of two men. Coming from just beyond the pantry doorway.

She hung back, pressing herself against the wall to listen.

"What the devil were ye thinkin'?"

"He's trouble."

"I know he's trouble. But it can be managed."

"That's what I was doin'. Tryin' to manage it."

"By killin' him?"

Carenza listened closer. They were talking about murder. This was something her father needed to hear.

"'Twould look like an accident."

"Not to the laird. And not to his daughter."

Carenza bit her lip. They were talking about *her*.

"I could explain it. Say 'twas an infection. Or 'twas worse than it looked at first. They'd trust me."

A chill shivered down Carenza's spine. That voice. It was Peris the physician.

"Ye know the laird has plans to make the man his heir, aye?"

"He can find another," Peris said.

"Not like this one. Have ye ne'er heard o' the Rivenloch clan? They're the king's favorites, for God's sake. They keep the border from bein' overrun by the English. A marriage into such a clan..."

"But if he finds out—"

"He won't. Because ye'll be careful."

"I don't like this."

"Ye don't have to. Just stay quiet. And don't do mad things like tryin' to kill a Rivenloch warrior."

The opium. It *had* been intentional. And if Carenza hadn't walked in when she did...

"The laird doesn't want him to go back to Kildunan."

"O' course he doesn't. Not when he's got his daughter waitin' on the prospective bridegroom, hand and foot."

"But he can't stay here," the physician complained. "He's too meddlesome. I can't work this way."

"He can't go back to the monastery."

"What! Why?"

"Father James is suspicious."

"Father James? Why?"

"Why do ye think? He's wonderin' why there's a Rivenloch warrior stayin' at his monastery."

"Laymen stay at monasteries all the time."

"Maybe in the infirmary. Not in the monks' cells."

"Maybe he's joinin' the order."

There was a dubious sigh. The same sigh Carenza had made at the absurd thought of Sir Hew donning a monk's robes.

"No one would believe that."

"I can't go on like this," Peris complained. "'Tis too dangerous."

"And ye think killin' a man in cold blood isn't? God's eyes, have ye no thought for your soul?"

"My soul is already damned from this nasty business."

The other man grumbled something under his breath that sounded like a curse. "Listen to me. I swear to ye, 'twill be done by Lent. If ye can just compose yourself for a few more months and keep from killin' anyone…"

"Compose myself? How am I supposed to do that?"

"I don't know. Maybe drink one o' those concoctions ye tried to give the warrior. Just lay low, and 'twill be right in the end."

There was a long silence before Peris replied with a despondent sigh. "Fine."

"Because we dare not do anythin' to rouse Father James's suspicions."

"I said 'fine'," Peris snapped.

"Good. Ye'll see. Everythin' *will* be fine. And in the end, if ye don't want a share o' the spoils, ye can stay here at Dunlop if ye like, with none the wiser."

"I didn't say I didn't want a share o' the spoils."

What they said after that, she didn't hear. They made their way along the passageway and up the stairs.

How long she'd been holding her breath, she couldn't

say. But once she could hear them no longer, she let it out on a shaky exhale.

Despite the chill of the pantry, she remained there for several moments, trying to make sense of what she'd heard.

Peris wanted to get rid of Hew because he was "meddlesome." What did that mean?

Whatever they were up to, Peris believed his soul was damned. Enough so that killing a defenseless man would hardly tarnish it further. What "business" could the physician be up to? What "spoils" did he intend to share?

She took a thoughtful bite of buttered bread.

Hew had spoken about a secret investigation. The monastery thefts. Could that be the matter they were discussing? But what could the physician have to do with that?

She had to share what she'd heard. But she couldn't go to her father. She didn't want him to worry. Not before she got more details.

She needed to tell Hew.

With any luck, he'd forget all about her indiscretions of last night, especially after she gave him this startling news.

She stuffed the bread into her mouth with a haste that would have horrified her father. Then she snatched up a block of cheese, a crock of butter, and tucked the rest of the loaf under her arm. Praying the two conspirators had had time to return to their beds, she stole from the pantry, across the great hall, and up the stairs.

"Sir Hew!"

Carenza's whisper was sharp and urgent enough to rouse him from a deep sleep.

"What is it?"

He pushed himself up, wincing as he forgot about his injured palm.

"I need to talk to ye."

Dropping some sort of parcels on the bed, she moved to the hearth and stirred the coals to life so they could see each other.

He raked his hair back and blinked the sleep from his eyes.

Carenza looked charmingly disheveled. He realized he actually preferred her that way. She might need to appear perfect for her clan. But he rather liked her imperfections.

She wheeled away from the fire and said, "'Twasn't an accident."

He was still half-asleep. "What are you talking about?"

"The opium."

Was she upset about what she'd said to him while she was drugged?

"There's no need to fret. I'll forget what you said last night. And you can forget what I said the day before."

"But that's just it," she said. She neared the bed and began unwrapping the parcels. "Are ye hungry?"

"In the middle of the night?" he asked. Then he realized he was. "I could eat. What have you got? And where did you get it?"

"Cheese. I've just been to the pantry," she said, drawing her eating dagger and slicing off a piece for him.

He shoved it into his mouth, talking around it. "The pantry? How did you..." How had she managed to escape? Some guard he was. He wondered if she'd been up for hours in an opium stupor, gushing to every man in the keep how much she wanted to kiss him.

"That's not important," she said. "'Tis what I heard that's important."

"What you heard?"

"Men whisperin'," she said, popping a piece of cheese between her teeth, chewing as she spoke. "One of them was Peris."

"The physician?"

"Aye. The opium that morn? 'Twas no accident. He was tryin' to kill ye."

"How do you know that?"

"He admitted as much."

"Why would he—"

"Ye know what I think?" she said, gesturing with a second piece of cheese. "I think he's part o' your monastery thefts."

Hew stopped chewing. His head was spinning. He already suspected the physician, simply because of his access to the monastery.

She took another nibble. "He was tryin' to get rid o' ye, because he knows ye're investigatin' the thefts."

He swallowed the cheese. "You said two men?"

"Aye. I didn't recognize the voice o' the second."

But it appeared she'd been right. There *were* two thieves.

She continued. "He was upset that Peris had tried to kill ye. He said 'twould draw too much attention."

"Attention?"

"Aye. He said ye were too important and..." She trailed off.

"And?"

She answered in a rushed mumble. "And that my father had designs on ye for his heir." But before Hew could begin to enjoy that heartwarming fantasy, she added, "He was also afraid 'twould draw the attention o' Father James."

"Father James?"

"Aye. He said the father was already suspicious about your presence at Kildunan."

He'd felt that. Father James's eyes missed nothing, and his mind seemed as keen as his gaze. If the father learned what Hew was investigating, it wouldn't be long before the king found out.

"So," she said, her eyes gleaming with intrigue, "what are we to do?"

"*We* are to do naught." This had become too close for comfort. "*I* will look into matters more deeply."

"Don't be ridiculous. Ye're bedridden."

"I'm not bedridden." Indeed, after he shook off the last of his sweating, shivering need for opium, he intended to get up and around and make himself useful.

"Ye need someone on the outside. Someone with unlimited access. Someone who can dig up more information. Someone," she said, raising her brows meaningfully, "they'll never suspect."

He hesitated. He hated to admit it, but she was right about that. Nobody would question Carenza's motives or suspect she was assisting him. Not only was she a woman. She was the laird's irreproachable daughter. It *would* help to have her poking her nose into things.

"Ye know I'm right," she added.

"What about the monastery?" he challenged her. "The second thief has to come from there, aye? They're not about to let a woman within the walls of Kildunan to question all the monks."

"The second thief doesn't have to come from the monastery. Peris has access. He goes there all the time. The second man could be the one who stashes or sells the valuables."

Hew narrowed his gaze. "Which one said Father James was growing suspicious—Peris or the other man?"

"The other man."

"Right. So he's the one with the knowledge o' what happens at Kildunan."

"Och. Aye." She thought for a moment. "Then I could find out who 'tis by questionin' Peris."

"He's going to wonder why. And eventually he'll know you suspect him of something. He's anxious and impulsive.

If he tried to kill *me*..." He let the sentence hang. The idea of Peris hurting Carenza was too awful to think about.

She scoffed. "He won't touch a hair on my head. My father would...string him up by his ballocks."

Hew choked back a laugh. He doubted the delicate maiden had ever voiced such a crude phrase aloud before. It amused him. It also flattered him that she felt safe enough with him to mince no words.

Still, it didn't feel right, getting Carenza involved in such a perilous game. She didn't understand the kind of men and the desperation she was dealing with. Hew did. He saw it every day, defending the border and keeping the peace.

"My lady," he decided, "this is not like reiving a coo. This is thievery on a grand scale, perpetrated against the church. Those involved will be severely punished. Maybe even hanged. That kind of threat will drive a man to do unspeakable things."

"I can look after myself," she assured him. "Trust me. Peris wouldn't hurt me."

"You didn't believe Peris would intentionally try to kill me either."

"I do now."

He shook his head. "I don't like this. If something were to happen to you..."

"If somethin' were to happen to me," she said with irritating practicality, "ye'd go to Kildunan and take your vows, the same as before."

That was the lie he'd told her. And to be honest, if something happened to her, he might decide to withdraw into the life of a monk and make his vow of chastity permanent. But that wasn't the way he felt now.

"I couldn't live if I lost you," he murmured.

When her eyes widened, he realized he'd bared too much of his heart.

So he amended his words. "For a knight to lose the lady he's supposed to protect is a disgrace."

"I see," she said softly, obviously injured by the retraction. "Well, no one said ye needed to protect me."

He wanted to go to her then. To take her in his arms and hold her close. To swear to protect her with his life. Forever.

But knowing what he knew now about her feelings... how much she desired him...how she'd imagined his kiss and longed for more...

Protecting her now meant protecting her from *him*. From his impulsive and intense nature. From his powerful passion. From the haste with which the storm of his desires could build and grow and overwhelm a lass.

He had to keep her at arm's length. Forget her seductive midnight confessions. Maintain a distance that would keep her honor intact.

He owed it to her father. He owed it to her.

"'Tis a knight's duty to protect all women," he told her.

Carenza's heart sank.

"O' course."

She'd spilled her innermost secrets to Hew. Shared her darkest desires. They'd kept each other's confidences. Saved each other's lives.

Now he felt as cold as the depths of a loch.

Was she truly just "all women" to him? Did he have no feelings for her?

His nonchalance hurt her. Then it irritated her. Then it made her angry.

She wouldn't let her anger show, of course. That was not the way a laird's daughter behaved.

But she intended to prove to him she was one woman who didn't need protecting.

She was not some helpless damsel in distress who needed a big, strong Viking warrior to rescue her. He had no authority over her. She need not abide by his wishes. She *would* investigate the thefts. She *would* question Peris. And if he didn't like it, he could mince off to the monastery and join the other monks who were hiding from the world.

"I should be goin'," she murmured.

"Going? Where? 'Tis the middle of the night."

"'Tis All Souls Day."

"I doubt the souls will mind waiting in the graveyard at least until dawn."

"It doesn't matter. I'm not tired. I slept enough for *two* days. Besides, 'tis always a difficult day for my Da. He still mourns my Ma."

Hew nodded and sighed. "'Tis hard to lose someone you love."

She wondered at that. Hew was yet a young man. What would he know about love and loss?

"Shall I leave ye the cheese?" she asked.

"Aye, thank you."

She started toward the door, then remembered. "I think ye're safe with Peris now."

"I'm done with opium anyway." He added softly, "But I think I would prefer your tender care anyway."

She bit her cheek, annoyed. What game was he playing? Aloof and distancing one moment? Warm and inviting the next?

She faked a smile of apology. "I really need to look after my father today."

He nodded.

She almost made it to the door before he said, "You won't do anything foolish like question the physician, right?"

She scoffed. "Don't be daft."

Damn. That was exactly what she meant to do. In fact, she'd thought of a way to squeeze the information from Peris as easily as getting milk from a coo.

Of course she wasn't going to tell Hew that. But he'd thank her later when she single-handedly uncovered the second thief.

The door closed.

Hew frowned.

Don't be daft, she'd said. That wasn't the answer he wanted. He expected something more reassuring.

Like *O' course I won't do such an unwise thing.*

Or *Nay, ye're right, 'tis too dangerous for a woman.*

Or *Why would I do that when I've got a strong, noble, chivalrous Rivenloch warrior at my beck and call?*

But nay, she'd left him completely without assurance.

And the more he thought about it, the more he worried that was exactly what she meant to do.

He popped the last bit of cheese into his mouth and threw aside the coverlet. His arms still burned, and he'd needed to change the bandage on his hand. But he couldn't afford to waste another day drowsing in the laird's bedchamber. Treachery was afoot. And The Woman He Loved was in peril.

CHAPTER 16

While Carenza freshened up in the solar, she considered the identity of the second thief.

Reason said it had to be someone Peris knew well at the monastery. Someone he'd known for a long time. Someone he trusted.

That ruled out the oblates and novices.

It also ruled out Father James, whom the thief had mentioned was taking too keen an interest.

That left the abbot, the prior, and the few dozen older monks who resided there.

Peris had been Dunlop's physician for as long as she could remember. Her father, hearing he was the best in the land, had summoned Peris when her mother had first become ill. But though his medicines and methods had been expert and thorough, she flagged under his care and eventually succumbed.

Still, her father had been grateful for his efforts. Peris had been the resident physician at Dunlop ever since. Aye, he had a sour, impatient nature. She attributed that to working with the ill and dying all the time. But he'd served the clan—and the monastery—with skill and devotion.

All she had to do was remind him of that loyalty. Of the great good he'd done in his lifetime. Once flattered, he'd naturally be too humble to take all the credit. He'd share it

Laird of Flint

with those who had helped him. His closest companions. His most loyal allies. His oldest friends at the monastery. Theirs were the names she needed.

When she emerged in the great hall, the servants were already up, shooing the layabeds out of their way as they stoked the fire and brought in bread from the kitchens. And to her surprise, taking a cup of ale from a blushing kitchen wench with his unbandaged hand was Sir Hew.

She furrowed her brows. What was he doing up and about? He should rest. He should heal. And he should get out of her way.

"Carenza, my dear," her father murmured as he approached. "Ye're frownin'."

She pressed fingers to her forehead. "Am I?"

He lowered his voice to a whisper. "Also, I fear ye have rats in your chamber."

She froze.

He added, "I'll have to summon the rat-catcher from the village."

Thinking fast, she said, "I'll do it on the morrow, Da. I have to go to the village anyway."

She had no intention of summoning the rat-catcher. But once her father was back in his own bed—an event that appeared to be imminent, if Hew's appearance in the great hall was any indication—she was sure he'd completely forget the matter.

"Fine." He glanced around the hall. "Och. I see our warrior friend is already up and about. He seems to have flourished under your tender care."

Had he flourished? Or had he forced his way out of bed out of pure stubbornness, just to keep an eye on her? She was beginning to think Peris was right. The Rivenloch warrior was meddlesome.

Before she could stop him, her father called out to Hew. Hew raised his cup in greeting and came toward them.

201

"I'm surprised to see ye recoverin' so well," the laird said.

Hew nodded. "Thanks to your generosity, m'laird, and some expert care." His gaze was warm as it slipped over to her.

"Indeed," her father said with a knowing smile.

Carenza found herself immediately furious again. How dare Hew feign affection for her—in front of her father, no less—when he clearly had no intention of following up or making any serious overtures toward her?

Her jaw was tight as she smiled and intentionally misunderstood him. "Oh aye, Peris is the best physician in Dunlop."

"Och, Carenza," her father chided, "ye know very well—"

"And here he is now," she interjected, grabbing Peris's arm as he passed. "We were just talkin' about your expert care o' Sir Hew."

Peris looked rattled. Anxious. And exhausted. Clearly, the last thing he wanted to do was talk. Especially not to the meddlesome man he'd tried to poison.

"Ye shouldn't be out o' bed," he grunted at Hew.

Whether he was referring to Hew's health or his meddling, Carenza wasn't sure.

"I feel fine," Hew said.

"That's the opium."

"I stopped taking it."

A look of disapproval crossed Peris's face. Still, he was a physician with a physician's concerns. "Must hurt like the devil."

"'Tisn't so bad," He gave Peris a wink. "Not as bad as having your heart broken."

Carenza almost groaned at that. The magnificent warrior had probably left dozens of heartbroken maids in his wake. But he'd surely never been the victim of a broken heart.

Her father, however, had.

"That," the laird agreed, growing suddenly solemn, "is the worst pain of all."

Carenza felt horrid for forgetting her father's suffering. She placed a gentle hand on his arm. "And we'll all pray for her today, Da." Then she turned to Peris. "Ye'll come as well, aye?"

He grunted in reply.

"If 'tis all right," she said to Peris, "once we're there, I'd like to talk with ye about...my mother."

She could immediately feel the tension in Hew. Like a wildcat about to spring.

His voice, however, reflected none of it. "Where is the graveyard?"

"Och," she said, knitting her brows with false regret, "'tis too far to go in your condition, I fear. But don't fret. We'll be sure to pray for the souls o' your clan as well. Won't we, Da?"

"O' course."

Fury flickered in Hew's flinty eyes. Fury and just a hint of reluctant admiration. He nodded his head, accepting his defeat.

Unfortunately, her father had an idea. "But...ye can ride a horse, aye?"

"Not well, with this hand, but serviceably enough, I suppose."

Her father decided, "Ye'll ride Carenza's palfrey then."

Carenza blinked. She wanted to scream. But laird's daughters didn't scream. They didn't even frown. And they definitely didn't complain when their father wanted to loan their palfrey to a distinguished guest.

Still, she almost choked on the smug look Hew gave her. She seized the cup from a passing servant's tray and buried her rage in a swig of ale.

The trek to the graveyard was delayed by a violent thunderstorm. Hew couldn't help but wonder if Carenza had summoned it to foil his plans. Lightning crackled overhead. Rumbling followed soon after. Fat drops of rain bounced off the courtyard grass. The clanfolk huddled in the great hall.

Meanwhile, Carenza's duty appeared to be comforting the young children frightened by the roar of the storm. She hugged them. Told them stories. And let them sit on her lap. But Hew could see tension in her mouth. She too seemed anxious. Who was there to reassure *her?*

It was a calling Hew couldn't resist. When she took a break in her storytelling, he placed a gentle hand on her shoulder.

"Are you all right, my lady?"

For an instant, he glimpsed raw fear in her eyes. In the next, it was gone.

"I'm fine."

"You need not fear the lightning," he murmured. "You're safe in here."

"I am. Aye." Her chin quivered once before she stilled it. "But what about the animals?"

Was that what she was worried about? The animals?

His shoulders softened. What a selfless and tender-hearted woman she was. What a rare and precious quality. He supposed he should have known. After all, who would go to such lengths to save a coo from slaughter?

"Don't worry about them," he said. "They seem to know how to stay out of harm's way." Then he tipped his head to whisper, "Otherwise, you'd see dozens of charred sheep by the side of the road after a storm."

One side of her mouth quirked up at that.

"Blackened ducks by the roadside," he added.

The other side curved up.

"And roast pigs ready for the table," he said.

She gave him a full smile then. A smile so brilliant and warm that he almost couldn't resist bending near and capturing her lips with his own.

But he had to resist. He had to bank the burning coals of his affection. Take his time. Temper his passion. He couldn't afford to make mistakes. The last thing he wanted was to drive her away by scorching her in the fiery blaze of his feelings.

So he mumbled, "I'm sure Hamish is fine." He gave her a nod of farewell before going to douse the flames of his desire with a second cup of ale.

Eventually, the weather cleared. The clouds shredded apart like wool, leaving patches of clear blue. The earth smelled ripe and mossy and fertile. And a few brave birds chirped defiantly from the woods.

The afternoon ride to the graveyard wasn't so bad. The church was to the west, an hour's walk away. Carenza's palfrey was mild and easy to handle, even with one hand. Hew maintained a slow pace, riding behind most of the clanfolk, who traveled on foot. They carried offerings of bread, as well as candles, which they would light in the churchyard to help guide any lost souls and use later to guide themselves home.

Carenza and her father led the procession. The physician positioned himself in the middle, far from them and far from him. He clearly wasn't interested in any interrogation today. Which made it even more critical that Hew keep Carenza from prying.

He expected, like a child with a clam, she would poke and prod and annoy Peris rather than gleaning any useful information. And her prodding would make him close his shell even tighter.

So Hew determined to stay close to her. He could draw her attention away if she became too inquisitive. Divert her probing questions with lighthearted commentary.

Distract her when she began to cross the line of safety.

Most of the day, she prayed with her father. Not only as an example to the rest of the clan. But because he seemed grief-stricken, as if he'd lost his wife, not years ago, but yesterday. Between prayers, she patted his hand and leaned her head against his shoulder, murmuring words of comfort to him.

But Hew wondered, who comforted *her?* Carenza had lost her mother. Hew couldn't imagine what it would have been like to grow up without the love of his mother. Lady Helena was a fierce fighter, but her love was just as fierce. And the things Hew had learned about women—about their vulnerability, their strength, their hearts, their minds—he could never have learned without his mother.

The All Souls Day rituals were unfamiliar to Hew. In his clan, descended from Vikings, they celebrated Alfablot, which likewise honored their ancestors. But it was a quiet and private affair conducted in one's household.

Nonetheless, he prayed silently for his grandfather Gellir. He'd never known the white-bearded giant. But the great warrior had been an inspiration to the Rivenloch clan.

It was nearly dark when, halfway through a prayer to Odin—for his grandfather had never much cared for the gods of the Scots, Hew glanced up to see Carenza ambling toward Peris. She whispered something to the physician. Then the two of them rounded the corner of the church, disappearing from view. He quickly ended his prayer and moved in their direction.

Halting behind the corner of the wall, just out of sight, he didn't hear her first words, but he heard the next.

"I don't remember much. I was so young at the time. But I do remember how ye stayed with her, day and night. How ye worked tirelessly, tryin' to save her."

Peris cleared his throat. "Your mother was a good woman."

"And ye were so kind and attentive. It must have made her final hours a comfort."

He was clearly discomfited by her praise. "I hope so," he muttered. "'Twas hard for the laird to see her go."

Carenza sighed. "But how much more difficult it must be for those who don't have a carin' physician to attend them in their final hours."

All at once, Hew felt awkward and out of place. She obviously didn't have an interrogation in mind. She was only sharing personal memories with her mother's physician and thanking him for his service.

Uncomfortable and unsure what to do, Hew took a sudden keen interest in the crow perched on the top of the churchyard wall.

Then he overheard Carenza say, "But ye do that at Kildunan, don't ye? Ye give all those wretched souls ease in their final hours."

"'Tisn't only me, m'lady," the physician protested. "All the monks are there to provide comfort."

"Och aye. But they don't all attend a dyin' man, do they? Is that not the purview o' the physician and perhaps the most senior clergy?"

The sly lass *was* prying. Poking her nose where it didn't belong. But she was doing it in such a clever way, Peris couldn't detect it. Indeed, the physician was answering her as readily as beer flowed from a tapped barrel.

"Certainly the abbot and prior are there," he told her. "And often the senior clergy take their turns at watchin' o'er the man."

"Ah. 'Tis so encouragin' to hear." Then she lowered her voice so Hew had to strain to make out her words. "In truth, I've often wished to give a tithin' to those who offer such charitable services. But my father insists 'tis an act of mercy, to be rewarded in heaven." She clucked her tongue. "Do ye think ye might give me the names o' your closest acquaintances among the clergy? I'd like to make a generous donation in their name."

Genius. The lass was as smooth as his axe blade. Her innocence and earnestness was allowing her to collect exactly the information they needed without the appearance of prying.

Once she got the names, of course, that would be the end of it. The rest was far too risky for her. He'd commend her for her efforts. Then he would take on the mantle of the mission, question the suspects, and solve the crime. Alone.

Carenza watched three emotions flit through the physician's eyes.

The first was annoyance, as if he resented being tasked with making a judgment about which acquaintances were his closest.

The second was envy, as if he deserved a donation for his efforts as well, despite making a generous wage from her father.

And the third was enterprise. He glimpsed a chance for profit. If not his own, at least a reward for his allies that he might leverage in the future.

Finally he nodded. "O' course, m'lady. As ye know, the abbot and the prior are always present. But three others come to mind who have oft been by my side with the dyin'. Brother Michael. Brother Robert. And Brother William."

"Michael. Robert. And William," she repeated. "I shall send a donation forthwith. But I pray ye keep my confidence. If my father should hear o' my generosity, I fear he might not wholeheartedly approve."

"As ye wish, m'lady," he said, stepping away.

She nodded and then whirled to leave. Rounding the corner of the church, she nearly collided with Sir Hew.

"What are ye—" she bit out between her teeth, then remembered her father might be watching. Gritting out a tight smile, she asked, "Listenin' around corners, are ye?"

"Michael, Robert, and William," he said. "That was brilliant."

She was shocked into silence. She expected a reprimand, not a compliment. Yet he seemed sincere.

"Truly brilliant," he repeated, shaking his head in wonder.

Her proud glow lasted a few precious moments.

"Now that we've got the names," he continued, "I'll question them on the morrow. 'Tis Michael, Robert, and William, right?"

"Nay!"

She winced at her own loud outburst. Then, before she could attract undue attention, she snagged Hew by the front of his plaid and pulled him around the corner of the church.

"Nay," she repeated.

He seemed puzzled. "Those aren't their names?"

"Aye. But nay, ye can't question them on the morrow."

She could see the pressure of ire building inside him, like a shaken bottle of wine, despite his steady tone. "And why is that?"

"Think about it," she explained patiently. "Ye—the man Peris just tried to kill, the one who's investigatin' the thefts—go to the monastery to question three respected monks. What will they assume?"

His brow creased as he digested her words. "Fine. Then I'll wait a day or two."

She shook her head. "Nay. I'll go."

"The devil you will."

"Listen. If I go, 'twill be to deliver the donation. Naturally, I'll want to meet the monks, to thank them for their service. And they'll wish to thank me for the tithin'. 'Tis far less questionable."

He looked pained. "I can't let you do that."

"Why not?" She held up a hand. "And don't tell me 'tis a knight's duty to protect all ladies." She still stung from that remark.

"I told you before, 'tis too dangerous."

"There's nothing dangerous about givin' a tithe to a monastery."

"If they suspect you know anything..."

"They won't. I won't give anythin' away. I'm a laird's daughter. I'm used to keepin' up appearances."

He seemed frustrated. "I don't want you entangled in any of this."

"I'm already entangled." Then she smiled. A genuine smile this time. "But don't worry. I'm brilliant. Or so I've been told." She reached up to give him a reassuring clap on the cheek.

He seized her wrist with his unbandaged hand. "I'm serious, my lady."

As he spoke, he began brushing his thumb idly back and forth along the inside of her wrist, the way she put a lizard to sleep by rubbing its belly.

"This is a hazardous game," he said. "If anything should go awry... If anything should endanger you... Bloody hell, if anything should happen to the woman I love..."

She gave a little gasp.

He halted the movement of his thumb.

Had he meant that?

He'd left the sentence unfinished. He clearly hadn't meant to blurt that out. But had he meant it?

She gazed into his eyes. Eyes that shone like molten silver. Eyes that suffered and smoldered and adored. And she saw the truth. He'd spoken from his heart. He *did* love her.

Carenza was never impulsive. She plotted and planned every move, every gesture, every expression. What to wear. What to say. How to comport herself. Such was the life of the clan's heiress.

But for the first time in her life she threw caution to the wind. Acted on instinct. And followed her heart.

Curling her fists in the front of his plaid, she pushed him back against the stone wall of the church, closed her eyes, and pressed her lips to his.

CHAPTER 17

It wasn't the first time a woman had stolen a kiss from Hew. Every time in the past, however, he'd known what to do.

He would immediately take charge, grateful to find a mate whose passion equaled his. He'd pull them into an intimate embrace. Sweep his hands into their hair. Slant his mouth across theirs. And feast on them with the hunger of a starving beast.

This time he felt utterly lost.

Carenza's kiss was careful, tentative, innocent. He doubted she'd ever kissed a man before.

His heart bellowed at him to seize the day. Slake his thirst for her. Take advantage of this moment.

Yet he hesitated.

This was not every woman from his past.

This was Lady Carenza.

The lady of his dreams.

His One True Love.

The lass he was afraid to lose.

The woman with the power to break his heart beyond repair.

For the first time in his life, he felt fear.

Fear that he would frighten her.

Fear that he would go too far, too fast.

So he withheld a measure of his passion from her. Instead of pouring all his desire into the kiss, he answered her with gentle caution.

He closed his eyes and moved his lips tenderly against hers. He took his time, relishing the sweet softness of her skin. The subtle perfume of her cheek.

He lifted his good hand and rested his fingertips on her jaw, as lightly as if she were made of delicate porcelain. Then he slid his hand tenuously into her hair, tracing the circle of her ear with a single finger.

She gasped and shivered.

Even that small response made his control slip. There was a tightening in his braies, and his veins pulsed with erotic current.

He groaned deep in his throat, fighting to hold back.

But it was too late. Something in his voice called to the primitive female part of her. With a small answering moan, she deepened the kiss. She began to consume him the way the fire had consumed his leine, eating away his will and leaving only carnal flame.

She clutched him closer, eagerly twisting her mouth to satisfy her hunger. Her breath came in fevered panting. With intuitive urgency, she leaned toward him, struggling to get closer.

Hew's heart pounded. Every bone in his body yearned to answer her craving. Every inch of his flesh ached to solve her womanly dilemma.

Yet he resisted. And it almost worked.

But then she captured his face in her hands. She pulled his head close. Opened his mouth with her own. Dared to let her tongue explore and taste and tempt him.

She tasted warm. Sweet. As delicious as the first cup of wassail at Yule.

And when she boldly pushed herself against him, molding her body to his, when he felt her supple breasts like soft pillows against his chest, he could no longer hold back.

Oblivious to the pain of his burns, he swept both hands into her silken tresses and growled against her lips. Delved his tongue into her mouth with starving need. And pressed against her belly with that part of him that wanted her most.

Carenza's head was spinning. But it was a delightful giddiness, the way she'd felt as a wee lass, twirling among the sheep in a grassy glen.

He'd said the words baldly. Boldly. He'd called her *the woman he loved.* Deep in her heart, she'd felt it, known it. But his constant denials and his variable affection had hammered at that belief. They'd almost convinced her he didn't truly care for her.

Now their embrace felt like a glorious celebration of the truth. The unlocking of a secret chest filled with treasure beyond her wildest dreams.

Her body hummed like summer bees as Hew dipped into the flower of her mouth to collect nectar.

Her veins gushed like a swollen burn in spring. Racing eagerly. Gathering speed. Heading to a destination unknown.

She couldn't remember how she'd come to be here. But she was certain it had been her idea. Now she felt as if she'd saddled a wild destrier and was clinging to him for dear life.

Still, she didn't want the breathtaking ride to end.

Hew's hands were strong yet gentle as he cradled her head.

Beneath her own fingers, his jaw felt manly. Firm and rough with stubble.

He tasted of ale and spice and restless hunger. And when he groaned against her mouth, it sent a sensuous current through her that drew from her an answering moan.

His chest was hard but yielding. She felt protected there. Yet where her breasts brushed against him, her nipples roused with heady longing.

But what filled her with the most thrilling heat and danger and excitement was the part of him that pulsed against her belly with eager need.

What she wanted, she could not have. Deep beneath the roiling waves of this sensual sea, she recognized that tragic truth.

Even now, though she felt far from the earthly plane, as if they floated together in heaven, she knew it could not last. No matter how much she wanted the feeling to go on. And on. And on.

And that was made painfully clear when she heard the distant voice of the laird addressing the clan. "'Tis sundown. Shall we return home?"

They broke from the kiss abruptly. Reluctantly. While lust still smoldered in their eyes.

How could it be sundown already? Surely they'd only begun to kiss. And she still felt full of light and warmth.

But as lovely as their embrace had been, duty descended on her like the dampening shadow of night.

She quickly adjusted her hair, praying it wasn't too out of sorts.

He quickly adjusted his braies.

"Forgive me, my lady. I should not have..." he said, leaving the rest open-ended, as if he wished to apologize for everything.

"Left me so unrequited?" she asked.

He blinked in surprise.

"I'll forgive ye this once," she told him breathlessly. "But I expect our *conversation* to continue in the comin' days."

It was a brazen thing to say, she knew. But Hew made

her feel brazen. And fearless. And brilliant. He made her feel like she didn't have to guard her words. Like she could speak her mind. And her heart.

For once, he was left speechless. Which rather pleased her.

Before she rounded the corner to join her father, she whispered to Hew, "I think ye should perhaps surrender your dreams o' becomin' a monk."

The walk back to Dunlop seemed miles shorter. Her step was so light and her mood so pleasant, she felt like she walked on air.

Indeed, as she carried her lit candle along the path, she had to remind herself that All Souls Day was a somber occasion. That perhaps she should be reflecting on those who had passed. Not grinning from ear to ear, obsessing over the man riding at the back of the clan on her palfrey. The Man She Loved.

Hew frowned in self-disgust.

Carenza didn't love him.

And if he'd only controlled himself as he intended, if he'd only maintained his honor and refused her kiss, she'd realize that.

Now she'd never know it was lust and not love that lured her. It was the hunger of her body, not the hunger of her heart.

She was too young, too innocent to realize that.

But he wasn't. He should have turned his head. Refused her.

It was what a gentleman of restraint and patience would have done. Hew, however, had never been able to act like a gentleman. He'd always let his passions take the reins. Sung Li, his aunt's teacher, called him *Baozhu*, saying he was as volatile as the fireworks from the Orient. Quick to ignite. Quick to explode. And quick to extinguish.

That volatility was what had earned him so many broken hearts. And this time he'd wanted so badly not to make a mess of things. He'd wanted to go slowly. To be her friend first. Her confidant. Her champion.

Later, when he knew her heart belonged to him, he would show her a measure of physical affection. Then he would kiss her. Take her hand. Hold her in a fond embrace.

But nay, he'd let impatience get the best of him. Again.

Now he feared her interest was only infatuation. After all, desire was new and fresh and exciting for her. Lust was a dish of delicious sweets she'd never sampled before. And she'd naturally imagine herself in love with any man who brought her such sweets.

But she would tire of them eventually. They all did. When there was nothing substantial beneath the honeyed exterior—no affection in the kiss, no cherishing in the caress, no heart in the embrace—what was once sweet would seem empty and ordinary.

He didn't want that to happen with Carenza. He cared for her too much. If she broke his heart, it would destroy him. Then he might as well join the holy order, for he would be unfit to be any woman's husband.

It was his own fault. He knew that. Aye, she'd made the first move. But she was untried in the ways of romance. He should have taken responsibility and refused her kiss.

He sighed.

That would have been impossible.

Her kiss had been heavenly. Her lips as plump and succulent as a ripe cherry. Her breath soft and sweet as she gasped against his mouth. And her tongue... Holy Mary, her tongue touching his had set off a lightning bolt of pleasure.

Her fingers brushing his face—at first as lightly as the wings of a butterfly, then with the strength of desperation—had made him shiver with longing.

But it was the brazen crush of her body against his that had sent him past the realm of resistance. Even as he relished her soft curves and engaging warmth, even as his cock strained at its linen prison, he'd dreamed of what it would be like to wake up with her each morn, to have her in his arms and in his life.

He shifted in the saddle. It would do him no good to revisit the moment. It would only serve to frustrate his already aching loins.

There would be no satisfaction tonight. Or for many nights.

He had to keep temptation at bay. And the only way to do that was to keep her at a distance.

Unfortunately, all his good intentions didn't even last a day.

Despite refusing the laird's bedchamber and sleeping in the great hall with the rest of the clan, Hew woke to Lady Carenza's lovely, smiling face. She crouched beside him the next morn with a bowl of steaming frumenty.

"I hope ye like cherries," she said.

His gaze lowered reflexively to her lips. What he thought was, *They couldn't be as sweet and delicious as what I tasted yesterday.* What he said was, "I do. Thank you."

"Would ye like me to feed ye?" There was a subtle smokiness in her eyes.

He very much wanted that. To stare into her eyes as she slipped the spoon into his mouth. To lick the frumenty from it while holding her gaze.

"That won't be necessary." He sat up and took the bowl in his bandaged hand, turning it so he could use the spoon with his good hand.

She leaned close and whispered, "I missed your snorin' last night."

He shoveled frumenty into his mouth to avoid having to

reply. It was warm and sweet. But not as warm and sweet as her kiss.

She murmured, "I had a dream about ye."

He almost choked on the frumenty. He'd heard that phrase before from lasses' lips. Usually in the privacy of a bedchamber. It was always followed by an arousing account of her dream coupling. And *that* was always followed by an actual coupling.

"Ye were in my bedchamber," she began.

The anticipatory tingling in his ballocks didn't bode well.

"Lookin' all bold and menacin' with your axe across your shoulders."

Was this going to be a plundering Viking dream where he seized the woman, tore off her clothes, and forced her to his will? He didn't much care for those.

"I had brought the rat-catcher in, as my father requested."

He stopped chewing the frumenty. The tingling had gone away. A rat-catcher? Where was this going?

"And sure enough," she said, "Twinkle made an appearance."

"Twinkle?"

"My pet rat."

He grunted. He dished up another spoonful of frumenty, not sure he wanted to hear a romantic fantasy that included a rat.

"Just as the rat-catcher was about to trap my poor Twinkle in his bucket, ye said, 'Allow me,' and ye raised your axe."

He furrowed worried brows and lowered his spoon. This had turned grim. Also, it didn't seem the best tale for breaking one's fast.

"And then ye turned it round backwards," she said with a grin, "and knocked the rat-catcher's bucket right out the window."

Her laughter was delightful and contagious. Even if her dream was the silliest thing he'd ever heard.

After she was done laughing, she gazed at him with adoring eyes. "Ye came to my rescue and saved my precious Twinkle."

Hew had never felt more like someone's hero. The way she looked at him. With warmth. And humor. And companionship. It was far more attractive—and dangerous—than the voracious glances women usually sent his way.

But how long would she look at him like that? Would her affection fade with time?

"For that, my brave knight," she murmured, "I shall someday reward ye." Her violet eyes simultaneously sparkled with amusement and shone with sultry promise.

Already he could feel his heart softening and melting and becoming vulnerable. She held it in the palm of her hand, like a fragile egg. If he wasn't careful, when she ultimately broke it, there would be nothing left but the shattered shell of a man languishing in a puddle of despair.

Carenza couldn't stop singing this morn. She rose at dawn and flitted from task to task like a happy butterfly visiting primroses.

After her curious dream, she'd given Twinkle an extra portion of her frumenty and reassured him that the ratcatcher wouldn't be visiting.

Then she'd brought Hew his breakfast.

Gazing down at him as he slept—with his mussed hair, his closed eyes, his open mouth—she'd imagined waking to that face each morn. And decided she liked the idea. Nay, she *loved* the idea. His was a countenance she'd never tire of admiring, even if it was accompanied by a snore loud enough to wake the dead.

She'd been tempted to stop that snore with a kiss.

But here in the great hall of Dunlop, she was the laird's daughter. Demure. Polite. Respectable.

Later she'd find a place where they could be alone, for she wanted to savor the thrill of his embrace again.

So she settled for slipping a few smoldering glances into her conversation, an extra morsel of breakfast for him to chew on.

Meanwhile, she went about her schedule. She slipped scraps to Troye behind the stable. Left several cherries atop the castle wall for the resident crows. Checked in on her pair of hibernating hedgepigs, huddled in their nest in the garden. Let the squirrel tug a stale oatcake from her fingers. And gave Hamish a good, long scratch behind the ears.

By the time she was done, her father was preparing to leave. Yesterday's lightning had struck one of the byres on the Boyle clan's land, so the laird and several Dunlop men were going to offer neighborly help. At least that was his story. She secretly suspected the men were only curious to see the storm damage. But the physician was going with them, so Carenza would be in charge of Hew's care. Which gave her an idea. A way she might forward her plan to get him alone.

It wasn't a moment too soon when she found him. He was seated by the hearth, frowning and picking at his bandage.

"Sir Hew o' Rivenloch," she mock-scolded him. "Just what do ye think ye're doin'?"

"Nothing," he said, abandoning his pursuit. "I'm just...restless."

She sat down beside him. It was probably torture for a warrior to be so inactive. Why he thought he could ever endure the tedium of being a monk, she couldn't imagine.

"What would ye be doin' if ye weren't injured?"

"I would have gone with your father," he sulked. "Been of some use."

"I doubt any o' them are goin' to be of use. They've only gone to gloat o'er the charred remains of Boyle's barn. Still..." She lifted his bandaged hand and studied it. "Ye might be healin' faster than ye think. Let's see how this looks. Come with me to the solar where the light is better. I'll change the bandage and—"

"Where's Peris?" he asked in surprise.

"He went with my father."

Hew let out a vexed sigh, which crushed her momentarily until he followed up with, "I was hopin' to question him."

"Ah. Well, 'twill have to wait."

Now she was doubly glad her father had taken Peris with him.

An axe-wielding Viking warrior might be accustomed to using intimidation to get what he wanted. But putting pressure on Peris would have been a mistake. Especially now, when they were so close to an answer.

Peris was as dangerous and impulsive as an anxious hound. Shivering in a corner one moment. Snarling and biting the next. Why else had he tried to solve his nervousness with something as drastic as murdering Hew?

If Hew started squeezing him for information, Peris would become even more wary and thus more threatening.

This part of the investigation was far better left in her hands. She would go to the monastery later today to deliver her tithing. And she'd employ a woman's touch to coax useful information from Peris's allies.

Meanwhile, she intended to use her woman's touch for something far more enjoyable.

"Come," she beckoned. "Ye can question him when he returns." Hopefully by then she'd have confirmed the identity of the second culprit.

She'd already placed the honey-butter mixture, linen strips, and a basin of clean water in the solar. She'd also told the servants she wanted privacy. So it took a great deal of willpower not to slam the door closed behind her, thrust herself into his arms, and immediately resume kissing where they had left off last eve.

She desired him. There was no doubt about that. But she found she *cared* more about him than she *lusted* after him. And right now he needed healing.

"Sit there," she said, indicating a chair near the window.

She opened the shutters to let in the light, filtered through a solid bank of white clouds.

Then she placed the basin on a nearby table and knelt before him.

She took his hand and carefully lowered it into the cool water, soaking the linen to loosen it from the blisters. With gentle fingers, she unwound the wrapping.

"I hope this doesn't hurt ye."

"'Tis fine." He was probably lying, she decided, for she could hear the strain in his voice.

"There," she said as she removed the last of the bandage. His palm was still raw and red, dotted with plump blisters. But the wound wasn't infected. "'Tisn't too bad, aye?"

He didn't respond, and when she looked up at his face, she could see his mind was elsewhere. His eyes were glazed, like the diaphanous silk of a veil that barely concealed what was beneath. But she could see what was beneath.

Arousal. Desire. Yearning.

Her gaze lowered to his slightly parted lips.

Then his gaze lowered to her bosom. She realized, kneeling before him, her leine had gapped away enough to display the upper curve of her breasts.

She should have gasped in outrage. Adjusted her garment. Scolded him roundly for leering at her.

But she didn't. Here, alone with him, she didn't have to keep up pretenses. Though her own brashness made her blush, she had to admit she enjoyed having him look at her that way. As if he wanted to tear off her clothes and ravish her.

Of course that wasn't going to happen. She *was* a responsible person, after all.

But she fully intended to kiss him again. After she finished bandaging his hand.

Pretending she didn't notice his stare, she placed the crock of the honey-butter mixture on her lap.

"Give me your hand." Her voice was breathy and alluring, even to her own ears.

He rested his hand atop hers, dwarfing it. How different from hers it looked. There was great strength in the sinews. The sun had weathered his skin. And calluses from wielding an axe thickened his fingers. She wondered how that hand would feel caressing the top of her breasts.

She took a deep, settling breath and tried to clear her mind. Then she dabbed her fingers in the honey-butter and began spreading it gently over his blisters.

He made no complaint. But she wasn't sure if that was because it didn't hurt or because he was distracted by the view. She didn't dare look to see if his eyes were still fixed on her bosom.

The silence was becoming uncomfortable, so she explained, "The butter is to keep the moisture in. The honey helps to keep the wound clean."

"To think I've been wasting it on oatcakes."

She smiled and glanced up at him.

He was gazing out the window now. The light caught his face, making his eyes shine like silver and highlighting his chiseled jaw and supple lips.

She shivered with anticipation. She needed to finish the task of dressing his hand so she could begin the next task.

Relieving some of her strain with a kiss as sweet as honey-butter.

Wrapping his hand again was a delicate operation. It was made even more difficult when she realized, kneeling before him, her eyes were at the level of his...

She gulped. She couldn't even think the word. She certainly wasn't going to stare at it.

Except she did.

There was nothing to see. Not really. He was fully clothed. His leine hung between his knees. And even if it hadn't, his trews surely covered everything.

Still, there was something forbidden and thrilling about stealing glances without his knowledge.

CHAPTER 18

Carenza was staring at his crotch.

She probably assumed he couldn't tell. But her gaze might as well have been a caress, the way it was affecting him. And her distraction became glaringly obvious, especially when she began wrapping the linen in a spiral up his wrist.

Part of him was amused. Nothing was more engaging than a woman interested in his body. Her curiosity was endearing and arousing. But part was afraid the change in him as he swelled with desire would show through his braies and trews and leine to horrify them both.

He had to distract her before he shamed himself and she wrapped the linen halfway up his arm.

"Are you planning to bury me?" he asked.

She started. "What?"

He raised his brows and looked pointedly at her linen handiwork. "'Tis beginning to look like a shroud."

"Och."

Flustered, she turned the loveliest shade of pink as she quickly reversed the winding and tied off the linen around his palm. Then, without a glance, she gathered her things and returned the basin to its place.

He couldn't help but be charmed by her blushing naivete. And he feared *that*—more than her beautiful face and her delectable curves and the lust in her eyes—was going to make her hard to resist. Like an exquisite itch he was forbidden to scratch.

Which reminded him... Now that his arms were healing, the itch was unbearable. He started sliding his leine sleeve back and forth along his arm to rub away the tingling.

"Does it itch?" she asked.

He nodded.

"'Tis good news. That means 'tis healin'."

He knew that. He was a warrior. He'd suffered countless wounds. Nonetheless, he replied, "Does it?"

"Aye, but ye shouldn't scratch it like that."

He knew that too. But it never stopped him.

"Here. Let me..." She started toward him, then changed her mind. "If ye'd remove your leine, I have some oil here that might help." She wheeled about and started searching through several vials of oils on the table.

Hew hesitated. Removing his clothing was a bad idea. They were alone. It was one less layer between them. And he was well aware of the effect a naked chest had on women.

But he couldn't think of an excuse that wouldn't make things more awkward. Besides, it was a weak man who couldn't control himself, just because he was missing an article of clothing or two. So without ceremony or fuss, he pulled the leine over his head and draped it over the chair beside him.

Surely she'd prepared herself for the sight of him. After all, she'd been the one to ask him to remove his leine.

Still, when she came near with the vial of oil, her step was halting, and her gaze skipped about like a gnat, deciding where to land. Then she closed her eyes. When her bosom rose and fell with a deep, steadying breath, he was instantly reminded of the peek he'd stolen down her leine. Her breasts had looked so round and soft and smooth. Like twin loaves of bread set out to rise.

Unfortunately, his loins were instantly reminded as well. He judiciously moved his arms between his knees then, blocking her view.

Carenza gulped. Had Hew grown even more massive since she'd last seen him without his leine? Perhaps it was only seeing him sitting up rather than sprawled unconscious on a pallet that made him seem more muscled. More forceful. More intimidating.

Her heart pounded. A sheen of light sweat formed above her lip. He looked to her like a dangerous animal now. An animal capable of crushing her.

Yet she felt more exhilaration than fear. She'd faced this beast before. Leine or no leine, there was no need to be intimidated. And she intended to get another kiss. So she shook off her self-doubt and held up the vial.

"Oil o' newt," she announced.

The look of disgust on his face erased all her fears.

A snort of a laugh escaped her.

"You're a wicked lass," he growled.

"Don't worry. 'Tis lavender. Perfectly pleasant."

She pulled a chair close to his and poured a thin stream of oil atop one powerful shoulder. Then, setting down the vial, she let her fingers catch the drop. With a light touch, she spread the oil down his arm.

"Does that pain ye?" she murmured.

He shook his head and closed his eyes.

She thought it would be quick work. Then she meant to proceed on to the kiss.

But she became fascinated by his body. The warmth of his flesh. The curves of his muscles. The subtle pulse of his veins. She explored it all with her hands, molding her fingers along each plane, smoothing and soothing his skin as if she sculpted him from clay.

Why the contact should affect her so, she didn't know. But soon she felt the eagerness in her fingers spread to a longing deep within her. The same longing she'd had when they'd kissed. A tightening in her breasts. A tingling in her nether parts. A fierce urge to be closer.

Her hands contacted the bandage then, and she picked up the vial to start on the other shoulder. His eyes were still closed. She wondered if he'd lied about the pain.

"Are ye sure it doesn't hurt?" Her voice came out on a rough whisper.

To her surprise, he replied with a self-mocking, rueful chuckle. "My arms? Nay, *they* don't hurt."

She smoothed the oil down his other arm. Her mind wandered, imagining his bulky arms, as unyielding as oak, enfolding her. Holding her. Protecting her. How safe she would feel in his embrace.

She slid her hand up along the inside of his arm, lightening her touch where the flesh was more delicate. As she reached the top, her fingers brushed the hollow under his arm, where a soft tuft of hair grew. Intrigued by the texture, she didn't pull away at once. She ran her thumb back and forth along the fringe.

Suddenly, he jerked and clamped his arm against his chest, trapping her hand.

She gasped. "I'm sorry. I didn't mean to hurt ye." She tried to slide her hand down.

He grunted and clamped harder.

She tried to wriggle her fingers out.

"Stop it," he bit out between his teeth.

Then she realized he wasn't in pain.

Sir Hew du Lac, powerful Viking warrior, was ticklish.

A slow grin found its way to her lips.

A grin he instantly understood.

"Nay," he warned.

But she wasn't about to heed his warning. She wiggled her fingers again.

"Wench," he hissed, squeezing harder.

"I'm tryin' to get them out," she told him with false earnestness, "but I just can't seem to…" She fluttered her fingers ferociously.

He grimaced. Squirmed. Chuckled. But he was helpless to pull her fingers away with his bandaged hand.

"Oh dear," she said, "I'm quite trapped under your arm. Perhaps if I try with my other fingers…"

"Nay!" he burst out.

"But I'm afraid I'm caught," she protested, edging her other hand closer.

He narrowed threatening eyes at her. "Don't. You. Dare."

Yet how could she resist?

"If ye lift your arm a wee bit," she offered, "perhaps I could withdraw my hand."

"*Will* you withdraw your hand?"

"Of course."

But there was still a mischievous twinkle in her eyes. She could feel it.

And he could see it. "I don't believe you."

"What?" She pretended to be hurt by his words. "I thought we were friends."

"And I thought you were a trustworthy lass."

"Yet ye're the one who's trapped my poor hand under your big, fat arm." She wiggled her fingers to prove it.

"Bloody—" He twitched again.

"I wonder if ye're ticklish under *both* arms," she mused.

"Nay!" he said on a laugh, reflexively clamping down his other arm.

But that didn't stop her. She was having too much fun. She walked her free fingers across his chest and began digging under his other arm.

"Nay, you don't," he gritted out, trying to fight her.

Her small fingers burrowed under his arm as easily as a mouse under a stump. And aye, he was just as ticklish there.

His laugh, peppered with oaths, was delightfully full-throated as he thrashed against her attack.

But then she made the mistake of letting the first hand slide free.

Now he could seize her with his unbandaged hand. And that was exactly what he did.

Her wrist was suddenly gripped in his iron fist. His eyes gleamed with triumph and a wicked promise of revenge.

She couldn't allow that. But there was one thing she could do to stop his vengeance. One thing that would destroy his resolve. The thing she'd been dreaming of doing all morn.

While one of his arms was clamped against his side and the other hand was busy shackling her wrist, she closed her eyes, leaned forward, and planted her lips squarely on his.

The combination of being weakened by mirth, stirred by battle, and overcome by love made Hew respond with more enthusiasm than he intended.

He knew it was wrong. He vaguely recalled something about keeping his distance. But he welcomed and deepened the kiss. His caution dissolved like mist as their mouths waged a gentle war and their breath mingled together in gasps and sighs.

Her fingers stopped their mischief then and dragged across his chest, rubbing with interest over his nipple.

Desire surged between his legs as her tongue delved between his lips. He released her wrist and lay his palm alongside her neck, holding her there so he could answer her hungry exploration.

Some faraway voice inside him was bellowing at him to stop.

But Carenza's mouth was begging him to continue.

Deaf to everything that would keep him from savoring this precious moment, he gave himself over to his passion. With a possessive growl, he sealed his lips to hers. Holding the back of her neck, he rose slowly to his feet.

Her hands crept up his chest, exploring him, kneading him. She looped her arms around his neck as if she never wanted him to leave.

Her kisses became greedy, frantic, and demanding, driving him mad with longing.

She leaned against him, pressing her breasts against his chest. And for a moment, it felt as if their hearts beat in tandem.

Then she broke away from the kiss and moved her mouth along his jaw. Down the side of his neck. Across his collarbone. Leaving a sensuous trail that left him breathless with arousal. She licked at the flesh of his chest, lowering her head to capture his nipple in her mouth, circling it with her tongue.

He stiffened and threw his head back, enjoying the playful curiosity of her lips.

Then she moved to the other nipple. She nibbled lightly there, teasing him, and chuckling low in her throat when he responded, hardening to a nub.

But that wasn't all that responded. The ache between his legs was growing sharper and more insistent.

He had to stop her. So he told himself. Over and over. Yet he might as well stop the sun from rising.

She pulled back then. For an instant, he thought she must have seen reason. Come to her senses where he had failed. When it came to temptation, she must be stronger than he was.

In that instant, he hoped he might be able to seize the reins of the runaway horse of desire. To stop both of them before they did something they'd regret. To stop things before they went too far.

But that instant passed. And in the next, she only made things worse.

Blushing at her own daring, she cast modesty aside. With frenetic fingers, she unpinned her arisaid and let it fall. Then she tugged the leine from off her shoulders until it perched atop her breasts.

Her glazed eyes compelled him to return the favor. To do for her what she had done for him. To finish what she'd started.

How could he refuse?

Her flesh was so soft. Warm. And willing. He longed to feast on her delicious skin. Almost as much as he longed to give her the gift of pleasure.

Still, he cared for Carenza. He loved her. If he gave in to his cravings, and she regretted it later, he wouldn't be able to live with himself.

So he managed to grate out, "Och, lass, are you certain?"

She licked her lips and nodded.

Every inch of his body sizzled with need. Fire burned in his loins. His heart galloped like a steed.

With any other woman, he would have dived in with all the force of his lust.

But with Carenza, he wanted to temper his passions. To go slowly and cautiously. To take care with not only her body, but her heart.

So, trembling with restraint, he slipped his hand gently down the front of her leine, freeing her breast from the linen.

She shivered as he bared her. Her tiny rosebud nipple tightened. She sighed as he lowered his head, brushing her delicate skin with his hair.

He placed tender kisses along the top of her bosom. Warmed her flesh with gentle breaths. Then he closed his lips around her nipple and bathed it with his tongue.

Her soft moan of delight gave him almost as much pleasure as the sweet taste of her. She arched toward him in invitation, and he swirled his tongue over her flesh. She gasped, fiercely clasping his shoulders, like an eagle holding onto prey. When he'd sampled his fill, he dragged down the other side of her leine, exposing her virgin breast, and began again.

Still, she couldn't be satisfied. Eventually, she craved even more. When he gave her breast a final kiss and moved his way back up to her mouth, she whimpered in complaint.

She pressed forward against him, searing his flesh with hers and driving him to new heights of torment. Her breasts cleaved to his chest like sun-warmed silk. And below, she surely could feel the pressure of his swollen cock low against her belly.

But despite her hunger, he knew there was no more he could give her. It was a risky game they played. They should go no further.

Carenza had likely never played at such sport before. Hew had. It was up to him to stop things.

Curling one of her hands in his own, he withdrew his lips from her mouth to bestow a kiss atop her knuckles. Then he firmly but gently nudged her away.

"Wait," she whispered, her eyes dulling with disappointment. "Don't go."

"I have to." It pained him to say the words.

"But I want to feel your arms around me," she gushed. "To keep kissin' ye for hours and hours. To lie with ye, heart to heart."

Her words were like ambrosia. But it was a love potion he dared not drink.

LAIRD OF FLINT

"So do I," he admitted. "But you and I, we're bound by honor. I cannot stain yours."

Then he released her hand to restore her leine, returning it to respectable order.

Carenza didn't want him to be right.

She felt as if she'd glimpsed heaven. Floated above the clouds. Sung among the angels. Never had she felt so loved, so cherished. And she didn't want that feeling to end.

But it had to.

"Ye're right, o' course," she said softly after her leine was set to rights.

As much as she liked to defy the constraints of nobility behind her father's back, she knew this was something quite different. Stealing coos and taming crows was not the same as dallying with a man.

Still, the idea of not kissing him again was too awful to contemplate. It was with sadness, shame, and regret that she pinned on her arisaid once more.

Hew slipped into his leine, concealing his magnificent chest and the formidable rutting beast beneath it.

It occurred to her that he must be suffering as well. She'd heard a man's ballocks could wither away from unrequited lust. She didn't know if that was true. But it seemed possible.

She straightened to her full height and clasped humble hands before her.

"I'm sorry if I enticed ye into somethin' ye didn't want," she murmured.

"Something I didn't want?" He let out a low rumble of a laugh. "Och, lass, you have no idea how much I wanted it. How much I still want it. How much I want *you.*"

Her heart flipped over. "Ye do?"

"I've ne'er wanted a woman more."

She didn't know how that could be true. Surely a warrior of Rivenloch could have any woman he desired. But he seemed sincere.

Then he stepped near and framed her face with his hands.

"'Tis more than wanting you, my lady," he said, gazing at her with eyes of liquid steel. "I've ne'er *loved* a woman more."

Her heart melted.

"And I've ne'er loved a *man* more." Even as the words left her lips, it seemed a silly thing to say. "Actually," she admitted, "I've ne'er loved a man at all."

He smiled. "Not even one of the Boyle brothers?"

She shuddered.

He hugged her then. A sweet, chaste, fond hug. A hug that may not have ignited her like the flint of his kiss. But a reassuring, protective, and loving embrace that she could definitely get used to.

"Will we marry, do ye think?" she murmured against his chest.

"Are you proposing?"

She wished it were so simple. It seemed to be so with most clanfolk. They were free to court and kiss and wed who they wished. They were even allowed to have a trial marriage for a year and a day. But she was the only daughter of a laird. And Hew was a border warrior from an illustrious clan. Their destinies would be determined by the king.

"I wish we could run away and be handfasted like the clanfolk," she said.

"I don't think the king would approve, ne'er mind your father."

"My father likes ye. He wants ye for a son."

"He won't like me if I run off with his daughter."

She shrugged. That was probably true.

She sighed against him. "What are we to do?"

LAIRD OF FLINT

"Bide our time," he said, lifting his hand to caress her hair. "First I have to complete my duty to the monastery and uncover the outlaw. Then we can ask my laird and yours to petition the king for permission to wed."

Her heart fluttered at the certainty in his voice. If all went to plan, this *was* going to happen. She and Hew would be married.

Still, it seemed somehow far-off and unattainable, like a rainbow glimpsed and never found.

An iron-gray cloud passed just then between the sun and the window, darkening the solar, and casting a pall over Carenza's good mood. She bit her lip. It felt like an omen. A warning that not everything was going to fall into place so easily. That what she'd found with Hew might slip through her grasp like sand through her fingers.

If that was so, then time was of the essence.

She pushed back from Hew's embrace and straightened with purpose.

"I have to go."

He looked disappointed. "Where are you going?"

"To the monastery."

His brows lowered in disapproval.

But before he could protest, she reminded him, "I told ye I was goin'."

"Alone?"

"I'll take Symon with me."

He let out a weighted sigh.

She soothed his discontent with a coaxing smile. "The sooner we solve this crime, the sooner we can be married."

He grumbled something that sounded like "There can't be a marriage without a bride."

She knew he was worried about her. But this was the easy part of the investigation. She was going to a monastery to give a sizable tithing to the monks. What could go wrong?

CHAPTER 19

Once Carenza handed the abbot at Kildunan a purse heavy with coin, he was more than happy to allow her entrance to the cloister. She requested to see the three monks Peris had named. The prior fetched Brother Michael first.

The elderly monk had bad eyesight, an arthritic limp, and a white fringe of hair.

In case he was hard of hearing as well, she said loudly, "I wish ye to know I'm makin' a sizable donation to Kildunan in your name, Brother Michael. Peris the physician was with my mother when she left this world. He told me ye too are often found by the side o' the dyin', givin' them comfort and easin' their souls. 'Tis for your great gift o' the heart I give ye thanks."

"Bless ye, m'lady." Brother Michael seemed pleased, though she wondered if he wasn't far from death himself. He had to squint to look at her, and one of his hands had a bad tremor. Still, his voice was strong enough. He might have been the one she'd heard in the passageway. It was hard to tell.

"If 'tisn't too much trouble," she said, giving him her biggest smile, one he'd be able to see, "can ye tell me about one o' your most memorable vigils?"

She wasn't sure whether the story would be of use,

but it might help to hear more of his voice.

"O' course, m'lady." He screwed up his face, thinking. "There was an elderly nobleman I remember. He claimed he had a son in the village, though he'd ne'er met him. I asked for his name and, by the grace o' God, I was able to find the lad." He seemed to drift off for a moment, lost in the memory. Then he blinked and finished the story. "I brought him to the man's deathbed, and they were able to make their peace before the Lord came down to collect his soul."

"How marvelous," Carenza exclaimed, placing a palm on her bosom. "But why had he ne'er met the lad before?"

Brother Michael lowered his voice and beckoned her close. "A man on his deathbed will confess all manner o' sins to a monk. To be honest, the lad was a by-blow. But the nobleman loved him as a true son all the same. I daresay the lad and his mother were pleased to be given a hefty portion o' the man's estate upon his demise."

"Indeed."

But was it the truth? Had Brother Michael had actually found the man's son? Or had he presented an impostor and split the inheritance with the lad's mother?

"What a lovely outcome," she said. "Thank ye for your time. And your generosity."

She decided Brother Michael might indeed have the wiles to cheat a man on his deathbed. It was less likely he had the stamina to smuggle valuables out of the monastery or to walk all the way to Dunlop to conspire with the physician.

The prior summoned Brother Robert next. He was a robust and jovial fellow with black hair and merry blue eyes. He definitely had the stamina to be an outlaw.

When she asked him for a story, the one that came to mind made him chortle with glee. When he spoke, it was difficult to compare his voice to the one she'd heard at Dunlop, because his mood was vastly different.

"I once sat at the bedside of a man who claimed he'd ne'er confessed his sins. Naturally, he wanted to do so, knowin' he hadn't long to live. So I offered to listen." The monk's speech was punctuated by snickers and chuckles. "He went on for half a day, listin' every wrongful act he'd done. Every hound he'd kicked. Every kiss he'd stolen. Every instance he'd labored on the Sabbath. Faith, ye'd have thought he was an outlaw bound for hell for all the 'crimes' he'd committed. But just when I thought he'd finished up, and I rose to go, he remembered a dozen other sins. I sat back down, and he told me about the innocent dragon he'd slain while the beast was asleep." He roared with laughter. "Then he told me how he'd wrongly accused his sister o' being a changelin', stolen the eggs from a gryphon, wounded the water beast o' Loch Ness, and fornicated with a selkie...in rather great detail." He guffawed at that.

Carenza blushed. She didn't know what to say.

Then Brother Robert's laughter died out. "The truth was the fellow likely hadn't anyone to stay with him. He feared if he didn't keep me entertained with his colorful confessions, I'd leave him alone." He shook his head. "I wouldn't have. What else has a monk to do?"

"'Twas good o' ye to stay with him."

She wondered if Brother Robert had enjoyed the man's salacious confessions as much as the man had enjoyed sharing them. He seemed too good-humored to engage in serious theft. On the other hand, he did reveal a rather careless attitude toward the dying man's soul, and if he shared the same unconcern for the sacred treasures of a monastery...

Brother William was her last interview. His countenance was somber and withdrawn. He made no eye contact, nor did he smile or speak.

He gave her mostly one-word answers, and only when she asked him to relate a story did his eyes awaken with interest. His voice, like the others, was unrecognizable as the man who'd spoken with Peris.

"I remember my first vigil," he said, his gaze focused on the ground, where he seemed to glimpse some distant memory. "'Twas one o' my fellows. A young lay brother named Liam. Too young and fair for death." His face took on a melancholy cast. "I held his hand as he lay dyin'. His skin was so pale, like candle wax. When he was awake, he wished to hear Bible verse. But he slept most o' the time, lookin' as peaceful as a bairn. His breath would sometimes stop for long intervals and then resume. Almost like heaven and earth were warrin' o'er him. Then, as evenin' neared, a rattle started in his chest, and the abbot said 'twas nearly time. But I couldn't leave him. Even if he'd ne'er wake again, I couldn't leave him, for fear the Devil, in his jealousy, might snatch up Liam's beautiful soul ere the angels could convey him to heaven." His eyes filled with tears.

Carenza placed a consoling hand on his arm, but he withdrew from her touch. She should have expected as much. Monks weren't used to a woman's comfort.

"What happened then?" she gently inquired.

"He woke once. And spoke his last words. Then he drifted into death's arms."

"What were his last words?"

Brother William sniffed back his tears and whispered, "He said, 'I've always loved ye.'" Then he cleared his throat and finally looked at her, stating adamantly, "The abbot said he was speakin' to our Lord."

She gave him a smile of compassion.

She might have said more, but the monastery gates suddenly opened behind her, emitting visitors.

Brother William's eyes went wide as he blurted, "Is that all, m'lady?"

She nodded, and he hastened toward the dormitory, as if he feared discovery.

When she wheeled around, she was face to face with Father James, flanked by two monks. He peered down at her with stern disapproval.

"What is a woman doing in the cloister?" he asked of no one in particular.

She gave him her most disarming smile. But for once, it didn't seem to work.

The abbot rushed forward to intervene. "Lady Carenza o' Dunlop, Father, the laird's—"

"I know who she is. Why is she inside the monastery walls?"

If Carenza wasn't already aware that Father James wasn't a suspect, she would have added him to the list. He'd never been a friend to women. But he seemed unnecessarily severe and hostile today. He was the sort of entitled clergyman who did as he pleased and took what he wanted. Could that include church treasures?

"Father," the abbot said, "Lady Carenza wished to give the monastery a considerable amount in tithin'."

"Ah." Father James's brows lifted a quarter of an inch. "And has she done so?"

"Aye."

"Then 'tis time for her to leave."

Carenza bit back a rude retort. It would do no good to make an enemy of the father.

"As ye wish, Father," she said with a respectful nod of her head.

As she picked up her skirts to start across the cloister, she heard him address the abbot.

"Where is that Rivenloch man?"

"At Dunlop, Father."

Carenza slowed her step.

"Dunlop? How long has he been there?"

She peered over her shoulder.

The prior joined the abbot and arched a judgmental brow. "Several days, Father."

"Two days," corrected the abbot.

"So has he decided against..." Doubt dripped from Father James's voice. "Taking his vows?"

The abbot stumbled a bit and replied, "Er...nay. He...still means to join the order."

"Then why is he at Dunlop?"

"There was an accident, Father," Carenza told him. "Sir Hew was badly burned."

The father scowled. He obviously thought women should be seen and not heard. Perhaps not even seen.

The abbot added, "It happened at Dunlop. The physician thought it best not to move him."

"So he intends to return?"

"N—" she began.

"Aye," the abbot interjected. "Aye, he should be well in...a day or two?"

The abbot was looking at her for confirmation. Confirmation she didn't want to give. She didn't want Hew to return to the monastery. She wanted him to stay at Dunlop. With her.

But she didn't want to endanger him or his mission. So she nodded.

"I would speak with him upon his return," the Father said to the abbot. "I find it curious that a border clan warrior would wish to join a holy order in the Highlands."

"So I've said many times," the prior smugly snipped.

To the prior's disappointment, Father James ignored him. Instead, he turned to Carenza. "You'll tell Sir Hew I look forward to his return to Kildunan."

Carenza didn't particular like being ordered about by a priest. But she bowed her head. Now was not the time to ruffle feathers. This time, however, she skipped the smile.

Father James clearly disliked her. Maybe he disliked all women. That was probably useful in his profession. But it rendered her best weapon—her charm—worthless.

Hew spent most of the afternoon pacing back and forth along the wall walk. He told himself it would help him recover from two days wasted in an opium stupor. After all, he was used to a daily diet of combat and lovemaking, neither of which he'd enjoyed for weeks. If he could neither wield his axe or ease his lust, he could at least ensure his legs didn't stiffen with disuse.

But that didn't explain why he kept eyeing the castle road every time a new traveler surfaced from the woods.

Carenza had been gone for hours. Soon it would grow dark.

Had there been trouble at the monastery? Had she raised any suspicions with her questioning? Had she uncovered the accomplice and unwittingly put a target on her back?

Bloody hell. He should never have let her go.

At the time, it had made sense. She'd convinced him it was perfectly safe. Reasonable. The best option. But perhaps it had only seemed so because he was basking in the afterglow of her caresses. Sometimes it seemed to Hew that when his blood rushed to his loins, it vacated his brain.

He wished he'd never involved her.

Just then, the Laird of Dunlop and his small entourage appeared over the rise, returning from the Boyle keep. Even at a distance, Hew could hear the men jesting and laughing. Maybe Carenza had been right. Maybe they'd gone as much to crow over the Boyles' misfortune as to lend assistance.

When his gaze returned to the road, Carenza had already emerged from the trees and was halfway to the keep.

LAIRD OF FLINT

By all appearances, she was safe and sound.

He let out a relieved breath. His shoulders dropped. Finally he felt like he could stop pacing. He hurried down to meet her in the great hall.

When he neared, her eyes lit up briefly, as if he were the only man in the room. But he wasn't. Servants hurried back and forth between them, preparing for supper and the return of the laird.

They couldn't talk here. She quickly ushered him upstairs to the solar and closed the door.

He feared she meant to begin again where she had left off. Kissing him. Embracing him. Caressing him. Actually, "feared" wasn't quite the right word for it.

But she had more important matters on her mind.

Without preamble, she said, "Father James was at Kildunan."

"Shite."

"Ye have to go back to the monastery."

"Now?"

"Perhaps on the morrow?" she suggested.

"Why?"

"He wants to question ye."

"Question me about what?"

"The same thing everyone has been wonderin'."

He furrowed his brow. What was she talking about?

She told him. "Why an illustrious warrior o' Rivenloch would wish to take holy vows at a Highland monastery."

He sighed. Of course hawk-eyed Father James would want to know that. "What did the abbot say?"

"He said ye *do* mean to join the order, that ye were only staying at Dunlop because o' the accident."

He nodded. That was good. But he still had to convince Father James he was sincere in his monkish pursuits and not doubling as a spy. It put him in an awkward position, keeping the abbot's secret. Hopefully, when he uncovered the perpetrators, he would be forgiven for not being entirely forthcoming.

"Did you learn anything from the monks?" he asked.

"Aye, though not enough to completely eliminate any o' them. Brother Michael is likely too feeble. But 'tis quite possible he's committed previous crimes. Brother Robert is a jovial fellow. But he seems irreverent enough to sin without battin' an eye. Brother William is quiet and tenderhearted. But he fled when Father James showed up, as if he had somethin' to hide."

Hew nodded. He knew all three monks, and he could guess what Brother William had to hide. Within the church, it was a sin worse than theft. But Hew wasn't going to be the one to expose the poor man.

"So what's next?" she asked.

"I return to the monastery."

She placed a hand on his chest and looked up at him with her wide violet eyes. "I don't want ye to go."

He enfolded her hand in his. "I don't want to go."

But Carenza knew better than to argue with him. She was bright enough to recognize it was a matter of safety.

"How can I help?" she asked. "What can I do?"

"Nothing. Not for a while. Perhaps a fortnight or two. We have to put Father James's fears to rest. Convince him my intentions are sincere."

She nodded and lowered her head. When she looked up again, there was a probing intensity in her gaze. She said softly, "What about your intentions as far as I'm concerned?"

That he could answer. He was even more sure of it now than ever. Now that he'd spent half the day pacing the wall in worry over her.

He lifted her hand to place a kiss on her palm, enclosing it there by folding her fingers over.

"You already have my heart," he said. "I intend to give you my hand."

It was a bold promise. One neither of them had the power to keep. After all, their futures were in the hands of the king. But Hew meant every word of it.

Carenza's eyes brimmed with tears of joy. "Then I shall have patience."

He kissed her brow. "What is a fortnight or two when we have our whole lives ahead of us, aye?"

A fortnight seemed like an eternity to Carenza. She'd never been in love before. And she'd only just begun to sample the joys of courtship. How could she survive without his smoldering glance, his warm embrace, his heart-melting kiss, his breathtaking caress?

"If we must starve for so long," she murmured, lowering her eyes to linger on his delectable lips, "then let us feast tonight."

Regret etched his face. "Och, lass, nothing would please me more. But we dare not."

"Why? No one will know."

"I will know."

"But ye mean to marry me."

"I mean to, aye," he said. "But every king who wages war means to win. That isn't always what fate decrees."

She rested her head against his chest. Listened to the steady beat of the heart he said was hers.

Fate wouldn't dare cross her. Not when their two paths had intersected at just the right time. Not when Sir Hew was a match her father actually wanted for her. Not when she was in love with a man who was politically perfect for her and her clan. It had to be. *They* were meant to be.

She knew he was only acting out of chivalry. He wished to protect her. To preserve her maidenhood. To safeguard her reputation.

But she didn't need guarding. She wasn't afraid. No one would find out. She was used to keeping up appearances, accustomed to hiding her emotions. Her trusty mask had always served her well.

She lifted languid eyes to his. "Just one kiss to remember ye by?"

He arched a scolding brow.

"One kiss…" Using the tip of her finger, she made a slow circle on the patch of bare flesh just above the neck of his leine. "To last a fortnight?"

He shivered. She saw his resolve wavering.

"And what if 'tis two fortnights?" he asked.

She gave him a sultry smile. "Two kisses?"

"You're a wily wench." He grabbed her finger to stop its circling. "Fine. One kiss." He lifted her hand and gave the tip of her finger a quick peck.

She widened her eyes in disbelief. Then she closed them with diabolical purpose. Seizing the front of his plaid, she hauled him forward and smashed her mouth against his.

She meant it to be a crude act of vengeance.

But that didn't last long.

Tasting him again revived her hunger. Had he been so delicious before? So savory? So mouthwatering?

Though he resisted at first, it was only a moment before he too began to feast on her lips.

Their labored breath coalesced. Their tongues entwined. Their bodies melted together.

Her senses responded quickly, knowing the path ahead. Passion's hum rang in her ears. Even within their linen confines, her breasts tingled eagerly. And betwixt her thighs an aching thirst begged to be quenched.

She couldn't wait. With fumbling fingers, she worked at the brooch of his plaid, sucking a sharp breath between her teeth when the point stabbed her thumb.

"Let me," he whispered.

He placed her injured thumb in his mouth, suckling it gently as he unpinned his plaid. Something about his intimate gesture was alluring. And when he began swirling his tongue around her thumb, plunging it into the deepest recesses of his mouth, she felt faint.

By the time he cast aside his plaid, she was aroused to a fever pitch. And when she began scrabbling at his trews, his eyes glazed over with desire.

CHAPTER 20

Hew's jaw fell open. He groaned as his long-neglected staff responded to her touch, pressing back against her groping fingers. Her warmth, her eagerness, her determination catapulted him to new levels of desire.

But long abstinence was making his response too sharp. Too swift. It had been too long since he'd enjoyed the attentions of a woman. And Carenza wouldn't know what to expect. He was likely to explode all at once, frightening her with his passion and leaving her unsatisfied.

That was the last thing he wanted. Better he should sacrifice his own satisfaction than leave her unrequited. Safer anyway.

So, though it took all his willpower to resist, he gently pushed her hands away. Swiftly, before he could change his mind, he lifted her up, turning to seat her on the chair. Then he dropped to his knees before her.

Her eyes were languid. Her mouth was rosy and wet. He caught the back of her neck and tugged her forward for a long, slow, passionate kiss.

Then, releasing her, he reached down to catch the hem of her leine. He lifted it, exposing her slender, wool-stockinged ankles, pausing to see if she would stop him.

She didn't.

He slid the linen slowly up her shins to where her stockings were tied.

Still she didn't stop him.

When he rounded her knees, she gasped. But it wasn't a protest. It was a gasp of anticipation.

Higher he slipped her leine, draping it above her knees, where the stockings ended and her flesh began. Then he moved his hands atop her knees to gently pry them apart.

She squeezed her eyes shut and instinctively resisted at first.

"May I?" he breathed.

After a moment, she nodded. Turning her blushing face shyly aside, she allowed him to spread her legs.

He bunched her leine around her hips then, completely exposing her to his view. Reaching his unbandaged hand behind her, he shifted her forward to the edge of the chair.

She was even more beautiful than he'd imagined. Her legs were long and lissome, and the nest of curls at their apex was dark and delicate. He lowered his head, stroking one silken thigh while he kissed the inside of the other.

The higher he moved, closer to the core of her need, the faster and harder her breath came and the more she opened to him. Her yearning fed his own. It pulsed between his legs.

Finally he reached the damp warmth of her womanhood, steeped with mystery, fragrant with longing. Drunk on her desire, he nuzzled her curls, tenderly parted her supple petals, and took a tiny sip of her feminine nectar.

Carenza gasped. His touch felt like lightning. A current shocking her to life. Sizzling through her body. Making her writhe in a torment of pleasure.

Just as quickly, his tongue came to soothe the burn, bathing her flesh with a healing balm.

And yet, it wasn't sweet relief she felt, but more exquisite torture. Like a punishing lash, he stroked her with his tongue again and again. And with each blow, she moaned in agony, sure she could endure no more.

She let her head fall back.

His breath was hot on her thighs.

Her face was hot with shame.

Nay, not shame. Something else.

Awe.

A great power was glowing inside her. A power he'd sparked the way flint sparked a fire. And now that he'd kindled the flames, there was nothing to stop her from bursting into a raging inferno.

She clutched the arms of the chair, fearful of what was to come.

But he clasped her fingers in his own, lending her reassurance. He would keep her anchored. He would keep her safe. He would be there for her.

She thought she could endure no more. But her body acted of its own accord. The power inside took control. She couldn't breathe. Couldn't move. She stilled as the flames roared higher and higher.

And then, with a taut squeal like a sleeping coal jabbed to life, she exploded into a thousand sparks. She gasped as waves of joy rocked her body and tossed her to and fro, shaking every last vestige of modesty from her.

How he managed to hold her, to keep her from flying in a thousand different directions, she didn't know. The throes of her desire were powerful and demanding. She could no more control them than she could stop the rain from falling.

But she didn't need to. Nobody but Hew was witness to her shattering. No one but he saw how she shuddered out of control, becoming a wild and wanton beast, and then gradually collapsed back into herself.

LAIRD OF FLINT

And he would safeguard her. He would keep her sins concealed. That the laird's daughter, who always comported herself with dignity, grace, and calm, had allowed herself to become passion's plaything would be their secret. No one else need ever know.

A sudden sharp knock at the door was all it took to destroy her sense of safety.

Panic leaped into her throat. She thrashed on the chair, freeing her hands and trying to tug her leine down.

"M'lady?" came a feminine voice.

Carenza opened her mouth to reply, not sure whether she should.

Hew scowled and put a finger to his lips. Then he whispered, "Who is it?"

"My maidservant," she whispered back.

He nodded. This was clearly not the first time he'd had to cover an indiscretion.

He called out, "This is Sir Hew. Lady Carenza allowed me the privacy of the solar to bathe. I hope 'tis all right."

There was a brief pause. Then she asked, "Do ye need help, m'lord?"

Carenza frowned. Did the saucy maid think while her mistress was away she could feast her eyes on the naked Rivenloch warrior? The man Carenza loved?

But Hew seemed amused by her expression. "Nay, thank you," he replied. "I'm nigh finished."

"What about linens for dryin'?" the maid asked.

Carenza's frown deepened.

Hew's grin widened.

"Nay," he called back. Then he turned a smoky, adoring gaze on Carenza. "I have everything I require."

At his words, Carenza's jealousy dissolved.

When they were wed, she supposed she'd have to get used to lasses staring at her handsome figure of a husband. Just as he would have to get used to the men who ogled her.

But their love had nothing to do with what others saw. The mask she wore as the well-behaved laird's daughter was not her true self. And it was the freedom and vulnerability to be exactly who she was without judgment—with all her naked flaws and faults, her shortcomings and her sins, her insecurities and her waywardness—that made their bond precious.

He pressed a fond kiss to her knuckles and smoothed her skirts back down over her legs before he stood to adjust his own clothing.

She stole a glance before he began to lace up his braies. Though his anatomy was as intriguing as ever, his proud lance had diminished now.

She felt a pang of regret. Hew had ignited in her the most beautiful bonfire. She still felt the ashes of passion drifting down around her. But she hadn't been able to grant him the same gift. Time had run out, and now the moment was past.

"I'm sorry," she murmured.

He paused mid-lace. "Sorry? For what?" He looked wary, as if he thought she might be sorry for engaging in such behavior.

But nothing could be further from the truth.

"I'm sorry I could not repay ye in kind."

He resumed lacing, and a wee smile played around his lips. "I assure you, 'twas nigh as pleasurable for me as for you."

She knew that couldn't be true. But it was kind of him to say so.

"Still, I would like to—"

"We dare not," he interjected, firmly but gently. "I should not even have done..." He paused to let his eyes graze longingly over her body. "What I did." He shook his head. "I leave for Kildunan on the morrow. And now I've made my time away from you even more painful."

"Then don't go," she blurted out, even though she knew that was a ridiculous request.

"I have to go." He slipped his leine on over his head. "You know that."

She lowered her eyes and nodded.

He reached out to cup her chin. "But not a moment will pass when I'm not thinking about you. About your bright eyes. Your sweet lips. Your tender touch. The way you feel in my arms." He rubbed his thumb across her lower lip and murmured, "I'll miss your kiss and the warmth of your heart next to mine. The softness of your breasts and the silkiness of your thighs." He lowered his voice to a whisper. "The taste of your womanhood upon my tongue."

She gulped. Already she craved him again. How would she survive two fortnights without him? How would she survive a day?

"We have to find a way," she croaked.

"A way?"

"A way to meet. I shall come to Kildunan."

He gave her a chuckle as he pulled his plaid over his shoulder. "We're absolutely not trysting in a monastery."

She didn't share his humor. The thought of waiting so long to be intimate with him again was unimaginable.

"It wouldn't have to be a tryst," she decided. "Surely we can at least meet somewhere for...conversation. Perhaps in the village."

"'Tis too great a risk," he said ruefully. "Father James has his eye on me. And you, my lady, can't go anywhere without an escort. The laird's daughter meeting the stranger from the monastery in the village?" He shook his head. "The gossip will spread like wildfire."

He was right. She knew it. But that didn't change the way she felt.

"Och, Hew," she said as tears welled in her eyes, "I can't bear the thought o' bein' away from ye for so long." She retrieved his brooch and came forward to pin his plaid. "How can fate be so cruel as to tear ye from my side when I've only just begun to love ye?"

Like a magical incantation, her words broke the last link of chain mail surrounding Hew's heart, leaving it completely unprotected. Now she could hurt him. Now she could pierce it with Cupid's arrow and leave him bleeding.

But as he always did, he couldn't stop himself from wagering everything on his heart. His love for Carenza felt so unique, so pure, so true, he convinced himself this time things would be different.

And as always, when he felt this way—over his head in the deep ocean of romance—his judgment was faulty.

He should have told Carenza to be strong. To have patience. To remember that absence made the heart grow fonder.

Instead he hauled her into his arms one last time, kissed the top of her head, and made a rash promise. "I'll find a way."

As it turned out, finding a way was more challenging than Hew expected. For more than a sennight after he returned to Kildunan, Father James was breathing down his neck. Inquiring into what aspects of a monk's life Hew was interested in. Asking for details about Hew's clan and his childhood. Even suggesting Hew might wish to show his serious intent by adopting the shaved tonsure of a monk.

Hew did not.

Finally Father James ran out of questions and left Kildunan for his next monastery inspection. After he was gone, the abbot privately assured Hew that he'd done well under the interrogation. He thanked Hew for keeping his secret. He even slipped Hew a congratulatory bottle of wine to enjoy in his cell.

Drinking three-quarters of the bottle in his bed late at night had probably been a bad idea. With only the pale plaster ceiling to look at, he quickly filled it with mental images of Lady Carenza. Of her smooth and lovely skin. Her shining violet eyes. Her cherry red lips. Her dark silken tresses. Her creamy breasts. Her sleek thighs. The soft mystery of her woman's flower, opening for him.

If he hadn't been in a monastery, he might have taken matters into his own hands then. Just the thought of Carenza had made him hard as steel.

He reached for the bottle again. Maybe he could drink himself into a stupor.

By the time he finished off the wine, he'd made a decision.

Now that Father James was gone, Hew would journey to Dunlop on the morrow. It had been a fortnight since he'd seen Carenza. The real Carenza. Not some sketches of his imagination drawn on the cell ceiling.

He'd give the abbot some excuse to go. He'd say the physician wished to check on the progress of his burned hand. Aye, that could work.

With that happy thought, he drifted off to dream about the woman he loved.

Unfortunately, in the middle of the night, he was awakened by the arrival of a guildsman in the infirmary. By morn, the physician was already at Kildunan.

Peris stayed the whole morn, tending to the guildsman, whom the other monks confided was close to death. Hew wondered how a physician willing to steal from the church and kill a man with poison had the moral fortitude to sit by a dying man's bedside.

Then a ghastly thought sent a prickling up his spine.

What if the physician was poisoning men in the infirmary? What if it was more than just the church treasures that went missing? Could Peris and his accomplice be murdering the nobles and robbing their corpses as well?

Suddenly Hew had a real reason he could give the abbot to travel to Dunlop—following up on a clue. While the physician was busy with the dying man at Kildunan, Hew could search Peris's quarters.

Even better, the lady of the castle no doubt had keys to all the chambers. Carenza could give him access to the physician's things. Looking for valuables among them wouldn't take long. And then...

Then he and Carenza could take their time reuniting.

At least that was what he planned.

But the instant he strode into the crowded hall of Dunlop and spotted Carenza across the room, his heart leaped, and he forgot all about the first part of his mission.

His ceiling portraits hadn't done her justice. Though her smile seemed strained as she spoke with two clanswomen near the stairwell, she looked more ravishing than he remembered.

A moment later, her meandering gaze halted on him. He saw her take a deep breath, and her tight smile broadened into a grin of pure pleasure.

He wanted to run to her. To sweep her up in his arms and kiss every inch of her face. To carry her up the stairs to her bedchamber and lock the door. To cast off his clothes and his inhibitions and make sweet love to her.

But they had to be cautious.

So he sauntered toward her, greeting clanfolk as he went, until he was close enough to see the shimmering delight in her eyes.

"Lady Carenza," he said with a polite nod of his head.

"Sir Hew," she replied in kind. "How nice to see ye. How long has it been? Thirty days? Three hundred?" She was teasing him.

He gave her a chiding smile. "Only a fortnight, my lady."

She sighed. "Is that all?"

"Is that Sir Hew o' Rivenloch?" her father suddenly bellowed, coming up to join them. "How's your hand, lad?"

Hew held up his injured hand. The blisters were gone and the skin had healed with little scarring. "Well enough to grip an axe."

"Good to hear." He clapped a hand atop Hew's shoulder. "'Tis time ye returned to us." He leaned close to whisper loudly, "My daughter missed ye somethin' fierce."

"Da!" she scolded.

"'Tis true, lass," he said. "Your smile's grown a bit dim."

Hew told him, "Alas, I fear I'm not returning just yet."

"What?"

"I've only come to fetch a few of the physician's things. He needs them at the monastery."

"I see," he said, disappointed. "Well, Carenza has the key to his quarters." He gave her a wink. "Ye can let him in, aye?"

"O' course."

He gave Hew's shoulder a squeeze. "Are ye sure ye won't stay? It can't be too excitin', mopin' about with monks."

"I'm sure."

That was a lie. He'd never been less sure. All he had to do was glance at Carenza's face to cast a thousand doubts on his decision to return to Kildunan.

When they were out of hearing of her father, Carenza murmured, "Is that true? Did ye come to fetch Peris's things?"

"Not exactly."

She smiled. She hadn't been so happy in a fortnight. Had it truly only been a fortnight? It felt like forever.

Then he added, "But I do need to see his quarters before we..."

"Before we...?"

The smoldering glance he gave her said everything. Her heart flipped like a fresh-caught trout. The blood sang in her veins. And her body awakened as if his gaze had physically touched her.

"I missed ye so," she whispered.

"It turns out you were right," he whispered back. "I'd make a terrible monk."

They reached the physician's quarters, and she opened the door with her key.

He stepped in and closed the door behind them.

She whirled about and immediately collided with him in an outpouring of affection. A fortnight's worth of yearning spilled from her like ale from an uncorked barrel. In his arms, she felt like she'd come home.

Hew responded in equal measure. Attacking her like a starving man at a feast. As if he could never get enough of her to fill the cavern of his heart.

Arms squeezed. Hands grasped. Mouths sought out flesh. Breath mingled in a whirlwind of desire. Their passion was frenzied and fearless, a ferocious storm they braved together.

As they kissed, he turned and backed her against the door. Then he used the deft fingers of one hand to gather her skirts, hiking them higher and higher. His other hand he crooked around the back of her neck, pulling her close. His body molded to hers, and she could feel the hard evidence of his desire against her hip.

He deepened the kiss. His tongue swept the interior of her mouth, and she answered him, snaking her tongue around his in a dizzying dance.

Then his fingers reached the hem of her skirts, and he rooted beneath them.

She stiffened as he threaded his fingers into the curls guarding her womanhood. But then, driven by instinct, she pushed against his hand. The pressure was divine. His fingers glided farther, urging her thighs apart and moving toward the center of her need.

Her mouth fell open. She let her head fall aside.

He swooped down on her exposed neck then, where his lips found a sensitive spot just below her ear. A place that stirred her senses. Made her head hum. And drove her to madness.

When he slipped his fingers between her wet nether lips, she pressed hard against his hand, stretching, yearning, aching for more.

He whispered in her ear, "Do you like this?"

She shivered, moaned softly, and nodded.

He moved his fingers over her then, stroking and circling her swollen flesh.

"You're so soft," he whispered. "So wet. So beautiful."

She should thank him. The laird's daughter was always gracious with compliments. But she couldn't center her thoughts. She could barely stand.

Instead, she clung more tightly to him. Squeezed her eyes shut as the lovely sensation betwixt her thighs grew more pronounced. More focused. More inevitable.

"Shall I go on?" he murmured, slowing his pace as her tension increased.

"Aye," she breathed.

"Are you sure?" he asked, stopping his movement.

"Aye," she insisted, on the edge of frustration. "Damn ye." The ache was unbearable. She tried to grind against his palm.

With a throaty chuckle, he resumed his motions.

Already primed, she burst rapidly into flame. She burned high and hot as she arched toward him, shuddering with sweet deliverance.

Afterwards, her knees turned to custard, and she collapsed against him to catch her breath.

"Och God, Carenza," he murmured. "You're magnificent."

She smiled weakly. But if he thought she was magnificent now...

She could still feel his iron-hard staff against her belly. She wondered... Could she give him the same kind of pleasure he'd given her?

While she rested her head on his chest, she perused the physician's shelves beside them. There was a row of oils—rosemary, lavender, hyssop, mint—with various medicinal uses. She'd once overheard two maids talk of pleasuring men with their hands and what kind of oil was best for the purpose.

Turning her attention back to him, she unfastened the leather belt at his hips and let it drop to the floor. Then she turned to force him back against the door and began gathering up his leine.

He paused her arm once to warn her, "This may be dangerous."

She gave him a one-sided smile. "Only if I do it right."

She pushed his leine up as far as she could and took a moment to worship his formidable chest with her lips.

"Hold this?" she asked.

He crossed his arms over his chest, holding the leine in place while she untied his trews and braies. His eyes closed, and his brow creased as she carefully slipped the garments down, allowing his rigid member to spring free.

She sighed in awe. Then she plucked the almond oil from the physician's shelves. Uncorking the vial, she poured a small amount into her palm. She wrapped her fingers around him as tenderly as she could. But he still quivered and sucked in a sharp breath when she spread the oil over his velvet-soft skin.

"Does that hurt?"

The last thing she expected was a weak chuckle of amusement.

"Och nay, lass. It doesn't hurt. Not e'en a wee bit."

Her confidence restored, she began moving her hand experimentally over his warm, firm flesh. He pulsed within her hand as she slowly drew up and down his length.

"Do ye like that?" she ventured.

"Mmm."

He opened his eyes a crack then, looking at her with such seductive adoration that all at once she wanted to be perfect for him.

But she had no experience with such things. "Will ye show me how?"

He nodded. Wrapping his free hand around hers, he guided her movements. The rhythm, slow at first, gradually increased along with the pace of his breathing.

Watching the changes in his expression, she grew enraptured by his sweet torment. Desire made a deep crease in his brow. Flared his nostrils. Tightened his jaw. The yearning in his face was beautiful. It mirrored what she'd felt. If coupling brought such sensations, how heavenly would it be to enjoy them together?

His breath suddenly hastened and deepened. The motion of his hand over hers became more rigid. He bent his head forward as if in anguish.

But it wasn't pain. In the next moment, his back banged against the door. His hips rocked forward as he erupted in spasms of release, groaning and spilling his seed over their joined hands.

"Oh," he panted, his chest heaving with exhaustion, "I'm sorry."

But Carenza didn't care about that. She was left speechless with awe.

He found a clean linen rag on the shelf and mopped up the mess. Then he let his leine fall between them and drew her into the circle of his arms.

She was still reeling with wonder.

She felt dwarfed by the magnificence of his passion.

Intoxicated by the heady power she wielded in her hands.

Honored by the trust he'd extended to her.

And reassured about his love.

She was reluctant to admit it. But being away from Hew for a fortnight had left her troubled by doubt. They'd *known* each other for less than a fortnight. Did he truly care for her? Or would time apart diminish his affection? What if absence made him forget her altogether?

Now, as he cradled her against his shoulder, she felt secure again, as if he'd never left.

CHAPTER 21

Hew held her close to his throbbing heart.

"I love ye," she mumbled against his chest.

That was how he knew Carenza was The One. What made her different from every other lass.

It was a sorry truth. One he'd only just realized. But no woman he'd ever courted had said those words so readily. It was always Hew who dove in head first. Hew who bared his heart. Hew who committed unreservedly to the relationship.

Indeed, he often frightened ladies off with the intensity of his devotion. As he'd learned often with lovemaking, women required time and patience. They were usually slower to arouse. And they never fell as fast or as far in love as he did. It seemed they preferred to dangle their hearts on a string, the way one teased a cat.

But Carenza had a passion and depth that matched his own. Though they'd known each other a short time, they'd fallen completely in love. And he didn't want that love to end.

"I love you too," he replied, snuggling her closer.

"I wish we could run away this instant."

"Me as well."

She turned her head to gaze up at him. "Do ye think your mother and father will like me?"

"They'll love you."

It was true. Even though she had none of his mother's warrior skills, Helena would respect Carenza. She had inner strength and a wee bit of deviousness that his mother would appreciate. As for his father, Carenza's charm and brilliance would win him over. Colin admired anyone with whom he could cross wits.

"Will your laird approve?" she asked.

"Aunt Deirdre? She'll just be relieved you're not English."

"I want to meet them," she decided.

"I want you to meet them."

"When?"

He loved her eagerness. But he had to finish his mission.

"As soon as I catch the thief. Och, bloody hell!" he said, holding her at arm's length as he suddenly remembered why he'd come to the physician's quarters. "I didn't tell you."

"Tell me what?"

He glanced around the small chamber for the first time. It served as the physician's apothecary. Most of it consisted of shelves lined with vials and jars, vessels of clay and wooden boxes, with labels identifying their contents. Dried flowers and herbs hung in one corner, and various desiccated frogs and fish dangled from another. Between them was squeezed a low, sagging pallet. Peris probably slept here to guard his precious potions.

"I need to search this room," he said.

Her interest piqued, she raised her brows as she realized, "He's at Kildunan."

"He's at Kildunan."

She wasted no time. While he fastened up his trews, she began searching the shelves. "What are we lookin' for?"

"Something. Anything." He began searching the second set of shelves. "I have a feeling they've been stealing more than just church artifacts."

"More? What more wealth could a monastery have?"

"I suspect he may be lifting jewels and coin off of the nobles who come to the infirmary."

She frowned, considering that. "Ye mean the nobles who...who don't survive?"

He nodded. He didn't want to tell her the second part of his theory. That Peris might be hastening their demise.

But as he scoured the shelves, he also looked for substances that could kill quickly.

There were several deadly ingredients. Belladonna. Cyanide. Foxglove. Henbane. Mercury. Monk's hood. Opium.

Of course, they were also used as medicines. Possession wasn't proof. Still, if poisoning had occurred, it made Peris the most likely culprit.

They made a thorough search of the physician's things. But they didn't find anything to condemn him. He had very little in the way of wealth, though he had a small library of medical texts. His clothing was well-made and tidy. His boots were in good repair. But because of his profession, he eschewed jewelry. There seemed to be nothing incriminating among his effects.

"He could have hidden them elsewhere," Carenza suggested.

"Aye, though it makes the most sense he'd hide them in a place kept under lock and key by day. The place he sleeps at night and can watch o'er them personally."

"True." She began pacing the small area between the shelves, rubbing thoughtfully at her chin. "Maybe he keeps them in his satchel."

"'Tis a possibility." Indeed, if he was using poison, that would surely be found within his satchel as well. "He always has it with him."

"Right. So how can we search it?"

"I'll find a way. I'll return to the monastery and—"

"Nay," she said, clutching at his sleeve. Then she gathered her brows. "I mean, must ye?"

Hew smiled. "The sooner we solve this," he said, reaching out to caress her jaw, "the sooner we can be together...for aye."

She sighed. "Then get out of here," she said, pushing him away. "Go on. Shoo."

He laughed.

Making sure everything was as they found it and their clothes properly fastened, they left and locked the chamber.

Carenza's father was almost as sorry to see him leave as Carenza was. But Hew vowed he'd return within a sennight. A fortnight was too long to be away from his ladylove.

Carenza watched for him, but Peris didn't return to Dunlop that night. She presumed that meant his patient was in critical condition and might not recover. But it also meant this might be an opportunity for robbery.

She wondered if Hew had found anything in his satchel.

The morn flew by. Noon came and went. The afternoon passed. Night fell.

The physician still hadn't come home to Dunlop.

Had Hew found the store of treasure on his person and exposed him to the abbot?

Or was Peris waiting for a safe time to return?

After he missed supper, Carenza stayed awake, warming her toes by the fire in the great hall as the hour grew later and later.

She was just about to drift off when she heard the front door open. It was Peris.

Shaking herself awake, she scrambled to her feet and smoothed her skirts. Then she picked her way through the dozing clan folk to intercept him.

"Psst! Peris."

He flinched once, but ignored her and kept on rushing toward his chamber.

Surprised, she hastened her pace. "Peris."

He didn't look up.

She knew he could hear her. Why wasn't he responding?

He seemed terribly nervous, which made the hair stand up at the back of her neck. Was it true? Had he stolen valuables off of a corpse?

Determined to find out, she followed him as he left the great hall.

"Peris!" she called out as he rattled his key in the lock of his door.

That he couldn't ignore. He licked his lips and turned the key. "Can it wait until the morrow, m'lady?"

When he turned to her, she could see tears standing in his eyes. Lines of worry and fatigue were etched in his forehead. Against her better judgment—after all, this was the man who'd almost poisoned the man she loved—her heart went out to him. She remembered he'd just come from the bedside of a dying man. And she remembered he'd looked exactly the same way on the day he told her father his wife was gone.

She asked him gently, "Did ye have a difficult day?"

"Aye," he said, dropping his gaze to the ground.

"A death?"

He nodded.

"Would ye like to tell me about it?"

"I'd just like to get some sleep, m'lady, if 'tis all right with ye."

She couldn't argue with him. A physician's life was chaotic. Late nights. Early morns. Births. Deaths. Impossible demands. Unreasonable expectations.

"O' course." She nodded her head in farewell. "Sleep well."

He entered his chamber and locked the door behind him.

She grimaced. She'd lightly entertained the idea of sneaking into his room while he was asleep and rifling through his satchel. But that couldn't happen now. And by the morrow, if he *had* absconded with any valuables, he would surely hide them before he emerged.

She let out an unhappy sigh as she climbed the stairs to her bedchamber. At this rate, it would be years before they solved the monastery thefts.

She couldn't wait that long. It wasn't that she cared so much about catching the thief. But every day wasted was a day she and Hew couldn't be together.

She had to do something. Find a way to speed things along. If she couldn't hurry along the investigation, perhaps she could expedite the courtship.

The weather conspired against Hew for several days. So much rain poured from the heavens, he began to grumble to the monks about the possibility of building an ark. Nearly another fortnight went by before the roads were passable and Hew could come up with a believable excuse to visit Dunlop again.

He claimed the laird had requested more honey. Since Dunlop frequently loaned their physician to Kildunan, the abbot repaid his services with honey collected and jarred by the monastery. So with his axe over one shoulder, a satchel of honey jars over the other, and a smile of anticipation on his lips, he made his way toward Dunlop.

Lady Carenza greeted him with a gaze of such adoration and yearning and eagerness, it would make a monk forswear his vow of chastity. Her face was bright with love and longing. Her smile twitched with secret promise. And he could see her racing pulse in the delicate skin of her delicious neck.

He ached to press a kiss to that spot. To pull her in and hold her close against his throbbing heart. To devour her mouth with all the hunger and passion he felt for her.

"Sir Hew!" The laird came down the steps, emerging in the great hall. "Ye've returned to us. But what have ye brought?"

He slipped the satchel off of his shoulder, rattling the jars. "Honey."

"Marvelous. Kildunan's honey is the ambrosia o' the angels." Then he turned to his daughter. "Carenza, will ye show Hew to the pantry so he can unburden himself?"

She gave him a polite smile and a nod. But Hew saw sparkling in her eyes and hastening of her breath that told him she was going to kiss him soundly as soon as they were alone.

So she did. He closed the door behind them. But the satchel of jars didn't even make it onto a shelf. He managed to lower it gently to the floor as she rained kisses all over his face. Then he completely forgot about it as she scrabbled breathlessly at his clothes, slipping her hands under his leine and into his trews.

Never had he come to life so quickly. Never had he dived so deeply into the pool of desire. All sense left him except one urge—to couple with her.

She would have let him. He knew that.

He had to be the strong one. But it was so hard to be strong when he was...so hard.

Knowing that swiving wasn't in their immediate future forced him to be creative.

He found an interesting use for one jar of Kildunan's honey. It turned out the laird was right. It *did* taste like ambrosia of the angels. Especially when licked off the breast of the woman he loved.

In the days and weeks after, they continued to play their love games. He visited at least once a sennight, and they reveled in each other's company.

They trysted everywhere. In the stable. In the buttery. Behind a holly bush. Against a fir tree. Under the moon. In the fog.

They celebrated their newfound romantic diversion. Experimenting with feathers. Fur. Mirrors. Scented oils. And handfuls of snow.

Still, more than anything, he wanted to be able to take Carenza's hand in marriage. To forge their futures together. To offer her his whole self—body and soul.

But despite all his best efforts, he continued to be stymied in his hunt for the church treasures. Unless he could locate them, there was no provable crime. He'd begun to wonder if the abbot had stolen the artifacts himself and only hired Hew as a foil to cover his tracks.

Then one midwinter day, when the snow had driven everyone indoors, and they were desperate to find a place to be alone, Carenza dug an old iron key out of a small wooden box.

She bade him follow her—at a safe distance—to the buttery.

But they weren't going to the buttery. The key fit the lock of a storage room located beside the buttery.

"'Tis where my mother's things are stored," she whispered. "My father locked them away when she died. And no one e'er goes in."

He frowned. Maybe there was a reason no one went in. "Isn't it...sacred?"

"Maybe to my father. But my mother lives in heaven, not on earth. They're just things."

He nodded. His ancestors took their things with them and lived in Valhalla, which sounded like a lot more fun than heaven.

She slipped the key into the lock. It opened easily enough. Then she pushed open the door. He winced, half expecting a loud screech to issue forth. But the hinges seemed to be well oiled. He wondered if maybe the room was visited more often than she thought.

This was the first time Carenza had seen the inside of the storage room. It contained everything that had belonged to her mother, crammed into a room half the size of a bedchamber. To her surprise, there was very little dust. The furnishings appeared as fresh as the day the door had been sealed. A pair of oak chests were draped with ornate tapestries and piled high with gowns of silk and velvet. A floor sconce with half-burned candles leaned against the wall. A wooden tub was filled to the brim with linens. A woolen arisaid partially covered a carved wood table which was topped by books and vials, combs and scissors, straw dolls and several pieces of her mother's jewelry.

Then she gasped as her eye caught on something of hers. Her childhood bed. Apparently, even that had triggered painful memories for her father. The day after her mother died, her father had ordered a new bed made for Carenza. The one she still slept in today.

She wondered...

She neared the bed and studied the coverlet. It was embroidered with wee animals. Hedgepigs. Hounds. Mice. Kittens. Sparrows. Piglets. She'd forgotten all about it.

"This bed was mine," she breathed.

Picking up the bottom corner of the coverlet to examine the stitching, he chuckled. "Of course 'twas."

But for Carenza, the presence of the bed represented more than just fond memories. She reached down and carefully peeled the coverlet back from the top. The linens were clean. And there were no fleas.

For weeks now, she'd prayed for patience. She'd waited for the monastery crime to be solved. For Hew's residence at Kildunan to be over.

It wasn't that she didn't love their inventive rendezvous. Like sparrows spreading seeds, they'd consecrated every corner of Dunlop with their love.

But the investigation could take years. It might never be solved. And Carenza was afraid if they waited too long, Hew would begin to think of her as his concubine rather than his bride.

It wasn't that he didn't love her. He adored her. But in the end, because he had to do as the king willed, he might be forced to marry another out of duty, believing he could keep Carenza as his secret mistress.

That would not do. She might not belong to an important border clan. But she was the daughter of Dunlop. She had a reputation to consider.

She decided perhaps she needed to hasten things along between them. And finding this bed among her mother's things...

This must be a sign from her mother. A message. Her blessing on their union. Carenza was sure of it. And now she knew exactly what she must do.

This was unexplored territory for her. And despite the closeness and affection between them, she felt anxious. Her heart beat more rapidly than it should. And her breath was shallow and shaky.

What if he refused her? What if she did something wrong? What if he was disappointed? What if she wasn't enough?

In the end, she decided it was a risk she had to take. She couldn't go on living in this purgatory of indecision, not knowing whether her future was secured.

In spite of her nervously pounding heart, she chose to keep things light and playful as always.

"This will be so much more comfortable than the holly bushes." She plopped down on the pallet.

"Or the buttery shelves," he said, sitting gingerly beside her, less trusting of the bed frame.

"Or the stable wall."

"Or the trunk of a tree."

"Or the doocot."

"The doocot?" He frowned. "We've ne'er trysted in the doocot."

"Nay?" she asked. "Och, that must have been my *other* lover."

"Wicked lass."

His gaze narrowed in warning. Then he began punishing her with tickles. He found all of her sensitive places. Under her arms. Along her ribs. Beneath her ears. Behind her knees.

"Do you surrender?" he demanded.

She giggled and gasped and shook her head.

He resumed until she could endure no more.

"Nay! I yield!" she finally cried out. Then she fell back onto the bed in a dramatic surrender, with one arm across her forehead.

He ceased his attack and gazed down at her with amusement. "Are you hurt, my lady?"

"I fear ye have wounded me sorely, sir."

"Then I must make amends." His eyes took on a sultry glaze. "Show me where you're injured. I shall kiss away your hurts."

His words sent a thrill of excitement through her. She turned her head and pointed to the side of her neck.

"There?" he asked.

She nodded.

He lowered his head and pressed his lips to the place where her pulse raced.

She shivered as her ears hummed in response. Then she

turned and bared the other side of her neck.

He kissed that side as well, sending an erotic vibration through her head.

"Here," she said, indicating her underarm.

With feigned regret, he furrowed his brow. "I fear I must remove your garments for that."

With feigned regret, she sighed. "If ye must."

He slipped the leine down her shoulders and off of her arms, lowering the neckline until it hung low on her breasts. Then he nuzzled each nook of her arm to plant a kiss there, though it came dangerously close to tickling.

He paused to look askance at her. "Where else?"

Blushing, she brushed across her ribs with her fingers.

He dragged the leine down slowly. As he grazed her nipples, she felt them tighten with yearning. He bunched the linen at her waist and dipped his head to lavish kisses along her ribs. His soft hair brushed her breasts with tantalizing tenderness.

"Where else?" he asked.

She rolled onto her side and pointed to the back of her knees.

He raised the hem of her leine, revealing her calves.

"Here?" he murmured against her skin.

She moaned in answer.

He placed rows of kisses behind each knee, then rolled her onto her back again.

"Anywhere else?" he whispered.

She bit her lip.

Holding her gaze, he slipped his hand down between her legs to caress her through her skirts. "Here perhaps?"

She nodded.

He got a mischievous glint in his eye. "I'm fairly certain I didn't tickle you here."

She squeezed her eyes as he pressed gently against her.

"I'm fairly certain ye did," she breathed.

"Are you absolutely sure?" he asked, rubbing across her.

"Aye," she said tightly.

"Very well then."

He rooted under the hem of her leine and tossed the fabric back to expose her.

She felt his breath like a warm summer wind blowing across her sensitive flesh.

He opened the petals of her womanhood and lavished his generous apology upon the bud of her desire.

Lost in a haze of love and longing, she rolled her head across the pallet and bunched the bedlinens in her fists. When she could endure no more of his intense attentions, she arched up off the bed. Then her body erupted in spasms of joy.

Lying on the soft bed, satiated, she felt a lovely sort of apathy. They were safe here. Nobody would intrude. She was free to be herself, pure and brave and naked. That sense of shamelessness inspired her to remove all her clothing. She wanted him to see her as she was. Wanted to be an Eve to his Adam. Wanted to feel his flesh against hers.

At first he only watched her. When she was completely undressed, she spread her limbs before him like a heathen sacrifice. Like she was his for the taking.

He looked at her with such ardor and hunger, it made her feel faint. One glance below his belt told her he was nigh bursting with desire. Yet he held back, trying to stifle his animal instincts.

"I want to see ye," she murmured.

His chest heaved as he gazed silently at her.

"Lie with me," she said.

She could see a battle raging in his eyes.

She clarified. "Now that we have a real bed, I want to feel ye next to me. To feel your warm flesh against mine. To feel our hearts beatin' together."

He still looked wary.

She let her gaze fall to the male part of him, straining against his trews with fierce need.

She licked her lips and whispered, "If ye like, we can lie together, and I can use my hand."

The silver flash of passion in his eyes was answer enough. He unbuckled his belt. Kicked off his boots, Stripped off his clothes. And when he wrested out of his braies, his cock—big and bold and brazen—almost gave her pause.

Was she sure she was ready for this?

But there was no time to reconsider. In the next moment, he stretched out beside her on the pallet. And though they hadn't yet made contact, she could feel the heat of his need like the glow coming off of a blacksmith's forge.

Suddenly he loomed large and imposing. She felt overwhelmed and overpowered. Despite his gentle, caring nature, being this close to his naked body reminded her that he was a fierce and dangerous warrior with Viking blood and shoulders like an ox.

What if he became angry with her?

But in the next instant, she forgot her fears. He draped one leg over hers and drew her close, taking her into the circle of his arms and cradling her against his chest. Strength and warmth and energy emanated from him as he surrounded her in his protective love.

He must have felt their combined potency too. He moved his hands over her, groaning at the sweet friction between them.

With bold purpose, she sought out his staff with her hand, wrapping her fingers around the firm column.

He gasped in awe.

But again she wondered if she'd made a mistake. He seemed impossibly big. What if she injured herself?

LAIRD OF FLINT

He took her hand and brought it to his mouth, using his tongue to make her palm wet and slick.

She found him again and began to move her hand in the rhythm he'd taught her.

He growled with pleasure and dug his fingers into her buttocks, pressing her hips toward his until they were flesh to flesh. There was just enough room for her hand to squeeze between them. Yet it still didn't feel close enough.

As she sensed the changes in him—his focused expression, his quickened breathing, his tightened muscles—she decided it was time.

She wrapped one leg over him and turned him onto his back, straddling his hips.

He stiffened in surprise and threw up his hands. But when she continued to stroke him and began rocking herself against his hips, he melted back into a sensuous languor.

She too found pleasure at the pressure of his body upon hers. She began climbing the mountain of erotic delight. The higher she climbed, the less control she had. Soon she was bucking and arching, searching for the right movement that would catapult her to the top.

And as she ascended, so too did Hew. His face was strained. His fists were as white as the bedlinens he clutched. As his cock thrust within her hand, his hips crashed into hers.

Finally, when her passions were stirred to a fever pitch and she sensed he was about to explode, she rose on her knees and aimed his dagger of flesh toward her womanly sheath. With urgent haste, she lowered herself onto him.

There was a wee pinch, less painful than a bee sting, and then a throbbing fullness.

He cried out, half in ecstasy, half in dismay.

Then he froze. A look of horror and disbelief crossed his face. A look that made her panic. Had she been wrong to do it? Did he think she was a shameless wanton? Did he despise her now?

Unable to endure his judgment, but unwilling to stop now, she closed her eyes and resumed her movements. He didn't resist. Soon the feeling of invasion became one of union as they strove together toward a common goal.

Whatever Hew thought of her, his body at least was delighted. He squeezed her buttocks as he thrust inside her over and over, and she rode him like a galloping steed, ascending that hill of desire once again.

When she reached the top, he stiffened at the same time. As waves of release crashed down upon her, he pulled out of her, pulsing and spilling his seed over his own belly.

Hew felt ashamed. And villainous. And spineless.

It had always been up to him to make sure he never harmed Carenza.

After all, she wasn't experienced. And he was.

Now he'd violated her trust. Compromised her virtue. Taken advantage of her in a moment of weakness.

There was no excuse for it. No apology that would suffice for what he'd stolen. No amends that would restore her virginity.

Still, he was a man of honor. He had to make the attempt.

Unable to look her in the eye, he murmured, "I'm so sorry, my lady. I ne'er meant to hurt you. I know better. I shouldn't have begun this. I should have had more patience. 'Tis all my fault. Will you e'er forgive me?"

"What?"

The odd tone of her voice drew his eye.

Carenza wasn't hurt. Or sad. Or distressed.

She was confused. "What is all your fault?"

He spread his hands to indicate their situation. "This."

She scoffed. "This is *your* fault?"

"Of course." These things were always the man's fault. Husbands never came after their wives when they were cuckolded. They came after the other man.

"But...I invited ye to this chamber, aye?"

"Aye."

"And I asked ye to lie naked with me?"

"You did."

"And who is loomin' o'er ye right now like a bloody conquerin' hero?"

He smirked. He could see her point. But he didn't have to agree with it.

"'Tis a matter of honor," he explained. "I should have prevented you. A man can't expect a woman to control her sexual impulses. 'Tis up to the man to..." He stopped, because she was giving him the most curious smile. "What?"

"It seems to me ye're the one lyin' in a pool o'," she said, glancing down at the mess he'd made, "sexual impulses."

That was a bit unfair. Indeed, he'd managed to curtail his sexual impulses at the last moment and pulled out before he could risk planting a bairn in her. Not all men would be so careful.

"Nonetheless," he said, "I apologize for neglecting my responsibilities. I can't undo what's been done. But I can assure you it won't happen again."

"It had better happen again," she said with a frown, "because there's somethin' ye should know." She crossed her arms over her breasts, which only made them look plumper and more tempting. "This was my idea. *All* my idea. I *wanted* this to happen. I *meant* for it to happen." She lifted her chin proudly. "I'm weary o' waitin' for criminals and kings and monks to steer my fate." She shrugged. "So did I seize the reins and ride away on a wild horse? Aye.

Maybe. But 'twas my choice. And I'd do it again. I *will* do it again. Many, many...many times."

Hew couldn't help but be moved. Carenza looked like a goddess, sitting astride him as if she rode into battle. Brave and beautiful and determined. Full of righteousness and rebellion. She might not be a warrior maid. But in this moment, he believed she had the strength of ten men.

Still, he wasn't convinced. No matter how tempting the thought of making love to her "many, many, many times" was, in their world it would brand her a wanton. That he wouldn't abide. He scowled and opened his mouth to counter her.

But she wasn't finished with her diatribe. And she wouldn't let him get a word in.

"We love each other, aye?"

He nodded.

"And we're married where it counts. In our hearts." She placed her hand over his chest, where that utterly smitten heart pounded. "Whate'er we do with our bodies must be right and pure, because we love each other."

She wove her words like a net around him. Lulling him. Luring him in. Trapping him.

He knew she was wrong. Things were never that simple. But he was already caught. And he had to admit he was not unhappy to be entangled in the net of her affections.

"Findin' this bed here..." She shook her head in wonder. "'Tis as if my mother herself has given me her blessin'."

"You think so?"

"I do."

Hew had other ideas about that. The pallet was horribly uncomfortable. If he hadn't been distracted by the lovely maid riding him, he would have moved to the floor.

"Because I've ne'er had a pallet poke me in the backside with such enthusiasm."

"What?"

"It feels like 'tis stuffed with sticks and stones."

"'Tis stuffed with goose feathers."

"Are you sure they plucked them off the geese?"

She moved off of him. "Let me see."

He got up from the bed and made use of a linen square from the tub to clean up.

She settled onto the pallet and began rolling back and forth.

"Och!" she said, arching up as something prodded her in the back. "What is that?"

She knelt by the bed then and began exploring the contours of the pallet with her hands.

"I think there's somethin' *in* here."

He knelt beside her and felt the same contours. "Or *under* it."

He slipped his hands under the pallet and lifted it up off the knotted frame.

She gasped.

CHAPTER 22

Though she'd never seen them before, Carenza recognized what they'd found at once.

A gold chalice. A silver cross. A jeweled Bible. And various pieces of costly jewelry—rings, medallions, brooches. They were piled on a large square of linen atop the bed's rope frame.

"The missing artifacts," Hew breathed.

"How did they get here? Only my father and I have a key to..." She shivered at a sudden chilling thought. "Ye don't think...?"

"That your father is a thief? Nay."

She had to admit it seemed improbable. She was glad Hew thought so too. But all evidence pointed to the Laird of Dunlop. Or his daughter.

"Then how...?"

Hew said, "Someone else has regular access to this room."

Their eyes widened simultaneously as they recognized the significance of that fact. With prudent haste, they began throwing on their clothes.

"Do ye think 'tis Peris?" she said, shimmying into her leine.

"That would be my guess." He pulled on his braies. "He could have easily snatched the key from your father."

"True." She slid her stockings up over her knees. "Da wouldn't even notice it missin'. I don't think he's come here since that day."

Hew stuck his leg through his trews. "The physician's accomplice. He said they planned to move the goods, right?"

"Aye." She tossed her arisaid over her shoulder, trying in vain to find the brooch to pin it together. "Before Lent, he said."

"So they mean to transport them from here within..." he said, tying a sloppy knot in his trews as he calculated the days. "A month."

"Which means we need to catch them in the act. But how? Post a guard at the door?" She shook her head. "My father would ask too many questions." She found the brooch.

"Nay." Hew shook his leine out and hauled it over his head. "I'm taking it."

"Takin' what?"

"The treasure."

She winced as she poked her finger with the brooch. "Ye can't do that. What if ye're caught with it?"

"'Twas stolen long before I arrived." he said, buckling his belt. "The abbot will vouch for that."

That made sense. Then a twisted thought coiled around her brain. "What if Peris's accomplice *is* the abbot?"

"I don't think so." But she could see there was a sliver of doubt in his mind. "The abbot wouldn't have put me on the task in the first place if he had something to hide."

"So what are we goin' to do with the treasure?"

"*We* are doing nothing," he said, arching an overprotective brow. "*I* have a plan."

"And what's that?"

He furrowed his brows. He obviously didn't want to divulge his plan.

"Damn ye, Rivenloch," she bit out, startling him with her oath. She startled herself almost as much. "I brought ye here." She pointed to the bed. "We just lay on that pallet together in nothin' but the skin we were born in. I shared my body with ye in the most intimate act a man and woman can perform. God's eyes, I gave my maidenhood to ye. Are ye goin' to tell me ye're unwillin' to share your plan with me?"

She could see he was taken aback by her fury. To be honest, so was she. But she had to admit she rather liked this new person she was becoming. Someone who wasn't afraid to speak her mind. To disagree. To get angry. To have opinions and ideas and dreams of her own.

He apparently liked her too. His lip curved up in a half-smile of approval.

"Fine," he said, telling her his plan as he gathered up the treasures in the linen square, tying a knot in the top.

She didn't like the plan. It was too risky. There were too many opportunities for mistakes.

But she knew it would do no good to tell him so. His mind was set. He was confident it would work.

The best thing she could do was make her own plan for when his failed.

Hew carefully poured the contents of the linen bundle onto the table of the chapter house. The gold gleamed in the candlelight, and the jewels winked up at the three witnesses.

"Ye found it!" the abbot exclaimed in stunned awe.

"How?" the prior asked, looking just as shocked. "Where?"

He didn't answer the prior. Instead, he addressed the abbot. "Is this all of it? All the missing items?"

"Aye, it appears so, but..." The abbot looked puzzled. "'Tis more than that." He picked up a medallion and a ring.

"These don't belong to the monastery. None o' these jewels do."

"'Twas a thief by trade, no doubt," the prior said, licking his lips. "A local outlaw."

"Did ye find the thief?" the abbot asked.

"I found one of them," Hew said, subtly bringing his axe down off his shoulder and testing the edge with his thumb. "He confessed."

The men paled.

"One o' them," the abbot repeated. "Is there more than one?"

"Aye. He had an accomplice."

"An accomplice?" the prior echoed.

"Did he name the fellow?" the abbot asked.

"Not yet." Hew pretended to examine his axe blade. "But I mean to return to Dunlop on the morrow. I'll convince him to clear his conscience. 'Tis only a matter of time. In my experience, most outlaws prefer to keep at least *half* their fingers."

Both men shuddered at that.

Hew shouldered his axe again and bid them farewell. Before he exited the chapter house, he turned.

"I believe you'll find the jewels belonged to your deceased infirmary patients."

Their jaws dropped in unison.

Hew returned to his cell. Now he had only to wait.

He'd made a large wager. It might not bear fruit. But if he was correct, the accomplice would be eager to act fast. Likely tonight.

As he suspected, a cloaked monk left Kildunan at nightfall, hurrying along the road as if chased by a pack of wolves.

But the beast on his scent was Hew.

Hew kept his distance. There was no need to further frighten the man. He was already headed into the trap.

The man naturally had no trouble negotiating the gates of Dunlop. After all, who would suspect a monk of foul play? The castle guards were probably used to his frequent midnight visits. To them, the prior appeared to be an exceptionally devoted man of the cloth, since he was always coming at the darkest hours to pray for suffering members of the clan.

Tonight, it was Peris who needed his prayers. And when Hew glimpsed the flash of a dagger blade in the prior's hand, he knew how the prior meant to relieve the physician's suffering.

He tracked the prior through the great hall to the physician's quarters.

Hanging back in the shadows, he heard the prior pound hard on the door. After several moments and an additional heavy round of knocking, the physician opened the door.

"What have ye done?" the prior hissed.

Peris sounded like any man wakened in the middle of the night. Stuporous and irritable. "What are ye talkin' about? And what are ye doin' here? I thought we agreed—"

"Bloody fool!" the prior bit out, brandishing his dagger. "Did ye think I wouldn't come after what ye did?"

"What the—"

The prior pushed his way in.

"Ye don't mean the guildsman, do ye?" the physician rattled on. "We agreed I could hasten him along with a few extra drops of opium. 'Tisn't the first time I—"

"Not the guildsman," the prior growled. "I don't care about the guildsman."

"Is it the guildsman's jewels? I swear I put them in with the rest."

"Och aye. Right before ye handed them o'er to Rivenloch."

"What?"

"He brought them to Kildunan, ye halfwit. Showed them to the abbot."

LAIRD OF FLINT

"What are ye talkin' about? They're right where I left—"

"Is that so?" the prior sneered. "So ye're sayin' ye *didn't* confess to Rivenloch and turn o'er the treasures?"

"What?" he blurted in amazement. "Why would I confess?"

"I should have known ye were a coward. Ye've been as twitchy as a cat for weeks now."

"Because I've been sittin' on top o' the spoils," the physician challenged. "Ye keep sayin' ye'll move it, but—"

"But since 'twas takin' so long, ye decided to wash your hands of it. Is that it?"

"Nay."

"Ye figured ye'd unburden your soul," the prior said, "and throw me to the wolves."

"I swear I don't know what ye're talkin' about."

"He's goin' to pry it out o' ye, one way or another."

"Who?"

"Rivenloch. All he has to do is pick up that bloody axe o' his, and ye'll be screamin' my name all the way to the garderobe." There was a sudden heavy impact, like the prior punching the wall, followed by a squeak from the physician. "But then ye know what happens? I tell them about your crime. They'll be interested to learn ye're a godforsaken murderer."

The physician choked on outrage. "God's eyes! Ye said it yourself. They were goin' to die anyway. I only put them out o' their misery."

"I don't think the law will see it that way. Which means ye're goin' to die. Probably by hangin'. 'Tis an ugly death, as I'm sure ye know. Ye'll piss your trews, and ye might strangle for an hour. So here's what I'm offerin'. I'm goin' to... How did ye say it? Put ye out o' your misery."

The physician gasped.

"But I'm a forgivin' man. It seems ye haven't given Rivenloch my name...yet. So I'm goin' to give ye a choice. Ye can either brew yourself a toxic concoction and die by your own hand, or I can slit your throat and leave ye bleedin'."

"Wait!" the physician barked in panic. "Wait," he repeated, clearly trying to calm himself. "Listen to me. I've said nothin' to Rivenloch. I swear. Absolutely nothin'. I stashed the guildsman's jewels away where I always do. And the treasure was right where 'tis always been."

"Are ye sure about that?"

"O' course I'm sure. Come. I'll prove it to ye. I'll take ye there now."

Troye lifted his head, suddenly alert.

Carenza coiled her hand in the hound's collar. She braced her other hand on the rim of the wooden tub behind which she was crouched and listened.

That had to be Peris. Once word got back to him that the artifacts were missing, he'd surely come to see for himself. Whether he would come with his accomplice, she didn't know. But one or both of them would likely flee once they discovered their crime was uncovered and their treasure confiscated.

With Troye by her side, she had the might and courage to face the outlaws before they were able to escape. The loyal hound was ferocious of growl, sharp of fang, and fiercely protective. The two of them could keep the thieves cornered until help could be summoned.

At the first rattle of the lock, Troye started growling.

The door swung open.

The hound immediately snapped and lunged at the two men—Peris and the prior.

The prior cursed.

Peris yelped in panic.

Carenza hauled back with all her might to keep the hound from charging.

The thieves would have exited back the way they came, but suddenly an immense figure filled the doorway. Hew stood glowering at the entrance, brandishing his axe before him.

Unfortunately, Carenza was caught in the backlash.

Peris, more threatened by Troye than a Viking, started kicking at the hound.

The hound caught the physician's calf between his teeth and began thrashing.

Screaming in pain, the physician wrenched a sconce from the wall and bashed it against the hound's jaw.

Troye went down with a whimper and was silent.

Carenza cried out. But before she could rush to the poor hound's side, the prior grabbed her arm and flung her against the wall. The impact sent stars exploding across her vision. Then she felt the cold, hard steel of a blade against her throat.

"Let me go," the prior said, "or I'll slit her throat."

"She's done nothing," Hew said tightly. "Your battle is with me."

"My battle is with anythin' and anyone who stands in my way," he corrected, prodding her hard enough with the point of his dagger to draw blood.

She'd just felt the prick when Hew hauled Peris forward by his leine and set the edge of his axe at the physician's throat.

"A hostage for a hostage," he bit out.

The physician squealed, rolling his eyes in fear.

But the prior was too concerned for his own survival to care about his accomplice.

"Go on," he growled. "Kill him."

Hew was afraid of that. There was no leverage against a rabid animal that was cornered and desperate.

His heart thundered. His breath froze in his chest. The single crimson drop of Carenza's blood rolling down the blade made him shudder with rage.

But in the end, there was only one thing to do.

Even though it went against his every instinct as a warrior, he couldn't let harm come to the woman he loved. The woman he intended to wed. The woman who meant the world to him.

He tossed his axe away and released the prior, who sank onto the floor.

"Let her go," he croaked. "I won't follow. I give you my word."

"Nay," Carenza sobbed in protest.

Hew understood how she felt. It was hard to surrender. To accept injustice. To fight for what was right and still fail.

But some things were more important than winning. Sometimes you had to pick your battles. *Amor vincit omnia* was more than just the Rivenloch creed. It was a truth. Love was the most powerful force of all.

For one awful instant, Hew feared the prior wasn't going to let her go after all. He hesitated. His eyes darted around the room. His hand tightened on the grip of his dagger.

Somehow Hew managed to keep his voice steady as he rasped out, "You don't want her blood on your hands. If you leave now, we'll remain here until dawn."

As further proof of his surrender, Hew raised his arms up and sat in the corner on one of the chairs.

It seemed an eternity before the prior finally decided he could make a clean escape. He shoved Carenza away from him so that she fell at Hew's feet. Hew curled his arm around her, less to protect her and more to keep her from lunging toward the prior to scratch his eyes out.

Still wielding his dagger, the prior slowly backed out of the room.

But he forgot about the physician, his accomplice, his partner in crime, that only a moment ago he would have happily allowed to be killed.

Peris was understandably bitter about that. And he was in no mood to forgive the prior. He seized Hew's axe where it lay on the ground and turned the blade upwards. Then he tripped the prior so that he fell backwards onto the edge.

The blow didn't kill him at once. Hew covered Carenza's face so she wouldn't see the prior's thrashing or hear his piteous screams. But within moments, the physician opened a double locket from around his neck and poured the contents—a white powder—into the prior's mouth. It must have been fast-acting poison. Foam spilled from between the prior's lips, and then he went still.

Hew wondered if this was the sort of mercy killing Peris had been doing at Kildunan in order to steal the nobles' jewels. It might be quick, but it was still murder. The physician would likely be tried and executed.

Looking into Peris's eyes, he saw the man's dark fate written there as well. Execution was not what the physician intended. Before Hew could prevent him, Peris opened the second side of the locket and ingested the rest of the powder.

Hew held Carenza close while Peris suffered the thankfully brief paroxysms of agony. The physician might have been a thief and a murderer, deserving of death. But at one time he'd cared for her mother. This was something Carenza didn't need to see.

CHAPTER 23

Carenza scratched Troye behind the ear as they stopped in a sunny spot of the rain-washed glen. He had only a wee scar left on his jaw from his violent altercation with Peris, thanks to Dunlop's new physician, Thomas. Thomas adored animals, to her delight, and could be seen tending to them as often as his human patients.

Since Kildunan didn't want it bandied about that they'd had a thief in their employ or that anyone had met an untimely death on their watch, the monastery thefts were mostly kept secret. Father James was never privy to the nefarious activities that had taken place at the monastery. The monks, for their part, kept silent. The treasures were quietly returned to their places, and the jewels were added to the monastery coffers to provide for the poor. The physician's death had been deemed an unfortunate accident, and the abbot declared simply that the prior had gone missing.

Of course, Hew informed her father privately about the investigation, since it centered on Dunlop and their physician. Carenza's part in solving the crime had to go unremarked. But she supposed that was for the best. Her father would never have approved of her taking such risks to life and limb.

Laird of Flint

Now that Hew's work for the abbot was complete, he could be released from Kildunan. And since her father was fond of the Rivenloch warrior, Hew was free to linger at Dunlop for as long as he liked.

Carenza smiled and tossed a stick for Troye. The hound galloped off across the grass toward the crumbled and rotting byre, scattering dewdrops in his wake.

It was so much more convenient having Hew stay at the castle. He was delightful company at supper. Inspiring to watch on the practice field as he battled alongside the Dunlop warriors. A joy with whom she planned to share the spring arrivals of hedgepiglets and fox cubs, squirrel kits and hares.

Best of all, now that Hew no longer had to keep up the fiction of aspiring to the church, he could begin courting her in earnest. He accompanied her to the village each week. Helped her father distribute gifts to the crofters. Rode with her across the countryside, making plans for the expansion of Dunlop once they were wed.

Of course, they still had to tryst in secret. The laird would have been mortified to discover his beloved daughter was not as lily-pure as he imagined.

But now that they'd made the mental commitment, it seemed ludicrous to waste weeks awaiting the king's permission when they could be enjoying each other's company.

Thankfully, they found ample opportunity. And soon it would be spring. So Carenza took small expeditions like this one with Troye to discover new locations in nature where she and Hew might eventually sample the wonders of the outdoors—in the crook of a tree, behind a thicket, in a fern-draped cave.

Troye came trotting back with the stick.

"Good lad," she said, patting his head. Then she turned and tossed it blindly in the other direction.

It didn't fly far. Hew had stolen up on her. It sailed about five yards to hit him smack in the middle of the chest.

As if that weren't enough of an insult, Troye lunged at the stick and nearly knocked Hew over.

"Troye!" Carenza scolded.

But she needn't have fretted. The Viking was as strong and steady as an oak. He was already laughing and scrubbing at the hound's face in good humor.

"Your da is looking for you," he said when he could take a breath. "Something about a missive."

She shrugged. A missive didn't sound so important. Not when she was alone with the one she loved in a beautiful sun-pierced glen.

"I'm sure it can wait," she purred.

He arched a chiding brow at her. "Do you think?"

She sidled up to him and walked her fingers slowly up the middle of his leine. "I do. And furthermore, I think I have just the thing to—"

Her words were interrupting by a sharp crack of thunder.

She gasped and clung tight to him.

In the next instant, the heavens opened. Fat drops of rain cascaded down over them.

She shrieked.

He seized her hand and pulled her along with him toward the abandoned byre. Troye dropped his stick and frolicked after them, thinking this was a new game.

By the time they ducked under the moss-covered timbers, they were already soaked. They huddled together at the open side of the byre while Troye ranged back and forth, barking at the rain.

The Laird of Rivenloch wore a Thor's hammer pendant to show her Viking bloodright. But at the moment, for Hew, the god of thunder seemed like a nemesis.

He hadn't had a moment alone with Carenza for days. Not since he'd made love to her in the moonlit shadows of the solar at midnight, nearly a sennight ago. And now the storm was conspiring against him, raising its wicked head to hamper his courting.

Their coupling that night had been magical. They'd soared through the heavens together, beating the air on silent wings of angels, singing a song only God could hear.

And afterwards, as they'd lain in each other's arms, gazing up at the jeweled firmament, one of the sparkling stars had happened to break free to streak across the sky like destiny's messenger.

They'd held their breath. He'd made a wish. And without uttering a word, he'd known. She'd wished for the same thing.

A lifetime together.

He'd written the missives that very night. Sent one to his cousin Feiyan and one to his aunt, Laird Deirdre. He no longer had the patience to wait for King Malcolm. He would obtain permission for the match from the Laird of Rivenloch instead and leave it in her capable hands to secure the king's approval.

The king could hardly refuse her, after all. The Rivenloch clan was the king's most powerful border ally. He would wish to keep such valuable vassals happy. And the fact that Dunlop himself was in favor of the match would surely work in everyone's favor.

But how could Hew explain that he'd fallen truly in love once and for all? Would anyone believe him? The best he could do was describe Carenza.

That had been nigh impossible to do in the space of a missive. Her qualities were infinite. Her beauty was inexpressible. Her character and charm and kindness were limitless. He could have spent a lifetime, writing tome after tome in tribute to Lady Carenza of Dunlop. Yet he dared not waste precious time trying to capture all of her on a single page.

Instead, he settled for a few heartfelt lines. They would have to suffice to convince Laird Deirdre that Carenza was The One. That Hew intended to make her his bride. That he expected the laird to procure the king's permission for the wedding.

She is beautiful and clever, he wrote, *wise and sweet, helpful and generous. She has a gentle nature and a ready smile. A man could hope for no more perfect a wife.*

Though it seemed early for a response, Hew couldn't help but hope that the missive that had arrived for Carenza was an approval of their match. And now he'd have to wait out the storm to find out.

Carenza was not going to let a good storm go to waste. No one would venture out in such a downpour. And until the rain stopped, they were essentially trapped here. Alone. Together. In an isolated, forgotten, abandoned shelter.

"I'm cold." She shivered and snuggled closer.

"I would build you a fire," he said, looking askance at the crumbling beams overhead, "but I fear 'twould burn down our shelter."

She shrugged. "There's more than one way to get warm."

His mouth melted then into a sultry grin. "Is that so?"

"So I've heard."

"Tell me more."

She did. She whispered a few suggestions involving the removal of their clothing. Then she murmured something she'd heard about the benefits of lying together, skin to skin. Then she mentioned various practices they might try in order to get their blood pumping more efficiently.

By the time she breathed the last idea into his ear—one about warming him with her mouth—he had picked her up and carried her off to the driest corner of the byre.

He laid out his plaid for a bed and stretched out beside her.

While Troye stared out at the storm and the rain made dull patter on the mossy timbers, they warmed each other in a dozen ways. With massaging fingers. And caressing hands. With tangling limbs. And loving lips. Finally, they merged in a molten mixture of fiery passion and steaming sensuality.

Their bodies joined in sublime bliss as they ascended to a place above the storm, above the clouds, a place where angels dwelt and love conquered all.

And when they fell back to earth, shuddering from their flighty brush with heaven, they clung to each other, holding onto the rapture they'd discovered.

Carenza opened her eyes and gasped at the sight. The rain had slowed now. Drops fell through the sunlight like precious crystals dripped from the dark clouds above. And beyond the trees, a rainbow arced across the sky, shimmering in vivid hues.

"'Tis a sign," Hew decided.

Carenza agreed. A rainbow was good luck.

It meant the storm was over.

There was smooth sailing ahead.

And hope was on the horizon.

They dressed and returned to the castle, arm in arm. The rainbow followed them all the way home.

But the instant she entered the crowded hall of Dunlop, Carenza sensed something was wrong. She could see it in her father's face. He looked...uneasy.

Her heart took a sharp dive. She extricated her arm from Hew's and came forward to greet him.

"Father?"

The laird gave Hew a quick glance, but just as quickly averted his eyes. Then he ushered Carenza aside.

"I need to talk to ye. Alone."

Hew nodded. Then he clasped his hands behind him, turning his back and walking away to speak with a group of clansmen drying their plaids near the hearth.

"What is it?" she asked.

"We've a missive from the king."

"The king?"

A dozen horrible thoughts ran through her head.

Had Malcolm ordered the Dunlop clan to fight for the English in Toulouse?

Did he mean to quarter English soldiers at Dunlop castle?

Had he decided her father should take a third wife, perhaps an English noblewoman?

"What does he want?" she asked.

"It seems the Rivenloch clan has been speaking well o' ye."

"Me?" She blinked in surprise. "But I've never met them."

"I believe Sir Hew has commended ye to his laird."

She smiled. That warmed her to her toes.

But melancholy lingered in her father's eyes.

"Then what's wrong?" she asked.

"The king has made ye a match."

A flutter of excitement made her heart flip over. Somehow Hew had managed it. He'd talked his laird and the king into approving their marriage.

"But that's welcome news," she gushed, clasping her father's hand even as he averted his solemn gaze. "Isn't it?"

Why wasn't he happy for her? Could it be he was feeling sorry for himself? Did he think she was abandoning him?

"Och, Da," she chided him, giving his beard a fond tug. "I promise I'll visit. 'Tisn't so far, and I'll have to come to Dunlop to see Hamish and all the—"

LAIRD OF FLINT

He clasped her hand to hush her, pulling it away from his face. She'd never seen him so grim, not since he'd said farewell to her mother.

"Ye should read the missive." He pulled a scroll from within his plaid. The red seal was already broken, but Carenza could see it had the royal insignia.

With trembling fingers, she took the vellum from him.

At first glance, it seemed an ordinary marriage writ. The beginning paragraph extolled Lady Carenza's virtues as a wife. Then followed detailed language about property ownership, coin exchange, the dowry price, and the line of inheritance. As she scoured the document, her eye caught on the names of the two parties involved, the Laird of Dunlop and the Laird of Rivenloch. All seemed in order.

But when she got halfway through the text, she saw a name that didn't belong there.

Gellir.

Gellir of Rivenloch.

She shook her head and reread the passage.

Sir Gellir of Rivenloch, the bridegroom.

Nay. That wasn't right. It was supposed to be Hew. Sir Hew of Rivenloch. She didn't even know Gellir. There must be some mistake.

She read on. But every mention of the bridegroom said Gellir. Hew's name appeared nowhere on the document.

Though she felt an uneasy queasiness in her gut, she couldn't help but assume it was a mistake. Someone had gotten the cousins' names mixed up. That was all.

She scrolled down to the bottom of the page. Laird Deirdre of Rivenloch's signature was affixed to the document. Surely she knew the difference between her son and her nephew. She wouldn't have accidentally promised the wrong woman to the heir of Rivenloch.

Her heart slowly sank to the bottom of her chest and remained there, as if heavy iron anchored it to the shadowy depths. When she lifted her gaze to her father, for an instant she saw her own bleak hopelessness reflected in his eyes.

But then the cold, hard truth fell over his face like a steel visor.

A laird couldn't be governed by empathy. A laird's power depended upon loyalty—his clan's to him and his to the crown. When it came to strategic alliances, the king knew best. And no amount of begging or negotiating or conniving would change that.

So as painful as it must have been for him to break her heart, her father straightened with pride, praising the king's wisdom and congratulating Carenza on her successful match.

Carenza felt numb.

By all measures but one, it *was* a successful match. Gellir was not only from a long line of warriors. He was the tournament champion of all Scotland. Instead of settling for the son of one of the Warrior Maids of Rivenloch, Carenza was wedding the son of Laird Deirdre herself. And when the Rivenloch clan chose a new laird, the responsibility would almost certainly fall to Gellir, making Carenza both the Lady of Rivenloch and the Lady of Dunlop. Their children would control the combined forces of Lowland and Highland warriors, securing the border for generations to come.

But that one measure—the measure of love—was all that mattered to Carenza. Her throat ached with betrayal, and her chest throbbed with heartbreak. Her eyes welled with hot tears, blurring her vision as she stared wordlessly up at her father.

He scowled once. Briefly. But she could read his expression.

He wanted her to understand this betrothal was a gift. An honor. A reward granted by the king.

To consider it anything less was disgraceful.

To accept it with anything other than gratitude was unseemly.

To welcome it with anything but the utmost enthusiasm was shameful.

As the daughter of the clan, Lady Carenza must proclaim her satisfaction with the king's choice. She must be thankful for his great care in choosing her bridegroom. She must convince the clan she was delighted with his royal decree.

Yet how could she?

For the first time in her life, Carenza couldn't mask her feelings. Her control slipped. Her brow crumpled. Her lower lip quivered. Heartache spilled over her eyes and trickled down her cheek.

Her father's brow darkened, and he swiftly pulled her into the shadows of the buttery before the clan could see her.

She was sure he was going to chastise her. Lady Carenza was supposed to be the clan's ray of sunshine. Their inspiration. Their joy. She wasn't supposed to frown or weep, show anger or cause unease.

But he didn't chide her. He only held her by the shoulders and regarded her with tired, sad eyes.

"I know ye're fond o' Hew," he murmured. "I am as well. And if 'twere in my power to give ye your heart's desire, I'd do so. Ye know that, aye?"

She nodded. But his kind words only made her sob more.

"But I can tell ye this. Rivenloch is beyond reproach. They're a clan o' great integrity and honor. Deep loyalty and courage. If Sir Gellir is half the man that Hew has proved himself to be, ye'll not be unhappy in this marriage."

He was wrong. She would never be happy. Not while

the one she loved with all her heart was not hers to have and hold.

She would *feign* to be content. It was what was expected of her. It was what had *always* been expected of her. She would smile and nod, act gracious and grateful, amplify her small joys and hide her deep disappointments.

But she would never be happy.

As she'd always known, her life was not her own.

For a brief sliver of time, Hew had made her believe she could express her own desires, follow her own dreams, dance to her unique music. He had made her feel as if she were worthy, by virtue of simply being herself.

But now reality buffeted her in the face, waking her from her foolish dreams and reminding her she'd never truly been the free-spirited Carenza Hew adored. From the beginning, she'd been carved into the perfect wooden effigy of the daughter of Dunlop. Beneath her velvet gown, she'd always worn the iron shackles of her station. She'd always borne the terrible weight of the clan on her shoulders. And she always would.

She sniffed back her tears and wiped the tracks from her cheeks. "I'll need a mo—"

"O' course." He turned to go, then returned to lean in close. "Would ye like me to break the news to him?"

She hesitated. His offer was tempting.

Hew would not take the news well. He'd likely explode. Bellow out in anger and fury. Rage against the king's decree.

Desperation would drive him to do something far more dangerous. He'd look for a way to gainsay the document his own laird had signed. Perhaps challenge the king himself.

Carenza couldn't let that happen. She and Hew had never been masters of their own fate. They'd denied it for weeks now. Believed they could make their own happily ever after.

But somewhere deep inside, she'd known all along it was just a fantasy. Kings played at chess, and nobles were merely their pawns. She'd only imagined it could be otherwise.

It was cowardly not to tell Hew herself. He deserved to hear the truth from her lips. Even if that truth was but a veiled reflection of what she truly felt.

"Nay, I'll tell him," she decided.

She swallowed down the last of her tears and gathered her courage. This would be the most demanding performance she ever pulled off. But everything depended upon it. The fate of her clan. The fate of Rivenloch. And the good will of the king.

Her heart caught once—when she saw Hew laughing and chatting by the fire with her clansmen. He looked so natural with them, they might have been his brothers.

How cold the hearth of Dunlop would be without the Viking warrior of Rivenloch.

She clutched the rolled parchment in her hands.

He glanced at it once when she came up, but said nothing.

It took all her will to maintain a calm expression. But she knew she had to be convincing. With a nod of her head, she beckoned him to follow her. She led him to the quiet alcove at the entrance of the great hall.

"Well?" he asked, his eyes twinkling as he arched a brow at the scroll.

Her heart plunged even farther into the miserable mire. She couldn't look him in the eyes. Not when she knew she was about to break his heart.

"We knew this day would come," she said, twisting the scroll in her hands. "We always said our fate was not our own. Isn't that right?"

She glanced up long enough to see a scowl furrow his brow.

"What has Malcolm done?" he growled.

She had to tame Hew's ire before it erupted.

"He's done what is his right to do," she said with a detachment she didn't feel. "He's chosen a husband for me."

Hew went absolutely silent.

The pulse in her ears was deafening. And her own flippant words sounded as cheap and meaningless as the jangling of a beggar's bell in a thunderstorm.

"But I want ye to know I've truly enjoyed our time together," she said. "I consider ye a cherished friend. And I will always—"

Hew snatched the scroll out of her hands.

The hammer blow to his heart had not yet landed. He was still numb. Or perhaps he had no heart left to break.

All he felt at this moment was fury as he frowned down at the document.

Bloody hell. Who did the English-loving King Malcolm think he was crossing?

Hew had written to his kin, singing Lady Carenza's praises. Had Feiyan said nothing? Had Laird Deirdre failed to intercede with the king on Hew's behalf?

Or had Malcolm slighted the clan, forgetting it was the Rivenlochs who protected his border?

What milksop of a husband had the child king chosen for his beautiful Carenza?

He scanned the words and let his eye fall on the signature at the bottom. His breath caught.

Laird Deirdre Cameliard of Rivenloch.

It was his aunt's hand and her seal.

Whatever had been done had been done with her permission.

Then his gaze traveled back up the document.

There were the blows of the hammer. Striking his heart. Over and over and over again.

Gellir.

Gellir.

Gellir.

His cousin. Carenza had been promised to his cousin.

Still there was no pain.

Only cold and hollow death dwelt in his chest.

He let the scroll fall from his fingers.

Carenza was saying something to him. But he was deaf to everything but the clanging of that name upon his armored heart.

Gellir.

Gellir.

Gellir.

He was beyond hurt. Beyond betrayal. Beyond rage. Beyond feeling.

Slowly, as if he moved through muck, he shouldered his axe and pushed through the doors of the great hall.

The sky was black. The clouds hung low. It was raining again. But he felt neither the wet nor the cold.

Anger burned low inside him like a glowing coal.

He strode across the courtyard, through the gates, past the road, over the rain-slick sward, climbing higher and higher, until it seemed he might be swallowed up by the clouds.

There, at the top of the mountain, all his pain and fury sparked to life. He raised his axe and, like a dragon breathing fire, bellowed in rage at the heavens.

An instant later, the god of his ancestors replied, sending down a bolt of lightning to kiss the blade of his axe.

Hew released the weapon just before the wood handle exploded and earth-shaking thunder rumbled down. Current crackled in the air all around him as he staggered back from the snapping whip of Thor.

When the storm receded, Hew was left among the black and smoking shards of his weapon, clinging to the crushed and broken pieces of his heart.

He looked toward Kildunan. He supposed the monastery would serve as his home now until the king found a bride for him. He wouldn't return to Dunlop. And he didn't have the stomach to speak to his treacherous Rivenloch kin.

His mouth turned down at the unsavory thought of marriage. He would rather take a vow of chastity than settle for a bride who wasn't Carenza.

One last bit of mockery awaited him. As he took his first steps toward Kildunan, he found a charred piece of his axe handle at his feet.

The remaining runes said Love conquers...

His words and his laughter were bitter. "Love conquers... nothing."

He crushed it beneath his heel as he walked toward an uncertain future.

Carenza wept every night.

For her lost love.

For the king's thoughtless decree.

For the Laird of Rivenloch's poor judgment.

For the cruel hand of fate.

For Hew, whose heart she'd surely broken, despite the fact that he'd left without a backward glance.

And aye, even for the man she was to marry, for though Sir Gellir might claim her hand, he would never possess her heart.

But weeping upset her father and troubled the clan, so she kept her sorrow to herself. By day she was kind and sweet, patient and charming. If the sparkle in her eyes was dimmed by the mist of melancholy, only the animals could tell. Hamish came to the gate for a scratch when she was near. The courtyard squirrel shared her litter of kits. And Troye followed her around the keep.

The clan was mostly excited about the Dunlop-Rivenloch union to come. Everyone had heard of Sir Gellir, the tournament champion of Scotland. It was truly an honor to be chosen to be his wife. To carry on his name. To bear his offspring.

She'd been thinking a lot about bearing offspring lately. She'd always kept close track of her courses, and she was supposed to start her menses today.

Naturally, it was also one of Carenza's busiest days at Dunlop. Easter. After the long period of Lent, almost everyone looked forward to the lavish feast where the Dunlop tables sagged with roasts and pies, eggs and cream, succulent meats and rich custards.

She never let a few aches and pains trouble her. It wouldn't be the first time she suffered the pangs of her courses while hosting a feast. With any luck, she would start her menses on the morrow, while the clan was recovering from their overindulgence today and she could lie down for a nap.

As she sat down beside her father at supper, she saw a familiar jar beside his platter of simnel cake.

"Is that Kildunan's honey?"

"Aye."

"Och, Da," she teased. "Have ye been squirrelin' it away?"

She expected him to give her a conspiratorial wink. Instead he said, "Nay. 'Twas an Easter gift from…" He cleared his throat. "From the monastery."

An awkward silence followed. She could guess who had brought the honey. And the fact Hew hadn't bothered to say good day to her was disheartening.

She should have let it go. She should have pasted on a smile to appease her father and murmured, "How kind."

But she was wounded by Hew's rejection. After all, soon

they would be cousins. Now she felt as if she'd lost not only a suitor, but a friend.

So instead she muttered, "He might have lingered long enough to say hello."

"I told him ye weren't here." He spread honey on a slice of simnel cake.

"What?"

He took a bite of cake and shook his head. "There's no sense in draggin' out the poor fellow's torment. Ye'll be gone in a fortnight anyway."

Spent in Hew's company, a fortnight would have been an eternity. Long enough to memorize every inch of his body. Long enough to speak aloud all the hopes and dreams they'd once had for the future. Long enough to make a lifetime worth of memories.

Now her father had stolen even that wee gift from her.

Her eyes filled with tears.

She couldn't blame the laird. He was doing what he thought best. Like culling coos, a quick blow and a sharp knife probably caused the least amount of suffering. But no one ever asked how the coo felt about it.

John the kitchen lad set a trencher of creamy mushroom, leek, and saffron pottage before her. Normally, she would have slurped up the velvety soup with enthusiasm. But today the strong aroma troubled her nose. She pushed the trencher aside.

"Simnel?" her father offered.

She nodded. He carved off a fruity slice for her and placed the honey within her reach.

Bypassing the honey, she nibbled a corner of the cake. But she had little appetite for it.

The next course was roast lamb, which she abhorred. She tried not to guess which spring lamb had been sacrificed as she tucked bits of meat into her napkin to sneak to the hounds later.

None of the subsequent courses appealed to her. Not the rabbit stew. Not the buttered vegetables. Not the capons. Not the cherry custard. Not the gingerbread. And even the fine French wine her father opened for the occasion turned her stomach.

She caught John's sleeve when he came to remove her untouched gingerbread. "Do we have any pickled eels left in the pantry?"

"I'll look, m'lady."

Her father chuckled. "Didn't get enough pickled eels durin' Lent?"

She gave him a sheepish smile. She supposed it was silly to crave something most of the clan was sick of, but they were the only thing that seemed worth eating.

That night, she wept again. For herself. For her husband to be. For Hew, whom she'd lost, not only as a suitor, but apparently as a friend.

Her menses didn't start the next day. Or the next. Or the following week.

By the time she packed for the journey to Darragh and bid her father farewell, there was no doubt in her mind.

Her breasts were sore. Her belly was troubled. And she had an unnatural craving for pickled eels and little else.

Sir Gellir of Rivenloch's bride-to-be was carrying a child. And it wasn't his.

CHAPTER 24

It was entirely Hew's fault. He saw that now.

It had taken him a long while to come to terms with that tragic truth.

At first he'd stewed in bitterness, sure everyone in the world had turned against him. Lady Carenza. Her father. His clan. His king. Even the gods.

But long days at Kildunan and a missive from Laird Deirdre had finally made him realize he had no one to blame but himself. And now, as he packed his possessions into his satchel to take leave of the monastery, he was even more certain he needed to unburden his conscience.

According to Laird Deirdre's glowing missive, Hew was the one responsible for Gellir's betrothal. It was his recommendation that had condemned Carenza to this fate. He was the one whose quill had set Lady Carenza's virtues to parchment. He was the one who'd painted her as an angel. A saint. A goddess.

He could see now what he'd neglected to clarify was that he meant Carenza was the perfect bride for *him*.

Hew.

Because of his careless omission, everyone wrongly assumed Hew had made the suggestion on behalf of his cousin, Gellir. After all, Gellir was the one in the most urgent need of a Scottish wife. He was a tournament champion and the heir to Rivenloch, a more valuable and vulnerable pawn when it came to the king's designs.

And before Hew could correct that error, Gellir—who trusted Hew's judgment when it came to women—had agreed to the match. And Laird Deirdre had been eager to petition the king on her son's behalf.

But—damn his eyes—Gellir could have *any* bride.

Women tripped over themselves to catch a glimpse of the illustrious champion Sir Gellir Cameliard of Rivenloch as he rode through their town. Titled ladies begged for an introduction. Wise beldams winked slyly at him. Maidservants freely offered their favors.

Of course, to the women's eternal frustration—and fascination—Gellir took no interest in any of them. He might be a model of chivalry, but he hadn't become a champion by letting himself be distracted by female attention. Every moment he wasn't waging battle in the lists, he was training for the next tournament. He lived, ate, and breathed knightly honor.

How unjust was it then that the glory-seeking Gellir should be rewarded with such a special prize of a bride? Gellir would have been just as content with a quintain cut into the shape of a woman he could joust against. He didn't deserve Carenza.

And she didn't deserve him.

Carenza needed someone who felt things as deeply as she did. Someone who shared her desires. Who understood her heart. Who appreciated her sensitivities. Someone who wanted more than a figurehead of a lady to bear his name and raise his bairns. Someone who appreciated her for the unique person she was.

Sentenced to a lifetime with Gellir, she would languish in loneliness while her husband pursued victory after victory. That was no kind of life for a creature like Carenza, who was made of passion and empathy and sacrifice.

Sacrifice.

Of course.

That explained her rejection that night. Her nonchalance. Her calm. The ease with which she'd accepted the king's decree.

Like all his past lovers, he'd assumed she'd grown weary of him or had never been as deeply in love with him as he was with her.

But now he could see clearly.

She'd thrust Hew away from her to preserve his honor. Masked her own broken heart to save his feelings. In the same way she hid her sorrow and ire and grief from her father, she'd tried to protect Hew from her distress at the betrothal. She'd pretended to be amenable to the terms. Sacrificed herself to please those she cared about. Her father. And Hew.

He'd decided he couldn't let her do that.

So he'd taken the honey to Dunlop.

Hoping for a chance to speak with her. To get to the truth of her heart.

What he would do with that truth, he wasn't sure.

Perhaps they would still part, but on better terms.

Perhaps she would assure him she'd weighed all options and made peace with this one.

Perhaps she'd beg him to speak to Laird Deirdre and alter the terms of the marriage.

He didn't rule out stealing her from Dunlop and carrying her off to be his bride. It was probably what Highlanders would expect from a warrior with Viking blood.

But he'd been too late. She was gone.

Now, if he wanted to ensure Carenza was content with her choice, he had to journey to Darragh and confront her in front of the man she was supposed to wed.

It was a daunting prospect. Not only would Gellir be there to argue his claim—and once he laid eyes on

Carenza, he'd not give her up lightly. But his fierce cousin Feiyan and her warriors would likely back up Gellir's claim to her. With weaponry.

Even worse, according to Laird Deirdre, they were to be married shortly after Beltane. The nobles of Rivenloch would be in attendance. They too would be fully armed.

As for Hew, he didn't even have his trusty axe anymore.

Nay, it would be far better to visit her by stealth. To choose a time when he could slip in to the castle unnoticed. Which was why he planned to travel to Darragh over the next several days and seek lodging in the village nearby until Beltane.

On Beltane eve, the gates of the castle would be flung open. Clanfolk bearing great torches would roam the hills with lowing coos. Wild bonfires would light up the night sky. The glens would be filled with drunken revelry. And no one would take note of a cloaked stranger traveling on the road to Darragh.

Carenza sighed as she climbed back under the bedlinens and eased her aching head onto the bolster.

More than anything, she hated to be a disappointment.

Her betrothed, Sir Gellir Cameliard of Rivenloch, deserved better.

She'd been so sick since her arrival at Darragh, she'd spent several days in her bedchamber, making frequent use of the garderobe.

It was bad enough that Gellir must think her an invalid. But she was made even more ill with guilt and shame, knowing she was sick with another man's bairn.

She'd seen her betrothed only a few times. He was classically handsome. Tall. Fit. Muscular. Striking enough that the young lasses of Darragh squealed behind their hands when he passed.

But he had a dark mane of rich brown. So he looked nothing like his Viking-blond cousin. Which would be troubling if she bore a fair-haired bairn.

Gellir's character had been mostly what she expected. He was serious. Noble. Polite. Obsessed with knighthood.

But he had a few unfortunate flaws. By his dour expression, she learned quickly why he was called Grim Gellir. The first time they'd met, he'd smelled of fish and didn't care what anyone thought about that. Now that he was off the tournament circuit, he seemed bored and restless. And she'd seen him squash a spider with his thumb.

Because she seldom saw him, she relied upon her maidservant at Darragh, a cheery, auburn-haired lass named Merraid, to tell her about her bridegroom-to-be. Merraid quickly became her close confidant, bringing her news and pickled eels and steaming baths.

Merraid waxed poetic when it came to Gellir. It was clear she bore great affection for the man, whom she'd known since she was a wee lass. Her stories gave Carenza some reassurance.

But the grave secret Carenza harbored gnawed at her conscience. And the more heroic Merraid made Gellir sound, the worse she felt about that secret.

Carenza soon discovered her delicate condition left her with raw emotions and a penchant for expressing them. One day she blurted out an awful confession to Merraid—that though she vowed to be faithful in body to her husband, her heart would always belong to another.

Kindhearted Merraid never judged her for that. But she *was* disappointed. And thereafter, the maidservant took it upon herself to kindle the romance between Carenza and Gellir.

As it turned out, Gellir was quite a poet. Though he didn't see her often, nearly every day he sent heartfelt verse. Lavish praises of Carenza's beauty. Humble declarations of his love. Effusive affirmations of his desire for her.

But in her vulnerable state, they only made Carenza feel worse. More cruel. More dishonest. More unworthy.

A disappointment.

She feared she was going to disappoint Gellir yet again tonight.

It was Beltane. And she felt miserable.

Normally, Carenza loved the holiday. Beltane was a season of rebirth and new hope. At Dunlop, she'd adorn the coos and sheep with hawthorn blossoms, deck the doorways and sills with gorse, and leave small pools of milk near rowan trees to appease the faeries.

It was a time for revelry and mischief. The clanfolk drank too much. Lasses flirted shamelessly, and lads showed off, leaping over the twin bonfires. Even the animals felt frisky. There was always a surge of bairns born in the months after Beltane—both beast and human.

But Carenza couldn't bring herself to celebrate. Beltane did not represent promise or renewal for her. Her new beginning was going to have a sinister start. She was going to be married in a matter of days to a kind and honorable man from whom she was keeping the most terrible of secrets.

She had good reason to conceal the truth. She meant to do what was best for Gellir, for Hew, for the whole Rivenloch clan, for her father, for her clan, for the bairn, and aye, even for the king himself. The only person for whom it was not best was her.

Still, it was a wretched way to start a marriage—with a lie.

Merraid poked her head in. "Are ye comin' to see the bonfires, m'lady?" Her eyes danced with pleasure, and Carenza wished she could join in the maidservant's delight.

"Nay, I think not."

"Are ye not feelin' well?"

"I'm sure I'll feel better on the morrow."

It was the lie she'd been telling for a sennight now. The truth was she didn't have the stamina to wear her usual mask of sunny disposition over her pervasive melancholy. And it was easier to claim she felt physically ill.

"Sir Gellir will miss ye at the bonfire," Merraid said, clucking her tongue.

"Ye can give him my apologies."

"I won't leave ye here alone, m'lady. Not on Beltane."

"Nonsense. I'll be fine. Ye go on and enjoy the festivities for me."

Merraid's eyes lit up. "Are ye sure?"

Carenza thought at least one of them should have fun this eve. "Och aye. Go on."

Merraid nodded to the hearth. "Ye'll want to douse your fire soon, so they can light the bonfire."

"Ye can douse it now if ye like."

"Ye won't grow too cold?"

She shook her head. In a few hours, someone would return with a brand from the Beltane bonfire to ignite her hearth, in the hopes of ensuring a fortuitous new beginning to the season. Until then, she should probably get used to the chill. After all, it was no colder than her icy heart.

Hunched over in a ragged cloak and without his famous axe, Hew found it ridiculously easy to blend in with the clanfolk at Darragh. He supposed that was the difference between living in the neighborly Highlands and on the border at Rivenloch, where one kept the gates locked against strangers.

Everyone was so preoccupied throughout the day with picking flowers and stacking firewood, decorating doorways

LAIRD OF FLINT

and gulping down ale, he was able to slip through the crowd without drawing attention.

Neither his cousin Feiyan, her husband Dougal, nor his cousin Gellir spotted him as he wandered the bustling courtyard at twilight. The Darragh clanfolk he hadn't seen in years, though he recognized one red-haired beauty, Merraid. Four years ago at the battle of Darragh, she'd been the brave wee lass who'd followed Gellir about like an orphaned pup.

Watching Merraid's comings and goings, he discovered she'd been assigned to Lady Carenza as her personal maidservant. But it appeared Carenza rarely left her bedchamber.

And now, at this late hour, when the bonfires were ready to be lit, the keep was nearly deserted, and Merraid disappeared upstairs, he figured Carenza must have decided to forego the festivities altogether.

He sighed from the shadows of the darkened hall. It seemed he'd come all this way for nothing. He was never going to get a better opportunity to speak with Carenza. And after tonight, she'd never be alone.

He had just pushed off the wall when he saw the glow of candlelight coming from the stairwell. Fading back, he watched the flicker dance into view.

Merraid emerged from the stairwell. She was by herself. She passed by without seeing him. And she seemed intent on exiting the great hall as soon as possible to join the others.

As the door closed behind her, Hew shifted his focus to the stairwell.

He took the spiral steps two by two.

He knew as soon as he tried the door that he had the right chamber. The soft floral scent that wafted out of the lightless room was all hers.

"Who's there?" she called out.

He wasn't sure what to say. If he told her who he was, would she sob with joy? Or scream for help?

"A friend," he mumbled.

She gasped. He heard rustling from the bed. "Hew?"

He frowned. How had she recognized his voice? Even his cousins had no idea he was among them.

"Is it ye?" she breathed.

He closed the door behind him. "Aye."

"Och, Hew." They were only two words. But into them was poured a deluge of emotion. Grief. Hope. Sorrow. Relief. Misery. Gratitude. Heartbreak.

Despite his intentions to remain aloof, to work things out logically, to have a calm conversation, his heart immediately went out to her.

He rushed to the bed, groping his way along the coverlet in the dark until she threw herself into his arms.

For a long while they said nothing.

She wept against his shoulder.

He cradled her head, growing more and more determined with every pitiful tear to play the hero and steal her away—his cousin, his clan, his king be damned.

Curse his cousin! How could Grim Gellir have made his sweet and precious Carenza so miserable? God's eyes! He hadn't even wed her yet.

Hew ground his teeth. He should never have let her go. Never have let her out of his sight.

Until now, Carenza had been able to conceal the strongest of her feelings. Aside from a few slipped confidences to Merraid, she'd bottled up her sorrow, her frustration, her heartbreak, her despair. And labeled them as sickness.

But now, in the arms of the one at the root of all those emotions, she collapsed into a puddle of raw emotion. All the heartsickness she'd hidden spilled out in its purest form as Hew held her. She no longer felt alone. She felt heard. Seen. Understood.

She didn't know exactly when the change happened. But in one moment she was raining tears upon his throat. And in the next she was lapping them up with tender kisses. The fists she'd clenched so desperately in his plaid found their way around his neck. Her hitching sobs became gasps of awe and need and urgency.

And then he began to respond.

With a low growl like a hungering wolf, he feasted on her again and again, savaging the tender flesh of her throat. His hands clasped and squeezed and caressed her, brushing aside linen to graze her bare skin. He tumbled her onto her back and fumbled beneath her leine, slipping his fingers up her thigh, closer and closer to where she wanted him most.

She couldn't wait. If she waited, she'd start thinking. If she started thinking, she'd hesitate. If she hesitated, she'd begin to regret. And she wanted to regret nothing.

So she took the reins. She scrabbled at his clothes in such a wild frenzy, he had no choice but to tear them off. She buried her face in his delicious flesh, kissing his chest, bathing his stomach, nuzzling lower.

He groaned and rolled her beneath him. Then, with a whisper of "I'll love you fore'er, Carenza," he sank deep inside her, sheathing his hungry cock and filling her thirsting womb.

It felt like coming home. Like he belonged inside her. Like this was right.

When they moved together, it was natural and perfect.

And when they gathered speed, it was with the grace and power of a falcon, its wings beating faster and faster, thrumming against the forces of nature to defy the pull of the earth and fly high into the heavens.

They dove together as well. He grunted, and she gasped

out a shrill cry of need before they dropped from the sky, shivering and circling and settling into a downy nest of release.

Their breath mingled and swirled as they clung to each other in the dark.

Carenza was afraid to speak. She wanted to preserve this moment just as it was. A moment where she would forever be with the man she loved. Where they had just experienced sublime happiness. Where it was their precious child growing inside her. Where the future was bright.

But Hew ruined that in four words.

"Come away with me."

Those four words brought the truth crashing down on her.

What they'd just done was not a divine act of love. It was practically adultery.

She withdrew from him, and it felt as if a chill wind instantly rushed in to separate them. A wind composed of remorse and disgrace, of horror and shame.

"I cannot," she said.

"We can leave tonight. This moment."

He made it sound so tempting. So simple.

But she knew it wasn't.

"I can't."

"Do you love him?" he asked.

"Gellir?"

"Aye."

"Nay," she admitted. "But he's a good man. I shall be content enough."

"God's eyes," he bit out. "You deserve happiness, Carenza. Do you not know that? You deserve a man you love with all your heart. Who loves you with every ounce of his being. Who will live for you. Fight for you. Die for you."

His words were like salt in her wounds, for she knew he

believed that was true. But she also knew it was not true for her. If a nobleman was the king's pawn, a noble*woman* was that pawn's slave. By royal decree, she belonged to Gellir. To defy that would bring dishonor to everyone she cared for.

"Even if 'tisn't me," he said quietly, "you deserve to be with a man you love."

Her heart cracked at that. She loved no one but Hew. But she couldn't tell him that. She couldn't enslave his heart in that way. She had to let him go. Give him permission to move on and find a wife of his own.

"I can't," she said.

When he would have argued, she seized his forearm to silence him.

"I can't," she insisted, "because I'm with child."

Hew's heart started racing. It shouldn't have been racing.

"You are?"

"Aye."

"Ah." At least his voice was calm.

But he was particularly grateful for the dark. It hid his ridiculous grin and the tears that were inexplicably filling his eyes. All at once, simultaneously overjoyed and distraught, he couldn't get words past the lump in his throat.

"I have to wed as soon as possible," she told him. "This child cannot be born a bastard. 'Twill already be early. I dare wait no longer."

He couldn't stop smiling over the idea that their love had made a bairn.

Or weeping over the fact he wouldn't be allowed to claim the child.

Unless...

"Who else knows?" he asked.

"No one. But I won't lie to Gellir."

Hew understood that. A marriage couldn't begin with deceit. "You won't have to."

Hew knew something about Gellir that Carenza didn't.

More than anything, his cousin was a man of morals. Without principles, without virtue, he was nothing. He would rather die than sacrifice his honor.

Even if she tried to hide it, Gellir would never be fooled into believing the bairn was his. He'd always know the child was not his true heir. He'd always know his bride had not come to his bed a virgin. While chivalry might prevent Gellir from interrogating Carenza, that knowledge would haunt him. He would be miserable in their marriage. As miserable as Carenza.

The clan would count the months. They'd assume either Gellir had planted his seed long before their marriage or Carenza had taken a lover before him.

Either assumption would be a blow to Gellir's pride. A stain on his spotless reputation. And that was something the illustrious Sir Gellir Cameliard of Rivenloch could not abide.

But Hew?

He wasn't the heir to Rivenloch.

He wasn't a tournament champion.

He wasn't a paragon of virtue.

Indeed, most people thought he was a philandering wastrel.

He had nothing to lose.

Suddenly inspired, he dug in his satchel and pulled out the wee parcel he'd been saving for months. He opened her palm, placing on it the gold ring he'd bought from the goldsmith's widow.

"Keep this until your wedding day."

"What?"

"Don't say anything to Gellir. Not yet."

"But—"

"I might have a remedy."

It took all his will not to sweep her up in his arms and bellow in triumph. But the fear that he might fail, that the odds were against him, that his efforts might be for naught, kept him from celebrating prematurely.

"Promise me," he begged. "Promise me you won't breathe a word to Gellir."

"If ye don't return before the wedding…"

He would. But he understood her reticence.

"If I don't return by your wedding day, then do as you must."

"Because I don't want him to get hurt," she explained. "Or disgraced. Or caught off-guard."

His heart melted. Carenza was so kindhearted and considerate. She'd already admitted she didn't love Gellir. Yet she was compassionate enough to want to keep him from harm.

"Don't worry," he said. "I'll look after him."

Gellir would be grateful to be spared the humiliation.

Hew wished he could linger at Darragh. With the Beltane fires burning outside, he and Carenza had the castle all to themselves. He yearned to make love to her again. To feel their hearts beat together. To let their moans mingle on the air. To run his hands over her belly, imagining the new life growing inside her.

But there was much to do.

CHAPTER 25

When the day of the wedding arrived, and Carenza still hadn't heard from Hew, she feared his plan had failed.

She still couldn't tell Gellir her secret. Not quite yet. Not while he could call off the marriage in disgust and leave her to bear a bastard.

She'd tell him tonight. After they retired to their bedchamber. And before they consummated the marriage. That was the only right thing to do.

But first, unable to endure the pressure of her guilt a moment longer, she decided she had to reveal the tragic truth to Merraid. That Carenza was pregnant by her lover.

The maidservant was understandably mortified. To Merraid, Sir Gellir had always been the perfect hero. Gallant, courteous, brave. He even wrote romantic verse. She couldn't comprehend how Carenza's heart could belong to anyone else.

She begged Carenza not to ruin his wedding night by breaking his heart.

Carenza argued that it was far worse for her to swive her bridegroom without telling him she was carrying another man's bairn. Indeed, it was because Gellir had been so sweet and patient with her, writing her verse that had been honest and kind, that she couldn't imagine deceiving him, even for a day.

Merraid suggested Carenza could perhaps delay the wedding night until they made the journey to Rivenloch. She could claim a few more days of illness. That way she and Gellir would have time to get to know each other—and perhaps fall in love—before she disclosed her secret.

It seemed a reasonable compromise, until Carenza realized she would be alone with Gellir. Merraid was not returning with them. How could Carenza break such devastating news to Gellir without his old friend Merraid nearby to soften the blow and soothe his broken heart?

It took some persuading. But the maidservant reluctantly agreed to come with her to Rivenloch, at least for a fortnight or so.

Then, resigned to her fate, Carenza picked up her mirror and began pinning pearls between her tiny looped braids. No matter how fraught she was with despair, she had to keep up appearances. She must look like a radiant and happy bride. The Rivenloch and Dunlop clans had already arrived.

Someone scratched at the door.

She checked her reflection, practicing a brilliant smile, one that would please her father.

Then she answered the door.

It wasn't her father.

It was a nun.

She dropped her smile. What was a nun doing here? Had she sensed Carenza's sin? Had she come to take her confession?

The nun gave her a perfunctory perusal from head to toe. "Lady Carenza?"

"Aye."

To Carenza's surprise, the nun pushed her way into the

chamber and shut the door behind her. She scoured the room.

"Ye have things?"

"Things?"

"Items ye wish to take?"

"Take?" Carenza asked. "Take where? Who are ye?"

"Sister Eve." She gave Carenza a decidedly saucy smile. The combination of her fresh face and the twinkle in her brown eyes made her look more like a courtesan than a nun.

Apparently, she expected Carenza to recognize her name. Could she be a Rivenloch clan member Carenza had forgotten to memorize?

Before Carenza could inquire further, Sister Eve rolled her eyes in self-disgust. "Och, Eve! Ye'd forget your own wimple if 'tweren't attached to your habit. I meant to say I've come from Sir Hew."

Carenza gasped, pressing a hand to her bosom. "Hew?"

"Aye. He bids ye come with me. We must make all haste." She glanced around the chamber once more. "If ye don't have any things..."

"Take me to him." What did things matter when the man she loved was waiting?

"Hold on. I've got somethin' for ye."

To Carenza's astonishment, Sister Eve reached under her habit, fiddled with some ties, and pulled out another habit. She tossed it onto the bed.

"Put this on."

The nun wandered to the window and peered through the crack in the shutters.

Carenza hesitated. A disguise? This seemed altogether too rash and mad and dangerous. She gulped.

"Where are we goin'?" she asked.

"Why, back to the nunnery, o' course." The nun turned and gave her an amused wink.

Carenza bit her lip. Running away. Was she sure she wanted to do that? Desert her bridegroom? And her clan? Risk everything on...

"Come." Sister Eve gestured her over with a wave of her hand. "Look."

Carenza joined her at the window and peered through the crack of the shutters. The Rivenloch clan was gathered in the courtyard. The men were bold and imposing. The warrior maids were impressive and intimidating. Seeing them made the breath stop in her chest. Was she sure she wanted to make foes of them?

Then her gaze landed on the Rivenloch man Eve was trying to point out.

It was Hew. He looked amazing. Dressed in resplendent attire for the wedding, with his hair pulled back into a formal braid, he might have been a Viking king.

He was mingling with the rest of his clan. But as she watched him, he crossed his arms and casually lifted his eyes to her window.

Her breath caught. Maybe he couldn't see her. But he knew she was there, watching.

He gave a subtle nod of his head.

"That's our signal," Eve said. "Hurry now and dress."

Her mind was made up. Aye, she *would* risk everything on the man she loved. She hastily donned the drab habit, hiding her meticulously plaited tresses under the ash-colored veil and leaving her intricately embroidered wedding gown in a pool on the floor.

Eve scooped up the gown, folding and concealing it under her own habit.

"We're to leave no evidence," she explained, though Carenza wondered if "Sister Eve" meant to keep the garment.

"Are you even a real nun?" she asked.

Eve pretended affront, but then admitted, "Sometimes."

Carenza felt a shiver of misgiving. Should she trust the lass? But then she remembered she herself had once feigned to be a cateran. She let out an uneasy sigh and straightened her spine. "I'm ready." Then she reconsidered. "Wait."

She went to the small wooden chest where she kept the ring Hew had given her and the verses from Gellir. She slipped the ring on her finger. She didn't have the heart to burn the pages. But she dared not leave them behind. She stuffed them down the top of her habit.

"All right."

They didn't dare interact with Hew for fear of drawing attention. Eve said he would meet them later at the convent. Still, it surprised Carenza how easily she could pass through the halls of Darragh as one of a pair of nuns. Clothed in dull colors, with her head covered and bowed, she moved through the crowded courtyard almost invisibly. And with all the flurry of preparations for the wedding, their departure out the gates of the castle was scarcely noted.

The journey south was taxing. Though her reasons for fleeing were noble, Carenza was all too aware that defying the king's will was treason.

But when she'd seen Hew's face, when she'd tried to imagine a life without him, she knew she had to take a leap of faith.

Now she'd leaped too far to turn back.

Riding away from Darragh through the woods on a stolen horse, Hew questioned whether he was doing the right thing.

He'd arrived for the wedding just this morn with the rest of the Rivenloch clan. But he'd begun plotting the daring escape days before then.

He'd secretly enlisted the services of an old acquaintance, Sister Eve.

Sister Eve was a nun with whom he'd accidentally—and temporarily—fallen in love years ago. Despite their mishap, they had remained friends. And though she was a less-than-devoted nun whose abbess had a hard time containing her within convent walls, when Eve put her mind to something, especially when there was adventure to be had, she was highly reliable and good at what she did.

It seemed as if all was going to plan. Sister Eve had replied to his signal. She would slip out of the castle with Carenza, and they would flee to her convent. Once the two of them were safely away—but before Gellir noticed his bride was gone—Hew would ride out after them.

But while procuring weapons for the journey from Darragh's armory, Hew had been waylaid by Gellir, who was already looking for Carenza. Anxious about his missing bride, Gellir was eager to alert both clans so a wider search could be started.

That was the last thing Hew needed. So he begged Gellir not to tell anyone just yet. He explained that the laird of Dunlop would go mad if he thought he'd lost his daughter, having already lost his wife. He said there was no need to panic the clans. Hew would volunteer to ride out and look for her quietly himself.

His cousin, however, was stubborn and principled. Gellir deemed it was his fault his bride had run away. Therefore it was his responsibility to recover her.

In the end, since Gellir refused to take nay for an answer, Hew had to resort to brute force. He imprisoned his cousin in the armory.

Gellir was naturally furious.

Hew understood. He felt sorry for him. But he wasn't about to let him go.

So he assuaged his cousin with a partial truth. He gently explained that Carenza was in love with someone else. He told Gellir he meant to reunite her with her lover. And in the meantime, he pledged to keep her safe.

Gellir, however, sternly reminded Hew he was not only aiding a runaway bride. He was defying the king.

Hew didn't need reminding. The idea already chilled his blood.

But despite all his misgivings, at that instant, Hew felt he was doing the right thing. He recited the Rivenloch motto back to Gellir. *Amor vincit omnia.* Love conquers all.

He doubted Gellir or anyone else would see things his way. But Hew's intentions were honorable. Carenza needed to have a father for her bairn, and she deserved to have a husband she genuinely loved. Gellir needed a wife who wouldn't mar his impeccable character, and he deserved to have a firstborn that actually belonged to him.

As for Hew, he cared little about his reputation. He wasn't important enough in the Rivenloch clan to worry about a fall from grace. As long as he could live with the woman he loved and be a father to their child, he would stay inconspicuous until the king's wrath blew over.

Still, when he thought about defying the will of two famously powerful clans—Rivenloch and Dunlop, absconding with the bride of the tournament champion of all Scotland, and disobeying the king's orders, he wondered if he'd brought enough weapons.

Carenza paid little heed to her traveling companion as they tramped along the rocky southern road. Sister Eve seemed awfully chatty for a nun, especially considering their perilous circumstances. She was going on and on about her sundry adventures, which seemed like more than one could squeeze into a lifetime.

As for Carenza, she was too nervous for conversation.

Sister Eve's gift of prattle and unruffled demeanor, however, were a blessing a few hours into their trek. A trio of Rivenloch men rode past, asking about a runaway bride. Eve did all the talking, pretending to give their questions long and thoughtful consideration, until they gave up and rode on.

From then on, Carenza had new respect for the woman. She wished she'd listened more closely to the young nun's colorful stories.

Indeed, she had to admit she was rather surprised when, a few hours before nightfall, they arrived at an actual convent.

"Sister Eve." The abbess looked weary, as if she'd been worn to a shadow. "What a lovely surprise."

"I told ye I'd be back. This is my cousin, Sister Agnes," she said without flinching, indicating Carenza. "She'll be stayin' with me for a wee bit."

The abbess actually looked pleased to see Carenza. "Welcome, Sister. I'm glad to see Sister Eve has kin for company. Someone to keep her on the straight and narrow path."

Carenza felt sick. She was hardly the one to keep anybody honest. Now she was defying royalty *and* deceiving the church. Nonetheless, she managed a weak smile.

Eve rubbed her hands together. "We're starvin'. Is Sister Eithne makin' her famed leek pottage this eve?"

Sister Eithne *was* making her pottage. Carenza was so hungry, it tasted as good as her favorite roast salmon. Fortunately, her hunger and Eve's chattiness prevented "Sister Agnes" from having to answer awkward questions. The nuns conversed in hushed tones around her, and soon Carenza grew sleepy.

Her eyes had almost drifted shut when Eve clamped her thigh under the table, bringing her awake again.

"Your pardon, Abbess," Eve said, "but Sister Agnes and I have had a long journey. We can scarcely stay awake. May we retire?"

The abbess gave her a pointed glare. "Will ye join us for matins?"

"Ne'er fear," Eve said. "My cousin has insisted upon it."

The abbess gave Carenza a smug grin. "Good."

As far as Carenza knew, Eve kept her promise.

Carenza, however, did not.

Well before matins, while it was still dark, Hew arrived at the convent on horseback.

Carenza could scarcely contain her relief and joy. How she'd yearned to fall into his arms. To feel his heart pumping with hers. And how she'd feared this day would never come. They embraced wordlessly, letting their eyes and hands and lips convey their longing.

"Och, ye two," Sister Eve admonished in a whisper. "Save it for after the weddin'."

Hew withdrew from their kiss. "How can I thank you enough, Eve?"

"Just give this wee one a proper da." She ambled close enough to place a tender palm atop Carenza's belly.

"I will," he promised.

Eve gave him a scrap of parchment. Then she handed Carenza's wedding dress, neatly folded, to her.

Hew read the parchment. "This is the place? In Mauchline?"

"Aye. I've told the father to expect ye in the morn." She winked at Carenza. "He'll marry ye then."

"On the morrow?" Carenza asked.

Her first thought was that wasn't enough time.

After all, she was Lady Carenza of Dunlop, daughter of the laird. She was representing the Dunlop clan. She had to look her best.

"The sooner, the better," Hew said, gazing down at her with love.

She squirmed. She wore a nun's gray tunic and a grayer scapular that was stained with leek pottage. Her once freshly bathed feet were caked with dirt. The pearls she'd pinned so carefully into her hair were lost. What remained of her braids had escaped her wimple in haphazard coils and springs.

Yet she knew he saw none of it.

He saw her shining eyes. Her gleeful grin. He saw The One he wanted to make his wife. The mother of his children.

And she knew in her heart of hearts that she would never be more beautiful to him than she was right now.

She gave him a smile so full of love, there was room for nothing else.

"What are we waitin' for?"

CHAPTER 26

Summer

Carenza cast a last handful of grain to the three hens scratching in front of the byre she'd begun to think of as home.

Nearby, Hew sat on a stump, weaving wattle by the morning light, making more panels to protect them from the elements.

In a way, it *was* home. This was the sagging byre with rotten timbers and a mossy roof where she and Hew had come long ago during the thunderstorm. The unexpected shelter at the edge of a forgotten jewel of a glen in the middle of the lush Dunlop woods. They'd made it their love nest that day.

Now it was a temporary refuge.

Remote enough to ensure their safety.

Close enough to her father's castle if anything should go wrong.

It also served once more as a cozy trysting place when, as Hew liked to jest, they wished to "relive their carefree youth."

In the several weeks since they'd hidden here, they'd swept out the byre and repaired the gaps with rough woven wattle, covering it all with camouflaging branches. They'd furnished their makeshift cottage with stumps and reed mats. Made a soft pallet of moss. Built shelves for the hens to roost in at night and hung fragrant herbs to dry in the corners.

Every day, Carenza collected the hens' eggs, picked greens and berries from the forest, and fished for trout in the nearby stream. When they needed other supplies, Hew crept out at night to the homes of nearby crofters, leaving behind ample coin for the clothing, food, and tools he gleaned. He'd brought home embroidery thread, and Carenza had embroidered the leine she'd promised him with flames around the wrists.

She'd never imagined she could be so happy, living in rags in a ruined byre. But after the father married them, she would have followed Hew anywhere. And the fact he'd led her back to a familiar place where she'd be close to her clan—and the animals she loved—meant the world to her.

They still had to conceal their whereabouts, of course. After Hew left Darragh, he'd immediately written—to the Rivenloch clan, to Gellir, to her father—assuring everyone Carenza was safe and telling them she'd been happily reunited with her lover.

But no one knew the identity of that lover. Hew's whereabouts were unknown, and by all accounts, he'd still broken the law. Any of the parties, including the parents and the king, might reasonably demand satisfaction and exact retribution for Hew's devilry.

So they hid together in the least likely place. Right under her father's nose.

Despite their proximity to Dunlop, clan news was hard to come by since they couldn't interact with anyone. Everyone knew Carenza, so she didn't dare stray from the byre. And a warrior of Hew's size would be memorable, even in disguise, so he had to keep to the shadows.

It was hard not to grow impatient for the end of their exile. But they had to wait until Sister Eve arrived. She was the only person who knew where they were. The only person who could let them know when it was safe for them to emerge.

"Do ye expect we'll hear from the sister soon?" Carenza asked, dusting the grain from her hands and rubbing a palm absently over her swelling belly.

"I hope so," Hew said as he twisted the branches together. "'Tis been weeks."

"Maybe she lost her way." The byre *was* quite secluded.

"I doubt it. Sister Eve could find her way out of a labyrinth."

"Ye don't think somethin' bad has—"

Their conversation was cut short by a distant rustling from the woods, growing closer.

They responded with practiced haste.

Hew knocked over the stump, sheathed his knife, and shoved the wattle panel into a gap in the byre.

Carenza spread the grain about with her foot, startling the hens, and unhooked the pair of fresh trout she'd strung up at the entrance of the byre.

The brush-rattling grew louder.

With a swift glance to be sure they'd retrieved everything, they ducked in to the byre. Carenza slid the wattle panel across the doorway. Hew pulled down the concealing branches.

Then they waited.

Carenza held her breath as the tramping abruptly stopped.

Someone hissed loudly from across the glen. "Psst! Hew!"

Hew peered through the gap in the wattle.

"'Tis her," he whispered, sliding back the door panel.

Carenza hardly recognized the nun as she came racing breathlessly across the glen.

She wasn't wearing her habit. Instead, she wore a rather sumptuous gown of crimson velvet, as fine as any Carenza had ever owned.

Her chestnut hair was long and loose and lush, hardly a short-cropped holy tonsure.

And nothing of the calm, cool, collected nun was visible in her manner as she charged toward the byre.

"I...don't have...much time..." she panted as she slid to a halt, scattering hens in her wake.

Not much time? She hadn't seen Sister Eve since the night they'd left the convent. And Carenza had so many questions. Not only about what had happened to Sister Eve's habit, but...everything.

What had become of Gellir? And her father? And the maidservant Merraid?

Had the Rivenloch clan returned home?

What was the disposition of the king?

Was it safe to leave the byre now?

Sister Eve was the only one who could tell them.

Eve glanced nervously over her shoulder. "May I come inside?"

Carenza welcomed her in.

Eve perused the interior and gave an impressed whistle. "Not bad."

Carenza smiled. It might not be a castle. But it was far nicer than any rotting byre deserved to be.

Hew dragged up tree stumps for the ladies and poured a cup of water for Eve, who was still casting an occasional glance toward the covered doorway.

"Were you followed?" he asked.

She shook her head and took a sip of water. "Not by anyone lookin' for *ye*."

Carenza wondered who would be pursuing a nun. Maybe the abbess?

"Ye seem hale," Eve noted with a twinkle in her eye,

swiftly changing the subject. "Motherhood looks good on ye."

Carenza blushed. She was still getting accustomed to this new and fascinating Sister Eve.

Eve drained the cup and handed it back to Hew.

"First things first." Eve came to her feet, arching a brow at Carenza. "I don't suppose ye have that habit I loaned ye?"

"The nun's habit?" Carenza said. "I do. 'Tis right where I packed it that night."

She went to the satchel that slouched beside the hens' roost and pulled out the folded bundle of gray linen. But when she handed it to Eve, several pieces of parchment slipped out, scattering on the ground.

Her breath caught. She'd forgotten all about Gellir's verses. She certainly hadn't meant for Hew to ever see them. She hadn't even meant to keep them. She'd only meant to remove all the incriminating evidence from Darragh.

Mortified, she blushed as she hurriedly scooped them up.

"What are those?" Hew asked.

Eve immediately sensed her discomfiture. "Och, those are likely mine. I'm always tuckin' scripture into my habits." She held out her hand to take the pages from Carenza.

Carenza shot her a glance of gratitude.

"Do ye mind if I change while we talk?" Eve asked.

Hew, whose patience would soon run thin, glowered. "Fine. I just need news from home." He turned his back so she could undress. "Gellir got my message after the wedding, aye? He knows I took the fall for Carenza's disappearance? He knows he's free from blame, right?"

"Och, 'twasn't so simple as that," she said, untying the silk rope girdle around her hips. "It seems ye and Gellir had the same plan."

"What?" Hew barked. "What did he do?"

"He ran off and left a missive sayin' 'twas *he* who broke off the betrothal with Carenza."

Carenza gasped. Why would he do that?

"He claimed he wasn't ready to take a wife," Eve continued as she pulled the velvet surcoat over her head. "He said he wished to sow his oats a while longer."

Hew grunted in disbelief.

She tossed the surcoat across the stump, which unfortunately scattered the pages again.

So Carenza hastily gathered them up once more. All but one. One of them landed at Hew's feet.

He picked it up and looked at the page.

She froze.

Not noticing, Eve carried on, changing out of her crisp white leine into the drab nun's garment. "He said when Carenza ran away in tears, he sent Sir Hew to retrieve her."

"What?" Hew snapped, momentarily distracted from the page.

"He took the blame," Eve said, "and made ye the hero."

"But that's not right," Hew insisted. "I was to take the blame. To make *him* the hero."

"I see." Carenza spoke the sad truth. "Gellir tried to save our honor."

"Wait, both o' ye," Eve said. "Ye've not heard the whole story."

Hew didn't know if he wanted to hear any more. How could things have gone so horribly wrong? Hew was supposed to have preserved Gellir's reputation. But now Gellir had destroyed his own good name, just to save Hew from blame. Bloody hell. Sometimes his cousin's sense of chivalry and self-sacrifice was excruciating.

"Meanwhile," Eve continued, donning her scapular, "the king has returned to Perth."

Hew straightened. "The king?" That could mean more trouble. While the king was in Toulouse, Hew was relatively safe. But if he'd already landed on Scottish soil...

Eve nodded. "O' course, some o' the lairds were not so ready to welcome Malcolm." That was likely an understatement. The lairds had been at odds with Malcolm since his friendship with the English king. "So there was a siege."

"A siege at Perth?"

"Aye," she said. "And your brave cousin?"

Hew shuddered. If he knew Gellir... "Tell me he didn't join the fighting."

"He did." She placed the veil over her head, tucking her hair under the edges of the cloth. "He couldn't leave the king undefended."

Hew let out a sigh. "Shite."

The last thing his cousin should have risked was getting caught in the battle between his king and his countrymen. But of course that's exactly what Gellir had done.

"I hope he's all right," Carenza said plaintively.

Hew heard the concern in her voice.

Though she'd been Gellir's betrothed, Carenza claimed she'd never been in love with Gellir. She said he was good and kind, noble and valiant. But he wondered. Did she regret leaving him now? Now that they were forced to hide in a dark, dank cavern of a byre without proper food or clothing or even a marriage bed? Did she ever wish she'd wed Gellir instead of him?

He glanced again at the page. It appeared to be some sort of verse. Love verse. What would a nun be doing with love verse?

"What *is* this?" he asked, holding it aloft.

"I told ye—" Eve began.

"Nay!" Carenza interjected. Her voice wavered as she said, "I can't lie to him, Sister." She came to him then and placed a hand on his forearm. "I can't lie to ye, Hew." She lowered her eyes, looking as if she was begging for forgiveness. His heart sank as he wondered what terrible sin she'd committed.

"That is verse that Gellir wrote for me when we were courtin'," she said. "It means naught to me. I swear it. I only took it from the castle so there would be no written record of his humiliation. No evidence left to shame him. And I didn't have the heart to burn such earnest and clever verse."

"Gellir?" Hew blinked. Clever verse? From his cousin? The idea was ludicrous. He snickered.

That reaction was clearly the wrong one. Carenza looked shocked and appalled.

He explained. "I hate to disappoint you, but these are not Gellir's words."

"What? O' course they are."

"Nay." He was sure of it. "My cousin has no talent for verse."

"Is this not his hand?"

"Maybe. But they're not his words."

"But he sent them to me," she said.

"Through a servant?"

"Aye, but..." She looked uncertain. "If he didn't send them, who did?"

From behind them, Eve let out a charmed giggle that made them both turn around. Thankfully she was fully dressed. "I think I may know." She skimmed the other pages, nodding as if verifying her theory. "By the way," she said, casually fluttering her hand, "Gellir is fine. *More* than fine." She looked up from the pages. "Ye see, at the siege, Gellir had an unlikely rescuer. A warrior maid."

"His sister Feiyan?" Hew guessed. "Laird Deirdre?"

Eve grinned. "His maidservant."

Carenza's jaw dropped in wonder. "Not Merraid?"

"Och aye. The wee lass not only fought at Gellir's back, she earned the respect o' King Malcolm himself." Eve began bundling up her discarded clothing. "The king gave her an audience, and somehow, with the help o' the Pope's emissary, peace was brokered between the king and the lairds."

Hew furrowed his brows. What was the Pope's emissary doing in Scotland?

"But the best part?" Eve teased. "When the king wished to reward Gellir for his loyalty, Gellir asked him to bestow a knighthood upon Merraid."

Carenza gasped. "And did he?"

Eve nodded.

Hew let out a low whistle. That kind of noble gesture was the stuff of legends.

"Merraid must be elated," Carenza said. "'Tis all she's e'er wanted."

"Och, that's not *all* she's e'er wanted," Eve said. "Since Merraid had just been dubbed a noble knight, Gellir asked permission from Laird Deirdre and King Malcolm..." She paused to wiggle her brows. "To marry her."

For a moment, neither he nor Carenza could speak.

When they finally found their voices, they both spoke at once.

"Gellir and Merraid?"

"Merraid and Gellir?"

And then Hew recalled when he'd left Gellir imprisoned in the armory, he'd been shackled to the redheaded maidservant. He hadn't had time to ask why.

Eve laughed in delight. "So ye see, ye've all come to happy endin's." She ruffled the pages in her hand. "And I'd wager the alms o' St. Andrews, 'twas Merraid herself who wrote these verses on Gellir's behalf."

"A maidservant writing verse?" Hew scoffed. "And why do that if she was in love with Gellir?"

Eve shrugged. "She probably didn't think she had a chance at him herself. But if she cared for him, she wanted him to be happy."

Carenza clapped a hand to her heart and let out a sigh.

"The words *were* written from the heart," she said wistfully. "Just not for me. How difficult it must have been for Merraid to be kind to me all that time when I was betrothed to the man she loved."

Hew knew just how she felt.

"We have to save these verses," she decided. "They truly *are* wonderful. 'Twould be a shame to lose them." Then her eyes lit up as she turned to him. "Perhaps one day we can return them to Gellir and Merraid ourselves, Hew."

He felt the weight of sorrow crush his shoulders. Eve had said they'd all come to happy endings. But that wasn't quite true. He and Carenza were still fugitives.

"'Tis not yet safe for us," he said gently. "The king—"

"Och, Eve!" Eve chastised herself. "Ye left out the best part again." She clasped prayer hands under her chin and smiled. "Merraid made sure ye and Hew would be forgiven for fleein'."

Carenza and Eve cheered in celebration.

Hew furrowed his brows. "That's good news. But I'm not sure it changes much. We might be forgiven for fleeing. But fleeing isn't the same as defying our lairds and king by marrying without permission."

Sister Eve flapped her hand at him in unconcern. "I'm sure 'twill be fine. The king's a romantic, after all."

But Hew knew affairs were seldom easily solved where royal decrees were involved. At the moment, all he and Carenza had was the wedding document they'd been provided. Not even clan marks were attached to give it authority.

He didn't wish to dampen their spirits. Eve had come to his aid when he needed her most.

But he questioned how much he should rely on her judgment as to safety in matters of life and death, considering a few things he knew about the nun.

For one thing, she seemed to be Sister Eve only when it suited her.

She somehow had an endless supply of clothing and seldom wanted for coin.

For a woman on her own, she traveled fearlessly far and wide.

And he had to wonder why she'd arrived in a sumptuous velvet gown and was fleeing again in a humble nun's habit, rushing off as if the Devil were after her.

But he didn't want to ask too many questions and risk offending her.

Instead he said, "I'm sure you're right. But I'd feel safer if we had the clan seals and royal approval on the wedding decree."

Eve shrugged. "Done. Do ye have the document?"

He fetched it from his satchel.

She took the scroll, lifted up her scapular, and stuffed it down the front of her leine.

Before he could utter another word and while Carenza's jaw still hung open, Eve whirled and headed for the door.

"You're leaving already?" he asked. Her hasty departure was highly suspicious.

"Aye."

"But you're coming back?"

"O' course."

"But your gown," Carenza said.

Eve took a considerate glance at the precious garment. "Hold onto it for me, will ye?"

Then, before Carenza could even close her gaping mouth, Eve peeked out the door and slipped out, continuing on her way, scurrying rapidly across the glen.

To Hew's surprise, Carenza was first to bring up doubts about their guest.

"How well do ye know Sister Eve?" she asked.

He didn't want to tell her how close he'd come to swiving Eve when he hadn't realized she was a nun. "Not terribly well."

"Do ye trust her?"

"To be honest, not completely."

"I know, aye? Where did she get such an expensive gown?" she asked, stroking the soft velvet as if it were a pet. "There was definitely someone chasing her."

Hew nodded. "I don't think she'd hurt a fly. She doesn't have a mean bone in her body."

"And she's a nun."

"Right." Hew didn't want to have that complex discussion right now. "But I'm not sure she always has her facts right."

"I'm glad she's goin' to get the permissions." She looked up at him with creased brows, as if she didn't want to disappoint him. "I know 'tis miserable for ye, living alone in the woods with only birds and squirrels for company. But I'd rather live here with ye till I'm old and gray than come out o' hidin' too soon and risk losin' ye."

Hew's heart melted at her touching words. If she realized how much he'd enjoyed sharing this laborious but rewarding adventure with her, she wouldn't have apologized. Mostly he was relieved he didn't have to be the one to dampen their plans to return to Dunlop.

"I love it here," he said. "You know that, aye?"

Her face blossomed into a pleased smile, as sunny as the primroses blooming in the glen.

"The fresh air," he said, stepping close to caress her cheek. "The peaceful woods." He wound a lock of her beautiful chestnut hair around his callused finger.

"Sparrow song. Morning dew." He tugged gently on her curl, bringing her close. "Sleeping when we're weary," he murmured. "Waking whene'er we wish." He lowered his gaze to her delectable lips. "Trysting when the mood..."

He never finished the thought.

Carenza finished it for him.

CHAPTER 27

Summer filled the glen with meadowsweet and bluebells.

Still Sister Eve didn't return.

Twice, against Carenza's wishes, Hew had risked a visit to the village alehouse late at night, heavily cloaked and stooped to hide his size. Yet he'd learned nothing about the king's disposition or the status of the laird of Dunlop or what anyone imagined had become of that Rivenloch warrior with the axe.

Carenza wasn't surprised. The men who exchanged gossip at a village alehouse were more likely to discuss the cost of bread and which neighbor was cheating on his wife than Scottish politics and nobles' marriages.

But she didn't mind. They'd transformed the byre into a home.

Meanwhile, summer ripened slowly into autumn.

The thistles in the glen flourished and faded. Bilberries and blackberries swelled and sweetened. Squirrels and hedgepigs and foxes had litters of young. Woodland birds retired their songs and muted their colors. And the trees changed out of their green gowns into shades of gold and scarlet that fluttered off like butterflies in the blustery wind.

Carenza's body ripened as well.

At first, it was no great inconvenience.

While Hew worked from dawn to dusk, cutting peat for their cook fires, gathering berries, fishing, and fetching foodstuffs and linens, she could still care for the hens and prepare the daily pottage and oatcakes.

But now she was simply unwieldy. She could no longer see her feet. Where in summer she might have skipped across the glen to gather bunches of wild garlic, the mere thought of trudging across the wet grass to admire the last persistent purple thistle was exhausting. And she was always hot, despite the cool autumn weather.

This morn, however, when she waddled out the door, there was a strange stillness in the air and a chill that made her wrap her plaid tighter around her round belly.

Hew was already outside, scowling at the sky.

"It feels like snow," she said.

He grunted.

"'Tis early yet," she remarked.

Nonetheless, the clouds were thick and bluish-gray, and it *did* feel like they might begin sifting snowflakes onto the earth at any moment.

He turned then to look at her. And she saw his unspoken fear.

It was the same fear that had lurked in the back of her mind for weeks. The one she'd kept cloaked in denial. The one they hadn't spoken about.

She could see now it was too late. The weather had turned. They'd never make it through the snow.

By her estimation, she would birth the bairn in a few fortnights. And if the snow started falling now, it could indicate a harsh winter where it might not melt until spring.

She'd foolishly hoped Sister Eve would return within the next fortnight with the approved document, to relieve them of their fugitive status and allow them to return home.

Laird of Flint

It had been her quiet wish to have their child at Dunlop—in the castle, on her feather bed, surrounded by the ladies of the clan—while Hew and her father drank ale and paced the great hall. She'd imagined presenting the bairn to her father. Dreamed of showing off the laird's heir to the people of Dunlop.

Now that wouldn't happen.

Her child would be born in a byre.

She wouldn't have a midwife.

And they'd probably be on their own for the first several months of the bairn's life.

Still, it wasn't a completely abhorrent thought.

The Christ child had been born in a byre, after all.

Her husband could serve as a midwife. That undoubtedly frightened him more than it did her. But Carenza had delivered coos and lambs and piglets all her life. She knew what to do.

And as far as being on their own, it might be pleasant to be alone with her wee family, out from under the influence of grandparents with strong opinions.

It wasn't ideal, but she could make do with this situation.

Even as she took a breath to assure Hew she would be fine staying in the byre, white flakes began to drift down between them.

Hew clenched his fists, as if priming to do battle with the elements.

"We need to go," he decided abruptly.

No question. No discussion. No hesitation.

She blinked.

Hew had made up his mind when he'd first risen and stepped outside.

He knew by the stillness in the air. By the cold. By the color of the clouds.

Snow was coming.

For several moments before Carenza arose, he'd stared at the heavy heavens, torturing himself with self-blame and self-loathing.

He should have taken her home weeks ago.

How could he have been so selfish? So irresponsible? So determined to watch out for his own safety that he'd trapped his innocent wife with him? So intent on keeping her for himself that he would sacrifice her happiness for his own desires?

What kind of savage was he to keep his pregnant wife in a hovel like this?

And what kind of father was he to endanger the life of his child?

He'd been a fool to delay so long. Before, coming out of hiding had meant risking his arrest. Now it meant risking the lives of Carenza and their bairn.

But he could afford to delay no longer. They had to go, no matter the cost.

"Go?" Carenza asked. "Go where?"

"Dunlop," he said, pushing past her to begin packing what they'd need.

"And risk the king's wrath? And our arrest? Nay."

"You needn't worry. None of this was your fault," he said, hauling out his largest satchel and stuffing it with wool plaids. "No one will blame you. Not your father. Not Gellir. Not the king. 'Twas all *my* doing."

"This?" she exclaimed, cradling her belly. "'Twas most certainly *not* all your doing. I seem to recall givin' ye little choice in the matter."

Hew seemed to recall that as well. But no one else would believe that. And that was as it should be. Carenza was too pure of heart to be branded a fallen woman or a wanton. He was much better suited to take on the burden. Many already considered him a boorish lecher anyway.

Nay, he didn't want to debate her.

"The hens will be safe enough inside," he said, adding oatcakes and a jack of ale to the pack.

"Hew," she said.

"We'll have to leave most of the linens."

"Hew."

"And I don't think we'll have room for Sister Eve's gown."

"Hew! Stop!"

He paused, but he couldn't meet her gaze. Couldn't stomach the guilt he felt when he looked at her.

"What's wrong?" she asked.

"What's wrong?" he echoed ruefully.

He'd woken up. He'd realized it didn't matter if the king condemned him. What was important was that Carenza was safe. Their bairn was safe. Dunlop's heir was safe.

Maybe by some miracle, Sister Eve had been right. Maybe all had been forgiven. But even if that seemed unlikely, even if it meant risking his life, Hew still had to take the wager.

If the worst happened—if he was immediately seized and put into shackles, carted away to a royal prison, and executed as a traitor—his dishonor would be only a wee blemish on Rivenloch and a worthwhile sacrifice for Carenza and their bairn.

Carenza might grieve for a bit. But she'd have their child to warm her heart and the love of her clan to surround her.

She'd be free to marry again. Indeed, if Sister Eve never showed up, it would be as if she'd never been wed. And a woman as perfect as Carenza—beautiful, sweet, kind, gentle, thoughtful, charming—would have men clamoring for her hand before Hew was cold in the ground, no matter whose child she named as heir.

As for Hew, he knew he would die a better man, just for the privilege of having spent this magical year with an angel.

He wasn't about to tell her all that. She'd only argue with him. And they didn't have time. The snow was falling fast now.

So he told her the most important part of the truth. The heart of it.

"The truth is I can't bear the thought of losing you, Carenza."

"Losin' me? Ye're not goin' to—"

"If anything happened..." he choked out, shaking his head. "If something went awry... If I lost you... If we lost the bairn..."

"We won't lose the bairn."

"I wouldn't be able to live with myself. I'd rather risk imprisonment than endanger the lives of my loved ones." He clenched his jaw as a knot rose in his throat. "You can't talk me out of it. So don't try. I've made up my mind. And I won't change it. I love you too much."

Her eyes filled with tears. "Och, Hew. I don't want to make ye suffer. I could ne'er cause ye distress. And God help me, I love ye more than—" She halted abruptly with a gasp and pressed a hand to her belly.

Hew's heart plunged. The blood drained from his face.

Dear God, was she...?

This couldn't be happening. Not here. Not now.

He held his breath and stared at her in horror for several agonizing heartbeats.

Finally, her face relaxed into a smile. "Just a kick."

The tension shivered loose like chain mail off his back, leaving him suddenly weak and vulnerable. And he knew at that instant he was doing the right thing by taking her home to Dunlop.

Carenza had meant to change Hew's mind. She'd intended to convince him they'd be fine staying in the byre. After all, this was her clan's land. She knew it well. The snow *had* come unseasonably early. But it wasn't the first time it had done so.

His fears weren't completely unfounded, of course. Births didn't always go according to plan. But she wasn't near her time yet, and so far she'd been healthy.

She would have argued that the risk of arrest was no less now than it had been months ago. So it seemed unwise to turn up at Dunlop when they couldn't be assured of a friendly welcome.

She'd intended to say all that.

But the moment she saw the sheer terror in his eyes and the pale cast to his face, she knew she couldn't. Putting him through that kind of fear over the next days and weeks would have been cruel.

She had a sense he was right about the blame. If Carenza waddled up to the castle gates with the heir of Dunlop in her belly, no one would put her in shackles. And that gave her a certain leverage.

She rubbed her palm over her belly, calming the bairn.

"He must be eager to go meet his grandfather," she said.

The relief in Hew's eyes was instant. And she knew she'd made the right choice.

She grabbed her satchel and tucked their pair of wooden cups into it, along with two wild apples and the verses Merraid had written.

Hew shouldered the large satchel. "She."

"What?"

"She's eager to meet her grandfather."

She grinned. "Ye think 'tis a daughter?"

"I *hope* 'tis a daughter." His eyes softened like melting silver. "I'd like another just like you."

She sighed. He always knew just what to say. Secretly, though, she wanted a son just like him.

Packing all they needed for the journey didn't take long. It was only a few miles to Dunlop. Still, it would be rough traveling, more than an hour over rocky ground and through dense woods. And Carenza would require frequent breaks.

They did leave behind Sister Eve's gown. Carenza wanted it to be there for her, if and when she turned up at the byre.

She said farewell to the hens. She figured they'd live like queens even without their human masters. After all, they had plenty of grain and the entire cozy byre to themselves.

Then she pulled her arisaid over her head, picked up her satchel, and slipped out into the feathery white.

"Hold on," Hew said.

He took her satchel and slung it across his back with his own. Then, before she could squeak in surprise, he swept her up suddenly into his arms.

"What kind of Viking's son would I be," he said, "if I couldn't carry off a wench?"

His ancestors would have been impressed. He carried her *and* their bairn all the way to Dunlop.

They passed through the gates of Dunlop and crossed the snowy courtyard without incident. When Hew carried her through the doors of the great hall to set her on her feet near the hearth, a sudden hush fell over the clanfolk.

"Carenza?" Her father looked stunned.

She'd been thinking about this moment all the way from the time they left the byre. She'd decided if they were going to do this, if they were going to march up to the gates of Dunlop and drop their fate in her father's hands, she would make it her mission to defend Hew with her life and the life of her unborn child.

"Father." She straightened and faced him squarely. "I have somethin' to tell ye."

"Ye're goin' to have a bairn," he realized.

"That's right," she said. "But I'll have ye know, if ye're not willin' to forgive Hew, if ye plan to turn him o'er to the king, I'll make certain ye ne'er see your grandchild."

"But—"

"I'll go into exile," she bit out. "And ye won't have an heir."

"But—"

"I know 'tis a harsh decision. But considerin' all Hew has sacrificed in the name o' love, 'tis the *right* decision. So what will it be?"

She braced herself for a challenge.

It never came.

Instead, her father looked at Hew. "'Twas ye all along, wasn't it? Her lover. Her caretaker. Her hero. I knew it." He came forward with watery eyes and a father's proud smile.

Against all odds, it turned out what Sister Eve had told them was true. All of it. Merraid the maidservant *had* written the verses. And fought at Gellir's back. And been knighted by the king. And brokered peace between the lairds. She was now married to Gellir and expecting a bairn.

Eve was even right about the king and the laird of Rivenloch forgiving Hew and Carenza for their reckless behavior, though they still needed the sealed marriage document to make their union official.

First, however, Carenza meant to write a missive to Merraid, apologizing for her hasty departure. Congratulating her on her marriage and her upcoming delivery. Commending her on her clever and passionate verse. And announcing her own marriage to the heretofore unnamed father of her bairn, Sir Hew du Lac of Rivenloch himself. Their marriages would make Carenza and Merraid cousins.

She smiled, imagining the stir her missive was sure to cause.

Carenza woke early on Martinmas morn. Not because she needed extra time to dress, which she did lately, since she'd grown to roughly the size of Hamish.

Nay, she didn't think she'd be going to Mass today.

What urged her awake was a twinge deep in her abdomen, the kind she got when her menses were beginning.

It was time.

The cramp subsided, and she levered herself out of bed.

She'd slept by herself for the past fortnight. In her condition, she found she grew too hot and restless with another person in the bed.

But she wasn't alone. Standing in the middle of the floor in the dim morning light was a rat.

"Not today, Twinkle," she told the wee beast. "Ye should make yourself scarce. The chamber's goin' to be full o' maids soon."

The rat didn't budge, only sniffed patiently at the air.

"Och fine," she relented, breaking off a crumb from the oatcakes she kept by the bed.

She tossed it to Twinkle, who scampered off through a gap in the garderobe curtain.

"And don't come back until everyone's left."

Then she summoned the maid, who called the midwife, who called another midwife, who called four more maids to assist. This was the Laird of Dunlop's grandchild, after all. They wanted no mistakes.

While the servants readied the chamber, stoking the fire, hauling water, bringing linens, Carenza felt more waves tightening her belly. As she'd seen the coos and sheep do, she huffed out her breath until they passed.

Between contractions, she thought wistfully about the marriage document. She had hoped it would arrive before the bairn was born. But no one knew what had happened to Sister Eve. Carenza hoped she was all right.

Someone was sent to wake her father and Hew, though she felt that was unnecessary. They might as well sleep. Birthing was usually an all-day process. Besides, Hew was already nervous about the ordeal. It seemed cruel to draw out his suffering.

At least they could keep each other company. As it turned out, they were nearly inseparable. And whether it was Hew's influence or the threat of losing her or the impending birth, her father had softened in his attitudes. He no longer cared if everything was perfect.

He made no mention of the missing marriage decree. By his behavior, he assumed they were legitimately wed. He already treated Hew as if he were his son. He'd even had Hew's precious axe replaced. Though he couldn't reproduce the runes, he'd had *Amor vincit omnia* carved into the handle.

He made no comment about Carenza's appearance, even though she knew she was as large as a coo and bedraggled as a molting owl. He was just thrilled to be getting an heir.

She breathed through another mild contraction. One of the midwives set up the birthing chair, though she wouldn't need it for hours. A superstitious maidservant slipped a dagger under her pillow, whispering that it would cut the pain. Another maid mopped Carenza's brow with a damp rag. The pain passed, and Carenza smiled. The quiet efficiency of the ladies around her was curiously calming.

"'Tis been hours," Hew growled in complaint as one of the maidservants tending to Carenza emerged onto the crowded great hall.

"These things take time, m'laird," she said.

"But she's all right?" the Laird of Dunlop asked.

"Och aye, she's fine."

Hew and the laird exchanged glances of dubious relief and returned to pacing.

Hew felt as if he were at his wit's end. His heart raced. Every nerve was on edge. Carenza was fighting a battle in her bedchamber. And there wasn't a bloody thing he could do to help her.

He shuddered to think what might have happened if he hadn't made the decision to return to Dunlop.

As for her father, he wasn't helping Hew's mood. His face was sickly pale with fear. He'd chewed his lip until it was raw. Even his hounds in the corner of the hall whimpered, sensing his unease.

The laird stopped him mid-pace, seizing his arm. "Do ye think we should fetch the physician?"

Hew wondered. It wasn't normally done. Physicians knew little about childbirth. That was a midwife's purview. On the other hand, this was his child and the heir to Dunlop. "I'm not sure. Should we?"

The maidservant suddenly appeared beside them again with a pair of ales. "Nay, m'lairds. 'Tis already crowded enough in her bedchamber. Here. Have a wee bit to drink. 'Twill help calm your fears."

"I don't want to calm my fears," Hew snapped, grabbing a cup and downing it anyway.

The maidservant didn't even flinch. Still, Hew felt remorse the instant he opened his mouth. He sounded like his mother, lashing out in anger at anyone in his path.

"Och, forgive me," he said. "I'm not angry with you. I'm just…"

"Ye're just a man waitin' for his child to be born."

"I was the same way," the laird confessed. "Fear dressed up as anger. This time, though, 'tis naught but fear for me."

The maidservant pressed the second cup into his hand. "This works for both. And ye might as well have a seat. Otherwise ye'll wear out the bottom o' your boots by the time this bairn comes."

They tried to sit. But the laird couldn't stop bouncing

Laird of Flint

his leg. And Hew kept standing up and sitting down, too restless to rest.

"Is it good luck or bad luck to be born on Martinmas?" the laird wondered.

Hew didn't know. "At this rate, the bairn won't come till the morrow."

"What if it doesn't? What if Carenza's up there in agony for a sennight?"

"It can't take that long," Hew scoffed. Then he reconsidered. "Can it?"

"Do ye suppose they have enough plaids?"

That was a consideration. It was snowy, and the bairn would be wet. "Should we gather more?"

They shot to their feet and began scouring the hall, demanding the plaids from clanfolk who warmed themselves by the fire. Whether they would be useful or not, it at least gave Hew something to do so he wouldn't go mad with worrying.

He'd gathered a heaping armful of plaids when the outer doors were suddenly flung open. A cold breeze rushed in to flicker the flames. A motley party of half a dozen travelers, cloaked against the harsh weather, pushed boldly inside.

Hew scowled.

What strangers dared to muscle their way so brazenly into Dunlop's hall?

Who deigned to meddle in their private affairs?

Incensed at their intrusion and forgetting this was not his keep, he called out, "Who goes there? Show your faces."

CHAPTER 28

"Hew?" Logan threw back his hood.

Hew dropped the plaids. "Logan?" It *was* his brother, although a taller version since the last time he'd seen him more than a year ago.

Logan loped forward with an enormous grin. He caught Hew in a rib-crushing embrace. Then he pushed away to arm's length to take a good look at him.

"So good to see you, brother," Logan said. "You're looking fit. Love *does* conquer all, aye?"

Before Hew could answer, he heard an unmistakable bellow.

"Dunlop!"

Aunt Deirdre? Was she here as well?

From behind his armful of plaids, Dunlop replied, "Deirdre?"

The clan cleared a path between the two lairds. Hew could see now the visitors were all from Rivenloch.

"Thank God ye're here," Dunlop said, handing the plaids off to a nearby clansman. "Ye're just in time," he rattled on. "We're not sure whether to call the physician. Or if we've got enough plaids. Or—"

"What's happened?" Deirdre demanded, as clear and efficient as always.

"'Tis my Carenza," Dunlop said. "She's goin' to have the bairn."

"Now?"

"Aye, and 'tis takin' so long, I fear—"

"Is it?" Deirdre asked in concern. Then she turned to the nearest maidservant. *"Is* it taking so long?"

The maidservant's eyes went wide. She'd likely never been questioned by a warrior maid. But Deirdre trusted her opinion more than a man's. Women knew more about such things. The maidservant bit her lip, glancing uncertainly at Carenza's father. Then she shook her head.

"Then there's time," Deirdre said. "Hallie?"

Hew's cousin Hallie came forward and pulled a scroll out of her satchel. She handed it to Deirdre, who handed it to Dunlop.

"I need you to sign and seal this," Deirdre said.

Dunlop frowned in confusion. "What is it? Can it not wait? This is no time for negotiations and contracts. As I've said, my daughter is in—"

"Aye, so you've said. And 'tis my nephew's bairn, aye?"

"Aye."

"Then I need you to sign and seal this."

She unfurled the scroll then, and Hew's breath caught as he recognized the document.

Dunlop raised himself to his full height, which was still just shy of Laird Deirdre. "With all due respect, m'laird, 'twill have to wait until—"

"Nay." She showed him the document. "Now."

Flustered by her bold challenge, Dunlop skimmed the parchment, then took it in trembling hands when he saw what it was. "Scribe!"

Hope swelled in Hew. Was their marriage going to be made real before the bairn arrived? That was his dearest wish for Carenza.

In the darkest part of his heart, he'd secretly feared God might punish him for his sin with the death of their child. Now at least that part of his dread might be vanquished.

The scribe arrived, bringing his quill, ink, wax, and the clan seal.

Logan sidled up and elbowed Hew with a grin. "A bairn already." Then he leaned close to whisper, "So tell me again how this vow of chastity works."

Before he could cuff Logan for his taunt, Hew's arm was grabbed by his sister Jenefer.

She was furious. But marriage had moderated her temper. Instead of using fists and bellowing, she was biting out curses between clenched teeth and squeezing the blood out of his arm with her archer's grip.

"What the devil were you thinking, you sarding cad?" she hissed. "I sat by while you dallied with half the village like a bloody rutting bull. I said nothing when you trysted with other men's wives and tried to bed a nun, for God's sake. A *nun*. But this, Hew. Lucifer's ballocks. This is beyond even you. Seducing your cousin's betrothed. A laird's daughter. Getting her with child and abducting her to live in exile. And all that without even securing a legitimate marriage. How could you?"

No one could get Hew's blood to boiling like his older sister. He was already on edge from the stress of the morn. And now his arm was tingling, and he couldn't feel his fingers.

It would feel good to engage her in battle. It wouldn't be the first time they'd settled their differences with blades. And a bit of violence might be just the thing he needed to get his mind off the turmoil upstairs.

"Do I need to defend my honor?" he bit out, skewering her with his gaze.

"Do you?" she bit back, burning into his eyes with a glare.

And then he took a breath.

Bloody hell. What was he doing? He didn't need to defend anything. Every step of the way, he'd done what he thought was best. Carenza loved him. And she was upstairs, fighting the battle of her life. The last thing she needed to hear was the clash of swords below from her husband's clan.

"Nay," he decided with a sigh. "I do not."

To his surprise, Jenefer backed down as well. Her eyes slowly turned from fire to molten wax. Her chin quivered. She released her grip and rubbed her hand along his arm in apology.

"I don't want to fight you," she admitted.

He smirked. "'Tis a good thing. You've drained all the strength from my arm."

"Och, Hew," she sighed, "I can't wait to be an aunt."

The document was signed and sealed. The laird of Dunlop handed it back to the laird of Rivenloch, who handed it to Hew.

"Your marriage is now official," she said. "My grandchild will be a Rivenloch."

She winked then, letting him know it meant more to her than that.

"Thank you both for your haste," Hew said. Then he glanced around the hall. "Where is Sister Eve?" He wanted to thank her and tell her about the gown they'd left in the byre.

Deirdre replied with a long-suffering sigh. "That is a tale for another day, one that is not yet finished."

Before he could wonder at her enigmatic words, his cousin Isabel crashed into him with a hug and a giggle.

"'Tis so romantic, Hew," she gushed, "like a Viking of old, abducting his bride."

"That's not quite how—"

"And Lady Carenza, trapped at Darragh, pining for you for days and days."

"'Twas only a sennight or so."

But there was no stopping young Isabel, who loved turning a wee spring into a raging sea.

"I told you you'd find The One," she said.

"You did."

Suddenly, a maidservant emerged from the stairwell into the great hall. The room immediately hushed. The maidservant froze, blinking in confusion.

Hew's heart was in his throat. Bracing himself for the worst, he finally dared to break the silence. "What news?" he croaked.

"Och," the maidservant said, exhaling in relief. "Nothin'. Lady Carenza is fine. I only came downstairs to get a wee bite."

After a collective sigh, the conversation in the great hall resumed.

Deirdre busied Dunlop with discussions of King Malcolm and the border and the English, which helped to keep his fears for his daughter at bay.

Logan caught Hew up on all the news from home, allaying his own worries.

Jenefer, Hallie, and Feiyan chatted with the Dunlop warriors, comparing weaponry and battle tactics.

Isabel nagged Hew for details about their romantic adventures. He finally told her some things were better left to the imagination.

The day dragged on and on. Food was brought out. Ale was poured. Some of the servants who had risen early for Martinmas napped along the wall and beside the fire.

Hallie wandered up to Hew. "How are you holding up, cousin?"

"I didn't expect 'twould take so long," he murmured.

"Nay?"

"I wish she didn't have to suffer so." He tapped the scroll against his thigh.

Hallie paused, frowning down at the document. "She doesn't know about that, does she?"

"The marriage decree? Nay."

She arched a brow. "I have an idea."

She took the scroll from him and made her way across the hall and up the stairs.

Of course, he realized. Carenza might never admit it, but as someone who had been raised to be a perfect laird's daughter, she was probably reluctant to give birth to a bastard child. Perhaps seeing the marriage decree, signed and sealed by the king, would relieve her conscience and make the birth easier.

Sure enough, when Hallie returned several moments later, it was with a brilliant smile.

"Sir Hew du Lac of Rivenloch," she announced, "you have a daughter."

The day dawned crisp and clear, with a fine coverlet of snow that reflected light into the crowded solar.

Carenza gazed at the Rivenloch clanfolk gathered around her and Hew—Laird Deirdre, Hallie, Jenefer, Feiyan, Logan, and Isabel—and felt as if she knew and loved them already. Hew had spent many hours in the byre retelling their stories. She couldn't wait to visit Rivenloch and meet the rest.

"What are ye goin' to call her?" Carenza's father asked as he smiled fondly down at the wee bairn cradled in his arms.

Carenza exchanged a secret smile with Hew, whose eyes hadn't stopped shining since she'd first shown him his daughter.

"We're namin' her Bethac."

"Ah." That was all her father could manage. He nodded, and Carenza saw his eyes fill with tears. But he was the

Laird of Dunlop. Strong and stiff and stoic. So he cleared his throat and quickly handed Bethac off to her grandmother, Laird Deirdre. Then he mumbled, "I'll make arrangements for the baptism," before he rushed out the door.

"Bethac?" Laird Deirdre asked.

Hew replied, "'Twas the name of Carenza's mother."

Everyone nodded in approval.

"'Tis a good name for a warrior," Deirdre teased, gazing down at Bethac with affection.

Hew asked her, "So what happened to Sister Eve? Why did the marriage contract take so long?"

"It seems while Sister Eve was attempting to get the marriage document sealed," Deirdre said, "she ran into Adam—"

"Adam?" Hew asked.

Feiyan glanced at Carenza and clarified, "My brother."

Carenza nodded. She already had Hew's cousins memorized.

Deirdre continued. "They apparently had a series of rather wild misadventures, and Sister Eve landed in...some serious trouble."

"What kind of trouble?" Hew asked.

Deirdre shuddered. "I'll leave that to them to explain. In any event, Adam managed to rescue her."

Carenza was glad to hear that. As odd as Eve was, she liked the lass, and she still wanted to return that lovely gown to her.

"After that," Deirdre said, "they procured the king's signature and seal by some rather questionable means."

Carenza furrowed her brows. Generally the royal seal was the last to go on a marriage decree. "But how did they get the king's seal before my father's?"

"Exactly," Deirdre said. "In any event, they rushed to Rivenloch for my seal. And we were forced to rush to Dunlop to get your father's."

Carenza felt awful about making the Laird of Rivenloch go to all that trouble, until Deirdre bent over wee Bethac and cooed, "But 'twas all worth it, wasn't it, my precious lass?"

Carenza added, "We're so grateful ye came. I'm grateful *all* o' ye came. I've so looked forward to meetin' ye."

Hew's sister Jenefer leaned forward eagerly. "I've been looking forward to meeting you as well, ever since I heard about your coo reiving."

"Aye," Feiyan said. "Is it true you were once a cateran?"

"Just for one night," Carenza said. "And only one coo in particular."

"Why?" Hallie asked.

"I raised Hamish from the time he was a calf, and I didn't want him to be culled."

By the expressions on the faces of the three cousins—Jenefer, Hallie, and Feiyan—they thought that was ridiculous. The warrior maids probably wouldn't hesitate to cull a coo, any more than they'd hesitate to kill a foe.

But Laird Deirdre came to her defense. "You know, 'twas a coo, Audhumbla, that licked the first Viking god into being."

"Aunt Deirdre," Logan chided, "are you sure you should be speaking of Viking gods in front of Hew? He's a monk now, you know."

"Logan," Hew growled.

"What was it like," Logan taunted, "that vast sea of men and not a selkie in sight?"

"'Twas worth the sacrifice," Hew told him, wrapping his arm around Carenza, "to end up with the most beautiful selkie of all."

Isabel clasped her hands and sighed.

"Well, that explains it," Feiyan said. "No wonder she had such a craving for pickled eels."

Everyone laughed.

Suddenly, Hallie hissed, "Nobody move."

Everyone froze with Rivenloch warrior precision.

Hallie had drawn her dagger, and was holding the blade, preparing to hurl it.

Then Carenza saw what was in her sights. "Nay!"

Hew reached out to halt Hallie's arm.

"That's a pet," he explained as the wee hedgepig continued to waddle along the wall, making its way to the corner and ducking into the wee box it was using for a nest.

The three warrior cousins exchanged glances that told her what they thought of having a hedgepig for a pet.

But Hallie put away her dagger, and Isabel changed the subject.

"What's this?" she asked, picking up Carenza's bestiary.

"'Tis a book o' all the beasts I've seen."

Since her return to Dunlop, her father had seemed far more lenient, willing to let Carenza express herself. So she'd brought her bestiary out of hiding and spent spare hours painting some of the animals she encountered near Dunlop.

Isabel leafed through the pages of illustrations and text about squirrels, coos, hedgepigs, crows, butterflies, and dozens of other animals.

"Did you make this yourself?"

"Aye."

"Wouldn't Ian love this, Hallie?" Isabel said. "He has a book full of notes like this."

Carenza decided she really wanted to meet Ian.

In the meantime, she had others she needed to thank.

"I still haven't seen Sister Eve," she said. "Does no one know where she is?"

"Nay," Deirdre replied. "The last we saw of her was when she brought the wedding document to Rivenloch."

"I might know something about Sister Eve," Isabel teased, drawing her toe across the floor and smiling the way she did when she had a secret. "I'm not sure exactly where she is. But I know who she's with. And I suspect by next year, we'll all be going to a nun's wedding."

What that meant, Carenza couldn't guess. All she knew was that she had never been happier.

She adored her quirky new clan.

She loved her precious new daughter.

And as for her fierce Viking warrior, fellow cateran, erstwhile monk, companion spy, devoted husband, and the proud father of the next generation of Dunlops and Rivenlochs, she believed Isabel was right. Hew du Lac of Rivenloch was The One.

The End

Coming soon...

LAIRD OF SMOKE

The Warrior Lairds of Rivenloch, Book 3

The intrepid son of Scots spies, Sir Adam la Nuit of Rivenloch hunts the most elusive prize of all—true love in the guise of a charming nun.

Thank you for reading my book!

Did you enjoy it? If so, I hope you'll post a review to let others know! There's no greater gift you can give an author than spreading your love of her books.

It's truly a pleasure and a privilege to be able to share my stories with you. Knowing that my words have made you laugh, sigh, or touched a secret place in your heart is what keeps the wind beneath my wings. I hope you enjoyed our brief journey together, and may ALL of your adventures have happy endings!

If you'd like to keep in touch, feel free to sign up for my monthly e-newsletter at www.glynnis.net, and you'll be the first to find out about my new releases, special discounts, prizes, promotions, and more!

If you want to keep up with my daily escapades:
Friend me at facebook.com/GlynnisCampbell
Like my Page at bit.ly/GlynnisCampbellFBPage
Follow me on Twitter @GlynnisCampbell
Follow me on Instagram @glynniscampbell.author
Follow me on Goodreads @glynnis_campbell
Follow me on Bookbub @glynnis-campbell
And if you're a super fan, join
facebook.com/GCReadersClan

ABOUT THE AUTHOR

I'm a *USA Today* bestselling author of swashbuckling action-adventure historical romances, mostly set in Scotland, with more than 20 award-winning books published in six languages.

But before my role as a medieval matchmaker, I sang in *The Pinups,* an all-girl band on CBS Records, and provided voices for the MTV animated series *The Maxx,* Blizzard's *Diablo* and *Starcraft* video games, and *Star Wars* audiobooks.

I'm the wife of a rock star (if you want to know which one, contact me) and the mother of two young adults. I do my best writing on cruise ships, in Scottish castles, on my husband's tour bus, and at home in my sunny southern California garden.

I love transporting readers to a place where the bold heroes have endearing flaws, the women are stronger than they look, the land is lush and untamed, and chivalry is alive and well!

I'm always delighted to hear from my readers, so please feel free to email me at glynnis@glynnis.net. And if you're a super-fan who would like to join my inner circle, sign up at http://www.facebook.com/GCReadersClan, where you'll get glimpses behind the scenes, sneak peeks of works-in-progress, and extra special surprises.

Milton Keynes UK
Ingram Content Group UK Ltd.
UKHW042145150524
442688UK00001B/1

9 781634 801447